The Cape Cod Blue

Selected Reviews

The Last Pope

"A truly great novel. I plan to make it my finest motion picture."
> —Martin Poll, producer of *The Lion in Winter*, starring Peter O'Toole and Katharine Hepburn

"A thrilling blend of history, religion, and human relationships."
> —*The New York Post*

"Packs a powerful punch … reminiscent of the Shoes of the Fisherman …"
> —Booklist

The Glass Tower

"Breathless introduction to the inner workings of big business …"
> —*The Times* Literary Supplement

"A vivid, fast moving story about people in PR."
> —*SHE* magazine

"[An] institution story perfected by Zola and none the worse for it … deftly, excitingly told."
> —*The Daily Telegraph*

"A sharp and entertaining first from Mr. Osborn, who is already an accomplished screenwriter."
> —*Lincolnshire Evening Telegraph*

Murder on Martha's Vineyard

"A good tale of mystery and murder. Its plot twists and turns in and out of an intriguing whodunit that packs a punch at the end powerful enough to floor one."
> —*Western Morning News*

"This well-plotted thriller makes compulsive holiday reading."
—*Salisbury Journal*

"This is the first entry in what might become a promising new series.... Osborn has created an interesting protagonist."
—*Publishers Weekly*

"Before settling down to read this book, take the phone off the hook, make sure all the doors and windows are locked, set a large medicinal brandy within easy reach, and prepare to let David Osborn scare your pants off. Highly recommended."
—*The Bloodhound*

"Delightful mystery is a zinger. Every one of its 258 pages says 'turn me.'"
—*Chattanooga New Free Press*

Murder on the Chesapeake

"Satisfying tale … intrepid sleuth."
—*Publishers Weekly*

"The tale is spun tightly and the main characters are engaging."
—*Chicago Sun Times*

Open Season

"A truly brilliant novel … an accomplished writer in all media, but ultimately a pro … a superbly organized book, brutal, chilling, but carrying a terrible conviction."
—*Canberra Times*

"As commercial and exciting a novel as can be found today.… It is shocking, savage, and graphic, a cruel book that spares little in detail. There is unbearable suspense, headlong action, and ends with a final ironic twist that will leave

the reader gasping. Osborn is a master storyteller and his remorseless style matches his remorseless narrative...."
> —*Abilene Reporter News*

"This well-plotted thriller makes compulsive holiday reading."
> —*Salisbury Journal*

"This is the first entry in what might become a promising new series.... Osborn has created an interesting protagonist."
> —*Publishers Weekly*

"Before settling down to read this book, take the phone off the hook, make sure all the doors and windows are locked, set a large medicinal brandy within easy reach, and prepare to let David Osborn scare your pants off. Highly recommended."
> —*The Bloodhound*

"Delightful mystery is a zinger. Every one of its 258 pages says 'turn me.'"
> —*Chattanooga New Free Press*

Murder on the Chesapeake

"Satisfying tale ... intrepid sleuth."
> —*Publishers Weekly*

"The tale is spun tightly and the main characters are engaging."
> —*Chicago Sun Times*

Open Season

"A truly brilliant novel ... an accomplished writer in all media, but ultimately a pro ... a superbly organized book, brutal, chilling, but carrying a terrible conviction."
> —*Canberra Times*

"As commercial and exciting a novel as can be found to-day.… It is shocking, savage, and graphic, a cruel book that spares little in detail. There is unbearable suspense, head-long action, and ends with a final ironic twist that will leave the reader gasping. Osborn is a master storyteller and his remorseless style matches his remorseless narrative.…"
—*Abilene Reporter News*

"David Osborn's story motif in *Open Season* is not new—the human set free to become the hunted, the quarry in a hunt made more exciting by the element of human intelligence and cunning on both sides. But Osborn who knows his way with a story and people and how to keep the suspense and relish boiling, gives it added spice and terror … one of the season's top novels."
—*Waco* (Texas) *Tribune-Herald*

The French Decision

"Osborn's novel shrivels the nerves … a gripping story skillfully developed … the ironic epilogue [is] even more explosive."
—*Publishers Weekly*

"An exciting, highly plausible Washington thriller …"
—Gore Vidal

"In a powerful story of industrial espionage which takes place in the United States and France, David Osborn examines American politics, the French economy, international high finance, and the Common Market as well as torture and love. He does it all with a gentle irony and without ever losing his perspective by deeply involving us in the troubled emotions of his hero, a young Arab posing as a Jew who takes American nationality to become a 'mole' in the service of French espionage.…"
—*L'Express,* Paris

"No better example of absorbing, fast-paced intrigue. Compelling to the last punctuation mark."
    —Clive Cussler

"Grisly serving of double-agenting and cat and mouse chases ... effective and understated ..."
    —*The Kirkus Review*

"fast-moving and hard to put down ..."
    —Associated Press

Love and Treason

"Spellbinding ... unbearable suspense ... compulsive reading ... what makes this novel even more than a thriller is the humanity of the characters...."
    —*The Pittsburgh Press*

"This is a first-class book. It has what one admires so often in English thrillers and finds so seldom in American ones: literate, accomplished writing which makes the plot more ingenious, the characterizations more deft and engaging, and therefore the thrills more thrilling...."
    —Michael Thomas, author of *Green Monday*

"There won't be a better book published in America this year.... brilliantly plotted ... infinite complications ... as audacious as it is original ..."
    —Alastair Maclean

"Taut and tender political thriller ... succeeds both as a thriller and a love story ..."
    —*Delta Air Lines* magazine

"Osborn captures the reader's interest almost at once and doesn't let it go."
    —*The Knoxville News-Sentinel*

The
Cape Cod
Blue

a novel by

David Osborn

Published by Dagmar Miura
Los Angeles
www.dagmarmiura.com

The Cape Cod Blue

First published 2017

ISBN: 978-1-942267-23-2

for Robin, with love

ONE

If you were to look today over an Adams mantel in the spacious living room of a vintage Nantucket mansion (which, with its lawns, gardens and out buildings is The Moorings), you would see a hauntingly lovely painting of a Victorian beach scene. A woman is seated beneath a blue and white umbrella with a small child who wears a straw hat with a blue ribbon. Both are looking across quiet blue water and a distant sandbar at a little lobster boat whose faded blue sail hangs limp in the windless air.

If you then looked from the painting through one of the three French doors, across a croquet lawn and beyond a grape arbor which borders a similar beach, you would see, in a near mirror image of the painting itself, the calm shoal waters of Nantucket Harbor. A long narrow bay, it extends nearly half the island's length and is separated from the Atlantic Ocean only by a narrow sandbar. On an early summer morning, you might also see, as in the painting, the shape of some little lobster boat or the splash of a white sail that would almost seem one of the cottony clouds brought to life by the early rays of the sun. You might see, too, a gull dipping its wings with the first breath of the on-shore breeze that would soon arise to sweep across beach, dune, and salt marsh and over the thickets of bayberry, cranberry bogs, and scrub pine forests that are the essence of the magical island of Nantucket.

On such a summer morning on Nantucket, sometime

before the painting changed so much in the lives of the Morse family, David, the youngest member, awoke with the sun on his seventh birthday. It was a Sunday, and the first sounds he heard were the muffled *chug-chug-chug* of a lobster boat and the distant outboard motor sound of someone in a skiff out to dig clams. He heard, too, the occasional screech of a gull above the muffled sound of the bell at the Catholic Church in the Town of Nantucket far down the shore. With them came his first thought; he was no longer six. Since yesterday when he'd become seven, and since he had learned to swim from the end of the dock to the shore, he was allowed to fish off the dock by himself. Last night at dinner, he'd only just blown out the candles on his birthday cake when Grandfather Darwin said so.

"All by myself, Grandfather?"

Darwin Morse was a big, bullish man in his seventies whose crown of thick thatched hair had turned white even before he'd been confined to a wheelchair by a stroke at Christmastime two years before. He'd beamed a rare smile at David. "Why not, my boy? Of course, you'll have to check with your father. But you can tell him I said it was all right by me." And that meant he could, even though his father wasn't going to like it.

Grandfather Darwin hadn't said anything about checking with his mother, but she had smiled down at him from where she sat by his side. She never argued with Grandfather Darwin, or with his father, and his father hadn't returned yet from the office where he'd gone for some kind of an "important business meeting," even though it was Saturday and his birthday.

"Gee, Grandfather, thank you." He'd shot a triumphant glance at Mr. Perkins, who stood a little distance from the table, his pinstriped trousers, pearl gray waistcoat, and butler's jacket complementing his usual severe expression. Only last week, Mr. Perkins had bet no one would allow him to go down on the dock and fish alone until he was at least ten.

"We'll have plates, please, Perkins."

"Very good, Mr. Morse."

His grandfather wheeled himself away from the head of the table and around to where David was sitting with his mother, across from Uncle Haydn and Gabrielle, the French lady who, Uncle Haydn said, was writing a story about the family for a newspaper in France and whom he'd brought out to visit several times. "And some champagne, please, Perkins. Haydn? Gabrielle? Felicity? Yes? Good This is an important moment, Perkins. Young men don't turn seven every day of the week."

"Yes, Mr. Morse. My thought exactly." And Perkins had nodded at Mary, who always waited on table, to bring the cake plates. When she came close to David and bent to put the plates by the cake, her starched uniform brushed his arm, and he could smell the brown kitchen soap she always used to wash her hands. Once when he'd had poison ivy, she'd given him a piece, telling him not to let Nellie, the cook, know, because Nellie was fussy about anything that left the kitchen, even a piece of soap. "Wet it and rub it on gently, Mister David," she'd said, "and it will dry that old ivy right out of yer."

David turned to where Mr. Perkins was taking a bottle of champagne from a silver cooler on a stand and was working out the cork. "You see, Mr. Perkins: I win. You said Grandfather wouldn't give me permission until I was ten."

Grandfather Darwin laughed and said, "I think Perkins was just getting your goat, young man."

Mr. Perkins didn't say anything, but David thought that he was hiding a smile. Mr. Perkins almost never smiled. He didn't speak much either, but when he did he had an English accent and once told David he'd come from a place in England called Dorset. He was always very punctual. He'd stand by the dining room door with his big gold railroad watch in his hand, and if anyone was even one minute late after he'd announced dinner, he would tell them so. Even Grandfather Darwin.

David picked up the ivory-handled cake knife Mary had laid next to the cake plates and began to cut into the cake.

When the first slice was a little ragged, his mother asked if he needed help.

"For heaven's sake, Felicity, stop babying the boy. If he's capable of hooking a fish, he's capable of cutting a cake."

David shot a grateful glance at his grandfather, and Felicity retreated. "Of course." Taken aback, she smiled polite surrender while brushing back a strand of her straight dark hair that had come away from a small gold hair clip and fallen across one side of her face. She was a slender, once quite pretty woman who was quietly unassuming and now sliding into middle age, always reluctant to reveal her inner feelings.

"It's okay, Mom, I can do it," David said and cut the cake for everyone, with her only having to help just once.

Mary served out the plates as he cut. When she brought one to Gabrielle, Gabrielle asked David if he'd take her fishing one day. He liked Gabrielle even if she spoke a little funny, but Uncle Haydn had said if he went to France and tried to speak French, the French people would think that he spoke a little funny, too. Gabrielle could beat the whole family at tennis, and his mother said she wasn't just beautiful, she was also the nicest person ever. She and his mother were best friends since Uncle Haydn had first brought her to The Moorings a month ago. But just the same, David thought, he wouldn't take her fishing. Fishing was for boys, not for girls. So he just smiled at her because it wouldn't be polite to say so and immediately wished he hadn't because of his front tooth that had fallen out just this last week.

Because of that, he suddenly thought of his father, who hadn't been there all day. Uncle Haydn said he'd called late last night, "after you'd gone to bed, David," to say he was stuck in town with urgent Carlyle business. He hadn't called again today, and in a way David was glad he wasn't there because his father was so strict. Even on birthdays. He always said birthdays were like any other day, and rules were rules. So just because he was seven he couldn't get away with things like jumping up and down on the living room couch or bouncing a tennis ball on the marble floor of the hall. Grown-ups, his father said, didn't do that, and boys weren't allowed to do it either. And if his mother pretended she hadn't seen, his father would get annoyed with her, too. But fishing would be all right because the only person he never got annoyed with was Grandfather Darwin. He was always polite with Grandfather and always agreed with him.

These were David's first thoughts for the day; remembering yesterday, and all the presents in the morning: the bicycle from Uncle Haydn and from Grandfather the super sling shot that could hit the garage from the house, the whole puppet set his mother had given him, the Swiss Army knife from Gabrielle, the crow caller from Asa, the gardener, and the super rubber sea monster to ride on when he swam from Mr. Perkins and the rest of the servants. And then there was also the big book from his father on the history of baseball, with a lot of pictures of players a long time ago. He really didn't like it very much because he'd never heard of them and, anyway, he didn't care about baseball in the first place, but he'd thank him just the same tomorrow when he came home and he'd say it was wonderful.

Presents, then later, dinner and cake with Grandfather Darwin and his mother and Uncle Haydn and Gabriel, the French lady, at the long mahogany table in the dining room where there was the huge painting over the sideboard of some river like the Amazon surrounded by jungle. His grandfather said it was by a famous artist named Church, and it had parrots in the treetops. It faced the three French doors, which, like the living room ones, looked across the lawn with its croquet stakes and wickets. Beside each door there was a small bronze statue on a little round table. One was a cowboy whose horse was rearing up at a snake. The other was an Indian who was huddled under a blanket on his horse which had its back to a wind and looked cold. Grandfather Darwin said they were made by someone called Remington, and Mr. Perkins said they were very valuable and he mustn't touch. Not ever. Just like—unless Mr. Perkins was with him—he should never touch Grandfather's big brass-bound cigar humidor which had been given to great-grand father by a friend called J. P. Morgan and had Grandfather's initials on it on a brass plate which Mr. Perkins kept polished so you could almost see your face in it. Mr. Perkins said that the cigars in it came from some place called Havana and each one was worth twenty dollars. And he also said that the Indian was caught in a blizzard out on the prairie and that Indians had hard lives. They didn't have any hot water or beds or even toilets. And they had to live in tents all year long. And sometimes they ate dogs.

Mr. Perkins was very strict about household rules, but that was all right because he was more like an uncle than a butler. Once he'd heard Mr. Perkins having an argument with Nellie, and Nellie had called Mr. Perkins a rich man's poodle. He'd asked his mother what Nellie had meant by that. His mother said Mr. Perkins came from a very poor family in England, people who had nothing and would always be poor; years ago, when still a boy his own age, Mr. Perkins had either to go to work in the coal mines or be a servant. He'd been lucky to be taken into a great lord's home to polish shoes and carry out ashes and to sleep on a straw mattress under the back stair. As he grew up, he'd learned all the many things a butler needed to know to make a big house run properly and had worked his way up to butler himself, which was a very important position because the butler was head servant. Nellie thought being a servant was hateful, but Perkins was proud to live where he was needed and respected and to manage a lovely home. "Everyone has to work in life for somebody," she'd heard him say to Nellie. "It's a privilege to serve people like the Morses." And his mother had told him, too, how very fond of him Perkins was. "He's your best friend in the world," she'd said.

After dinner, Uncle Haydn pushed Grandfather in his wheelchair out of the dining room and across the hall to the living room where everyone sat on the two long couches each side of the cocktail table and talked, and because it was his birthday he was allowed to stay up an extra half hour before his mother took him upstairs to bed. Uncle Haydn had taught him how to play chess, and got out the big ivory chess board so he could play Grandfather Darwin and whispered moves to help him win. Uncle Haydn was his favorite. If he did anything wrong or broke a rule, Uncle Haydn would just smile and give him a hug and tell him to be more careful next time.

That was last night.

Then, all of a sudden, his next thought made him forget last night and cake and winning a bet with Mr. Perkins and sit straight up in his bed and almost shout "hurray." Before he'd fallen asleep, he'd promised himself that the very first thing in the morning he'd go fishing. And so he was going to. And right now. And all by himself when the whole house was asleep and especially before his father, whom he'd heard finally come home after he'd gone to bed, might awake and see him going down to the dock alone and stop him.

David threw off the covers and raced into the bathroom, and then came back and took off his pajamas and quickly got into his clothes: his underpants and T-shirt with the picture of an iron tower on it that Gabrielle had given him and said was the famous Eiffel Tower in Paris, and then his socks and his jeans and his sneakers. He knew he should brush his teeth because he remembered Mrs. Rhinelander was coming down to The Moorings from Boston for lunch, and she would almost certainly ask him if he had. She always did, and she always told his mother that she should make sure he brushed his teeth three times a day because little boys were always putting dirty things in their mouths. He wondered if Mrs. Rhinelander brushed her teeth three times a day. You couldn't tell if they were white or if they were actually yellow like old Asa's, because all her bright red lipstick always smeared onto her teeth.

He hated Mrs. Rhinelander. She was always so bossy, and

she disapproved of everything, like when Gabrielle made a mistake in English, even though a very small one, and then got annoyed with his mother when she stood up for Gabrielle. His mother said she might marry his grandfather someday, but David was sure his Grandfather was too smart to do that.

Once, just to avoid Mrs. Rhinelander, he had hidden inside the tall clock in the front hall and risked being sent to bed by his father with no supper for doing so. His father liked Mrs. Rhinelander and was always terribly polite to her. When he asked one day "why," his father had said, "Because she's very correct socially." And when he'd asked his father what he meant by "socially," his father had only said, "Never mind, David. When you grow up, you'll understand."

He had asked Mr. Perkins one day if Mrs. Rhinelander kept balloons or maybe basketballs in her dress because she was so big out front, and Mr. Perkins had turned away quickly and Mary, polishing the hunt table in the living room, had stifled laughter. His mother said Mary came from County Donegal in Ireland, where they always shrieked when they talked or laughed because the wind blew so hard all the time off the Atlantic Ocean that nobody could hear them otherwise; and a lot of trees there couldn't grow because of the wind; and the sheep had to hide behind stone walls to keep from being blown away.

When he left his room, David was careful closing the door behind him so it wouldn't make a sound. He crept past his mother's and father's rooms down the corridor that led to the upstairs hall landing where there were doors to Grandfather Darwin's suite of rooms and to the guest rooms. Over a table against the wall between them his mother had hung a framed watercolor she did of some seashells. He had stopped to look over the balcony down into the hall below with its black and white marble squares that Uncle Haydn said they ought to use as a checker board, and he had noticed the flowers in the big blue vase on the hall table that his mother had arranged yesterday after Asa had gathered them from the garden, when the tall clock struck six.

Its deep, booming sound made him jump. Inside. Outside, he didn't move. He could hear his heart beating and feel it against his ribs. He was sure the clock would be heard by everyone else in the house, even though it was only six, and they'd come running, and he'd be told it was too early to be up and be sent back to bed.

But nobody came. The only sound inside the house was the clock's slow, hollow tick-tock, tick-tock.

Still making sure to keep very quiet, David went to the head of the wide, soft-carpeted stairs that swept in a long curve down to the hall. He decided this was not the time to slide on the banister, and started down. Halfway, Gauguin appeared from his dog bed that was in Grandfather Darwin's study next to the guest bathroom and out of sight from the landing above. The moment he saw him, David almost ran the rest of the way down, praying with every step that Gauguin wouldn't bark hello and give him away. Gauguin was getting old and beginning to show white around his black muzzle, and he wouldn't retrieve any more like Labradors were supposed to. Asa said it was because when you got very old you got tired and didn't feel like running around, and he'd wondered how Asa knew all that because Asa wasn't really old himself, not the way Grandfather was, even if he took off his straw hat while weeding the flower beds so you could see he was all bald on top. Grandfather was so old he'd had a stroke.

But Gauguin only wagged his tail and, after David reached the bottom of the stairs and gave him a hug, lay down in the middle of the floor when David went to the hall cupboard.

His drop-line with its heavy lead sinker was wrapped carefully around a little wooden frame. It sat on a shelf along with his mother's gardening basket and gloves and scissors that she used to cut flowers with and just above his father's golf clubs and some raincoats hung on hook. He reached up and got down the drop-line, being careful not to jab himself with the barbed end of the hook which he'd tucked into the wound-around line when he'd finished fishing the week before with Uncle Haydn but which stuck out halfway.

Back in the hallway, Gauguin was still lying where he'd plunked down on the middle of a white square. When David came out of the closet, the dog looked up at him and slowly thumped his tail on the marble floor, and David knew Gauguin was hoping he'd get him a dog biscuit from Grandfather Darwin's study where they were kept in a big jar. Or maybe a cookie from Mr. Perkins's butler's pantry, but he decided against it. Mr. Perkins might already be up, or Nellie the cook, or Mary, and he didn't want to have them say, "Good Morning, Mister David," which they were certain to say, and, "What are you doing up so early?" because he'd have to answer, and if either his mother or father happened to be awake, they might hear him. So he pointed to Gauguin's bed and pushed him toward it because he didn't want Gauguin going with him. Gauguin would almost certainly bark at some seagull sitting on the hand railing of the dock, and he didn't want anybody to wonder why Gauguin was outside and look to see and then see him.

But Gauguin followed him just the same when he crossed back over the hall to the wide double doors that led off the hall to the living room. He decided to leave the house by one of the French doors there because it wouldn't make as much noise opening and shutting as the front door did. Once in the living room, he was wondering how to get rid of Gauguin when he remembered that just before his mother had taken him up to bed, and Grandfather and she and Uncle Haydn and Gabriel were still sitting around talking, she'd rescued from Gauguin a bowl of nuts on the glass cocktail table and put it up out of his reach on the mantelpiece. He could see it there, directly below the big painting that Grandfather loved of the old-fashioned, square-rigged men-o'-war ships in the midst of a battle. Standing on tiptoe, he got it down. He took out a couple of the biggest nuts, carefully put the bowl back on the mantel, and dropped the nuts on the floor right in front of Gauguin. When the dog at once dove to pick them up, he made for the French door as quickly as possible without bumping into any of the furniture and knocking things over. He got the door open and was out before Gauguin realized he'd been tricked and left behind.

On the flagstone terrace, he paused long enough to look out across the bay. The early on-shore breeze coming in from the Atlantic hadn't started yet, and the water in the harbor was as smooth as glass. He'd be able to see clear to the bottom and watch the fish coming after his hook. But he'd have to hurry. So he bounded down off the terrace and ran across the lawn as fast as he could, dodging croquet wickets and stakes. If anyone saw him and called out, he'd pretend he didn't hear them, and the farther he was away from the house and the closer he got to the dock, the greater chance he had of telling the truth.

He didn't stop until he'd gone under the grape arbor and was on the beach wall by the gate Grandfather had put across the foot of the dock to keep his father and Uncle Haydn off it when they were his age. Nobody had ever bothered to take it down, and over the years its big iron handle and lock had got so rusty you had to be a grown-up to open it, and then it sagged slightly on its main post so that the bottom of it scraped on the dirt and gravel where there'd once been grass, and the heavy rusty hinges made a terrible sound he was sure would wake up the whole house, even if he could open it. So he pushed his drop-line between the two bottom slats of the gate so that it fell onto the worn planking of the dock itself and then, with a last look back at the house, he climbed over.

The dock, weather-worn from several score of storms, was long and narrow. It began at the low wall separating the beach from higher property and the grape arbor and went at least fifty feet, Uncle Haydn said, out over the water. It had handrails on both sides and stood on barnacle-crusted wooden piles nearly four feet above the water at high tide and at low tide a good deal more. At the end, there was a hinged ramp that went down to a square float on eight barrels. That was where everyone swam from rather than from the beach itself, which was often littered with flotsam and seaweed and where you could cut your feet on broken shells. The ramp had wheels on its end where it reached the float, so as the float rose with the tide it would flatten out, and when the tide was out it would become steeper. Tethered to the float was the fast little Chris-Craft motor launch David's father and his uncle Haydn used for waterskiing and to reach the *South Wind,* his father's sixty-foot ketch, moored across the harbor close to the Coatue bar where the water was deeper. David wasn't allowed in the launch and had once risked his father's wrath by slipping behind the wheel when no one was looking to pretend he was driving it.

Before he went out onto the dock, David dropped off the beach wall onto the beach to one side of it. The tide was just beginning to ebb, and he ran quickly along the beach to an outcropping of large rocks where, below the high tide mark, he found a cluster of periwinkles. He pulled some loose and jammed them into one pocket of his jeans. Next, scouring the sand, he found a fist-sized stone which he slipped into another pocket and then ran back to the dock and down the ramp at its end onto the float.

There, he put one of the periwinkles on the smooth boards and, taking the stone from his pocket, smashed its shell and pulled out the periwinkle. Holding it fast, he pushed the point of his drop-line hook well through the periwinkle so the barb wouldn't let it come off. At the edge of the float, he lay flat on his stomach, his head out over the water, and slowly unwound the drop-line with its heavy sinker off the frame and looked down.

For a moment he saw little. The tremor of the line made by the descending sinker and hook first rippled the water's mirrorlike surface. When the water calmed, it reflected the sky, making the surface shine a silvery blue and still hard to see through. David inched forward a little, holding his free hand out over the water to shield the water from the sky.

And then he saw—deep down, just off the bottom where his hook was. Saw and for a moment didn't understand. A wheel and what seemed a pile of cloth.

His scream had already begun to rise in his throat and fill his whole being when a fish poked hard into one of his grandfather's dead, staring eyes.

TWO

The evening before this terrible event, David's father, Chase, finally showed up after David had gone up to bed. He was concern itself, asking a dozen questions: Had David had a wonderful time? What had he done all day? Did he like all his presents? He thanked Haydn for playing surrogate father and apologized for his absence, which he excused as unavoidable. "You put me in a spot that's sometimes too hot to ignore, Father," he said to Darwin, "when you insisted I take over Carlyle."

Throughout the hour before she and Haydn, and later Felicity, excused themselves, Gabrielle felt a vague unease at Chase's interest in David's birthday and his general affability. She wondered if any of the others felt the same. It almost seemed to her as if Chase were putting on a skillful act to hide that he was troubled over something he didn't want anyone to know about.

Later, in the Blue guest room she'd always been offered on previous visits to The Moorings, and listening to the soft sounds and smells of the sea, Gabrielle found sleep difficult. David was wonderful, the classic small boy. He reminded her of Tom Sawyer, always with his shoelaces untied, a normal amount of dirt on his face, hair unruly, things forever tumbling out of his pockets, his shirttail adrift—and, in spite of all that, miraculously unspoiled. But Chase and Darwin, Chase and Felicity, Darwin and Haydn, Haydn and Chase? There was always such an undercurrent of conflict. Bad enough her feeling of guilt making public some of family intimacies she'd slowly learned about and sent in almost daily reports to *France Aujourd'hui*; worse were her feelings where Haydn was concerned. Saying goodnight to him, whether at the Moorings or in New York, and keeping a distance between them was becoming increasingly difficult. An affair or an infatuation was one thing. She'd weathered that with a number of interesting men, but it was different with Haydn. He was the first in her life about whom she felt a desire for permanence and, no matter how hard she'd tried to resist, she had fallen in love and hard almost from the day they'd met. She could handle it, she had enough Gallic toughness in her for that, except that Haydn's almost ardent attention didn't help. She had enough common sense to know that many seemingly sincere men mistake sexual desire for love, and she wasn't going to risk her hard-won position as a journalist in the utter emotional destruction she'd feel if it turned out that for Haydn she was only a casual affair. Reinforcing her caution was that Haydn knew quite well her visit was brief. She would be returning to France as soon as she'd finished up a full report on the family and the Carlyle auction house. So when he made a first tentative pass at her, she had ducked, even though it had taken everything she had not to respond.

But supposing she had succumbed? Would it also have been an affront to get involved with Haydn when a guest in his family home? She didn't think Darwin would have minded all that much. He was an American *aristo*, to be sure, and they all pretended to hold to a standard in manners superior to anyone else, but somehow she felt he was a little different from the rest when it came to affairs. He'd had a few himself, she suspected. But what about Pamela Rhinelander, the Boston socialite who had her sights set so hard on Darwin that when she came down to The Moorings she bossed the servants around as well as Darwin, as though she had already won him. She was sure that Pamela Rhinelander, if she learned there was sex in the Blue Room, or even sex someplace else with Haydn, would somehow use it to get at her. Without mincing words, the woman had made it quite clear from the moment Haydn had introduced her that she didn't think anyone who wasn't American, or, if a foreigner, didn't have a title, was socially acceptable. Pamela Rhinelander was so impressed with titles, especially English ones, that she had cultivated a phony English accent and kept two yapping little Corgi dogs in imitation of the British Queen Elizabeth.

Gabrielle's thoughts wandered then to the strange circumstances that had brought her to America and into the bosom of the Morse family. Her mind left the present to pick out scenes like a roving camera from life even before *France Aujourd'hui*: her home in France, the run-down, centuries-old château on the Cher River near Tours that so badly needed repairs her impoverished father couldn't afford. If someone had told her two years ago that she would find herself involved in all the complexities of a famous American family on the island of Nantucket off Cape Cod, she would have simply laughed. Two years ago, she didn't even have the job. Two years ago, she was just out of journalism school in Paris and up on the roof of the château with her father replacing broken tiles and talking about how to get employed when her mother, in her apron and holding a mixing bowl and spoon, had emerged from the kitchen and called up to her to come down.

"Gabrielle! Ecoute! Il y a un monsieur a l'appareil qui te demande."

"C'est qui, alors?"

"Sais pas. Quelqu'un de *France Aujourd'hui*."

"J'arrive, Maman." And she'd climbed down off the roof into a never-dreamed-of job and then into a never-dreamed-of future when she was unexpectedly summoned again, only six months ago, by *France Aujourd'hui*'s severe and legendary senior editor, Bernard Bligny, to his cluttered office on the top floor of the weekly magazine's old building on the Rue St. Antoine in Paris. Heart in her mouth, she'd obeyed with no inkling of what lay in store for her. All she'd been able to think was that she somehow hadn't sufficiently backed up with facts her conclusions on the article he'd assigned her to do on price gouging at the *marché aux puces* at the Porte de Clignancourt.

The venerable editor had been in his shirtsleeves, his feet up on his desk, reading *Le Monde*. When he'd tossed the Paris daily to one side, put his feet down, stamped out the *Gauloise* he'd been smoking, and smilingly asked her if she'd like to do an article in America, she'd at first thought she'd misheard him.

"Alors, jeune fille," he'd demanded, "how would you like to go to America? The United States, New York, and some place called Nantucket!" And without waiting for her to reply, "Yes? Good. I want you to do something on a major auction house, Sotheby's or Christie's or Carlyle. We'll run it as a weekly series, so you'll need to file reports on a regular basis. They should be not so much on how the auction business works, everybody's done that, but human interest stuff, something on the people who run the show. Carlyle, for example. It's a family business, has been for four or five generations. Huge. Offices in London and Rome and here in Paris, yes, but the family's in New York. A Chase Morse is currently in charge. His father, Darwin, is a legendary name in fine arts auctioning. He had a stroke and was forced to retire. Yes, try them. We have a connection there, Morse's youngest son, I believe, name of Haydn. Yes, Like the composer," he laughed. "I'm told his mother was listening to a Haydn symphony when he was born. He doesn't actually work in the business; he operates his own show, sells antiquarian books and paintings. Begin with him. Dimitri, downstairs, you've met him; he covers whatever scandal is brewing at the Hôtel de Ville, he can give you an introduction. He knows this American fellow quite well, apparently. They did a bicycle tour of Crete together two years ago."

A week later, in New York, she'd found Haydn's unassuming bookshop-gallery, surprisingly with a French name, La Rive Gauche, in the eighties on Columbus Avenue, and had for a moment thought she was back in Paris visiting Shake-speare and Company on Quai des Grands-Augustins. The place, although crowded with paintings as well as books, was so similar in atmosphere.

Expecting Haydn to be as formidable himself as Dimitri had described his family, she was more than surprised when a quiet and reserved young man, whose light stammer, when-ever nervous, matched a slender, scholarly appearance, empha-sized by old corduroys, a sweatshirt, and unruly brown hair in need of cutting, modestly revealed himself as Haydn Morse. She was even more surprised when she discovered that he not only spoke fluent French but had spent two years studying art history at the Sorbonne in Paris, that he painted on the side and saw himself as one day residing permanently in France.

During the week that followed, he made sure she felt wel-comed. He took her all over town, to lunch and dine at places she found no different than the fun places in Paris she haunted; and once he drove her to a delightful country inn up the Hud-son River valley. "Just so you don't think everything is New York," he'd said.

During working hours she met and interviewed his brother, Chase, at Carlyle House, the New York headquarters of the great auction establishment. Like Haydn, in his thirties, but three years older, he was courtesy itself. He arranged for her to interview any department head who she thought would be helpful to the article she'd come to write. But she sensed constraint between him and Haydn, with Haydn guarded, as though avoiding saying anything that could be misconstrued; and with Chase, she thought, slightly condescending about Haydn's lesser, small-shop role in the art world.

She came away from the meeting having found the two quite unlike in nearly every way. Chase was big and ruggedly handsome, with a football player build and impeccably dressed and groomed, as though he'd stepped out of an advertisement for the best in Wall Street wear at work while at home his clothes were the best of the top designer casual wear. Where Haydn was quietly modest and self-effacing, almost taciturn, but hiding nothing of himself, Chase, in comparison, although projecting well-mannered self-assurance, was at the same time guardedly reserved, so that one never quite knew what he was thinking. She found it extremely difficult to interview him. Responses to her questions were always, she sensed, faintly tinged with condescension. No answer ever contained more than the barest skeleton of the information she sought. Statements from herself, calculated to elicit more helpful reaction, were invariably greeted with silence, so that she found herself babbling on embarrassingly. Soon she got the feeling that his manners and courtesy were a kind of armor to mask class intolerance because she didn't fit in with his elitist social standing which, she discovered, was exemplified by the *New York Social Register*, the private telephone directory of the fast-fading so-called "society."

It was available, she learned, only to those who "belonged," giving them an exclusive and restricted status they felt placed them above everyone else. It told you, in a listing, a man's college, his year of graduation, who his parents were, his mother's maiden name, the names of his children, his wife's education, and her maiden name. Even more exclusive was the *Blue Book*, which listed only one hundred of New York's most "socially acceptable" families, and which Pamela Rhinelander lived by, limiting her friendships to those listed in it. Gabrielle wondered how she, or any others in either listing, could continue to believe that the world those books represented was still of any importance. Haydn had turned his back on all of it long before he had finished studies at the exclusive boarding school to which he'd been sent. He rarely visited The Moorings, and then apparently only to see his nephew, David. Gabrielle had to believe his staying away was also due, in part at least, to a strong distaste for Chase's barely concealed patronizing as well as Darwin's relentless domineering, even when good-natured.

She felt she couldn't live with either herself.

She soon learned that the senior Morse, ever since the stroke had confined him to retirement and a wheelchair, simply overrode everyone, especially Chase, whom, Haydn said, he had virtually ordered to the helm of Carlyle. Iron-willed, he forced people either to do everything his way or suffer an open breech with him. He did it less with Haydn than with anyone and even less where she was concerned, Gabrielle reflected. At times he'd shown her a rare softer side. If she'd summoned the courage to dispute him, he'd been politeness itself in respecting what she had to say. She couldn't help wondering, however, if he liked her for herself or if he wanted to portray himself favorably because she was doing an article about the family and, in spite of his son's obvious interest in her, would soon be gone.

One day when Haydn took her for a picnic on one of the long, empty surf- pounded beaches on Nantucket's southeast coast and she'd asked him, he'd been candid in answering her. "Personally, I think he likes you," he'd said. "But he mostly connects you with me since I brought you out here. In his mind I'm more or less dismissed because he thinks I've ruined my life by taking up art and running a bookstore. Hence, in a way, you're not worth his time either."

"But why would he dismiss you for being an artist? His whole life has been art."

"Ah, yes. Art. But not the people who create it. He sees the artist as some kind of a social freak. Like Van Gogh about to cut off an ear. Or Gauguin, retreating to Polynesia to revel among bare-breasted young beauties."

"So you get spared and Chase gets bullied unmercifully. It doesn't make sense."

"I don't disagree with you. He dismissed my mother the same way. My father, bless him, is someone who can't think outside of his own particular formula of what people should be."

Later that evening, when she was alone with Felicity, who was giving her some cream for a slight sunburn, Felicity remarked that Haydn, in his liberal attitudes, was much like his mother, Ariel, who had come from an old New Orleans family of French and Spanish nobility. Gabrielle could learn little of the woman except what Haydn and Felicity had told her. Ariel's own family before her marriage were either dead or dispersed to the four winds. Several editors of her work she had interviewed said she had an extraordinarily fine mind burdened by temperament as well as friction with the various lovers she had taken after her divorce from Morse. She had been born to prestige and wealth, to be a "society" wife, and had been renowned for that and for her considerable beauty as well, and for being an outstanding a horsewoman.

Then in a kind of epiphany—a revelation of the shallowness of her life—she had abruptly turned her back on all of that. Even before she and Darwin divorced, she had become her own person, a liberated woman long before her time who no longer felt she had to defer to a husband when deferring meant being subservient to male chauvinism. She had identified with liberal causes, focusing her attention on struggling young artists and writers, and writing serious poetry and several novels herself. In her last few years, before a toxic combination of alcohol and prescription drugs brought on by the pain of a bungled back operation tragically ended her life, she had also become a highly vocal advocate of laborers' rights, ardently espousing the cause of commercial cannery workers in New England fishing ports.

Chase saw her change as an acute social embarrassment and a threat to the protection of his own social standing. When Ariel and Darwin divorced, he virtually rejected his mother and never saw her except for brief formal visits every Christmas, and then only because Darwin insisted on it for David's sake.

Gabrielle learned from Haydn, and later from Felicity, however, that there was a reason behind that, a sad one. To her surprise Haydn told her that Chase had started off in life quite differently. "Actually," he'd said, "my brother deep down is, or at least used to be, more like my mother than I am." Chase, it seemed, had once shown signs of real artistic talent. He had taken photographs that earned the praise of the great Walker Evans, a friend of Ariel. He was inventive, building his own shortwave radio when only eleven or twelve, and he was adventuresome and imaginative.

"But Haydn, what happened?"

"Me," Haydn had replied bluntly. "For reasons I've never really understood, she found me perfect. Perhaps it was because the burden of a first child is always more than that of the second when a woman is finally used to the endless struggle with a tiny ego and all its demands. In comparison to me, maybe Chase and everything she'd been through with him, learning motherhood, was suddenly resented. She bullied him incessantly, morning, noon, and night. He could do nothing right, poor guy. And I saw him begin to withdraw more and more into himself and to distance himself more and more from Ariel and everything she represented, especially when she began lavishing praise on me. So when in prep school he became conscious of a different world than the one his mother was always extolling, he sought safety in it."

Poor Chase, Gabrielle thought. Unattractive as she found his arrogance and patronizing air of superiority to be, it was hard at the same time not to feel a certain compassion for him. The knowledge emphasized to Gabrielle what she had already realized; in writing about the family she was going to have difficulty separating what was grist for the public from what she morally felt she had to keep to herself in order not to betray information given to her in confidence. She wanted to point out to Haydn that his brother had clearly swapped being bullied by his mother for being bullied by his father. Out of the frying pan into the fire, she thought. But she didn't, because, in a way, it also meant sharing her dilemma as a journalist with Haydn, which might make her relationship with him even more intimate and thus more disturbing than it already was.

The gulf between Chase and Haydn, the two so different in nature to begin with, had widened irreparably since they left school. The lives and characters of those they counted as friends were miles apart. Beneath Haydn's mild and academic exterior, Gabrielle soon discovered not just the heart of a lion but a fiercely independent nature and an iron determination. His social acquaintances, many of whom he'd introduced to her, represented a rainbow spectrum ranging from artists and writers to scientists, inventors, and people in theater or films. Chase's friendships, on the contrary, were virtually restricted to former college classmates from *Social Register* backgrounds, the Princeton Club or the Union Club, and to a handful whose origins he disregarded when their stellar performance on Wall Street impressed him or proved useful. Now, save for their sharing a father and time off at The Moorings, the two brothers rarely spoke, other than exchanging trivia or when Haydn would rise in defense of Felicity when Chase would unfairly disapprove of something she said or did, or all but sneer at her vibrant and protective love for their son.

Gabrielle saw Chase's attitude toward his wife, as well as toward women in general, as cavalier and frequently embarrassing to others. Was it a natural reaction to Ariel, a misplaced arrogance toward all women as a kind of revenge against her? She was constantly surprised at Felicity's lack of reaction to some of his affronts, although she noticed that Felicity rarely showed Chase the warm and generous disposition with which she rewarded others. Gabrielle wondered, too, that while surrounded by wealth beyond the wildest dreams of most and a social position many women may have envied, Felicity seemed to detach herself from all of it as of no importance. She showed little interest in social affairs and little for clothes or jewelry. She wore the minimum of makeup and dressed simply, with clearly no interest in fashion. Creatively talented, she instead immersed herself in painting excellent watercolors of flowers and in turning out decorative ceramics on her potter's wheel.

Altogether, Gabrielle could only wonder at her marriage. She and Chase seemed more social acquaintances than husband and wife, and they had separate bedrooms and baths.

Thinking, then, about what she would e-mail to Bernard Bligny the next day, Gabrielle eventually fell asleep. Awaking, she at first thought the scream she heard was in her dreams, and then that it was the cry of a sea gull. And then realized it was human. What on earth had happened? An accident? Some kind of terrible trouble? When its sheer terror finally jarred her into reality, she heard voices, suddenly, Felicity's and her husband's.

Felicity was crying out over and over, her voice wild with fear, "David, David!" And Gabrielle heard Chase say, "For God's sake, Felicity, calm down," and irritatedly, "What the devil has the silly child gone and done now?"

Gabrielle rose quickly and threw on her robe. Out on the landing she ran into Haydn. "Hay, what's happened?"

"I don't know. It sounded like David."

"He's up already?"

"Down at the dock, I think."

"Is he hurt, or what?"

"Don't know."

The screaming was fainter here, barely audible out of the room where the window was open. Haydn ran down the stairs and she followed. In the hall, Perkins appeared from his pantry, his shirtsleeves rolled up and without his jacket and tie. Gauguin was running to the living room and back, barking.

"Perkins. Do you know what's happened?"

"No, sir, Mr. Haydn. I've just heard it myself. Is it David?"

Haydn didn't answer. He raced into the living room, threw open a French door, and bolted outside. Gabrielle followed him, colliding with Perkins and almost falling.

"Sorry, Miss."

She didn't answer. She ran after Haydn across the terrace and then the croquet lawn, cursing her robe, which kept opening to expose her very short nightdress which kept riding up from her thighs. She could see Felicity and Haydn, already by the gate barring entry to the dock. And David. Felicity had fallen to her knees and was holding the boy tight against her. He had stopped screaming. When Gabrielle drew up to them herself, David was gasping for breath and babbling something that was incomprehensible. Felicity's kept saying, "It's all right, darling. It's all right. We're here."

Chase joined them, towering over both David and Felicity. In his short terry cloth robe, his muscular dark-haired legs looked incongruously out of place. "David, where are you hurt?" And then, "Come on, boy, pull yourself together. Answer me! What have you done to yourself?"

Haydn knelt next to David. "He's not hurt, Chase."

"What do you mean, he's not hurt? What do you think he was screaming for?"

Haydn said, "What's happened, David? I think he's just had a bad scare, Chase."

"Oh, for Heaven's sake, Haydn. Of what?"

It was Perkins who opened the gate barring the dock.

Chase said, "Perkins, come back, please. I'm sure you have things to do in the house."

The butler didn't answer and headed determinedly toward the distant ramp and float.

"Perkins!" Chase gave up on him, muttering annoyance at being ignored, "Bloody man." And then said to the others more moderately, "Now, look. Let's everybody calm down. Felicity, do get David to make sense, will you? So we can all go back to bed. And what was he doing down here in the first place at this hour?"

Haydn said, "Fishing, I suspect." He put a gentle hand on David's head. "Were you fishing. David?" He looked up at Chase. "Father gave him permission last night at dinner."

Gabrielle saw Perkins disappear down the ramp to the float. Something—instinct, intuition?—told her that Perkins was the one person who knew that was where the trouble lay, whatever it might be. She followed. When she got to the ramp herself, Perkins was kneeling at the edge of the float by David's drop-line frame. He was looking down at the water. As Gabriel started down the ramp toward him, he stood and turned. His face was ashen.

"Perkins, what is it? Mr. Perkins?"

When he didn't answer, she knew it was very bad. There was a ringing in her ears, her mouth turned to sand. She pushed past the butler and knelt at the edge of the float and looked down into the water herself, shielding the water from the sky, as David had done. She hadn't been a journalist for very long, but had already seen a lot she would have been happy to forget: the mangled bodies of kids in highway accidents, the bloated corpses of the murdered, photos at work that would never be shown to the public, of soldiers ripped to shreds by shrapnel. But now, when she saw what David had seen, and Perkins, she rose and had difficulty in breathing. She moved to Perkins, who stood rooted with shock where he was when she'd pushed by him. She saw tears streaking his always immobile face, and she touched his shoulder. "I'm so sorry, Mr. Perkins. I'm so terribly sorry."

She went up the ramp slowly. Nothing seemed real, the dock, the lawn, and house beyond. At the top of the ramp, she met Haydn.

"Gabrielle, what's happened?"

She blocked him from going down. "Haydn, don't go down, please don't. You mustn't."

He stared, tried to go past her, but she still wouldn't let him. She put a restraining hand gently against his chest and felt her heart break for him. "Haydn, it's your father. He—he's gone."

THREE

The police came. And an ambulance. The shrill, pulsating scream of their sirens could be heard for minutes before they finally arrived, beginning as a distant whisper, then louder, a sound that in the softness of the early morning seemed intrusively alien. Mercifully, they silenced as they entered the front gates of The Moorings. There was then only the crunch of driveway gravel as their tires passed over it and as they came up to the circle in front of the house and parked with the heavy sound of car doors slamming as officers and paramedics emerged.

But the silence didn't last long. A cub reporter for a mainland newspaper who was visiting the island got wind of what had happened. Hoping to ingratiate himself with the Associated Press, he quickly punched in their number on his cell phone and let them know that there'd been a death on the Nantucket estate of Darwin Morse, possibly even Morse himself. Before the day was out, the media circus descended on The Moorings.

Unlike the police, however, any discomfort the news-hungry journalists might have felt for intruding on such obvious wealth and social status was overcome by aggressive brashness. A dozen or more, flown in by their papers or news syndicates, quickly swarmed the property. Some, ignoring the yellow "Police activity" tape stretched across the driveway, managed even to get into the house, looking for servants to corner in hopes of revealing some family scandal.

Darwin gone, Chase took over and quickly searched out the Nantucket Police officer who seemed in charge, to say, flatly, that if the reporters along with television cameramen weren't shown off the property immediately and held off it, that he would see to it there'd be trouble. The Morse family had political clout with the governor as well as in the federal government.

Chase's demand served to create hostility between him and the police. Darwin Morse had been a deeply respected and much welcomed lifetime resident of the island, as other Morses had been before him, right back to his great grandfather. Bill Booker, acting police chief in the absence of his boss in hospital recovering from a heart attack, was already doing his best to restrict the rampaging media, not only in order to protect the privacy of the family but to keep it from disturbing the rest of the island as well. The tranquility of Nantucket, as long as he was in charge, was not going to be disrupted by an uncontrolled media circus. He had issued particularly strict orders that any paparazzi were to be warned off in no uncertain terms and, if necessary, an excuse found to lock them up.

Thus, even before Chase threatened, the unwanted reporters and TV personnel were in retreat to the outer limits of The Moorings where, in hushed groups clustered around their cars or broadcast vans, they issued first hourly then daily reports concocted out of thin air or from rumors they could dramatically embellish. Drownings among established socialites didn't occur every day, especially among the highly circumspect elder generation. It was open season on the Morse family in favor of a public who could never get enough whiffs of scandal on the rarified mountaintops of society.

Like many resort places, Nantucket had the usual town-and-gown social division. Bill Booker, a square-shouldered, good-natured yet slightly laconic man of forty, was strictly "town" and a fourth generation islander who had quarterbacked on the high school football team. He was the son of a man who had served a good number of years as deputy chief in Nantucket's fire department, and he had chosen police work after various jobs in one of the boatyards where he had worked installing and repairing maritime navigational equipment. Looking for a more diverse and interesting career, and without a college degree, he had enrolled in the state police academy at New Bedford, from which he'd graduated with flying colors, and at twenty-two signed up with the island police. Within a year he married Ellen Parker, the daughter of a captain on one of the car ferries of the Steamship Company connecting Nantucket to Falmouth on the Cape. By the time the couple had been together eighteen years, they had three children, all boys in middle and high school, and Booker, who had found nearly every aspect of police work interesting, was deputy chief.

Booker still had a closely intimate relationship with his wife. Ellen was a pretty and youthful woman whom he adored and who had become the ultimate soccer mom. Both parents took an intense interest in their boys' studies and school activities, and when the call came of a serious incident at The Moorings, Booker had been up since dawn readying fishing tackle for a day out at sea with Ellen and the boys on his brother's game fishing boat. It was the season for the bluefish to run, and they expected some great catches. Trying not to hear the groans of disappointment, he asked Ellen to refrigerate his share of the box lunch she'd put together in case he got home for dinner, switched on the roof and interior flashing police lights along with the siren in his unmarked car, and headed from his small unpretentious clapboarded home off Macomet Avenue across town for Polpis Road, which bordered Coatue Sound.

Booker had never had any problems with the social division of town and gown. His easy attitude stood him in good stead on an island visited by the superrich and where a number of the same lived permanently. Police work had taught him that no matter what the wealth or lack of it and no matter how high or low in social standing, people were still prone to the same passions, the same strengths and weaknesses, and except for the habitual criminal class, of which there were virtually none on Nantucket, could all get into the same kinds of trouble.

With accidental death almost immediately ruled out after the most cursory questioning put to family members and servants, it hadn't taken him long to conclude that, impossible as it seemed, Darwin Morse had either been murdered or was a suicide. Homicide seemed the far more likely of the two. It was almost inconceivable that a man whose very essence was said to be positive by all who knew him, and who had just spent a pleasant evening with his family, could have wanted to kill himself. Booker had met Darwin Morse twice at civic affairs gatherings, for Morse had always taken a serious interest in the lives and goings-on of the permanent island population and had generously contributed considerable money to various civic organizations. He had come away from both meetings with the impression that he'd talked with a lion who savored life above everything.

Besides this, Morse was in his seventy-eighth year. His stroke had left him partially paralyzed and unable to tend to his most physical needs. If indeed he had wanted to make suicide a route out of life by drowning himself, he would have had to get himself in and out of the elevator between his ground floor study and his upstairs bedroom, and silently. This at about one in the morning when, according to the medical examiner, he died. And then what? How on earth could he have traversed in darkness not only the house but the lawn, with all its croquet wickets, then opened the awkward gate fencing off the dock before negotiating the dock itself and finally descended onto the float by the ramp? This ultimate obstacle was at a steep angle due to the tide being on ebb and very likely slippery as well from the night fog that often fell over Nantucket this time of year.

Receiving his report to that effect and late that day, the district attorney for the Cape and Islands and the ultimate authority where any suspicion of crime on Nantucket was concerned flew down from his headquarters at Barnstable on the Cape. With him came a state police detective lieutenant and two forensic troopers from CPAC, the crime prevention and correction unit. Their job—to assist Chief Booker in his investigation.

While Booker appreciated the help and warmly welcomed the DA and his state police colleagues, he had a hunch that no amount of routine forensic and basic investigatory work was going to be of any real assistance to him in getting to the bottom of the patriarch's death. Although it all had to be done in order to provide solid facts for a jury, in the back of Booker's mind the thought persisted that only luck and intuitive guesswork, along with a thorough analysis and understanding of the character of everyone who could possibly be suspected, would ultimately reveal the truth and bring about justice.

While uncharacteristically cursing all socialites for whatever national attention they drew down on themselves, Bill Booker knew it would do him little good with the district attorney, who ruled his professional life, to say he was unprepared to discuss the case with the media. Accordingly, and accepting the medical examiner's temporary conclusion prior to autopsy that Morse had drowned, he reluctantly joined the DA and the state police detective lieutenant in facing the bank of microphones and television cameras, all too common in such circumstances, to present a report to the nation and the world beyond. Fielding a withering barrage of impossible-to-answer questions, he rendered the conclusion that Morse had been murdered by persons unknown but that the police hoped to have a serious lead in the near future. It was a formula the media had heard often enough where other famous crimes were concerned, but as Booker steadfastly refused to accommodate them further, they were stuck with it and could do nothing except continue to prowl the exterior limits of The Moorings.

Booker waited for what he thought was a decent interval

to allow the family to bury the patriarch, to come to grips with their grief, and to let the media become so bored with standing outside the property in a vigil so unrelentingly tedious that many left voluntarily or were called off by their various news editors to cover events elsewhere. Then, aided by CPAC detectives and forensic experts, he set to work. He had the "how" Morse had been murdered: he had been cold-bloodedly pushed off the float. Strapped firmly, as always, to his wheelchair, the weight of it insured he'd stay under to drown. What was left was the daunting task of ascertaining the "who" and the "why."

When her husband got his teeth into any ordinary felony, Ellen Booker was used to resigning herself to his total concentration on it. From experience she knew that if he didn't spend most of every evening at police headquarters, he'd hog the kitchen table at dinnertime with his laptop, if not at his PC in what they laughingly called his study, a glorified broom cupboard into which he had managed to squeeze a desk and chair. The day after Darwin Morse was laid to rest in a private cemetery on Nantucket, Ellen Booker picked up the telephone and started arranging endless bowling and movie times for herself and her brood. Before she left the house that day, she confronted her husband.

"Bill, honey. Why don't you skip this one?"

"Do what?"

"Recuse yourself."

"On what grounds?"

"Knowing the family. Being too close to whatever. I'm sure we could come up with some reason."

"You must be kidding."

"Sweetheart, this isn't ordinary felony. This is big-news homicide. Look at all the biggies at the funeral. Chase Morse threatening you with his palship with the governor and the war you've already had with the media. You were even on the front page of the *New York Times* and the *Wall Street Journal.* You're a good cop, everyone says so, but you weren't trained for this sort of thing. It's going to drive you nuts."

"Couldn't care less. And Morse can go fuck himself."

"Don't be stupid. More likely he can fuck you."

"Ellen, slow down, okay? I'm not backing out of this. I'm in charge of the police here until Chief gets back, if ever. It's my job, okay? I'm not walking out on it."

Ellen knew her husband well enough also to know when to shut up. The cornered quarterback who could still come out fighting from his own ten-yard line and win a game was written all over his face. Maybe he'd calm down a bit in a day or so when the going got even rougher and see the light. She sighed, "It's all yours, sweetheart," kissed his forehead, and headed out the door.

Looking at her retreating back, Booker had a dismal feeling that she might be proved right. The worst part of this wasn't the media, though. The worst part was going to be the dreary, boring, endless collecting of evidence, evidence, and more evidence. And paperwork. Goddamn, how he hated paperwork, all of it probably a total waste of time but just the same required. Experience had taught him that even minor felony cases could keep him busy for hours filing reports left, right, and center. There were times like this when he wished the hell he'd stayed in the boatyard.

Staring blankly at the screen of his computer, he had a brief picture of the lost day out in the sound with the boys and his brother after bluefish, then pushed it out of his mind and tried to add things up, see where he stood. A coroner's autopsy, confirming the medical examiner's initial report of death by drowning, had revealed no toxic substance or drugs of any kind in the deceased, which might have rendered him unconscious when he was wheeled down the dock to his death. This meant one thing; in the absence of any outcry or even a feeble struggle, Darwin Morse had known his murderer. It also meant suspecting a daunting number of people who had not been in the house, along with those who had been, since Morse during his life had amassed a considerable number of business acquaintances as well as cronies whose names sounded like a who's who of America's Northeast establishment and nearly all of whom he would have greeted without fear or a hesitation that might have alarmed the family dog.

Outsiders also included the old man's nurse, Marie Costello, who came every weekday morning to rouse, feed, and bathe the old man and look after him during the day before returning to her home and husband in their cottage in Siasconset, a village at the eastern end of the island. Booker knew Marie: a first class woman, you couldn't find better, her husband a joiner at the local boatyard and an occasional lobsterman. She was from an Italian American family who threw great red wine and pizza blowouts in the summer and had once told Booker that she liked old Morse, that he was kind in his gruff way to his servants and others but rough on his sons, especially the older one, which she thought was maybe due to his wife having left him.

Also included was Thomas Mason, the chauffeur who lived alone in a two-room apartment above the garage. Booker had learned of his prison record in an automatic database checkup when Thomas had once got himself a parking ticket. He'd met and talked to Thomas at the time and had come to the conclusion that Thomas was a man who might conceivably rob if forced to, yes, but murder, never. The man's work with SHEP, the Society Helping Ex-Prisoners, down in Newark, was certainly a plus in his favor. Just the same, he made a mental note that the man had had the weekend off and supposedly had been away when Morse died, but perhaps not. A third person was Asa Hammond who, like Costello, did not work weekends. Booker deemed the elderly groundskeeper, a somewhat eccentric native of the island, utterly incapable of killing anyone save his implacable enemies, the moles who tore up the Morse estate lawns.

If Morse had met an outsider, Booker wondered what the stricken old man might have been up to that he didn't want his family to know about and that had caused someone to take the risk of coming to his home to kill him with all his family present. Morse would have had to be expecting him or her, Booker thought, and pictured the patriarch giving whomever it might have been telephone or e-mail instructions as to where to meet him. This could hardly have been in the bosom of the family bedroom area upstairs, so Morse would have had to do what Booker had already dismissed as virtually impossible—namely and without making a rousing noise, get himself downstairs on the elevator and even out onto the terrace, if that was where a meeting was planned. But a check of Morse's computer as well as phone calls had shown that no message had been sent to anyone arranging a rendezvous. A further check on names from Darwin's personal phone book showed none of those listed had booked passage from the Cape to Nantucket either by air or sea during the two weeks previous to the murder.

Within days, Booker turned his methodical attention to the family, but only routinely, because he had little hope of getting any leads. Families like the Morses, he knew, were so insulated by wealth and heritage from the middle-class world he himself lived in, and often even from their own class, that they tended to close ranks to any strangers, particularly the police, either with a wall of silence or noncommittal, often hostile stances.

Skipping the grandson who had discovered the dead man under eight feet of water, he began with the young French journalist who was doing a story on the Morse family and their Carlyle auction business and had been the Morse family's weekend guest. Following his interview with her, he carefully and tactfully interviewed each member of the family in turn, and the servants as well. He used Darwin Morse's book-lined study to do it, seating himself behind the dead man's massively ornate nineteenth century desk, one previous owner of which had been Theodore Roosevelt. Being thus in the virtual presence of the deceased, he'd considered, might slightly unnerve those he interrogated and cause them to say things they would have otherwise intended to keep to themselves.

But as he had envisioned, he got nowhere. He came away with the same impression he had of celebrities on television whose personal lives were so carefully kept hidden that an adoring public could never know who they really were and what their real lives were like.

Each one he interviewed, except for the eldest son, attested to the fact that they had gone up to bed before ten o'clock.

"Maybe the whole family got together and did it," Ellen had joked one morning at breakfast.

"Not funny," he'd grumbled, and the eldest of the boys had nearly choked on bacon trying not to laugh.

Chase Morse, who had assumed control of the Carlyle auction concern two years before when his father had suffered the stroke, had come back from a business meeting in New York in time to chat briefly with his wife and brother and the French woman. When the others retired for the night, he had stayed with his father, first to talk about the auction business that had kept him away that day and then to put the old man to bed. He said Darwin Morse was in good spirits from the birthday dinner of his grandson and had given no indication whatsoever that he planned to meet with anyone that night. For him to do so, he'd added, would have been most unusual, if not impossible. Like the others, Chase reported he had heard no strange or disturbing sound from his father's bedroom or from any other place in the house.

It was the same story with the servants, none of whom had any apparent motive and about whom the district attorney's office uncovered relatively little in the way of interesting facts when an investigation into their backgrounds was broadened. The butler, Mr. Arthur Perkins, had come to the Morses with the highest recommendations from the Rothschilds, for whom he had worked for many years in England. He'd chosen to come to America in order to see a sister who had married in the States, decided to stay, and had been sent to the Morses by a leading domestic employment agency in New York. The chauffeur, Thomas Mason, somehow managed the exhausting quick turnaround weekend to far off Newark, New Jersey, and SHEP where a checkup revealed he indeed had been. A close scrutiny of the cook, Nellie Reilly, revealed only an overweight woman with a bad temper, and the parlor maid, Mary O'Donnell, had come to the Morse family directly off the boat from Ireland twenty-five years ago. Morse was her first employer; she had no relatives in the States and never went anywhere on her day off except to her room, where she was an avid fan of the TV soaps and evening reality shows.

Added up, none of those who were in the house when Darwin Morse had gone to his death seemed to have any reason or chance to have been implicated.

Further, in looking into the dead man's will, Booker found little to incriminate any beneficiary. In tangible property, Morse had left two exceedingly valuable paintings, one by Cezanne, the other by Pissarro, to his alma mater, Princeton University. His personal belongings, his gold watch, binoculars, favorite twelve-gauge shot gun, and the quite extensive collection of major jewelry he'd given his wife, Ariel, which, during their divorce, she'd returned to him, he'd divided between his daughter-in-law, Felicity, and his son Haydn, with the stipulation that Haydn was to give his share of the jewelry to a wife if and when he married.

Where greater sums were concerned, he had willed several hundred millions to Princeton and to foundations in which he'd always had an interest. He had also left the very substantial sum of three hundred million to the Carlyle Foundation, established by him many years before to benefit educational scholarships and talented and aspiring young artists.

To his sons, Chase and Haydn, he left half each of his estate's residue of fifty million dollars. To Chase, in addition, since his son Haydn had expressed a desire to live in France, he left his yacht *South Wind* along with The Moorings with the stipulation that on Chase's death both would go to his grand-son, David. Finally, he had bequeathed twenty-five thousand dollars to each of his household servants as well as to Asa Gardner, Thomas Mason, and Marie Costello. He had also remembered, with generous legacies of ten thousand dollars each, a dozen local tradesmen who for many years had provided the necessities and service for the maintenance of The Moorings.

It was when Booker ascertained that Haydn Morse apparently wanted to expatriate himself and live in France, where he planned to use his inheritance to paint free from any financial worry, that his natural wariness of all foreigners surfaced. He thought for a moment that he'd found someone with a possible motive for something as heinous as parricide.

His suspicion was dispelled, however, when he interviewed Morse's doctor. The elderly physician who had tended to Morse's needs most of his adult life revealed he'd recently had a frank talk with both brothers in which he'd told them that their father perhaps did not have more than a year or two to live. Booker reluctantly had to consider that this might possibly let Haydn Morse off the hook, for he could see no immediate reason why anyone would risk murder for something he would get so soon anyway.

As for the deceased's eldest son, Chase Hewlet Morse, whom the deceased had honored with the stewardship of Carlyle, he was already extremely wealthy, drawing a salary of well over a million and a half dollars a year as CEO of Carlyle while annually reaping five times that as the lion's share of the famed auction house's profits.

"Crime passionelle?" Ellen suggested one night at dinner.

He'd started thinking the same. "Possibly," he'd agreed, even while thinking that trying to sort out emotions among people who made a life habit of hiding them was going to make the whole business even more difficult.

FOUR

On Friday morning, two days before Darwin Morse died, and a day before his grandson David's birthday, an incident took place that might have helped Booker in his investigation.

At eleven o'clock in the morning, Chase, in impeccable business attire, walked into the building known as Carlyle House. An imposing ten-story boxlike glass structure, it occupied nearly a half block on Second Avenue on Manhattan's East Side, not far from Sotheby's, one of Carlyle's chief rivals. It was set back from the avenue by a formal Japanese garden, a creation of the famed architect Hokido Akinari. A center fountain cut from New England pink granite by sculptor Hiram Rosencranz, renowned for his Holocaust memorial in Cracow, graced the garden as support to a magnificent LaChaise bronze statue. Both works were clearly reflected in the building's bluish mirrored glass surface, unbroken save for two tall bronze doors, copied in style from those in Florence by the Renaissance artist and sculptor Lorenzo Ghiberti. Decorative only, the doors were flanked on each side by real ones, mirrored panels which, at the command of a remote held by a uniformed doorman, slid open in magical silence at the approach of visitors.

Such a modern monument to a famed fifth generation business belied Carlyle's humble origins. The auction house began as a small private art collection during the nineteenth century, the property of one Harold Carlyle Morse. The second son of Henry Morse, Earl of Litchfield, Harold emigrated to the United States in 1826 when, although left the collection in his father's will, he lost out on everything else in primogeniture to his older brother, who was indifferent to art. Soon marrying the enormously wealthy daughter of a multimillionaire coal magnate, Harold settled into a life of leisure in a magnificent neoclassical structure on Fifth Avenue where his neighbors bore such names as Astor, Fiske, and Morgan.

It was his son, Geoffrey Carlyle Morse, who was credited with actually founding Carlyle. A compulsive gambler, when Harold died he was obliged to auction off his father's art collection to silence creditors. Fascinated by auctioning, which he saw akin to gambling, Geoffrey went into the business and was able to leave to his own son, at the turn of the century, a modestly profitable auction establishment.

This son, Aldrich Hewlet Morse, unfortunately found botany and literature far more interesting than either art or auctioneering. Carlyle Auctioning, as it was then known, stagnated. In turn, his son, Carlyle Hewlet Morse, ran it down even further in following in his father's naturalist footsteps. But fate fortunately then took a hand in the auction house's fortunes when his socialite wife produced yet another male in the Morse line. She named him Winthrop to honor an ancestor, but Aldrich gave him the second name, Darwin, to honor the memory of the man he considered the greatest in the millennium. To his wife's endless irritation, he insisted on calling the child Darwin right from birth, and it stuck so firmly that when in college the young man legalized it as his first name.

With Darwin, through a five generation leapfrog of genes, the run-down auction establishment's fortunes changed for the better. Darwin inherited not only his great grandfather's love of auctioneering but his great-great grandfather's love of fine art. Driven by an irrepressible ego, an unquenchable competitiveness, and by a limitless capacity for hard work, he not only put Carlyle back on the map but in a lifetime of dedication turned it into a world class institution that rivaled both Christie's and Sotheby's. Although Carlyle expanded into both real estate and yacht brokerage, art remained Darwin's principal interest. As a hands-on CEO, he could claim, before his unfortunate stroke, never to have missed a single auction in over fifty years of managerial prowess.

Arriving regularly at seven thirty in the morning, Monday through Friday, and rarely, if ever, leaving before seven or even eight in the evening, his presence was felt in every department. He knew the first names of every employee and, more often than not, the names of the husband or wife of each along with those of their children. With little tolerance for sloppiness, he drove all who worked for Carlyle as hard as he drove himself, but he was nevertheless loved as well as held in awed respect.

Unfortunately, once again genes intervened. The ones that gave Darwin his great love of art and auctioneering were lacking in his son. Chase, with a Princeton BS and a Harvard MBA, had little if any interest in auctioning outside of what any particular item was worth. This was especially true of auctioning of the arts or creative crafts. Art and craftsmanship, along with all the people involved with them, were to him completely alien to his concept of the narrow, isolated world of his own kind. Except for the rare magnate saluted by Wall Street, real estate and yacht brokering were the province of people he regarded as failures.

With the exception of brief apprenticeships at Credit Suisse and Citicorp, unsuccessful stints achieved solely through nepotism, and with Darwin constantly raging at his son's inability to stick with either job, Chase since college had led a life of playboy indolence until one day, finding an income from trusts and an allowance from Darwin insufficient for his lifestyle, he seized at a chance for major money which appeared as a brokerage position after six months provisionary training with the investment banking firm of Kleinmann-Roth. With it came the promise of a potentially golden future with an annual income that could well develop into several millions. There was also the promise of an eventual senior partnership and endless stock options through loans in the many companies controlled by Kleinmann-Roth. Intrinsically more important to Chase, however, than the potential riches was the socially dominant position the wealth would give him vis-à-vis his college classmates and in the exclusive world to which he belonged. Chase suddenly saw himself as becoming more prestigious than his celebrated father.

But only a few weeks away from the promised brokerage, all abruptly ended when Darwin unexpectedly suffered a stroke and, ignoring all protests and pleas, insisted Chase abandon a future in investment banking to take over Carlyle. Unable to find the courage to defy his father, hating himself for the fear and subservience Darwin chronically instilled in him, Chase suffered further indignity from the wrath of Kleinmann-Roth at the time the firm had wasted on him. A senior partner there, who had gone out on a limb to hire him, made it more than clear that he'd never be taken back and, worse, that word would be passed to Goldman-Sachs, Lehman Brothers, and others that Chase Morse was unreliable.

Equally galling was the threat to his relationship with a fellow Kleinmann-Roth trainee.

Courtney Sherwood was tall, slender, beautiful, and blond and came from a socially distinguished mainline Philadelphia family. To Chase she represented the best of two worlds—exclusivity and sex with no obligation. Before his marriage to Felicity, they had enjoyed a casual off-and-on affair when classmates at Harvard. Brightly brash, Courtney, too, had squandered postcollege years. When she married a highly successful plastic surgeon, she saw no reason to halt their occasional clandestine meetings, and it was she who usually and unabashedly called Chase herself to suggest they meet. For, where Chase's marriage, in his eyes, had always been a union in name only for the sake of producing an heir to Carlyle, Courtney's marriage was to her a purely social convenience.

There was no love between them. Their bond was fierce competition; their relationship, even in sex, was an endlessly challenging game of one-upmanship in which each sought to outdo the other. When Courtney, out of boredom and desire to be free of her husband's tight rein on the marital purse strings, had joined Kleinmann-Roth, Chase had found additional reason to do so himself.

During the summer, the six-bedroom family apartment Darwin Morse had always maintained was kept open and staffed with a housekeeper, for Chase only went the occasional weekend to The Moorings, even though the trip in the company Dassault executive jet was less than forty-five minutes. On East End Avenue, the apartment commanded a view of the mayor's house on Gracie Square as well as the East River. It was a condo where most of the tenants either knew each other or were ultra-fussy about who the other owners were. During the long summer months from May through October when the family were at The Moorings, Chase often found this inconvenient. Last night he'd slept in a different place; a terraced apartment on the thirtieth floor of a high rise building on East Seventy-Fifth Street and York Avenue that Darwin before him and now he himself kept for the entertainment of those in business whom they did not wish to intrude on their family turf. It had two bedrooms, a large living room, a study–TV room and dining room, and a view of all of Midtown Manhattan. A fashionable interior decorator had turned it into a showplace. He and Courtney found the setup ideal.

There were more times than not, however, when it was impossible or awkward for them to meet, and Chase, who saw no reason either for fidelity or to suffer being lonely, often sought feminine company elsewhere. He shied, however, from seeking it in celebrity and upmarket bars or restaurants such as the Polo Lounge or the Aspen Room, where he was almost always assured of picking up someone to liaison with him, even if just for a one-night stand. The risk of this sort of bed-mate demanding more than just that and putting him in possible social as well as legal jeopardy was too great. He'd found that just as much pleasure could be had in occasionally using one of the better escort agencies that abounded in Manhattan and provided stunningly lovely young women quite willing to provide more in service to a well-heeled client than being a gracious dinner companion.

The girl who'd spent the previous night with him had given him an exceptionally good time. The memory of her was a partial panacea for the slight champagne hangover he now suffered, and ushered into Carlyle House by an obsequious doorman, he took little note of the vaulted, three-story spaciousness of the main entrance graced at one side by a two story-high banyan tree artificially lit with life-sustaining ultra-violet rays, its multi-trunk base surrounded by a stone fountain bowl on which floated a variety of exotic tropical water flowers. Opposite, across the hall, was a long counter on which were displayed a full score of catalogs for as many different auctions, as well as expensive brochures for Carlyle's yacht brokerage and real estate department. In the hall's center was a wide teakwood island, the receptionist's post. Its modernity, expressed by computers and other electronic equipment as well as by the stark simplicity of its design, matched the pale travertine marble walls of the hall, the sole decoration of which was an impressively large, fifteenth century Flemish tapestry. Suspended on the room's back wall above a brightly lit escalator leading up to the principal auction rooms on the second floor and flanked by elevators, two to each side, it depicted a *vendange*, the wine grape harvest. With the vineyard and its workers expressed in the most carefully woven detail, its colors paled by age, it blended perfectly with its modern surroundings, and indeed seemed to express full compatibility with so many of the historic items there at Carlyle House to be auctioned in a world unimagined at the time of its creation.

Chase's attitude toward the employees of Carlyle matched his regard for the servants at The Moorings. Distant civility was in order not because you felt it but because it was required of you by your position. On entering that Friday morning, he paused long enough in heading for the elevators to return the smiling "Good Morning, Mr. Morse" from the several uniformed security guards as well as from the two trim and fashionably turned out young receptionists whose job, besides lending chic to the establishment, was to keep unwanted visitors away and to allow the privileged ones access to whomever they had come to see. Several of the latter, waiting for appointment times to come due at a bank of Noguchi-designed leather and chrome couches and chairs in an alcove near the banyan tree, were reading the *New York Times* or clutching briefcases while listening to discreetly muted classical recordings piped in through hidden speakers.

The auction house had been opened for business since nine. Chase's normal hour of arrival for his dutiful day as CEO was ten o'clock or later. Today, it was nearly eleven. A silent and softly lit elevator took him rapidly up from the ground floor of Carlyle House with its huge storerooms and shipping access bay hidden deep in the building behind the main entrance hall. It rose past the second floor with its auditorium-sized two-story-high main auction room and several smaller auction rooms along with display rooms where the interested could view what would be presented at a forthcoming auction. It glided effortlessly on upward past a multitude of executive offices and conference rooms where experts in nearly every form of artistic expression could authenticate or appraise whatever a potential client, or simply the curious, could inquire about, whether it be a nineteenth-century French impressionist, a flintlock rifle, a massive cathedral organ, or a miniature cameo locket containing silky strands of hair once adorning the head of an eighteenth-century lady in the court of Louis XV.

When the elevator finally slid to a gentle stop on the tenth floor and its doors opened, Chase stepped into a world that emphasized Carlyle's international prestige. Here, in an executive reception room graced with deep-pile carpeting, Thai silk draperies, and brocaded upholstered couches and chairs, he was greeted by a second receptionist as fashionably attractive and immaculately groomed as her counterparts below. On seeing him, she rose immediately from behind an Empire desk that had once been the property of Napoleon's famed general of his armies, Marshal Ney.

"Good morning, sir."

"Good morning. Is Selma in yet?"

"Yes, sir. Miss Freedman came in some time ago."

He pointedly glanced at his watch. "I'm late. Banking business downtown. And I've a pile of back work. So spare me any interruptions, okay? Absolutely none. Not from anyone."

"Yes, sir."

"Good girl, make sure you do." He pretended a laugh. "Unless, of course the building catches fire."

She forced an indulgent smile in return. She had long ago seen Chase's courtesy and polished good manners as covering the darker reality that he disdained her as a social inferior. The job was good, however, and she didn't intend her own rather low opinion of him ever to show.

While Chase took a moment to straighten a magazine on the glass table between two couches, for he hated even the slightest untidiness, she held open the door to the foyer of the executive suite. The door had hardly closed behind him when he was confronted by Selma coming into the foyer from her office, separated from his by a conference room.

"Oh." In that one word there was a mixture of faint scorn, condescension, resigned tolerance, and annoyance at his being late. "Good morning, Chase." She didn't smile, and her look matched her words, although she managed not to glance at her watch. Graying and well beyond retirement age, everything about her, from her short-cropped hair and sequined harlequin glasses that hung perpetually when not fastened onto her hawkish nose from an embroidered chain around her neck, was in severe contrast to the opulent modernism of the foyer. And her stocky figure, barely disguised by the functional clothing, whether dress or mannish suit, that she always wore, stressed the matriarchal and proprietary efficiency of her personality.

Selma Freedman had been his father's personal assistant for nearly forty years, and Chase hated her. He hated her not just because she was a constant reminder of Darwin's revered status at Carlyle, but for what he saw as her apparent assumption that she had more moral authority over Carlyle than he did, an attitude he saw emphasized, to his endless fury, by the warm respect and deference given her every day by nearly all of Carlyle's employees. She had stayed on the job well past retirement age only to help with the transition from his father to him, to make sure he got the hang of things and Carlyle didn't lose ground to Christies or Sotheby's. He hadn't objected because to do so would have brought unbearable wrath from Darwin down on his head. He justified this surrender to his father by persuading himself that it was only because her encyclopedic knowledge of every working function of Carlyle and the entire auction business as well as her intimidating quality when it came to any negotiations made it possible for him to cut down on the long hours of work that his function as CEO called for.

With effort, he managed a pleasant good morning in return. And added, "Don't say it. I'm late. Is there anything I missed?"

"Horst Von Ludlow called." Selma wouldn't let him off the hook and pointedly emphasized the time, now making a show of glancing at her watch. "At about nine thirty. He wants you to call him back. And we have a meeting with DeWitt at twelve. He wants to discuss the Millet."

Chase remembered that DeWitt Bouchard, the chief auctioneer, had said that the recently discovered Millet, which had been given to Carlyle to auction, had to be the French artist's greatest work as well as one of the very greatest paintings of the nineteenth century. Bouchard would want to discuss promotion. A work of inspired force, it representing a peasant woman washing clothes at a stream on the edge of a field where harvesters reaped grain. Once part of the collection of a prominent German Jewish family, it had disappeared when its owner was dragged off to the Holocaust during World War II to show up hanging in Adolph Hitler's alpine retreat at Berchtesgaden. Then, at the war's end, it disappeared a second time, finally to be recovered only recently from a politically prominent German family. This had happened after a highly publicized lawsuit by the rightful Jewish owner's heirs when the European Union Art Recovery Council produced evidence that one of the family, a former Nazi high official, had removed it from Berchtesgaden on Hitler's demise. A major Hollywood producer was already having the story scripted. Both *Time* and *Newsweek* had run features about it.

"Sure," Chase said. "You know where to find me." And throwing another smile her way, he went into his own inner sanctum, shutting the door firmly behind him.

FIVE

For Chase, this was usually the worst moment of the day. His office had been ordered redone, in keeping with the reception rooms, by Darwin when he'd surrendered leadership. Chase could not escape the feeling, whenever he entered it, that it wasn't his, it was still his father's. Darwin's domineering and demanding character spoke to him from every foot of deep pile carpeting, from the desktop, wind-swept clean save for an engagement pad, a telephone, and his computer, and especially from the wall on which the decorator, at Darwin's insistence, let remain a Picasso from the artist's "Blue" period along with a Gorky and a de Kooning.

Usually on entering, Chase would stand a moment rooted midway between his desk and the doorway, looking out at the roofs of the buildings across Second Avenue, visible beyond the entrance garden with its statuary through a wide floor-to-ceiling glass window. He hated the view. He couldn't look at Second Avenue without thinking of Wall Street and Kleinmann-Roth, of being forcibly reminded of what he was missing out on. Most days the anger and resentment he felt at his father would be invariably fired by Selma and become so bitter he could nearly taste it. Okay for Darwin, he'd think. Darwin had escaped. He'd had a stroke and copped out, leaving him free for years, regardless of what his stupid doctor said, to throw his weight around and lord it over everyone at The Moorings the same way he had at Carlyle, compulsively always having to be right and control everyone. Never mind that he was stuck in a wheelchair and had to have a nurse.

All that for the old man, great, but what about himself? Faced every day now and for years to come with the dreary business of getting rid of all the art nonsense other people needed to dump, for whatever their reasons: the need of money, mostly. And putting up with all the lucky bastards, nouveaux riches or Asians or Arabs, usually, who had really big money just to fritter away the way they'd play the stock market.

That was the way he'd think on most days. Quickly dismissing Second Avenue and all it reminded him of, he'd throw himself into his high-backed leather desk chair to curse the day his father had endured the stroke and curse Darwin's flatly commanding him to take Carlyle's helm. "This is a family firm, Chase; don't you ever forget it." And curse that once again he'd abjectly and cravenly, as always, surrendered to Darwin.

He'd cursed the future it had cost him, and, thinking of the years ahead, he'd curse his marriage he couldn't get out of without bringing the wrath of Darwin down on his head. "She's a fine young woman, Chase, who has given us an heir to take over after you're gone, and don't lose sight of that either, or you'll hear from me."

But all that was nothing to knowing that the world Kleinmann-Roth represented had passed him by. Even if he somehow found the courage to defy Darwin or after Darwin died could possibly persuade Kleinmann-Roth to take him back or some other investment firm to take him on, he would now be too far behind the fast-track successes of all his former peers to catch up. Besides the label of unreliable, he'd be seen, too, as an outsider from the "art world," condemned to watching Courtney soar from triumph to triumph.

Imagining her hurt more than anything. How long would it be before she'd decide their "friendship" wasn't exciting anymore, that he was a loser, and before the ultimate humiliation of her taking up with some guy who was hitting it really big.

When, except for Darwin and damned Carlyle, it could have been him.

That was the way he usually thought and felt. Today, however, was different. Today the view of Second Avenue almost looked good; the Picasso also. Today was the day when all his misery was going to be reversed.

The expected call from Horst Von Ludlow was going to change everything. He'd planned to call Horst himself, and he could easily guess why Horst had called him. He didn't need to feel like a trapped animal any longer. He could forget his anger and resentment at Darwin, the boredom of his marriage to Felicity. All that was virtually past. He wasn't going to fall behind Courtney. It was going to be the other way around.

He sat up forcefully, laughing aloud with the sheer joy of it, and pulled his personal Tiffany address book from a drawer and found the number he wanted. This was the day, the hour, when he could stop taking orders from Darwin Morse and begin life without him.

Horst Von Ludlow was senior partner in Von Ludlow, Grissinger, Schornhorn and Bork, AG, the most reputable and prestigious private bank in Germany. They had handled Carlyle's foreign portfolio for Darwin and, before Darwin, for Darwin's father. They had survived both the Depression and the Nazis. Besides Carlyle, they had as clients a score of foreign nations as well as some of the most important and influential banks in Europe. They specialized in oil and handled major Mideast interests, especially for clients on the Arabian peninsula. Last year alone, they had pulled in six and a half billion dollars for one Saudi family on a half-billion-dollar investment.

Chase punched the buttons on the phone panel, first to exit the United States, then the international code for Germany, the area code for Munich, and finally the number. And waited, hearing the phone ringing and feeling anticipation building.

The phone answered. A German voice. He heard the words "Von Ludlow, Grissinger, Shornhorn undt Bork." The rest would be "AG and "Good afternoon" for it was four in the afternoon in Munich.

He didn't bother to try to communicate in German. They all spoke English. "Good morning. Mr. Von Ludlow, please."

"Right away, Mr. Morse." The operator's panel had registered his caller ID and instantly referenced it to a database of special clients privileged to be admitted to the inner sanctum. There was the sound of interoffice ringing, and then another woman's voice, saying, he presumed, "Mr. Von Ludlow's office."

He replied abruptly. "Chase Morse for Mr. Von Ludlow."

"Oh, yes, Mr. Morse. One moment, please, sir."

He waited. Horst Von Ludlow came on the line. "Chase! How are you?"

"Good, Horst, good. You called. Don't tell me we've struck our first gusher?" He laughed at the incredible pleasure of it. There was a silence. He said, "Horst?"

He heard a brief exchange of low voices, then the German came back, his English more noticeably accented now. "Chase, look, I'm afraid the news isn't so good this morning."

"What do you mean?"

"Tundra Oil. We heard about it late last night. It won't be out in the papers your way until next week, but you might as well get it now. The Russian government has seized it."

A shadow of coldness began to steal through Chase's body. "What do you mean, seized it?"

"Just that, I'm afraid. Putin signed the executive order yesterday morning, Russian time, and the government walked in an hour later and seized everything. All of Tundra Oil's assets."

"They can't do that."

"I know, but I'm afraid they can, Chase. Russia isn't Germany or the U.S., you know. They still have, what can I tell you, certain attitudes?"

"Hold on Horst. I have eighty million invested in Tundra Oil through you."

"Ja, ja, I know, I have a big slice of investment capital in them myself."

"You're saying the Russians now have my eighty million investment by simply walking in and taking it?"

"Well, yes, Chase. I'm afraid so."

"Look, Horst, That was my money, not Carlyle's. And the only reason I sent it over to you was that you guaranteed the investment."

"Ja, Ja, Chase. Of course. And it was a good one. Tundra Oil was a steal, Chase. And you stood to make it back ten times over, maybe more within the year. But I couldn't and didn't guarantee what the Russian government would do. We had no inkling even the day before yesterday when I talked to Tundra."

"Horst, I didn't come to you. You called me and told me you had a sure thing."

"Ja, ja. But I did warn you there might be some risk. You know, Russia is Russia. Look, Chase, you used to be in investment banking, try to understand. You're not the only one. Nor are we. We have a dozen clients who've lost a lot more than you. I can name you investment firms, good ones, all of whom have had the same bad news. There's a major French banking consortium that will probably go under because of it."

"Horst!"

"We'll appeal, of course, but to be honest the chances don't look good. The Tundra Oil offices have been closed and sealed, everything in them taken away. And the principals have been arrested for fraud. Boris and Serge. You met them."

Chase had a flitting memory of the Russians, graying, serious men, British tailoring, the epitome of modern European capitalism, one with a degree from Harvard. "Horst."

"Chase, we'll get you something else. Recoup. Give us a little time. Okay? Meanwhile, Putin will have to compensate eventually if he doesn't want to frighten off future investors. Give it a couple of years, maybe less."

"Horst."

"Yes?"

"Fuck you."

He slammed the phone down. The son of a bitch. The lousy, rotten, Kraut bastard. He'd promised. A sure insider thing. Couldn't miss. Eighty million bucks invested with a guarantee it would be a half billion or more within a year. There'd be buyers for his share all over the place. And with even a quarter of it invested in the Nigerian wells, there'd be another half billion only months later.

He sat for a long while, too numb even to feel anger. Nothing seemed real except fear. The room he sat in, his desk. Nothing. Minutes ago, he'd had a ticket to freedom. He'd been going away, leaving all this he hated. Now he wasn't. He'd been going to tell Darwin to go to hell. He would have made more money in a year than Darwin had made in his entire life. He'd been going to hit the investment banking world so big it would have made everyone at Kleinmann-Roth insignificant. The comeback kid. They'd be falling all over themselves even just to say they had known him once.

A picture floated behind his eyes someplace, obscuring his vision of the office. Courtney: chic and trim in her Balenciaga suit, expensive jewelry flashing, her smile radiant, laughing at him. Then Darwin. Glowering, red-faced with anger, his great bulk hunched in his wheelchair. "Thought you could one-up me, did you Chase? Well, you'll keep on doing as I say or else."

The shadow of coldness in him grew colder. Fear began to claw, an animal deep inside him. There was a sound in his head, a rapid drumbeat that echoed. And the darkness behind his eyes again, almost obscuring objects in the office, making everything seem suddenly far away. He wanted to get up, to move. He had to get out of there. But he couldn't. He felt pinned to his leather chair. Anyway, go where? Home? Yes, he should. It was the boy's birthday tomorrow, Darwin would never forgive him if he didn't show up. But he couldn't, he just couldn't. How could he show up with this inside him?

Jesus Christ! Eighty million. How could he ever replace

it? And Darwin would find out. Somehow. Sure as hell. And then the board of directors. It was only time before it would all come out, that he'd milked the Carlyle pension fund, a short term "loan" that could be kept hidden for a year, anyway. But he didn't have a year any longer; he didn't have anything, and Darwin would disinherit him sure as fate, with all the social disgrace incumbent on that, and unless there was some kind of a miracle, word would get out. Then, faced with certain prosecution, he could forget any last hope of a return to banking, any dreams of power and prestige. He would be blacklisted everywhere, ruined.

A panorama of visions tore through his mind. Courtney again, laughing, then friends at Kleinmann-Roth standing about reading the headlines, adding it all up, merciless. Next, the ugly New York courtrooms: the sleazy clerks and bailiffs, half of them couldn't speak proper English, judges from Brooklyn or some other back of beyond who'd got to sit on a bench through city politics and who hated the rich and anybody Ivy League, the twisting lying media, goddamned vultures. And jail, himself thrown in with all the scum.

The panorama got worse and worse. It forced a thought finally. Don't wait for that. Get out. Now. Take what liquid assets he had, jump country. But even as the thought appeared, he knew it wouldn't work. You couldn't hide forever. Others had tried and failed. And what about money for day-to-day living? What he could take with him wouldn't last a year. Then what?

When Selma came in an hour later to remind him tartly of their meeting with DeWitt Bouchard, she found him still sitting behind his desk in his high-backed leather chair, staring at the Picasso she knew he hated. From his expression, she also knew that whatever he was thinking couldn't be good. "Bouchard will be up in a few minutes," she said. "He's bringing young Brian Grey from Fine Arts and someone from PR. We'll meet in the conference room." She went back to her own office to wait for the auctioneer.

SIX

A t two thirty that same Friday, Gabrielle left Rockefeller Center and Christie's, where she had been given a guided tour of the facilities of Carlyle's second great rival by a fellow Frenchman in the fine arts department, who had teased her mercilessly for doing a story on the competition. She successfully flagged a cab on Sixth Avenue and fifteen minutes later found herself at Haydn's La Rive Gauche. He'd planned a vacation from the fourth of July to the fourteenth, France's Bastille day, and had decided "to start things off right" by arranging for her to see the famous Millet coming up for auction at Carlyle.

Gabrielle was excited at the prospect. She had loved paintings since childhood, when her father had introduced her to an endless banquet of beauty on the walls of the Louvre. While working for *France D'Aujourd'hui,* she had frequently taken her lunch hour there, often so fascinated as she sat on a bench staring at some great work that her sandwich would lie undisturbed in her lap. To have a private viewing of the Millet was something she'd never dreamed could happen.

She found Haydn, busy as usual. An elderly woman customer, a volume of Proust in hand, wanted to know how the Hudson translation of Proust compared to that of C. K. Scott Moncrieff. "In my view," he told her, "there's no comparison, and besides, Hudson only translated one volume, *La Prisonière,* I believe." Accepting the woman's effusive thanks and sending her off with his young assistant to collect the other six

Modern Library volumes of the great work, he turned at once to Gabrielle. "How was Christie's?"

"I prefer Carlyle."

Haydn laughed." Before we go," he said, "I've a little something for you to celebrate Bastille Day in advance. I think you'll like it. I do." From behind the counter he produced a small oil portrait in an antique frame not much bigger than a magazine cover, of a bespectacled old man wearing a stocking hat and peering over an open book at a young woman whose shawled bosom was decorated by a rose.

"Like it?

"Oh, Haydn, it's lovely."

"It's all yours."

"You mean it, really?

"Of course, Something to remember La Rive Gauche by."

"As if I could ever forget it." Gabrielle spoke lightly but inside felt a twinge of guilt. She'd seen so very much of him since they'd first met, and now this lovely painting. Was it right for her to accept a gift? Wasn't that compromising her as a journalist? Hadn't she perhaps already done so? All the lunches and dinners. But worse by far was the pain she felt in his not saying "me, too." Didn't that reinforce her fear that to him she was probably only a passing interest in his life, nothing more? The thought of returning to France when her work on Carlyle was finished and leaving Haydn behind, perhaps forever, instantly darkened her pleasure over the little painting as well as the excitement of seeing the famous Millet.

As she struggled to come to grips with her conflicting emotions, Haydn said, "This painting was once a landscape. Nothing particularly exciting, but it needed cleaning and a bit of repair. The restorer discovered it was painted over what you see now, which he said was a far better work. So good-bye landscape."

"They can do that with a painting?"

"Not always. But there have been some famous discoveries

that were hiding behind something completely different. I've seen one painting simply tacked over another on the same stretcher."

Watching him wrap the painting back up, Gabrielle thought how much he cared about so many things, in his modest self-effacing way: books, art, sailing—especially art, which it seemed to her Chase really didn't care much about at all. Astonishing, she thought, considering his job. It made her wonder more and more how there could be such a difference between two brothers.

They took the painting out to his car, parked around the corner on a side street. It was a beat up old Jeep Cherokee whose red paint had surrendered any sign of luster to years of sun and rain. Refusing to turn it in for something newer and more reliable, Haydn would always say, "You don't shoot a favorite horse just because it's getting old."

Heading across town for Carlyle House, Gabrielle's excitement returned. "When did the Millet come in?"

"Two days ago, I'm told. Lufthansa. It was picked up at the airport with a Brinks armored truck."

"A truck? But it's so small."

Haydn laughed. "Twenty-one and a half inches by seventeen. Not as large as some of his landscape paintings, or ones of farm workers harvesting, *The Gleaners* or *The Angelus*, but of major interest because he basically was not a portrait painter. Whatever, with all the hype and history behind it, it's worth more than the cash they pick up from a half dozen department stores at the end of a big sales day."

"Really? How much?"

"I'm not sure, but certainly millions. A portrait by Eakins recently sold for seventy million and a Picasso for a hundred."

Reaching Carlyle House, Haydn parked in its underground employee garage. Going upstairs in the elevator, Gabrielle unexpectedly felt a little nervous, wondering at the last moment if she might be causing trouble by privately seeing the Millet. She said, "Are you sure your showing it to me won't be a problem for you? I mean, Chase won't object for some reason?"

"Chase said no problem. I think it's the first time he's actually shown any interest in any painting. Anyway, he's not here. His office told me he's taken off for the day."

On several previous visits to Carlyle, during her first ten days in America, Haydn had escorted her on a tour of a score of different departments, from painting and statuary to ceramics, antique weapons, carpets, firearms, and furniture, each managed by a world-class expert. He'd arranged, also, for her to attend an evening "by invitation only" auction of important French impressionists. Held in the main auction room, it had drawn a glittering crowd of art experts, collectors, and celebrities from around the world. Afterward he had introduced her to DeWitt Bouchard.

An austere imposingly tall gray-haired man, the legendary auctioneer had the kind of quietly authoritative manner Gabrielle found intimidating. Everything about him, from his impeccable British tailoring and carefully cultivated Mid-Atlantic accent to his unfathomably expressionless face made her feel that purely out of politeness he merely tolerated her and whatever she said. Haydn had told her that with simply a glance he bullied people into bidding when they really didn't want to. Attending the auction and meeting him and exchanging a few clichéd politenesses, she'd been able to see that for herself.

"I understand you are doing an article on us," Bouchard had said.

"I'm sure I can't be the first," Gabrielle replied. She'd always found that modesty about any article, no matter how important, got her better results in interviewing than if she made it look as though she were doing her subject a favor. It put the person in the driver's seat and gave him a chance to expound.

DeWitt had smiled condescendingly. "Of course not, but what the French think of us when it comes to art is always important to us."

It didn't fool Gabrielle. Actually, you don't mean a word of that, she thought. You don't like the French because they won't defer to you.

Getting off the elevator from the garage at the ninth floor, Haydn was greeted, as on her previous visit, with warm familiarity by many when he stopped a moment to ask about them and their work. It almost seemed as though he was in charge of the place and not his brother and, as they headed for DeWitt's office, a nagging question that lurked deep within Gabrielle slowly came to the surface: Why did Haydn want to leave all this and go to France to paint? She couldn't help but think how comfortable he seemed when at the office and how happy at The Moorings, sailing or puttering about with his nephew.

These thoughts were fleeting, however, for she hadn't forgotten that she'd decided last night to anchor her whole story about the Morse family on the forthcoming auction of the famous Millet, and in a few minutes she would actually see it.

The auctioneer was at his desk in his Louis XIV office with its heavy tied-back damask drapes and fabric-lined walls. Hung ostentatiously with seventeenth-century pink-fleshed opulent nudes by such post-Renaissance romanticists as Watteau and Fouchard, and including one minor work by Poussin, it was a world apart from what lay outside, across the Carlyle forecourt on Manhattan's Second Avenue.

"You'd like to see the Millet, Haydn tells me," DeWitt said, rising and putting aside a folder he'd been studying.

"I'd be thrilled. I understand it only came in yesterday."

"Indeed." DeWitt turned to Haydn. "We have it in the vault. Shall I lead on?"

They took the elevator down to the third floor to a small carpeted lobby. From there they turned down a corridor A few feet along it, the auctioneer stopped, took out his key ring, selected a key, and opened a door. Gabrielle following Haydn, found herself in a small silent lobby in which the only decoration was a Chippendale table and on it an open leather-bound register book. DeWitt signed his name and, glancing at his watch, jotted down the time also. Then on a panel above it, he punched in a five-number code. A soft hum and a click and the door sprang ajar, bank-vault thick and heavy. DeWitt pushed it open all the way, reached around the door jamb, and clicked a switch, flooding with bright light a small undecorated room lined with security boxes like those in a bank vault. Against the back wall, next to an artist's easel, were two wide shelves. On them, carefully placed upright, were a number of paintings, each wrapped in protective padded quilts.

"Let's see," the auctioneer said. "Degas, Chavannes, Corot … ah, here we are." He extracted a painting and deftly removed the quilting to reveal the Millet in an old and ornate gilded frame. He casually set it on the easel.

Gabrielle's first impression was similar to what she'd felt when first seeing the *Mona Lisa* at the Louvre. What was all the fuss about? Millet's painting was of a kneeling peasant woman looking up from her work at the edge of a shallow rocky stream. Distantly behind her could be seen reapers at work in a field of yellow ripened grain. Nothing else. There were no other people near her. She was alone. Next to her and partially hidden by river grass, a large basket of wet laundry waited to be taken away. One of her work-reddened hands held the shirt she had been scrubbing and pounding on a flat rock. The back of her other hand was against her brow. Weariness or holding back perspiration? Perhaps both. A heavy, wooden scrubbing brush with worn bristles lay by her side at the water's edge.

But then, staring at it, Gabrielle began to realize that, like the *Mona Lisa*'s, the woman's expression was magnetic. Across her face and in her eyes there was expressed in all its entirety the lot of the earth's downtrodden: the weariness, the sorrow, the anger and defiance, the resignation and acceptance. As Gabrielle looked, one emotion seemed to sweep across the woman's face to be replaced by another. It was as though she were truly alive, and was facing an unwanted observer whom she did not wish to intrude into a world wholly personal to herself.

Almost unable to tear her eyes away, Gabrielle couldn't find words to express what she felt, what the painting transmitted to her. She could only utter a few banalities. "But it's so beautiful," and "incredible." Later, she thought, she would try, in attempting to explain to Haydn what the painting made her feel, to understand that herself.

She heard Haydn say, "What's your estimate?"

And DeWitt answer. "I won't take anything less than seventy million. I hope for ninety."

"That's a hell of a lot," Haydn argued, "for a Millet."

"Not when you think it's one of the few portraits he ever did and of the hype that's built up since it was recovered." The auctioneer laughed. "I told one Japanese client what I wanted to get for it and he never blinked an eye. Besides, Chase has ordered the PR guys to pull out all stops to help it along. I think we could possibly go even higher. Look what our competition got for that Picasso. One hundred million. Makes you think, doesn't it?" And when Gabrielle expressed awe, he added, "It's not impossible, you know. Nothing is in this business. Depends on people's moods, what's in fashion, that sort of thing. And especially trends in the market. Most major paintings these days are seen as a commodity. They're not bought because the buyer loves the work. They're bought as an investment to be resold at profit. And every time they're sold, the price goes up."

"You're leaving out what you goad them into," Haydn said.

DeWitt put on a modest expression. "I'll pass on that, Haydn."

The painting was wrapped again in its quilting and put back into the partition on the shelf; the vault doors closed on it. Gabrielle thanked DeWitt for allowing her to see it, and on the way back up to his office, where she said good-bye to him, asked him a few perfunctory questions about himself: what it was in auctioneering that he loved the most, how had he got started in it, what were one or two memories of his most sensational sales, could he tell her of one awful disaster? Expecting glib or super-ficial answers, she was surprised when in spite of all his austerity of manner and seeming indifference to the esthetics involved in his profession, he was indeed impassioned with art and was a virtual encyclopedia as to its history down through the ages.

"Why is that so surprising?" Haydn said when she told him. "To make this business work, you have to be a good salesman, yes, but if you don't care about art, forget it."

Gabrielle didn't reply, for Haydn suddenly looked uncom-fortable, and she knew it was because he had just inadvertently condemned his brother. The remark had made her uncomfort-able, too, but for a different reason. Both were silent as they rode the elevator upstairs to the executive suite, where he wanted her to meet Selma Freedman, Darwin's administra-tive assistant of many years. Filing preliminary reports on the Morse family, Gabrielle realized, was just as she had feared. It was becoming more and more difficult as she became increas-ingly aware of family tensions. It had been one thing to write of the family history and about the functioning of the great auction house. It was becoming quite another to write about the family itself without betraying clearly confidential family matters. The question of where she should draw the line was constantly with her. Where did her loyalties lie? To Bernard Bligny and *France D'Aujoud'hui*, to her career as a professional journalist, or to the Morse family who were virtually treating her as though she were a member?

There was momentary relief from her troubled thoughts when she met Selma, who had been on vacation during her previous visit. "She's a Jewish matriarch and runs the place," Gabrielle remembered Haydn explaining. "Always has. She started off as Dad's secretary back in the old mechanical-type-writer days, and now with him gone and typewriters, too, she's a sort of unofficial senior vice president, although for some reason Chase won't formalize that with her name on the direc-tory or on her business card. I was never quite sure whether she worked for Dad or whether Dad worked for her."

She'd laughed and said, "They were a team."

"More than that. They were like an old married couple. She was indispensable to him. And vice versa. If they weren't fighting, they were extolling each other. One reason Dad's as cranky as he is at home, ordering everyone around nonstop, is that Selma isn't there to tell him to damn well shut up and behave. You should make a date with her for lunch. You'll get more out of her about Carlyle than from me or anyone else."

Face to face with Selma, who rose at once from behind her cluttered desk, Gabrielle so immediately liked the frosty, authoritative, no-nonsense older woman that she forgot to be frightened of her. Beneath the exterior there was caring and warmth. She had no trouble seeing why Haydn was so fond of her, and where he'd picked up all the rich Jewish expressions he often used—*mensch* and *pisha* and *mashugana*.

The meeting was brief. Selma had to prepare for a business appointment away from Carlyle House. Before Haydn and Gabrielle left, however, she promised Gabrielle to find time to talk at length about her view of the family and the business and admonished her to "tell that old tyrant, Darwin, if he doesn't behave, I'll come up and set him right."

Collecting the papers she needed for the appointment when Haydn and Gabrielle had left, Selma mentally reviewed the brief meeting with the younger woman. They had only exchanged polite introductory remarks, but Selma hadn't been where she was at Carlyle for forty years without learning to see quickly through whatever mask people put on to get a keen sense of their real character.

What a shame, she thought, that Chase couldn't have married such an intelligent and level-headed modern young woman. Things might have been different at Carlyle if he had. Felicity was okay; Felicity was a darling, everyone loved Felicity. So good, so unassuming. A darling and a wonderful loving mother even if overprotective of David. But Felicity was far too unworldly, too sheltered, to stand up to Chase, let alone manage him. Felicity should have been married to some nice, ordinary person, someone she could mother and who would have put her on a pedestal and worshipped her.

She picked up her phone and dialed.

When the number answered, she said, "I just met the French girl who's doing the article on us, well, the family, mostly, I understand. She's headed your way for two weeks, I take it, for Haydn's vacation.

Darwin said, "I asked Haydn to bring her up. Damn nice girl, I think. The times she came before, I spent hours with her. Family history and all that for her article. Just the sort of young woman he should marry if he has any sense. He ought to get her in the sack and tie her up right now. But you didn't call me about that."

"No, I didn't."

"Problems you can't handle without me, I presume."

"I could say something rude in response, Darwin, but I won't."

She listened to him laugh and mentally took a deep breath, dreading the real reason she'd called. Three months ago, Chase had had an unnecessary and nasty row with a favored buyer. It caused Carlyle to lose the man as a client. Darwin, unable to let go his lifetime stewardship of Carlyle all the way, had ordered her to have a tap put on Chase's office line.

"Waller can do it for you. Pay him whatever he asks, and tell him if he doesn't keep his mouth shut he's out of a job."

It had done no good to protest that it wasn't a moral thing to do, or that for his own sake Darwin simply had to learn that he was no longer in charge of Carlyle; that for better or worse he'd turned it over to Chase and couldn't rightly supervise everything Chase did, and that none of that was the real reason for her protest. She couldn't tell Darwin the real reason: that there'd come a day, she was sure, when Darwin would find out things about his son that he wouldn't really want to know, things that Chase's mannered courtesy and class high-mindedness hid from most of the world but had never hid from her. There was a dark side to Chase that occasionally frightened her.

That day had come, and she felt sick at what it obliged her to reveal.

SEVEN

"Darwin, we may have some trouble."

"Oh?"

Selma took a deep breath and launched in. "I checked this afternoon on the tap you insisted I put on Chase's phone. I don't think you're going to like what I heard."

"Which is?"

"It's got to do with Chase."

"Of course it's got to do with Chase. Who the hell else? Get to the point, woman, damn it! What's he screwed up this time?"

"He bought into Russian oil. An outfit called Tundra."

"And you're going to tell me it blew."

"I am."

"How did he get into it?"

"Horst Von Ludlow."

"Horst?!"

"I know; you can't get them straighter. It looked a good deal, but Putin went and seized the company."

"How much, Selma?"

"Eighty."

"Million. You wouldn't have called otherwise."

"Yes."

There was a silence during which Selma could almost hear the old man thinking. Why hadn't she had the nerve to talk him out of monitoring Chase? He was sick and old and needed to rest on his laurels in peace and quiet. Not get news like this.

Damn Chase; he wasn't worth one tenth of Darwin.

Darwin finally spoke. He said, "I don't like it, Selma. Chase never had eighty million of his own, nothing near it. And no collateral sufficient for a loan of that amount. Where the devil did he get it from? Check this out with Karl Bracer. See if he has any thoughts. Call me back as soon as you can."

It was the old Darwin taking charge once more, and she prayed not for the worst. "Will do," she said. She heard him hang up, and put her own receiver down. The patriarch hadn't said why he wanted her to check with Bracer. He didn't have to. She'd heard it in his tone of voice, loud and clear. He was guessing that Chase had somehow tapped Carlyle for the money, figuring to put it back when he cleaned up with Tundra. If so, the auction house could be in dead trouble, although Darwin could bail it out from his personal fortune, and would if it were the only way.

But talk to Bracer? She'd thought to check with him herself and had dismissed it as a waste of time. If Chase had indeed got the money from Carlyle, Bracer, of all people, almost assuredly would either have known of it or be involved in it himself. Whichever, the secretary-treasurer would be the last to admit anything untoward on his watch, and certainly not guilt, if that were the case. Darwin had asked her to do the near impossible. If she were to learn anything, she'd have to be a virtual mind reader and extraordinarily careful in any questions she asked. For two reasons it wouldn't do to let Bracer know that Chase's affairs were being looked into. If guilty, Bracer would be alerted to cover against any future investigation. If innocent, he could well use Chase's trouble to his advantage. As a general rule in life, Bracer had got where he was by doing just that.

She shuddered. She would hate to be in Chase's shoes in the confrontation that was sure to take place between father and son. Darwin had never felt the same fatherly warmth toward Chase that he felt toward Haydn, regardless of thinking Haydn a dead loss when it came to Carlyle. He'd forcibly put a reluctant Chase in charge of the auction house, ignoring all her efforts to talk him out of it. "You're wrong about Haydn," she'd insisted. "He's got it in him if faced with the challenge. Try to persuade him."

It had done no good.

"Nonsense, woman. I love him but he's a goddamned artist. The house is full of his junk. Okay stuff, but nothing great. Second tier. No money in it. He's no Pollack or Rivers or Gorky. Never will be. Anyway, he's not interested, he's made that perfectly clear. Right?"

"Probably not, but you could at least try to get him to change his mind," she'd said. "And what's wrong with being an artist? You sell their work every day."

"Their work. Not them."

"Maybe his painting is just a defense."

"Defense against what?"

"You. Who else?"

"Oh, sure, sure." His laughter was laced with sarcasm.

She hadn't argued further. She'd seen the uselessness of trying to tell Darwin that it was his whole manner that had brought Haydn to disdain the world he and Chase stood for. Why else the stammer that Haydn had mostly overcome? But Darwin never saw causes in people, or any complexity. If they didn't fit his conception of what they should be, he simply wrote them off. And that was *his* weakness, the one from which she had protected him the same way she'd managed to persuade him to keep at bay that clutching society horror, Rhinelander.

"Don't worry, Selm. She hasn't a prayer."

"She thinks she does."

"That's her problem."

It was Selma's turn to say, "Oh, sure, sure." But she didn't. A small light winked on her desk. Reception. She activated her intercom switch. "Who is it?"

Reception's soft voice said that Lou Waller would like a quick word with her. Reluctantly, Selma told the girl to send him in.

She knew exactly what Waller wanted, and when he appeared and stood slouching before her desk in his shirt-sleeves, she barely said good morning before she got out her office checkbook, all the while averting her eyes from him.

"How much did we say?"

"A thousand. You already paid me five hundred."

She quickly wrote out the check, forced when handing it to him to take in his slouching unmuscular appearance, the colorless gray-white of his face, his too long sideburns and lank dark hair and his overbite teeth and receding chin. If he hadn't been a computer and electronic genius that kept that side of Carlyle functioning perfectly, she would have rid herself of him long ago, the same way she would have junked an ugly soup bowl or hideous vase. The thousand dollars was his off-the-record fee for putting a tap on Chase's telephone.

He took the check and asked "Any problems with it?"

"No."

"How long do you want it kept on?"

"Until I tell you to stop." Selma glanced at her own telephone panel. One of the extension buttons now silently patched her in to Chase's personal phone.

"I'm taping all calls like you asked. That could become expensive."

"That's my worry."

He shrugged. "Suit yourself. Just let me know."

When he'd gone, she called Karl Bracer. "Karl? Selma. Could you spare a moment."

"For you? Always."

Fifteen minutes later Selma knew with sinking heart that Darwin was right. She blamed him for the careful questions she put to Bracer. The old man, she said, wanted to know if there were any unusual financial problems Carlyle might face that he should know about. Darwin was being Darwin, she apologized, and as usual fussing unnecessarily, bored with inaction, she guessed. When Bracer, as she expected, declared total unawareness of any irregularities in the auction house's bookkeeping—"I'd be the first to know, Selma"—she was certain he either was fully aware of Chase's disaster, or that he was involved in the Tundra deal himself and covering. She could smell a lie a mile off and was now virtually certain that Chase had indeed got the money from Carlyle, although how remained hidden.

From her questions and Bracer's answers it was clear to her, also, that Bracer knew that she was on to what had happened with Tundra Oil. She failed, however, to ask herself how he could have known that.

When weeks before she asked Lou Waller to put a tap on Chase's telephone, the computer engineer had hardly accepted her first hush money check and slouched from her office when he was on his way to Bracer. In the past, Bracer had found Waller a willing source of information on a good number of company matters. The computer expert not only had free access to every department of the giant auction house, he also had no trouble hacking into e-mail exchanges.

"There's something afoot you might want to know about, Mr. Bracer."

"Oh? What's that?"

"It's a bit tricky."

Karl Bracer was adept at reading faces. Even Lou Waller's. "It's like that, is it?"

When there was no answer, he reached for his checkbook. "You've been working pretty hard lately, Lou. I think you're due for a bonus. In my experience, people generally have a pretty good idea of what they think a bonus should be. How about yourself?"

Lou Waller had smiled and told him, and Bracer had written a check.

EIGHT

Haydn lived in a spacious airy loft on cobble-stoned Franklin Street in Tribeca, an area of southern Manhattan that was once New York's principal warehouse district and had now become fashionable with artists, advertising, television, and film people. Haydn's building had stored furs and olive oil, and a faint odor of both still lingered in the walls. His corner loft apartment consisted of two very large open rooms and a bath. The larger of the rooms served as both living and dining room with a modern kitchen alcove behind a counter. The smaller one, the bedroom, was virtually unfurnished except for a dresser, a bed that was low, boxlike and king-size, and a modern love seat. He'd had the original wood flooring sanded and clear varnished, the walls painted an off-white with Japanese roll-down bamboo blinds on the windows. In the living room there was only a wide couch and several deeply comfortable chairs in coarse white cotton, and a Shaker-style dining table. The few wall hangings were collages: important modern photography of abstract still lifes, and posters, carefully selected for their artistic value.

There were pictures on the dresser. One was of Felicity, about whom Haydn said, "She's not what she seems on the surface. I adore her. There's real hidden value there." The other was another photo of an exceptionally beautiful dark-haired woman (in her late thirties, Gabrielle guessed) whose eyes expressed a rare intensity. "Ariel," Hayden explained. "I never knew anyone quite like her. She could drive you crazy, but you always forgave her because there was so much in her that was so vitally important. She set a very high standard."

Gabrielle loved the place. She'd been there several times when Haydn had invited friends to dinner: people he thought she'd like to meet, not for her story but just for themselves. He was a charming host and a good cook, and it had been fun shopping for the food and then getting everything ready with him before guests arrived, and helping him clean up afterward. Evenings there were so relaxed compared to the formality of The Moorings, and they had given her a real insight into how many Americans lived and thought. It had been a struggle, though, after one evening to resist Haydn's tactful suggestion that she abandon the dreary Upper West Side hotel that the New York representative of *France Aujourd'hui* had arranged for her.

"That dump they've got you in is plain awful, Gabrielle. You could have the bedroom here. The couch is plenty large enough for me. I've often slept on it when I put friends up for the night."

She'd kept it cheerful. "A night is not a week or longer, Haydn." And was grateful that he hadn't persisted.

Today, she had arrived breathless and late from being taxi-stranded in Midtown gridlock to find Haydn just closing up his overnight suitcase. As soon as he and Gabrielle left Selma, they had hastened to their respective apartments to pack up whatever they would need to wear at The Moorings, Gabrielle not forgetting an informal cocktail dress (Darwin liked to dress for dinner) as well as a cardigan and a light jacket because nights on the island could be chilly even in July, and Darwin had said they would perhaps go for an evening cruise on the *South Wind*.

It was only two thirty in the afternoon, but Haydn urged her to hurry. She didn't question the need, but she wondered why. They were flying to Nantucket in the Carlyle executive jet, and the flight took only thirty-five minutes. She found out, however, as soon as they were in the old Cherokee and headed, she thought, for the maritime terminal at La Guardia Airport, where the jet would await them.

Haydn stopped at a deli to pick up some sandwiches. "Better than what they sell at McDonalds," he said.

Gabrielle was surprised. "Do we need food for such a short flight?"

"I'm afraid we're driving. Chase said he needed the plane. I'm sorry. I guess I was too angry about it to tell you. I tried to get seats on a commercial flight, but no luck. This is a big holiday weekend. We may be able to fly from Hyannis on the Cape. If not, we'll have to take the boat."

She realized, then, that the phone call he'd received on his cell on the way out of the Carlyle building must have been from his brother or from the pilot to tell him so. It must have also been the reason he'd suddenly become so distant and unresponsive to her chatter about what they would do during the long days ahead. She hadn't wanted then to ask him what the call was about. For all she knew it was from an old girlfriend or something else not her business, and she refrained now from any comment. The drive, Haydn said, would take four hours just to the Cape, perhaps longer. They'd be fighting holiday weekend traffic all the way. And if no flights to Nantucket were available and they had to take a ferry—even the fast passengers-only one—that would be another hour, perhaps more. She determined, however, not to let it spoil Nantucket for her, although it was hard not to resent Chase from finding an excuse for keeping the jet for himself, this of all weekends, when she and Haydn had always flown up before.

Why he had was obvious, she thought. Being able to say yes or no arbitrarily to the plane added to Chase's need to flex his power, which she sensed he never really felt secure about, having been virtually forced to follow in Darwin's shoes at Carlyle and ending up being Darwin's puppet. She had come to think that Chase, for all his amiable deference to his father and seeming respect for him, might somehow actually be frightened of

Darwin. Every time she'd seen them together, she'd thought Darwin's behavior toward Chase extraordinarily heavy-handed, even downright bullying. Mindful of what Haydn had said about Ariel also bullying Chase, she'd found herself wondering how Chase then managed to stand it all over again from his father. Why else but fear? And no matter that on the surface he seemed to take no offense; deep down he also would have to harbor deep resentment. Anyone would.

The thought was disturbing. It would mean there were two Chases—the composed, handsome Ivy Leaguer who seemed so arrogantly self-confident, the other some lost and tormented inner person living in a darkness that kept him well hidden from the world. There had been the occasional classmate like that, she remembered, back in school in France: broken birds who, starved of love, had turned to secret hate and anger. And what about the father? She could only think that Darwin either had to feel some terrible competition from the son, and perhaps always had, or possibly resented him because Chase, coming before Haydn, had totally detracted from Ariel's interest in him as a husband.

It all came back to the mother, she thought—every time she tried to figure out the family dynamics. If only Ariel were still alive. How fascinating it would have been not just to meet and interview her but to see firsthand how her two sons and once husband would react to her.

Once free of New York and in the flow of traffic rushing northward into New England on Interstate 95, she fell asleep. She didn't really wake up until they crossed the Bourne Bridge, which spanned the Cape Cod Canal, and were on the Cape itself.

"You shouldn't have let me sleep, Haydn."

"Why not? You were tired."

She wanted to stop right there and have a frank talk about how she felt, how he felt, clear the air for herself. Instead, she stared at the road ahead, coming back slowly to full consciousness as they branched onto Route 6, heading east for Hyannis on the Cape's south coast. Luckily, once there, they found that Air Island had put on extra flights, so that when they finally arrived at The Moorings, a mile beyond the Town of Nantucket with its old New England houses and cobbled streets, it was not yet dinnertime, and the sun was still well above the waters of Nantucket Sound to the west.

Thomas met them at the airport with Felicity's station wagon, and in minutes they were driving through the estate's imposing front gate, its two massive gateposts topped by large stone gargoyles pirated by Darwin's father from a twelfth-century French church. At the end of the long gravel driveway, flanked by gnarled old apple trees that nearly shut out the evening sky, they came abruptly on the house and behind it, on a branch of the driveway, the garage that had once been a stable. Both, in the weathered-gray age of their shingled exteriors and roofs, seemed never to have been built but to have grown naturally by themselves out of the windswept soil of the island, just as had the surrounding scrub forests, salt marshes, and cranberry bogs.

Getting out of the car, Gabrielle was at once enveloped by the heady all-embracing smell of boxwood that formed a waist-high hedge each side of the brick walk to the front door. The smell merged with that of the seashore and the freshly mowed grass of the lawns into a perfume she found sheer heaven. There was peaceful silence, too, after the noise of city and traffic, a silence broken only by the occasional cry of a gull, the distant muffled sound of a powerboat, the hissing whisper of wavelets encroaching on the stretch of sandy beach where the property met the water of the wide harbor, and the far-off heavier sound of surf on the Coatue sandbar protecting it.

The Moorings was an oasis, a world of its own. At the end of the nineteenth century, when he had come to Nantucket to fish and observe seabirds, Geoffrey Morse, Haydn's great-great grandfather, she'd learned, had bought an eighteenth-century farm house, now the kitchen and part of the upstairs of the present dwelling. His son, Aldrich, had added to the house to bring it to its present size before turning it over to Haydn's grandfather, Carlyle. It was easy for her to understand why Darwin loved the place so, and why Haydn, too, still felt such a deep attachment to it. Every tree and bush, every flower bed, nurtured over the years into seductive maturity, spelled five generations of one family. In a world at times so unduly harsh and strident and hostile, it seemed sanity and safety.

To her shocked surprise, she found Chase had already been there for several hours and that he'd left New York in the company executive jet at the same time they had. Haydn managed to swallow his anger. "I thought you said you were going to Washington."

Chase was apologetic. "I'm truly sorry. Last minute change of plans. I tried to get in touch with you and couldn't. Going to the airport when I could have stopped you, I found I'd left my cell phone behind, and once at the plane, it was really too late. You were undoubtedly too far up the pike to make it worth turning back."

It didn't ring true to Gabrielle. She was sure Chase had never intended them to take the plane in the first place. The explanation was plausible enough, however, and left little for Haydn to say, but Gabrielle was sure his thoughts about it were the same as hers. It made her wonder how devoid of feelings Chase must be not to be concerned, except as a meaningless formality, about what effect his actions or words might have on others.

The greeting she received from Felicity and from David made up for it. Felicity's warm sisterly embrace made her realize how fond she'd become of her. And she found David adorable when, before they had even got out of the car, he rushed to remind her that it was his birthday tomorrow and he'd be seven and to tell her and his Uncle Haydn everything Asa had said during the past week.

"Asa said moles eat dirt and can hear you walking around

on top of them, and do you know what? He found a humming-bird nest in the trumpet vine and it had three eggs in it. Asa said they were smaller than my thumb nail. And when they hatch he'd show them to me, but he couldn't until then because it might scare the mother bird away, and they'd all die."

She and Haydn went at once to their separate rooms to unpack; hers the Blue guest room with its lovely faded wallpaper and view of the harbor, and with flowers on the dressing table and the canopied four poster turned down for the night; Haydn's, the room of his childhood, was just down the hall. She had hardly finished when Mary came to tell her that Mr. Morse Senior was out on the lawn, and would she join him for tea. "And if you need anything in the night, Miss, there's just the bell here 'n I'll come right up. Not to mind the hour, Miss. I'm a light sleeper."

She met up with Haydn, and they found Darwin in his wheelchair at his favorite spot just where the dock began and under the broad leaves of the grape arbor that shielded him from the last of the evening sun and from the dying afternoon breeze off the ocean. With him at the tea table with its padded tea cozy and plates of little sandwiches and cookies was Marie Costello, his nurse, who politely rose at once to say hello before returning solicitous attention to Darwin. Gabrielle liked the big bosomy Italian-American woman; there was a wonderful warmth to her. Haydn said she'd taken the job because her husband was laid off work in the boatyard and they needed the money. That was hard, Gabrielle thought. And at the same time reminded herself that her mother had taken a job assisting the village baker when her own father, who was clerk to the *notaire,* had been obliged, when business was bad, to take a hefty salary cut.

"She's a saint, that woman," Haydn said later. "She dresses and undresses him, she manages all his toilet problems and helps him from his wheelchair onto the shower seat, and then back onto the chair when he's through, and dries him off. I don't know what we'd do without her."

Poor Darwin. Gabrielle could only think how awful it must be to be old and sick and unable to do so many of life's private and functional necessities for oneself. And how additionally painful to a man used to being a demigod to whom everyone bowed and deferred.

It was during that time an incident occurred which she found disquieting and would long remember. David had eaten earlier and gone to bed to be certain he'd get enough rest for his big day on the morrow, when he would be able to stay up late for his birthday cake and ice cream and eat with the grown-ups. There was just herself, Felicity, Haydn, Chase, and Darwin. Conversation had been mundane, first about repairs needed to the tennis court, then Haydn had turned to Chase to ask him whether he planned to join the New York Yacht Club Cruise that year. The Cruise was an annual event when a fleet of sailing yachts of all sizes raced in various classes, beginning far down Long Island Sound and ending at Bar Harbor in Maine. Darwin had suddenly interrupted. Before Chase could answer Haydn, he said, "I take it you're planning to be here tomorrow for your son's birthday."

All evening, Chase, who had been pleasant enough albeit his usual formal and unbending self, had nevertheless seemed slightly remote from all of them, as if he saw nothing of interest in whatever they were talking about. At Darwin's interruption, he came to life and stiffened visibly. "Of course, Father," he said, and Gabrielle thought he struggled to hide immediate resentment. She was taken aback herself by Darwin's tone. She thought it embarrassingly heavy-handed in its insinuation that Chase was an inadequate father.

There was an awkward silence which Darwin broke. He sniffed and then said, with a kind of deliberately put-on casualness that in its very manner was equally provocative, "I had a call from Karl Bracer this afternoon. What would that be about?"

For a second Chase simply froze. He was being served

mashed potatoes from a silver dish by Perkins, and the serving spoon stayed suspended half way between the dish and Chase's plate as though a film had stopped on a single frame. Then he continued helping himself, putting the serving spoon back in the silver dish when finished, making his father wait. Gabrielle had the strong impression that he'd been caught by surprise and needed time to recover.

"Bracer? Good heavens! I have no idea, father. What did he say?"

"He didn't. Thought you might know. He just said he wanted to come out and talk to me."

Chase was reflective. "Odd. He might want to discuss retirement. I'll have a word with him. I don't want him bothering you. Some of these people still can't get it through their heads that you're not there any longer". He held up his empty wine glass. "Perkins?"

Gabrielle glanced at Haydn. He was staring fixedly at his plate, and when he raised his eyes to meets hers, they were without expression. Next to him, Felicity looked uncomfortable. The exchange clearly had all the marks of a challenge by Darwin, who again broke the silence. With a noise of dismissal, he returned to the subject of the annual New York Yacht Club Cruise. The fleet was currently in Buzzards Bay, having come up from a night's harboring at Block Island. Tomorrow it would sail for Martha's Vineyard, anchoring in the Edgartown harbor, where there would be a party in the fleet's honor at the Edgartown Yacht Club. Then, it would sail on to Nantucket. Darwin, still playing the team coach and captain, suggested that if Chase didn't want to join it for a few days when it continued north, perhaps Haydn might. The *South Wind*'s presence with the Cruise was almost a tradition, and people would wonder why it wasn't joining this year. "Show everyone that if I'm laid up it doesn't mean my family is," he said.

Chase didn't rise to this further bait with its accusatory tone. "I most certainly intend to go," he said. "Wouldn't miss it for anything." He smiled at Haydn. "And if Hay wants to go, I think he and I can manage to take turns at the helm, right, Hay?"

Whatever had passed between him and Darwin seemed to have been completely put aside, Gabrielle noted. Chase had returned to his usual well-mannered and confident self and readily joined in discussions about which sails to take and what to provision the yacht with in the way of food and drink.

Later, when Felicity had taken Darwin off to bed and Chase had gone up, too, Haydn asked her if she wouldn't like to come along on the cruise. She was thrilled. "*France Aujourd'hui* would love that," she said.

"And you wouldn't?"

She laughed. "Try me." And then lowered her voice. "Hay, what was all that at dinner? The someone who called from Carlyle."

"Karl Bracer?"

"Who is he? You never introduced me to him."

"Probably because I don't like him. He's the secretary-treasurer."

"Why don't you like him?"

"I don't know. Bad vibes. He's one of those people where everything is a front, and you never know who they really are or how they really feel. Don't think he likes me either. His office is virtually autonomous. The board loves him because he's always been highly successful with Carlyle investments. My father claimed he was a whiz with figures."

"Do you know why he called?"

"Haven't a clue. Maybe he was just being polite. Come out and pay a social call. After all, he owes his job to my father. They worked together for over ten years."

She persisted. She'd thought about the brief exchange between Chase and Darwin, and she thought it odd that Haydn hadn't noticed anything in Chase's reaction to news of the call. She said, "Chase didn't like it."

He smiled. "Caught that, did you? Chase doesn't really

like anything that's not Chase, especially when it brings in my father. And especially today. Something's eating at him."

"You noticed that, too?"

"Sure."

"What do you suppose it is?"

"Who knows? I long ago stopped trying to figure out what makes my brother tick."

It was the closest she'd ever heard to his being openly critical of his brother. She decided not to pursue it. Upstairs in the hall outside her room, saying goodnight, she managed to duck a pass he made, which she stopped herself just in time from accepting. "Behave," she said. She quick-kissed him on the cheek and without another word quickly went into her room, closing the door firmly but softly behind her and leaning against it, breathless, until she could collect herself. Most men would have given up on her by now. Haydn didn't seem to have. It was making it more and more difficult for her to keep a wall between them.

Even when she'd settled into bed and turned out the light, she found herself wondering about the exchange between Chase and his father, until finally the faint sound of waves on the shore and the far off moan of the Great Point lighthouse foghorn at the farthest tip of the island lulled her to sleep with her last thought that tomorrow would be David's birthday and a wonderful day for all.

NINE

Early in the morning while Gabrielle still slept, Felicity awoke in her room down the hall. The sun was just rising out of the Atlantic, throwing a long swath of crimson along the harbor. It filled her bedroom with the soft light of summer and early-morning freshness. At the same time it was a surprise. Facing her window, her eyes still half closed with sleep, she saw that her curtains were open, and she remembered she'd closed them when going to bed because the moon, turning the room and everything in it a pale pastel gray, had made her feel lonely and depressed. Then, with a start—she had just remembered it was David's birthday—she heard a sound close by. She turned quickly and sat up to see her husband fully dressed and rummaging through her handbag.

"Chase?"

"My car keys. You took them yesterday because you said it was blocking your station wagon."

She got out of bed, threw a robe over her pajamas and went to her dresser where she'd left them. "Here."

He snatched the keys from her hand. "Next time leave them in the car, okay? Or is that too much to remember?"

Felicity glanced at her bedside clock. It said ten past five. She didn't feel like speaking to him; having him come in and wake her was bad enough. But curiosity got the better of her. "Where are you going?"

"New York."

"At this hour? Why?"

"Business. I'll be back for dinner."

She felt an immediate knot of anger. "Chase, it's David's birthday."

"I'm aware of that, Felicity."

"You promised him you'd take him sailing."

"I'm aware of that, too. Haydn can take him."

"It won't be the same, and you know it."

"Well, blame Darwin. Not me. I was quite happy at Kleinmann-Roth."

The anger in her boiled up, choking back any answer, but she had to keep it going. She had to make him change his mind. It wasn't just missing David's birthday, it was his rarely ever spending any time with David at all, and boys needed fathers. Haydn was wonderful; she knew he'd take David sailing, so at least the boy wouldn't miss what he'd been looking forward to for days. But it wouldn't be the same as if his father took him.

She tried to keep it low key. No point in a confrontation. "Chase, can't you possibly delay New York?"

His answer was to look at her and turn on his heel.

"Chase. Don't walk out. We're talking about our son."

That did it. As he went into his room, she grabbed her hairbrush from the dresser and threw it at him. "You rotten bastard." The brush flew uselessly against the door as he closed it. She rushed to yank the door open

"Chase!"

He glanced back at her. "That's right. Make a scene and wake up the whole house."

Disbelieving, suddenly numb, she watched him disappear into the hall and knew it was useless to follow. Her eyes swept the room, the mussed up bed covers, the clothes he'd worn yesterday thrown half on the floor and half on a chair waiting for someone else to pick them up and put them away. The half open door to the bathroom where he'd left the light on. She hated his room, every inch of it. She hated him. She couldn't stand the framed photos on his dresser, taken at the party given for him two years before when he'd had to leave Kleinmann-Roth. One showed half a dozen men in tuxedos surrounding Chase and grinning at the camera. The other was of Chase and two men and a woman. Everyone had signed the photos. The woman's name was Courtney Sherwood. She was tall and beautiful, dazzlingly blond, expensively dressed and jeweled, and exuded the kind of confidence that made her look as hard as nails, someone who had the world by the tail at thirty and didn't give a damn for anyone. She remembered how Chase had relished telling her the woman was making close to five million dollars a year. She was married, Chase said, but Felicity had always suspected him of having an affair with her. Sometimes she wondered if he still was. If so, and looking again at what she saw as cold hardness in the woman in spite of her bright smile, she guessed Chase had met his match there. She had to be a woman who chose her bedmates and when it suited her.

Several years ago, shortly after David was born, she had discovered a package of condoms in the drawer where Chase kept his handkerchiefs, and she'd had to face the fact that she wasn't imagining that he was adulterous. It was real. And if not with the Courtney woman, then with someone, perhaps even a number of women. It brought back what she'd always tried to bury deep—the misery of their honeymoon.

Trying not to dwell on her reaction back then to his betrayal and to the utter sterility in their marriage now, she returned to her own room and sat at her dressing table. A tired, almost middle-aged woman with dark circles under her eyes and crow's-feet starting stared back at her from the antique gilt-framed mirror Haydn had found some place and given her for her birthday. How had she ended up like this? Every day a futureless treadmill. The frustration of it. The loneliness. If it hadn't been for Haydn and David, she thought, she would have left long ago. She ought to take David now and run, but how could she? They'd take David from her no matter where she ran to; Darwin would, and build a fortress wall around him with money and lawyers. And when Darwin died, David would be at the mercy of Chase.

She got up rapidly to stop thinking of it and went to her bed and tried to talk sense to herself. Chase was the way he was. Feeling out in the cold in a marriage that wasn't a marriage except in name and social appearances only wasn't going to change it, or anything else in her life. You had to live with the hand you'd been dealt. That's what her mother had always said. So forget trying to hope Chase could turn into someone he wasn't, and stop crying about it. Chase was Chase. He was president and CEO of a world-famous auction establishment, and she and their child lived in his beautiful family home and lacked nothing. Today she had sailing with Haydn and Gabrielle to look forward to. They'd make it fun for David. He was fascinated by Gabrielle being French, and that she was able to speak to Haydn, who also spoke French, and he wouldn't be able to understand a word.

There was no way Felicity could know that a woman was the last thing on Chase's mind. Swallowing his flared up resentment at her angry protests at his having to go to New York, hating that, like it or not, he was stuck with her the same way he was stuck with Carlyle, he went quickly and silently downstairs.

In the front hall, he picked up the phone sitting alongside the *Social Register* on the ornate little telephone table and punched in a three-digit number. When his call was answered, he made it short. "I'm going to the airport, Thomas. Right now. I'll take the Jag."

He didn't wait for the "Yes, sir" but hung up, punched in another longer number, waited a moment, then with a totally different, almost apologetic tone, he said, "Peter, good morning. It's Chase. Look, I'm truly sorry to wake you, but I have to hit New York urgently. Yes, now, I'm afraid. I just got a phone call. Can you? Good fellow. Thanks so much. I'm on my way."

Hanging up, he thought, There's going to be the devil to pay when the rest of them get up and find out I'm not here, but to hell with it. This is more important than any birthday, no matter whose.

He went silently across the hall and through the dining room into Perkins's butler's pantry, where he helped himself to a handful of cookies. When he left the house, it was through the silent kitchen where the hanging burnished pots and pans, along with the huge Aga range and various appliances, waited silently for Nellie and her kitchen maid to begin their day.

The garage, which lay a few hundred discreet feet away and set back from a far side of the lawn, was approached by a gravel path bordered on each side with flowers and boxwood. The path cut past a palisaded enclosure surrounded by an arborvitae hedge. Within the palisade were several rows of laundry lines where the household sheets and towels and other linens were dried by the sun and freshened by the sea air. Darwin refused the use of a dryer except in the winter or when it rained. "The sun, everybody, the sun," he'd exclaim. "It's the source of life and health. Not some damned electric machine churning away in the dark." And he'd smile triumphantly at everyone's forced agreeing expressions.

The garage housed four cars. Above it, under the wide cedar-shingled roof, was a chauffeur's apartment. Thomas, who lived in it, had had a futureless part-time limo driver job until Darwin hired him without references. In a stroke of good luck, he happened to have been available as an instant replacement for his predecessor, who had simply packed up and left one day without giving notice, causing Darwin considerable inconvenience. Desperate for a better job, Thomas had nevertheless told Darwin that he was an ex-con who had done a ten-year stretch for armed robbery. Darwin liked the honesty and decided to give him a break, and a grateful Thomas had lived up to the trust, soon making himself almost indispensable to the whole family. Always prompt and instantly available, he drove carefully but with adequate speed; he kept the cars immaculately clean, his own short and nearly bald-headed person impeccably neat in his uniform, and took charge of any baggage, briefcases, or packages and cheerfully ran any errand requested.

When Chase appeared, he was already downstairs, trying to look alert. Awakened from a dead sleep and with barely time to dress, he'd got out the deep blue Jaguar convertible and was making certain, with a damp chamois cloth, that the windshield and side mirrors were crystal clear.

Last night he had come back after two days off during which he had made his usual eight-hour boat and bus trip trek to Newark, New Jersey, and the offices of SHEP. Coming out of jail, reformed and proud of the high school diploma he'd earned while there and, with the help of the prison pastor, deeply devout, he had vowed to give part of whatever he earned in the future to helping ex-cons like himself who found themselves abandoned by wife, family, and friends and homeless. Through Darwin Morse, he had found everything he'd lost except a wife, and there was hope in a widowed waitress at a dockside diner in Nantucket town.

"Good morning, Sir."

"The airport, Thomas. I'll drive."

"Yes, sir."

Chase got in the Jaguar, waited impatiently for Thomas to skirt quickly around the back and get in the passenger seat, then shot off, barely giving the chauffeur a chance to close his door.

"Going to the city, sir? Seems a shame on a day like this, young David's birthday and all that."

"I'm afraid business doesn't always recognize birthdays, Thomas."

"No, sir. That's right." Thomas finally picked up on the cold dismissal in Chase's tone and didn't speak further.

At the front gates, Chase slowed and put out a hand to stop an incoming pickup truck. It pulled alongside. Marie Costello was at the wheel, her hair still in curlers hastily half-covered with a scarf when she'd seen him. She wasn't wearing makeup, and she suddenly looked old to Chase.

"Good morning, Mr. Morse."

Chase didn't respond. He glanced at his watch. Darwin usually awoke at six. It was five-forty five.

He said, "I'm going to New York. Be back this evening. Any problems, you have my cell number."

"Yes, sir."

Chase accelerated away. At the airport, the Carlyle Dassault Falcon 50EX trimotor executive jet waited on the tarmac where it had parked the night before. A ground crew, alerted by the pilot, was already undoing its mooring ties. Chase dismissed Thomas. "I'll call when I'm ready to be picked up, Thomas."

"Yes, sir, Mr. Morse. Have a good flight, sir."

The plane's uniformed crew of three pulled up in two cars moments after Chase arrived.

"Good morning, sir." That was Peter Doyle, a once Navy F-16 carrier pilot with several thousand hours of flight time. He was echoed by his copilot, Randy Speers, also once Navy, who had flown for Delta Airlines. With them was the cabin hostess, Helen Chen, a trim young woman who had worked for United.

Chase returned the greetings and apologized for getting everyone out of bed on such short notice. This wasn't Thomas. Or even Perkins. These were professional people who demanded respect and courtesy and with whom it made him feel good to be friendly, be one of the boys, even if Carlyle was paying a small fortune in salaries for their service.

While the pilots filed a flight plan, Chase went aboard the sleek eight-passenger jet with Helen Chen. "Helen, a cup of your wonderful coffee would do me a world of good."

"I'll get one right now, sir." She lived half a mile from the airport. Also sound asleep when Doyle had called to tell her that the boss had an urgent appointment in New York, she'd skipped her usual morning shower and somehow managed to dress and put on the rudiments of makeup in time to arrive when the two pilots did.

Chase dropped into one of the six plush and deeply comfortable lounge chairs, four of them grouped around a small conference table. He snapped on a seat belt and closed his eyes, planning what he had to do. Bracer's call to his father infuriated him. What the hell had he called about? It couldn't be personal. Bracer had no relationship with his father outside of Carlyle. Something else? Something that had to do with Carlyle when Darwin ran it? Bracer's needing information he couldn't get elsewhere or from anyone else because Darwin had kept to himself so much that was vitally important to Carlyle?

Or none of that. Chase felt a wave of cold rise up from the pit of his stomach, a cold that clutched at his throat and suddenly made his chest feel heavy and breathing difficult. Was it sheer coincidence that Bracer called the same day Horst Von Ludlow called? It had to have been.

Or was it?

His mind in a turmoil, he hardly heard the pilots come aboard and was only aware that they were readying to taxi to take off when Helen Chen slammed shut the cabin's heavy pressure door and swung the locking handle into place.

The Dassault's motors whined to life. Chase tried to think. Suppose Bracer had somehow found out about Putin's seizure. But how? Bracer knew about Horst since Carlyle had done occasional legitimate business with the man, sure, but he'd never discussed with Horst Bracer's involvement in prying loose the eighty million from Carlyle's pension plan. So Horst couldn't have called Bracer. And Bracer couldn't have picked up the news from the papers. It wasn't due out until next week.

Then a memory flared, focused a picture in his mind, first fuzzy, seen through a mist, then sharp. Like a color slide. Himself and Bracer in Bracer's office six months ago when they'd suspected their European furniture expert of deliberately undervaluing a near priceless item up for auction and getting a kickback from the successful bidder. Bracer had laughed and said he'd soon fix the guy's wagon. He'd get the company's communications technician—what was the idiot's name?—to bug his telephone and next time catch him in the act.

Had Bracer bugged his office, too? If so, he could well have hacked into Horst's bad news. And if the Russian oil deal was actually why he'd called Darwin, then what the hell was he playing at? Was he crazy? Christ, he was in it, too. For twenty-five percent. He was the one who had done the actual dirty work, covering the sudden reduction of investments in the pension plan.

Chase felt the executive jet swing around to face down the runway into an early morning wind coming from the north. Its brakes eased it to a full stop, its three motors throttling back to almost a whisper as Doyle waited for tower clearance. Chase realized he'd been holding his breath. He cursed and tried to relax and breathe normally and looked at his watch. Six thirty. Bracer was in for a surprise, he thought, the rotten bastard. What a fool he had been to think he could do any kind of a deal with him and not get screwed. Stick to your own class, Darwin had always told him. And Bracer didn't belong. He was public high school and state college, and what had his father been? Some little pharmacist, if he remembered correctly. So socially, no way, forget it. Except a once-a-year token invitation to the kind of party his father always gave to those to whom he felt he owed something. Bracer would have seen through that. He'd probably always hated the Morse family for it, so it was a fair guess that he wouldn't have made the call unless he had something nasty in mind.

The Dassault's brakes eased off, its motors roared to a muffled scream. It surged forward, forcing Chase back into the softness of his leather seat. Its landing gear on the rough surface of the runway vibrated throughout the cabin before, in what seemed seconds, its nose lifted sharply, the runway disappeared and it shot upward at a steep angle.

Maybe it was revenge, Chase thought. Sure, that could be it. Reveal Russia's grab and Carlyle down eighty million. Preempt before Darwin heard of it from elsewhere—auditors maybe, or somebody on the board. Get points for doing so and his own back for not being awarded with the CEO job at Carlyle. Lie his head off to exonerate himself from all guilt while at the same time twisting Darwin into knots of his usual fatherly rage, so that it would be all those prep school years all over again.

It would be like the time he'd been up for serious discipline for cheating on an exam when he hadn't, and when Darwin had refused to listen to his protests of innocence and had sided with the school. Just the way he'd always sided with that German governess—what was her name? Baldweg? Whatever. Damned Nazi bitch. Complain about her taking the belt to him, or twisting his penis if he missed the toilet bowl slightly; complain and he'd get a lecture from Darwin on how to behave himself, Darwin threatening more punishment of his own and saying that what he needed was a tough Marine Corps drill sergeant to straighten him out.

A million other times, the same story. Always wrong. Somebody else always right. He didn't have the job because Darwin appreciated his ability. He had it because Darwin wanted Carlyle to be his lasting legacy. If the Morse family lost control of Carlyle, the world would soon forget Darwin Morse as the man who made Carlyle what it was today. For Darwin, that would be like being buried without a tombstone or no obituary in the *New York Times*.

The memory of Darwin sticking him with Carlyle was almost too painful to bear: Darwin back home from the hospital, threat of imminent stroke death barely over, wheelchair-bound but still in charge. "Carlyle's yours now, Chase. See you do right by it."

"I don't want it, Father."

The bulldog jaw going slack with astonishment, the gray

eyes burgeoning into outrage. "What the hell do you mean, you don't want it?"

"Just that. I'm not you. I'm a banker. I don't like auctioning."

The helpless bulk in the wheelchair going rigid then: face red, eyes like colorless marbles, a moment's terrible silence in which he could only hear his own heartbeat hissing and drumming in his ears, and fear rising up to choke in his throat.

Then, "Don't like auctioning?! Well, get this, Chase. And get it straight. Too damn bad what you like or don't like. Carlyle doesn't leave this family." All that with the cold, triumphant smile of winning.

"Father, I'm working for Kleinmann-Roth and doing well."

"You heard me."

"What about Haydn?"

"Haydn's incompetent. Artists don't know up from down. You take charge, Chase, or you're out of here. No Moorings, no money. And nothing when I cash in, either. On your own. Permanently. No mistake about it." A harsh laugh. "Might do you the world of good. Find out what reality was."

Oh, yes, indeed, as if you knew yourself. What this is really all about, Darwin, is your lining me up to be your surrogate while you keep running the place. Do this, Chase. Do that. Did you do what I told you to do, Chase? Why not? Don't argue with me. Just do what the hell you're told, dammit. That's what it was going to be.

So if Bracer had spilled, he'd be a fool to expect any mercy. Darwin would side with Bracer. He would lower the boom on him just the way he had threatened. He'd be out on the street in a flash with Felicity and the boy. On his own and stuck looking for some stinking stupid job to keep a roof over their heads until he managed to get back into banking and then having to take shit from some boss with half his breeding and education. And forget appealing to the Carlyle board of directors. Darwin might be in a wheelchair, but he still had clout. Most of them were old cronies he'd put there.

The cold fear in Chase became a leaden feeling. It spread slowly and insidiously into his limbs until he felt numb, his whole body. His mind, too. He couldn't get his thoughts straight. He tried not to think of his friends at Kleinmann-Roth, their laughter, or the misery the last time he'd had sex with Courtney. Right in the middle of it, her legs tight around his back, her pelvis thrusting up hard against him, her vagina clamping like a vise around his penis, she'd suddenly said triumphantly, "Guess what, Chase. You're getting it from Kleinmann-Roth's new five-million-dollar winner." And through her laughter and as she came, Darwin's voice, Darwin shouting something unintelligible, his voice thick with anger.

When Helen appeared from the galley with the coffee he'd asked for, he said, "Helen, would you mind awfully if I changed my mind and had a Bloody Mary instead?"

She gave him a warm smile. "No problem, sir." And took the coffee back to the galley.

That's better, he thought. She knows who's really boss when she sees him. She knows who's really in charge.

When she returned with the Bloody Mary, he drank it slowly, allowing the warmth of the Vodka to seep through him, dispelling some of the cold, lessening the weight on his chest. He forced himself to relax, to see some light in the darkness. What the hell, Darwin wasn't God, was he? Not really, even if he saw himself that way. And Darwin or no, he wasn't going to give up what he had. Not ever. Darwin had brought him up to have it, and he wasn't going to give it up. Not for anybody or anything. He'd find his way out of this mess. Whatever it took, he'd manage it. Meanwhile, maybe, just maybe, he was being paranoid and Bracer's call was completely innocent.

Yet even as he thought that, a last glimmer of light went out. Bracer had never done an innocent thing in his whole life. To think anything else was a delusion.

And Darwin came back into his mind, Darwin wheeling his chair around to face him and shout

TEN

Where the sky, a cloudless vast hemisphere of light blue, met both land and sea, a yellowish haze promised another hot day. The Dassault Falcon, cruising at over Mach 0.8 at twenty-five thousand feet, took less than forty minutes to reach New York and set down at La Guardia's Marine Air Terminal in Queens. Once in the air, Doyle had phoned ahead to a Carlyle chauffeur, who was always on tap to deliver Chase's BMW convertible he kept garaged at Carlyle when away, and the car was waiting for him when they landed. It was ten minutes past seven.

Keeping the chauffeur with him, Chase pulled up fifteen minutes later at a new twenty-five-story apartment building on Central Park West and Eighty-First Street, close to the Hayden Planetarium and the Museum of Natural History.

It was still not seven thirty. Save for a few eager joggers headed for Central Park, the street, like the rest of New York on this holiday weekend, was virtually empty. Chase told the chauffeur to wait, got out, and was intercepted at the door by a burly uniformed Irish doorman whose rheumy eyes and mottled complexion betrayed a drinking problem. "Good morning, sir. Who was it you wished to see?"

Chase was ready for the question. He told the man Kurt Bracer and flashed his business card. Carlyle owned the building.

"Oh, yes, Mr. Morse. Mr. Bracer hasn't left yet. He said last night when he came in that he was going to Paris for the French independence day. What they call Bastille day or something, I think he said."

"Bastille day, yes." Chase felt a flood of relief in hearing that Bracer hadn't left yet. He'd taken a chance coming down unannounced. He hadn't wanted to warn Bracer and had prayed that racing into New York at this hour wouldn't turn out to have been in vain. Bracer was taking two weeks off and was flying first class at Carlyle expense on an Air France flight that didn't leave until six in the evening. There'd been no guarantee, however, that he'd still be in New York this morning. He could have decided to spend Friday night on Fire Island, enjoy the beach today, and go to the airport directly from there, accompanied by the lover he kept hidden from Carlyle, as well as the rest of the world. Business-wise, Bracer had found it politic to stay in the closet while maintaining a completely "straight" demeanor.

Chase told the doorman he didn't wish to be announced and at the elevator told the half-asleep elderly operator "Penthouse" and rode up to it.

The penthouse lobby serviced only two apartments, Bracer's and somebody unimportant whose name Chase couldn't remember. Against one wall, papered in a delicate golden pattern of leaves, there was an expensive Empire side table adorned with the chiseled stone head of an unknown Roman that had come from the ruins of Pompeii. On the wall opposite, a polished pink marble shelf supported a large Chinese Ming period bowl that floated fresh-cut exotic flowers which were replaced every other day by building maintenance.

The doors to the two penthouse apartments were oak-paneled with expensive British brass hardware. Directly facing the elevator, they were virtually side by side, an architectural arrangement Chase thought ridiculously inconvenient. You were trapped, like it or not, in a "neighbor" situation you couldn't escape. Given the fair chance of running into the other occupant, serious privacy simply didn't exist.

The little lobby was deathly still, its air stale. No sound came from either apartment. He briefly ran through a checklist of his leverage over Bracer then rang the doorbell, the faint sound of its ring beyond the heavy door penetrating the silence like a muffled shriek. He waited ten seconds before he rang it again, half smiling to himself in the knowledge that Bracer was probably thinking it was either a building employee or an urgent delivery, maybe a FedEx.

He was right. For a second or two when he opened the door, but not more, Kurt Bracer's expression, like the flick of a whip, gave away first his astonishment at Chase's completely out-of-context presence on his doorstep then, because of it, acute anxiety.

Gaining the kind of control that had enabled him to climb to the top of Carlyle from relative obscurity, he managed four words and a smile. "Chase! What a surprise." He was wearing nothing more than boxer shorts that made his thin angular frame with its soft muscles and white skin look more naked than it was. His face was stubbled with unshaven beard, his thick graying hair, usually so carefully combed, was disheveled. Chase had never seen him in anything but an immaculately tailored business suit and for a moment hardly recognized him.

"Good morning, Kurt." He smiled and strode past him into the penthouse apartment.

Bracer, as unobtrusively as possible, hurried to block his way from going beyond the foyer. "Could you tell me what this is about? I have a guest staying."

"Get rid of him. We need to talk."

"What about? For heaven's sake, Chase. It's Saturday and I'm off for a day in the country before my plane tonight."

"I'll wait in the living room."

Bracer saw there was no use in protest. "Okay. Would you want coffee?"

Chase didn't, but he said, "Why not?" for no other reason than to inconvenience Bracer.

When Bracer hurried off, Chase entered a living room furnished in expensive yet neutral English regency, the floor covered with a handwoven oriental carpet. Wide sliding glass doors to the terrace gave onto a magnificent view of Central Park and beyond the park's leafy coverage Manhattan's upper east side, beginning with Fifth Avenue. A little sterile, but pretty damn nice anyway, Chase thought; not quite on a par with the family apartment overlooking Gracie Square and the East River, but as nice if not better than the business apartment on East Seventy-Fifth Street.

He turned from the view to activate the television set, recessed into a wall between two nineteenth-century land-scapes of the English countryside. When a documentary film on illuminated medieval manuscripts appeared, he realized that it came from a DVD which Bracer hadn't finished watch-ing. When had Bracer got into that sort of thing? And why? He'd never seen him show any interest whatsoever in any art, not even in any of the great works they dealt with. Bracer's sole interest in art, like his own, was finance.

For a moment Chase watched as more shots of priceless old manuscripts flicked by along with shots of European mon-asteries: Gregorian chanting monks filing along ancient stone loggias, the poplar-dotted hills of Tuscany, the vaulted arches of French cathedrals. He switched it off. Whatever Bracer's interest, it wouldn't pay to be caught looking at it.

It wasn't more than ten minutes before Bracer was back with two mugs of coffee. In the interim, Chase could hear another man's voice and what sounded like a dispute, with Bracer mollifying someone's indignant protest at being roused out of bed a half hour early. And then doors slamming before silence descended again.

Kurt Bracer came back in. He'd got into a pair of chino pants and a loose sports shirt and had combed his hair, but he still looked almost a stranger to Chase, who had made him-self comfortable in an upholstered chair. Bracer didn't sit but stood, his legs slightly apart and his arms folded aggressively across his chest. "Okay," he said. "You're here. Please proceed with whatever."

Chase chose his words carefully. "Let's start with your call to Darwin. I want to know exactly why."

The smiling response was measured. "You know something, Chase? I really don't think it's any of your business. I worked for and with your father for over ten years. If I want to talk to him, that's my affair."

"Come off it, Kurt. You have nothing in common with my father except Carlyle, and since he retired he regularly gets a full report from me as to everything Carlyle is doing business-wise: its balance sheet, profit picture, up to date prospects—all that as reported to my office by you and DeWitt. So where does that leave us? With something you needed to know that Darwin had kept to himself? I doubt it. Clearly not liking Darwin, you have consistently tried to avoid any further contact with him once he retired. You're a logical person, Kurt, and logically you would have come to me, and you didn't. That leaves the deal you and I have. So let's stop fencing and put a few cards on the table, shall we? Is there some incomprehensible reason why you would want to go running to anyone about our deal, let alone behind my back to my father?"

"All right, if you wish, and, as long as you want to put cards on the table, we could start with my cut."

"Ah. Indeed. Then this is a crude gun-to-my-head attempt to get more, right? Up the ante, or I tell Daddy his son has bitched up his precious Carlyle? But don't just drop in on him. Call him first as a warning to me to discuss things?" Chase forced a laugh. "I'm surprised, Kurt, frankly. I would have thought a man with your acumen in business would have seen that ploy as a two edged sword."

Bracer put his coffee mug on a table, making Chase wait. When he'd settled himself, he assumed an air of patient tolerance. "Not quite, Chase," he said. "Good try, but not quite. My twenty-five percent that we agreed on for my expertise at tapping the Carlyle pension fund—I'm not going to see even a penny of it, right? As of a couple of days ago when you called Munich and conversed with Horst, I'm now not going to get anything. Nor are you, correct?"

Chase stared at him, unable to think of any reply. He'd been right to foresee that Bracer might have got hold of the Russians seizing Tundra. And to have guessed how he had done it when Horst didn't know Bracer was in it and when there was no earthly reason that Bracer would have called Horst. He said, "I take it you bugged my office."

Bracer shrugged. "Whatever. So let's discuss where we're going from here. The eighty million we 'borrowed' from Carlyle is eventually going to surface. Helping yourself to employee savings is only safe until there's a run on the fund in general, half a dozen employees retiring at once, say, and having to cover their rights with other corporate money and then disguise what that money was actually for."

Where earlier he'd been certain he had Bracer cornered, Chase now had a sickening sense of being cornered himself. He tried not to show his feelings and assumed an aggressive posture.

"Since you were clever enough, if you can call eavesdropping clever, to find out about Tundra, suppose you tell me where you think we go from here. In your devious accountancy machinations, where does Darwin come into this?"

"I should have thought that obvious."

"Your brand of deviousness never is."

But it was. Chase knew exactly what was coming and knew he should have realized as much.

He heard Bracer answer him. "I happened to have made it my business years ago, Chase, to inform myself as to exactly how much money Darwin Morse actually had. Five years ago he was worth close to a billion, with several hundred million of it relatively liquid. Knowing Darwin, and I know him well, I can't imagine he's lost any of it."

So that was it—get Darwin to cover the loss personally. Chase managed a laugh. "You're telling me that you actually think my father will cover an eighty million corporate loss with his personal money?"

Bracer smiled in return. "To avoid the discovery that Carlyle's employees will get nothing when retiring of all the money they've faithfully put into a pension fund, and the disgrace of having his son and inheritor of Carlyle the one responsible? What do you think?"

It was hard to think. Sudden fear of Darwin pushed everything else aside; there was only Darwin backing up school discipline and complaining governesses; Darwin endlessly catching him trying to escape Darwin-style humiliation and punishment.

"I think you're a double-crossing, two-faced bastard, Kurt. That's what I think."

When Bracer just shrugged, fury choked Chase. "How do you propose to exonerate yourself in Darwin's eyes? You were in this as much as I. As a matter of fact, you were the one who came up with the idea. 'All I want,' you said, 'is enough to close the deal on my retirement home in the Caribbean. Five million of my twenty will do it. The rest will be for living.' That's exactly what you said."

"I don't deny it. And that's all I do want. And don't worry; I don't propose to exonerate myself at your expense. I don't have to. Darwin can think what he likes of me. Come on, Chase. Instead of fighting me on this one, join me. Darwin may rant and rave, he's good at that, but do you honestly think that he's going to risk seeing Carlyle dragged through a scandal for what in his eyes is a mere pittance of eighty million? And he's hardly going to the board with this either, even if he could. I don't care how many of them are cronies. If he did, it would make him look a fool for ever putting you in as CEO, and he'd be taking the risk that some board member who wasn't a crony, and there are several, would blow a whistle on the whole works and bring in the law. Hey, don't lose any sleep, Chase. Darwin isn't the Darwin who used to run Carlyle. We're talking about a decrepit old has-been in a wheelchair with a nurse feeding him chicken soup."

Staring at Kurt Bracer, Chase had a dull feeling of déjà vu. The time came back to him when, years ago at prep school and captain of the debating team, he'd gone into a major debate with another school—was it Andover? He'd felt dead sure of himself but with every advantage had come out the loser against a token black kid, one on a full scholarship who had come from some Philadelphia slum. The boy had torn his every argument to shreds. And even now Ariel's voice ringing in his ears, "Times have changed, darling. Get used to it. The world belongs to everyone, finally, thank heaven." His fury over her lack of understanding, her support of people who didn't count instead of himself. The anger, remembered, choked once again. There was a way out of this, there had to be. But he needed time. "Okay, Kurt. You're probably right. But I insist on one thing. We wait until you get back from Paris."

Bracer shrugged. "Why not? Give you a chance to figure out how to break it to him."

Being in the same room with Bracer had become unbearable. Chase rose and abruptly left the apartment. Undeterred, Bracer came into the elevator lobby to see him off and to have a last word. His tone was hard and unforgiving. "Don't get any ideas in your head, Chase, when we get the money, to figure some scheme to cut me out of my share. Two can play at that game. I've taken the trouble to look into your preference for whatever isn't Felicity."

To Chase's relief, the elevator arrived. He stepped into it "Enjoy Paris, Kurt."

When the elderly operator closed the doors on him, Bracer, returning to the apartment, allowed himself an indulgent smile, and going to the refrigerator in the kitchen, helped himself to a beer and silently toasted himself with it.

So much for the spoiled rich Ivy Leaguer, he thought. The gold-spoon-in-his-mouth Chase Morse was finally going to get pulled down a peg. He could hate Carlyle all he wanted, but now he was going to have to eat a lot of humble pie and do a lot of crawling to hang onto everything Carlyle meant: his million-plus yearly salary and his huge slice of the Carlyle profits, the executive jet at his service and all the other perks, the luxury hotel suites when he traveled, the five-star restaurants, his cruising about on a million-dollar yacht with all his society cronies, and using the Seventy-Fifth Street business apartment for a sex hideaway. And if he thought he could con Darwin with a trumped-up story, that wasn't in the cards. Bracer was pretty sure he knew who was responsible for bugging Chase's office. If he was right, Darwin would hear all about Tundra in a surprisingly short time, if he hadn't already.

As Bracer began to pack for Paris, he found himself more than relieved that he would be away when the confrontation between father and son took place.

ELEVEN

A s Chase came out of the building, he was observed by two New York City plainclothes cops of the Midtown Manhattan major crime unit. They were staked out in an unmarked car about half a block away. One was Detective Sergeant Aaron Klein, a veteran of the Desert War, beginning to gray at forty-five and to add weight to his generally slender frame. Good humored and given to bantering with his colleagues, eighteen years as a police officer had turned him cynical about people and persuaded him to be chary of believing anything until it was proved otherwise. He had a half-finished coffee in one hand, a nearly finished sugar bun in the other. He'd picked up both two hours earlier, before the stakeout. His fingers were all sticky with the bun's sugar, and the stakeout was getting on his nerves. He'd been against it when it was ordered up. "What the hell's the point?" he'd complained. "The guy never gets out of bed before eight."

"Now, just who that might be?" The sudden remark came from his partner, Detective Georgina White, who sat behind the wheel. She was a young, exceptionally pretty African-American officer who didn't look at all like a cop. In her late twenties, she had a celebrity figure, and when off duty wore her straight dark hair in bangs and styled to just below her ears in a pageboy. When working she usually tied it back in a short pony tail.

"Jesus, Georgie, Who cares?"

"I do. I swear I've seen him somewhere before. And if you don't care, you ought to. Who comes into a residential building at this hour, gets challenged by the doorman, meaning he doesn't live there, and then comes back out in thirty minutes?"

"Delivery?" Klein said facetiously.

He and Georgie, as everyone at the Midtown major crime unit called her, had been partners for five years, and he was only beginning to get used to her endless curiosity about everything that didn't seem worth being curious about, but invariably turned out to be otherwise.

Georgie laughed. "Yeah, champagne and caviar. Goes with the BMW convertible. I'm going to check his license."

"Because you think he came to see Bracer?"

"Head of the class, Aaron."

"Oh, come on."

"Come on yourself." Georgie got on the phone. When someone answered she said, "Hi. It's Georgie. Listen, got your computer fired up? Do me a quickie. New York license CRL3689. Sure, I'll hold. No, on a stinking stakeout; like me and Klein had nothing better to do. Crandall loaned us out to the art squad. Yeah, suspected trafficking in stolen illuminated manuscripts. You know, what the monks back whenever used to handwrite and illustrate. Worth a fortune, apparently. Sure, I'm holding. Take your time."

Her casual tone and the brief exchange reminded Klein of a similar moment. In their first year together, Georgie, still a rookie he felt unfairly stuck with, and worse, a female, had been on the phone digging license information when they were caught in the alleyway. She'd dropped the phone as casually as putting a fork down on a plate and then just as casually put a bullet through the windshield of the crazy who came at them with a car, using it as a weapon to smash both of them, with the alley not wide enough to get out of the way and no doorway to duck into. Right through the windshield and smack between the bastard's eyes. The car ricocheting from wall to wall and slowing enough for them both to throw themselves on its hood as it ground to a stop. Georgie then dropping her compact Beretta back into her shoulder bag, cool as ice. Himself awed, giving her a big hug and thanking God for her as a partner. He'd never got over it.

Holding, Georgie came to life. "Ah—got it? Who?" She fast scribbled a name onto her notepad. "Okay. Great. Listen, thanks a pile. I owe you one. Sure, you too. They say it's going to be a stinker. Nearly a hundred. Bye."

She clicked off. Klein said, "So?"

"Chase Morse. Bracer's CEO."

Klein came alert—fast. "Well, well, well. Birds of a feather?"

"It's a nest to get into, that's for sure."

"Do we have anything on Morse?"

"On the books? Nothing. Took over from his dad two years ago. Was in investment banking with Kleinmann-Roth. Has a brother runs a bookshop and a part-time sack mate left over from Kleinmann, Courtney something. *Social Register* type gone serious over big money."

Klein was awed. "How do you get to know all these things?"

Georgie laughed "A good cop's handbook. Supermarket celebrity rags." She scribbled a note in her book and looked up to stare at the building where the janitor was now hosing down the sidewalk. "Number one, making business calls at seven thirty on a weekend? Watch out, Mr. Morse. You've got the NYPD on your ass."

"Yeah, but let's go careful. Bracer's one thing. Messing around with the Morse family—who knows what they have for political clout."

"I plan to check that out."

Both then sat in silence, keeping an eye on the building, thinking their own thoughts: Klein wondering about his wife and two rambunctious sons spending six weeks as they did every summer in a rented cabin by a New Hampshire lake. He found their absence heavy going. Georgie was wondering if her boyfriend was up yet and praying he'd not shoved off for work forgetting to turn off the stove's burners after he made himself breakfast. He ran a small business making custom-ordered picture puzzles and was branching out into doll houses for children. For the purpose, he'd rented space in a Brooklyn warehouse.

At eight thirty, two men came out of the building, one with several pieces of expensive matching luggage. Bracer and friend. The doorman hailed a passing cab, and they drove away in it.

Klein wrote down the time in his notebook; Georgie did the same in hers. Klein said, "Okay, let's go home. On the way I'll check airport security and find out where he's going."

"Roger," Georgie said. She started up the unmarked car, and they headed back for their precinct.

TWELVE

In the aftermath of Darwin's tragic death and the preparations for his funeral, Felicity found herself dwelling more and more on two things that replaced any anger and frustration she felt about her husband with a dark and tormenting suspicion.

One was a vague memory of awakening in the early dawn that terrible morning by the need to go to the bathroom. On glancing briefly out the window when returning to bed, she'd seen someone, a man, coming across the lawn to the house from the grape arbor. She'd taken a sleeping pill the night before, and still heavily sedated, she'd tumbled back into bed to sleep instantly and soundly until awakened by David's screams. She'd completely forgotten that moment; it was like a dream remembered, but it finally surfaced to her consciousness days later.

In the half light, who was it she had seen? It had to have been someone familiar for her to go back to bed without worry. Some neighbor? But there weren't any who would have trespassed at that hour. Who else? Asa? His work day started at eight. Could it have been the lobsterman who often tied up his boat at the dock in the very early morning and came up across the lawn to deliver lobster to the back kitchen door? Heart in her mouth, she had asked Perkins if any lobster had been delivered around David's birthday or even since. His answer of "no" was one she desperately had hoped not to hear. The hazy picture of the man crossing the lawn, identity still unclear—who was it? Who? Increasingly, an answer cried out to Felicity—an answer she found it almost impossible to face or share with anyone.

The other thing that turned suspicion into a sickening dread was something that had occurred the evening before, when David's birthday was finally over. She had tucked him in bed far later than usual, and Haydn and Gabrielle had come to kiss him good-night and wish him happy birthday a last time. They had gone back downstairs, and Chase had finally appeared, contrite over missing the birthday and with questions as to how it had all gone. There'd been general conversation for a while, she and the others filling him in. Finally, Haydn and Gabrielle had gone on up to bed, leaving her alone with Chase and Darwin.

Felicity had learned to detect even the most subtle change in Chase's moods, especially anger. How many times had he suddenly lashed out at her when she had disagreed with him or had showed him wrong in something. One moment he would be affable and friendly, circumspect in whatever he was saying, the Chase everyone thought they knew; the man she thought she'd married. In the next, there would be a sudden and almost volcanic explosion of rage. Once, sailing with Darwin in the *South Wind* between Martha's Vineyard and Nantucket when David was still an infant, Darwin had corrected Chase in an argument. He'd then gone below to the salon to check their chart, and Chase had muttered an angry response only she had heard. Letting down her guard, she'd said, "Please don't be upset, Chase. It's not really important, is it?"

They were seated side by side in the cockpit, Chase steering the boat with one arm resting lightly on the wheel. He'd shrugged and had gone dead silent and then, without warning, there'd been a sweeping backhand that had drawn blood in her mouth and left her with a swollen lip That and other incidents had taught her to recognize certain signs of danger: Chase staring straight ahead in dead silence, not looking at her, a muscle in his cheek twitching, all the color drained from his face, his eyes suddenly losing their light.

She'd seen those signs last night. With Haydn and Gabrielle no longer there, Chase had lapsed into relative silence, speaking only in response to Darwin's demanding questions about affairs at Carlyle, and then grudgingly. It was obvious that something was weighing heavily on his mind and that Darwin was making him more and more uncomfortable. He had fixed himself another drink when in an awkward silence Darwin asked about the forthcoming exhibition of the rare Millet portrait which was scheduled to be auctioned off in a few weeks' time. Chase's answer was perfunctory. He'd put his drink down preparatory to going upstairs himself, when Darwin said, "Stay a moment, Chase. I think you and I have something we need to discuss. Felicity, you wouldn't mind? Chase can see me to bed."

She'd taken the hint. She'd risen, collected her crochet frame, kissed Darwin on the brow, and with a murmured good-night, left the room. Doing so, she happened to glance back, and to her shock saw the familiar twitch in Chase's cheek, his eyes go dead, his color pale.

Later, she was to remember the anxiety that had surged in her as she got undressed and brushed her teeth. The telltale signs she'd seen in Chase were due to Darwin, not her. The old patriarch's manner had sounded falsely affable, as though he were covering disapproval of something. And she'd thought that Chase was probably in for one of Darwin's heavy lectures on how to run Carlyle correctly. But she doubted Darwin would suffer from any confrontation between them. Chase, she thought, was probably too frightened of Darwin for that. He'd take out all his fury on her or David. Her heart sank when she thought of what he might be like tomorrow.

Felicity was right in seeing Chase's mood change. He had been swept by such instant seething anger that he was scarcely aware of her departure. A sound like wind rose in his head and with it a steady drumbeat; he felt a repeated tick in his cheek as though half his face was jumping. Without looking at Darwin, and with each word taking effort and echoing in his head as if repeated by someone else, he said, "What is it this time, Father?"

Darwin's first response was a brief snorting laugh, one tinged with contempt and disdain. Then he answered as though to a child. "From your expression I suspect you know very well what we have to discuss. But we're not doing it here. The walls have ears. I'd be obliged if you would wheel me out onto the lawn. It's a warm night. We can talk at the grape arbor or perhaps even down on the dock if I should find you raising your voice."

The old man wheeled his chair toward one of the French doors leading out to the terrace. Infuriated at not having the courage to disobey, Chase went to hold open the door and help his father navigate first out onto the terrace, then across the terrace onto the lawn, and as in a dream, weaving Darwin's chair over the darkened grass toward the grape arbor so as to avoid the croquet wickets made barely visible by light from the house.

It had to be about Tundra. What else? It simply had to be. Darwin always punctuated his worst discoveries of wrongdoing and subsequent punishment with dramatic gestures like this; wheeling out into the night so as not to be heard. Bracer said he hadn't told him, but Bracer surely lied. His phone call to Darwin must have been that. What else? But no, that couldn't be. Bracer was too shrewd to risk incriminating himself. He'd hold what he knew like a mailed fist under the table only to be used if driven to it. Then how had Darwin found out? And had he gone on to guess where he'd got the money from?

The question repeated itself over and over. The words became a dark shawl that wrapped themselves around his panicked mind in a mantle of uncertainty. Until showing through it there was a face at first barely seen; a face and a voice. Selma Freedman. Had she got onto it somehow?

They had reached the grape arbor. Darwin glanced back at the house where upstairs bedroom lights were still on, "Keep going, Chase. Down onto the dock. The night air off the

Atlantic will take whatever we say out to sea."

Numbly, he obeyed, got the gate open, rumbled the chair slowly down the length of the dock. At the head of the ramp to the float, Darwin ordered him to stop, slamming his hands onto the chair's wheel rims to make sure he was obeyed.

There was light from a three-quarters moon that from time to time was darkened by drifting small clouds. It was enough for Chase to see his father's face, his massive, dominating body. He wanted to turn and run. He couldn't. His feet and legs were lead.

Darwin said, "I understand you've had a bit of trouble, courtesy of Mr. Putin."

A glimmer of hope suddenly. Just the thinnest ray. Darwin was so quick with his knowledge about Putin that perhaps, only perhaps, this was all he knew.

The thin ray of hope quickly shattered.

"How do you plan to pay Carlyle back, Chase? And don't tell me you didn't have your hand in the till because you don't have eighty million of your own."

Chase found his voice. Darwin was guessing. He couldn't have proof that he'd got it from Carlyle. He was just fishing to flush him out. That was an old trick of his. Make it look like he knew when he didn't. Pull you in that way. "I didn't touch Carlyle, Father. I borrowed it."

"You borrowed it, did you? I see. And from whom? And with what for collateral? From whom, Chase?"

Another fleeting glimmer. He could be right, this could be a trick. Darwin possibly didn't know. How could he? Bracer wasn't that stupid. And how could Selma have learned?

He became aware of the night around them, the soft sound of waves on the beach and lapping the piling of the dock. From far off there was the bark of a dog and very faintly, drifting on the still night air, someone's laughter down the shore. He felt unexpected strength surge.

"From whom, Father? Friends. You wouldn't know them."

That was it. Sound confident. Take charge. The way Darwin

always did himself. "Look, I don't see any point in this, Father. Yes, I lost my shirt, so did a hell of a lot of other people, including some big French consortium, and Horst himself, for that matter. It will be in all the papers next week. I took Horst Von Ludlow's advice; you always have yourself when it came to investments. This wasn't some back-alley deal. But it's my problem, Father, not yours. Now I'm going to wheel you back to bed. We can take it up again in the morning. If you wish."

The wheelchair didn't budge. Darwin said, "Hold it, Chase, and stop trying to play me for a fool, because if I know anything about you, I know when you're telling the truth and when you're lying. Your so-called *friends* you got the money from; we're talking Carlyle, right? And don't tell me otherwise."

"Father …"

"I'm waiting, Chase, and I haven't got all night. How do you plan to put the money back?"

All the uncertainty swept in again. A suffocating wave and his will gone. Darwin taking over. Darwin always took over. Somewhere in him a silent voice cried out, "Don't let him do this. Fight back. This isn't school or college. This isn't then, this is now."

The voice stilled. A steel band drew tight around his chest. "Father." He couldn't speak more. He could only stare down at the ghostly wheelchair figure. Stare helpless in loss, unable even to move an arm. Nothing was real.

Darwin spoke again, voice cold with anger. "Okay, Chase. I'll give you until morning. If you can't come clean by then, you'll find yourself locked out."

"Locked out? From where?" But he knew. From Carlyle, and the hated Carlyle was better than obscurity, better than being out on the street, on his own and no one.

"Where the hell do you think?"

"You can't do that."

"Can't I?"

"You're not in charge any longer." He'd started to cry and

couldn't help it. "I am. Father, You can't take that away."

"I can't?" That laugh again. Contempt. Disdain. "Correction, Chase. Get something straight You're only up there in my office on probation. I may be in a chair, but I still run Carlyle."

"That's not true."

"No? Try me. Or better, care to try the board?"

A memory. His father a towering figure, coming off the tennis court. "Come on, Chase. Let's have it." Himself a little boy who'd snitched a tennis ball. "Let's have it, boy. The truth never hurts. Hand it over and you can go have your supper."

Believe him. He's smiling. Trust him.

"There you are, son. That's better, yes?" The smile vanished. "Now go to your room and write 'I'm a rotten little thief' one hundred times. There'll be no meal until you're finished."

Then, and now Carlyle. He looked out past his father, the wheelchair and the dock and into the night at the tiny star that was the distant *South Wind*'s mast head, riding light. The yacht was his. He tried to hold onto that and couldn't. He was going to lose it. He was going to lose everything. Blacklisted in banking and without even his income from hated Carlyle. Incongruously, a picture of Helen Chen serving him vodka that morning flashed behind his eyes, then flitted away.

Nausea swept over him, the roar of wind in his ears again, the drumbeat. There were blows against his cheek, his body was someone else's. Darwin would make him nothing. Someone out on the street job hunting. Someone else the boss. Do this, do that. Some faceless nobody, ordering.

"Chase, answer me, dammit."

Stop Darwin. Stop him. Shut him up.

"Chase!"

Someone seizing the wheelchair suddenly, spinning it toward the ramp.

"Boy, what the hell …?"

Someone's voice screaming in his head. "Stop him. Stop him."

Someone pushing the chair hard. Hurling it down the

ramp. The float, rushing up, the heavy splash, the shower of water, a muffled cry. An explosion of air and water, the chair rising, pushing it down again under the dark surface.

Then nothing. The silence of the sea at night. Silence except the beach he was walking on. The faint hiss of sand as waves swept in and out again. How long had he walked? The moon way down on the horizon. The night air chill. A faint gray crack of dawn on the eastern horizon. His shirt and trousers damp with sweat.

Remembering, finally. Numb. Darwin wasn't any more. In the morning someone would find him. Asa maybe. Even himself. Darwin would be there. But wouldn't be. Darwin wasn't any more.

He came slowly back up the beach. His tasseled city shoes were filled with sand and his feet were agony. He took the shoes off, climbed up over the sea wall, and walked across the lawn to the darkened house.

THIRTEEN

Thursday, July 7th. Among those who did not attend the funeral of Darwin Morse when three days after his death he was interred at the Morse family private cemetery not far from The Moorings was Jason Olenski. The scion of a prominent establishment family, he was a product of the same New England prep school attended by Chase Morse and subsequently, with considerable artistic talent, graduated with a bachelor of fine arts degree from Brown University. Olenski was not, strictly speaking, his real patronymic, however. Olenski was his mother's maiden name which he had adopted, feeling it was more in keeping with his overly romanticized dream of life as an artist. His mother was the great-granddaughter of a once-prominent Russian nobleman who, during the Bolshevik revolution of 1917, fled Russia under the threat of either Siberia or a firing squad. Jason's actual name was Curtiss-Pelham, his father a corporate attorney and a member of the socially prominent Curtiss-Pelham family of Baltimore.

Ignoring his father's wise note of caution—"Do you really want to paint, or are you just enamored with the idea of being an artist?"—Jason flamboyantly proclaimed himself a painter whilst a regular attendant of all the smart cocktail parties among the social circles of his peers in New York. In the summertime he frequented East Hampton and Blue Hill in Maine.

To the astonishment of many, Jason seemed, for a while at least, to turn out some quite reasonable canvasses. He even had mild critical success in one or two minor exhibitions. It didn't last, however, and for good reason. Jason soon learned he couldn't actually paint well enough to sell work which, supplemented by a private income from an inheritance, would enable him to maintain the lifestyle in which he'd been raised. In desperation, he took to copying the unknown works of minor artists of the nineteenth century wherever he found them and claiming them as his own. Perhaps even to his own surprise, he became first good at this fraudulent occupation, then very good.

This bent also didn't last. He ran out of unknowns whose work came up to the standard of those he had previously plagiarized. In appearance and value his choice of paintings deteriorated, and with it the aura he had created for himself among those ignorant of important art. Having developed an expensive drug habit which along with a lavish lifestyle helped him run through most of his inheritance, Jason continued to decline rapidly until finally the ax of disaster fell. He was revealed as a copyist and forger when, in order to recover his reputation, he took a chance and copied an obscure painting by Jules Garnier, a not-very-well-known French impressionist but one of considerable talent and with a certain appreciation not just by his peers but also by modern connoisseurs.

The painting was recognized by, of all people, Darwin Morse, who didn't hesitate to denounce Jason during a socialite-studded cocktail party, bellowing out for all to hear, "You have no damned right to call yourself a painter, Olenski. A painter creates. You create nothing but forgeries and copies of other's work. Have you no shame?"

Oddly it was Chase, his former classmate, who saved him. Perhaps only to spite Darwin, Chase deviously suggested that Jason not only admit to having copied Jules Garnier and others but candidly claim he had done so in order to bring to the works of relatively unknown artists the recognition they justly deserved and to boast that he was such a good copyist that he had fooled everyone except a chance expert.

It worked. Defeat became victory among the gullible in the shallow social circles in which Jason traveled. And when Chase made a public fuss, again probably to spite Darwin, and to Darwin's disgust and annoyance ordered a copy of a well-known Pre-Raphaelite, Jason soon found himself in demand and back on his feet financially. For there was a growing market among those who could not afford great painting, and soon, while some audaciously claimed his meticulous work that hung on their living room wall as original, others, more honest, readily and even proudly admitted their acquisition was a copy which enabled them to enjoy great art at a reasonable price.

Shattered dreams, however, are a bitter pill, and one Jason found it nearly impossible to swallow. The pain of seeing a great masterpiece or even of hearing the artist's name became nearly unbearable. Worse was the growing relative fame of some of his contemporaries. In spite of his talent being channeled in a direction that at least provided a moderate income, he compensated for his lost dream of greatness by clinging to the illusion that he was a serious artist and did so by developing the sort of bohemian lifestyle he had always romanticized great artists to lead. He gave up a fancy Upper East Side Manhattan apartment and found himself a miserable little one-room studio in Chelsea, which only served to increase his sense of inadequacy and depression.

Strikingly handsome, with a slender, athletic frame, deep-set eyes, and a proudly prominent nose above a sensuous, full lipped mouth, Jason let his hair grow long, shaved only intermittently, and rarely changed the baggy chino pants he adopted in place of Brooks Brothers flannels. T-shirts, often sporting dubious slogans, replaced button-down poplins or Lacoste polo shirts, and his feet habitually sported open-toed sandals.

Clearly headed nowhere, he was rescued by a very worldly woman ten years older than him who was everything he was not or unable to be. Her name was Renata. She was of Greek and Armenian heritage, a big statuesque and handsome woman with very short dark hair combed forward, Roman-style. Once a student of the famed European sculptor Brancusi, she had abandoned Paris and Rome for New York and the dollars there that her considerable talent and ability as a sculptress guaranteed. Becoming reasonably established, first by doing busts of well-known people, she branched off into large statuary for the plazas or courtyards of important buildings. Charging a small fortune for her work, she soon became well known and much in demand.

Disillusioned with the influx of expensive commercial and residential living in once quiet Tribeca and by nature careful with money, she looked for a place where she could get what she felt was important space with real character. It didn't make any difference where it was as long as it was removed from what she called the "appalling hyped up dishonesty of the beaten art track" in Manhattan. Brooklyn or Queens or the Bronx would be fine. She didn't have to worry about isolation. The world, she knew, would come to her. Space was what she needed. Space.

She soon found it in a nearly abandoned Bruckner Boulevard warehouse by the rail yards that bordered the Harlem River, that decaying industrial waterway that separates the unfashionable Bronx from upper Manhattan, and conveniently reached by the Willis Avenue Bridge only a short distance away.

It was a huge, airy, high-ceilinged place that had once provided storage for oriental carpeting and more recently the manufacture of outdoor neon advertising fixtures. It consisted of two very large, undecorated whitewashed rooms, one with wide floor-to-ceiling windows letting in north light and which had once been open-door hoist entrances for materials too large or two awkward for the elevator. It perfectly fitted Renata's needs. She sculpted in both clay and stone, and when in stone, often made quite a bit of noise, of which old-fashioned hammer and chisel were only a small part. Modern electric-powered tools, especially saws that cut stone, had caused endless complaints from her former neighbors in Tribeca.

Renata had no use for fashion where her person was concerned, nor for interior decor. The very essence of her being was creativity and work. One room, separated from the other by a wide arched opening where a heavy café curtain served as a door, was graced only with a king-size platform bed, a pine dresser, a chair, and a Victorian washstand. One of two small walk-in storerooms in this space served as a clothes closet; the other housed a galvanized steel stall shower, an ancient bathtub on legs, a sink and toilet, the latter activated by an old fashioned pull chain attached to the tank situated some five feet above the commode.

The room with the two windows was both Renata's work and living place. Currently, it was dominated by an eight-foot-tall nearly finished statue, in clay and to be cast in bronze, of two massive-bosomed and wide-hipped nude women, both resembling Renata herself. They stood defiantly, legs planted firmly apart, one with a hand resting on the muscular shoulder of the other. Everything else in the room was relegated to relative insignificance by the nudes as well as by the room's size. There was a copper kitchen sink on one wall, above which was hung a string of onions and some exotic Central American gourds along with a classic flamenco guitar rescued from a pawn shop. Close by, there was a large coal range converted to gas and a refrigerator of dubious age. Not far away, there was a pine trestle table with several straight-backed chairs, and against wall space between the windows, a worn couch, the faults of which were covered with a heavy cotton blanket and flanked by two upholstered chairs of equal vintage. These three huddled around a long irregular-shaped slab of marble supported on each end with concrete blocks. Steam pipes traversed the ceiling from near the battered steel of the entry door to descend the wide wall space by the kitchen sink and then disappear into the uneven surface of a wide plank floor.

Renata was a sophisticate. Well read, with a liberal and agnostic outlook on life and a firsthand knowledge of important European capitals and resorts, she could hold her own in any dialectic combat or discussion. When working, as she was at present, and unembarrassed by human nudity in either herself or others, she invariably wore nothing other than a clay- or rock dust–spattered leather apron that protected her front from her neck to below her knees. If at leisure and not going into Manhattan socially or on business, when she always dressed stylishly, perhaps in a sensuously low-cut dress by someone like Armani, she donned a pair of men's shorts and covered her expansive and beautifully sculpted bosom, of which she was inordinately proud, with a barely buttoned man's white shirt. For dinnertime company with close friends in the art world, she wore either a caftan or a loose fitting Mexican tunic woven of coarse cotton. A free thinker when it came to sex, she would from time to time take on a new lover when it amused her, discarding them with equal casualness when they became too dependent. She drank only occasionally and then wine or vodka but incessantly smoked Balkan Sobranies, the dark tobacco cigarillos.

Jason came into her life at a perfect moment for her as well as for him. Renata, although possessed with a flamboyant ego, was not an unkind woman. Where Jason was seen as a pariah and scorned by nearly the entire art world, she not only saw talent and energy but felt truly sorry for him. Being half Armenian she knew what it was like to feel an outcast. She saw, behind Jason's chauvinistic arrogance and cavalier attitudes, a lost and disillusioned man, one of deep sensitivity and more importantly one who inside a hard protective shell was desperately lonely and above all needed the security of love and tolerance. She saw, too, that although Jason ranted against the great masters of art, calling their success and fame hype or good luck or gallery and auction commercialism, there was certain reverence kept hidden behind his bluster in the meticulous way he copied their work, making certain that every brush stroke did justice.

Jason's sad plight intrigued Renata and aroused in her a

woman's protective and maternal instincts. Her bed life being empty of the male sex for some time, she took him on as a lover, and finding him satisfactory, allowed him to move into the warehouse and set up an easel that didn't interfere with her own work and her need for space. He thus occupied a substantial corner of the huge main work room.

That either loved the other was doubtful. Perhaps neither had ever loved anyone. But that they were welcome fixtures in each other's lives was without question.

Jason had not forgiven Darwin for his shattering denunciation. The day after the patriarch's funeral, Renata, who had once spent a night with Darwin and still cherished a soft spot for him, was unable to resist reading aloud the names of all the important people, as reported in the *New York Post,* who had flown to the Cape to attend the obsequies. In a small way it was reminding Jason who in reality was boss between them, and Jason pretended not to hear.

He had pulled two chairs from the kitchen table and was seated on one before a lowered easel. On the other, next to him, were two empty beer cans and a cracked saucer occupied by three or four marijuana roaches along with a still only half-smoked joint. Tired of goading him and without a response, Renata came over, removed an unlit Balkan Sobranie from her lips, helped herself to the joint, and dragged deep. "If you'd gone to the funeral yesterday, you might have picked up some work."

"Yeah? Who from?"

"I just read you a bunch of names. Billionaires."

Jason didn't answer. He was copying a Van Gogh from a photograph. It didn't seem quite right to him, and he was thinking that he really ought to go once more to the Metropolitan Museum of Art and study the original, perhaps sneakily photograph it with his digital. His buyer, an Oklahoma banker, was paying him three thousand dollars for the job, which to date had only taken him a few days.

"Jason?"

"Please. I'm busy."

"It says the cops don't have any clues. I mean, who do you think did it?"

"Did what, for Christ sake?"

"Pushed the old man off the dock."

"Who the hell cares? I wish I had."

"That's how he died. He drowned. I mean, they say he wasn't dead first. Poor old Morsey. What a horrible way to go"

Getting no further response from Jason, Renata put down the newspaper, returned the joint to the saucer, and wandered over to the kitchen stove to light the dead Balkan with a kitchen match. She was used to Jason's occasional and rather tedious moods of rebellious independence. He'd pulled one a week ago when she'd had some important gallery people in for dinner, and she'd come close to throwing him out. "Do you want lunch?" No reply. "Jason? Lunch?"

He responded to the slight severity of tone. "I'm okay."

Renata gathered together her patience, took two glasses from where they had been drying on the sink's drain board, and filled them from an opened bottle of red wine. She took one back to Jason and put it down next to him by the saucer of roaches. Returning, she drank briefly from her own glass, then went to the fridge, where she took out a half-empty can of refried beans, a plastic container of sour cream, and a bag of grated Mexican cheese. She lit the oven to briefly warm some taco bread and began to make wraps. She'd hardly finished when the house phone rang. She let it ring several more times before crossing the room to where it sat on the floor by the couch.

"Renata speaking." A look of surprise came over her face. "Oh, hi. Yes, he's right here." She took the phone over to Jason and on the way, just before she handed it to him, she said to it, "I'm sorry to hear about your dad. Are you okay? … Good." And then to Jason, "It's Chase."

He took the phone. "Yeah, Chase. What?" He listened and said, "Sure. Any time. Sure. That's okay."

He hung up and held out the phone to Renata.

"He's coming over."

"When?"

"When he gets through work."

"He's working? So soon after? Is he going to want to eat?"

"He didn't say."

"Well, in case he does, you'd better go out and get another bottle of wine."

Jason's response was hopeful. "Would you mind doing it? I've got to finish this damn thing." And then, "Please."

Renata studied him, eyed her own unfinished work, shrugged and went into the walk-in closet in the bedroom where she shed her work apron, found a pair of shorts on a peg, and put on an oversized white shirt, closing it with only two buttons. On a shelf there were various drug paraphernalia, including a five-gram bottle of cocaine and a tiny spoon. Jason had bought it only that morning. Renata didn't do drugs except on rare occasions, but she didn't like Chase, whom she saw as a self-important bore, and decided to fortify herself with a snort. She filled the little spoon from the bottle, sniffed it hard up one nostril, did it again, put the bottle away and went back into the studio to take a look at Jason's work, which she found quite amazing in its seeming authenticity.

"It's even better than Van Gogh himself. You ought to charge the Okie double."

When he didn't answer, or even look up, she slipped her feet into his sandals which he'd removed, grabbed up a worn canvas shopping bag from the kitchen table, and without another word, went out.

When the door closed behind her, Jason stopped painting for a moment. He appreciated Renata no end; he enjoyed her company, her brilliant mind and talent as well as the very good and frequent sex they had together, which almost always happened in the midst of work, when Renata would suddenly strip off her apron and lead him to the bedroom. Above all he appreciated her having taken him in. He had a problem, however: feeling constantly dependent on her financially. He yearned to be at least halfway equal in earnings and often found himself trying to devise ways to be so. Her goading him about the Morse funeral and the wealth attending it had galled.

It was nearly two hours before Chase showed up. In his business suit, starched white shirt and expensive necktie, and custom-made shoes, he looked completely out of place in the warehouse studio. After casual greetings, during which he showed no interest in Renata's unfinished work and offered only a frozen smile for her condolences, he put down his Gucci briefcase and a small package and took a painting from a large shopping bag.

Using Jason's straight-backed chair as an easel, he stood the painting up so Jason could have a look.

Jason said, "Whose is it?"

"It's unknown. Late nineteenth century. A sticker on the back says it's called *Cape Cod Blue*." Chase tried to keep his tone friendly. He hadn't liked Jason all that much in school, and even less after Jason announced his name was no longer Curtiss-Pelham but Olenski and that he was an artist. Now he felt nothing but contempt for what Jason had become—bohemian trash, and worse, a traitor not just to his family with all its tradition but to his class. How could anyone live like this, and with a libertine like Renata, who was clearly so much older? Sure, if you only went for sex with her statuesque type, but other than that, who gave a damn if she was constantly in demand, that she'd known Picasso and had studied under Brancusi and that her work frequently got attention in the art section of the *New York Times*? How could anyone live with someone so independent and bohemian?

Jason cast a professional eye on the painting. Not a masterpiece, he thought, but nice; in fact extraordinarily nice, a beautifully painted piece and something almost anyone would be happy to hang over their mantelpiece. It was unsigned, which meant it had relatively little value compared to its artistic worth. There were paintings like that, fine works that got lost in the backwaters of the art world. It represented a beach someplace on a sun-drenched, placid saltwater sound. In the foreground, framed by scattered dune reeds, a woman and a child, their dresses and hats late Victorian, were shaded from a brilliant summer sun by a blue and white striped beach parasol as they sat watching an old-fashioned lobster boat near a distant sandbar, its tattered blue sail limp in the still air. The picture was cheaply framed, the frame, part of it broken, barely molding around its stretcher.

Jason picked it up and turned it over to look at its back, where there was a yellow sticker. "Yeah, *Cape Cod Blue*. That figures. Except it could be a beach almost anyplace. Up for auction, is it?"

"You might say that."

"When?"

"Two weeks. It's not signed. Any idea who the artist might have been?"

Jason shrugged. "How would I know? Ask your pet idiot, Bouchard."

"He's too busy with the Millet to be interested."

"Frame's junk."

"I'm changing it."

"What's the reserve?"

"Not much. I think three thousand."

"Who's the owner?"

"Not important. It came from some old lady's estate in Chicago along with half a dozen other pieces, watercolors, mostly, and some furniture."

Jason stood back and eyed the painting again. "I think it's American. One of the women impressionists. Not Cassat. Somebody else."

"Why do you say a woman?"

"Hunch. Brush strokes. You want it copied, or what?"

"Yes."

"Why?"

"I'll get to that later. How long will it take you?"

"I've got the Van Gogh to finish first."

"Forget Van Gogh. I'm in a tight time frame. You can slip this in, come back to that."

Jason sighed, leaned back and studied the *Cape Cod Blue* again. "How tight?"

"By next Tuesday. Five days."

Jason laughed. "Good-bye."

"Ten thousand dollars."

There was a pause while Jason digested this. Bells rang. Clearly Chase was under some kind of pressure. He said, "I don't know what you're up to, Chase, but you must really want it bad. Okay. Make it twenty and Thursday, and you're on. That's only a week, and that's pushing it if you want it to really look authentic. It has to be chemically treated to make it look genuinely aged like the original, crackle the paint and all that, and a special varnish. You don't want Bouchard sniffing it out, do you?"

Chase didn't like it, but he agreed. "Twenty and Thursday it is, then, and not a minute longer. Let's have a drink and I'll fill you in on some other details."

Jason turned to Renata. "Could we open the new bottle?"

"Of course." She went and fetched the bottle, an opener and two glasses, put them down on the chair next to Jason, and had a look at the painting. "How about making a copy for me while you're at it? I'll hang it here over the sink. Chase could give it to us for Christmas and write it off his taxes." She laughed at Chase's frozen smile. "I'll be in the bedroom if you need me. Maybe in the shower."

When she'd gone, Jason said to Chase, "All right. I'm all ears."

Chase said, "First of all, the copy has to be a half inch wider.

Does that pose a problem?"

"A half inch? Shouldn't. I'll do a quarter each side."

"Do you have treated canvas?"

"Of course."

"Okay. I want you to put it on a stretcher that's exactly this size." Chase took out his wallet and produced a small slip of paper which he gave to Jason. "But exact, Jason. To the millimeter."

"You must think I'm a bloody carpenter."

"You can do it. Now, when you've finished the painting, I want you to take out almost all the staples holding it onto the stretcher. I need to take it off the stretcher and fast."

Jason gave Chase a long hard look. "You're planning to cover another painting with this, aren't you." It was a statement of fact, not a question.

Chase managed a thin smile. "You want the twenty thousand, Jason, you'll keep questions like that to yourself."

Jason took a roach from the saucer on the chair and lit it. "I heard you."

"Good. Next step. I want the painting delivered to my office at exactly twelve on Thursday. Not eleven thirty, not twelve thirty. Twelve."

"Not a problem."

"But covered over with another painting."

"Why so?"

Chase pointed to the *Cape Cod Blue.* "It's not supposed to be out of the building. Security has orders to check everything coming and going. I can get away with it, but they'll want to know why you have it. So slap one of your own over it. I'll alert security you're bringing me a painting I might want to buy." He glanced at the *Cape Cod Blue.* "The paint on your copy won't still be tacky?"

"I'll use a fast drying varnish when I age it. What do I do with the original?"

"Burn it."

"You're kidding."

"No, I'm not."

Jason's expression showed what he felt: destroying a painting like this, almost any painting, somebody's creation, was sacrilege.

"One more thing. Get a haircut and wear a suit. No, not one of your Brooks Brothers numbers you used to wear; they don't look *artist* enough. Wear this." Chase held up the small package he'd brought. "And shoes, if you still have any." From his dispatch case, he took out a small bottle and a calling card, which he handed to Jason. "When you come to Carlyle House, I don't want you using your own name. The card says you're Ari Pindar with an address in Chelsea. Okay?"

Jason studied the bottle. "What the hell is this?" he demanded.

"Hair coloring. You're going to be two or three shades lighter."

"Are you crazy? What the hell for?"

"I don't want you recognized."

"Well, forget it, Chase."

Ignoring him, Chase ripped open the small package and pulled out a suit he'd got from a rack in a thrift shop.

Jason took one look and said, "And I'm not wearing some stupid car salesman's suit either."

Chase said dryly, "For twenty thousand, Jason, I get extras. If you don't like them, I can make other arrangements."

Jason saw Chase was clearly up to no good, but Carlyle was his, and he could probably get away with almost anything he wanted. Just the same, there might still be risk. He'd find a chance later to hit him for more money.

After he'd gone, Renata came back to look at the *Cape Cod Blue*. "Jason, I was listening, and I don't care if he told you to destroy it. If you do, you can say good-bye to me. When you're finished copying it, I'm hanging it up." She pointed to the blank wall over the sink and stove. "Right there."

Jason shrugged. Her tone of voice brooked no argument, and he'd learned there were times when it was suicide to defy Renata. "Okay. Just so long as you promise to take it down whenever he comes over."

He took the painting from her, replaced the Van Gogh with it, and after a last, venomous glance at the bottle of hair dye and one at the suit he'd tossed onto the couch, he set about making a stretcher for the copy to the exact measurements Chase had given him.

FOURTEEN

The following day, a Friday, Selma Freedman came out of her West Eighty-Third Street Apartment, walked to the Seventy-Ninth Street crosstown bus stop and, as she had done every Monday through Friday for almost forty years, took an eastbound bus that traversed Central Park to Manhattan's east side. She got off at Second Avenue and walked the few blocks to the Carlyle auction building. Passing through the front garden with its giant La Chaise statuary and its Hiram Rosencranz fountain, she felt an acute sense of emptiness and stopped for a moment simply to stare around her. The weather had cooled slightly. There'd been a thunderstorm during the night with lightning crackling into the tops of tall Manhattan buildings and rain filling its gutters. Now the air was clear.

Today would be her last day at Carlyle. With Darwin's death, something in her had died also. It was impossible to work there anymore. As long as he lived, and even though confined to a wheelchair at home, his presence was still felt everywhere at Carlyle by everyone. To her it was as though he were still sitting in the front office, and not his son. With him gone, however, there was now nothing but the stark reality of Chase, his clear dislike of the job and barely concealed bitter resentment at having been forced into it by Darwin. To Selma, the father had been everything, the son an impossibility that threatened to bring the business down. Then, too, she had stayed long past retirement age, and she was tired.

She stood for a minute or two longer, staring around her at the facade of the building and at the garden itself, knowing that after today she might never see either again. She was planning to leave soon for Vancouver in Canada to live with a sister there. Glancing back once at the early morning bustle on Second Avenue, she took a deep breath, nodded "good morning" at the smiling doorman, whom she was going to miss along with so many others, and entered the building.

When she crossed the top floor reception room, she found the young receptionist subdued. This meant that, surprisingly, Chase was already there. An instant later she was told, "Mr. Morse came in a few minutes ago and said when you arrived to tell you he'd like to see you."

Selma enjoyed an inner smile. Did he, now? Fancy that. She wanted to see him herself. She had already written out her letter of resignation the day after Darwin's funeral. In it, she'd said it had been a lifetime of pleasure to work for Darwin Morse, that she had stayed on after his departure to help in the transition, but now with him gone and Chase apparently settled in, she planned an immediate retirement. Chase's asking her to see him facilitated her handing him the letter earlier than she had planned. His reaction would tell her if she would have the day to do a round of departments and say good-bye to those with whom she'd worked so closely for so long. But a sense of foreboding told her that she wasn't going to have that luxury. Reaching her office, she went to her desk and started to bring up her e-mail to see who had already tried to reach her, then withdrew her hand from the mouse. They would have to learn to get along without her, and now was as good a time as any. She'd told no one she was leaving. It would come as a numbing surprise to many, although she knew there would be a handful who would be delighted. Trying to accommodate Chase when he'd first taken over, she'd had to be uncharacteristically heavy-handed to achieve compliance with some of his operational wishes.

She put away her handbag, took the letter of resignation in

its envelope from within a drawer of her desk, and laid it on her blotter. Her eyes went to the small framed photograph of herself and Darwin taken some years before on a company outing. Darwin had an arm around her shoulder and a broad smile on his face. How difficult to think of the old tyrant dead, that he was gone, that he simply wasn't any more and never would be. Her thoughts went to the funeral service in the early New England Church, and to the interment in the Morse family private cemetery, where the dozen or so dead lay silently beneath weather-worn headstones. It had been hard to see Darwin's dark coffin resting above the freshly yawning grave, the family grouped together on one side in front of the many notables who attended, among them the dreadful Mrs. Henderson, dressed appropriately in black, Selma thought, but surely more in mourning for lost hopes of Darwin's money, since for all her snobbishness she had little of her own, than Darwin, and thus would probably never be seen again at The Moorings. Across the grave were the servants, the Carlyle staff and Karl Bracer, flown back from Europe along with many townspeople standing in mute homage.

Haydn had insisted she join the family. "You're one of us, Selma." It had comforted her to be with Felicity and her son and Haydn and with the several cousins, some nieces and nephews, the children of Darwin's brother who had died some years before, with his never-married sister, still living and looking bent and parchment gray and terribly aged, and with the young Frenchwoman whom she hoped Haydn would marry and who had been shocked into deep-blushing but silent anger when someone had tactlessly suggested she'd have quite a story for *France Aujourd'hui*.

Staring at the coffin, Selma had felt too numb for grief. She could only feel surprise. She had kept thinking, "Darwin Morse is in there. Darwin." She had, until then, she realized, always believed that he would forever be around and thunderously vibrant.

A fog had swept in from the sea, shutting out the sun and adding to the somberness of the day by coating with a sheen of wet the old lichen-covered apple trees and the thick privet hedge that surrounded the little cemetery, the fresh mowed grass between the graves, and the flowers heaped on the coffin. After the ceremony, everyone had gone back to The Moorings to have something to eat and drink, putting on a brave face, holding back in rigid New England protestant fashion any outward display of sorrow or grief.

Knowing how devastated Felicity must be, she had wondered at the woman's appearance of calm, put on with effort, she thought, for the benefit of her son. She knew that Felicity had always seen Darwin as a protective barrier between herself and her husband. Part of what she had to be feeling, Selma thought, was utter vulnerability. She'd wondered about David, too. The little boy at times had looked bewildered at the composure of the grownups around him, as though Darwin had not died after all. And she felt for Haydn, keeping his grief to himself. She could see from the way the French girl protectively stood close by him, and with her whole demeanor trying to lend him strength, that he probably suffered more than anyone.

And then there was Chase. No wondering there. She couldn't imagine him grieving for anybody. But his face seemed suddenly not only old and haggard, as though he were tormented by some secret inner demons, but also terribly degenerate. It was as though the shock of Darwin's unexpected and ghastly death had ripped all superficiality away to expose the ravages of a coldly adulterous lifestyle. Throughout the funeral, he spoke to no one, and anyone speaking to him received only a monosyllabic answer.

A light flashed on her desk telephone's panel. She pushed in the lit up button and picked up the receiver.

"Could you come in, Selma?"

It wasn't a question or request. It was an order. She said, yes, hung up, and with her letter of resignation, headed for

Chase's adjoining office. This is it, she thought. Forty years are ended. She remembered wondering occasionally over those years what the end would be like. And here it was, the finality in all its ugliness. She couldn't believe it was actually happening. But it was.

In the foyer, she was stopped by Lou Waller abruptly exiting Chase's office and slamming the door behind him. He was sweating and mopped at his forehead with a handkerchief. "The sonofabitch just fired me," he said. "How do you like that? 'You don't work here anymore, Waller, collect your pay and get out.' That's what he said. Just like that. I went in and he looked up from his desk and said, 'Good morning, Waller. You're fired.' The sonofabitch."

Waller was still muttering when she went into Chase's office herself and shut the door behind her.

Chase was seated at his desk. He was staring, as she'd seen him the week before, at the Picasso. With Darwin gone, he's going to have that down, she thought. And probably the other paintings, too. "Good morning, Chase."

He didn't answer. She might not have even been there. She said, "I understand you just let Waller go."

He turned slowly to face her. "The first of many. Darwin doesn't run Carlyle anymore."

Selma offered him her coldest smile; there was no point in pretending friendliness where there was only enmity. "I presume I am among them," she said.

"I'm afraid you presume correctly."

Selma smiled again, this time inwardly as well as continuing to offer the put-on one. It was good, really good, to have beaten him to the punch.

"It's mutual, Chase. I decided several days ago that you could do without me. And, I might add, vice versa." She handed him the envelope with her letter of resignation. "As you'll see from the date, I typed this the day before the funeral." She added, "My pleasure."

His expression reflecting he'd been one upped partially made worthwhile the misery of the two years she'd suffered him sitting in Darwin's chair. He hadn't been able to find words to respond. She left him in silence without another word herself or so much as a backward glance, and returned to her own office to clean out her desk.

When she'd gone, Chase sat in silence, eaten by the bitter gall of being bested by her. It was as though Darwin himself had put him down. Darwin, always right, always in command. While Selma was still in the office, her very presence had somehow made Darwin be there, too.

Thinking of Darwin, remembering his "no escape from me" tirades, Chase's head began to pound, pain lancing his temples. There were sounds again: the drumbeat, the rushing wind, the sea, the churn of small waves on the beach. And, mixed in, voices raised in anger. Whose? Darwin's? His own? The office darkened around him, seemed almost night, his desk far away. The voices rose, unintelligible, strident. Darwin. Yes, bloody Darwin. Darwin lecturing, patronizing, threatening. Darwin, always right. And suddenly the rumble of wheels, a dizzying descent in which everything seemed jumbled and confused. Then, the splash. The sound of heaviness hitting down into deep water, the water coming back up at him. Sheets of it. Drenching, soaking, and filled with the strident voices that now flailed like a whip, mocking. Darwin laughing, face distorted as if seen through a curtain of water and pointing at him. The laughter rose to a terrible babbling sound before it whispered away into merciful silence. Silence, except for the wind that rushed through his head until it also slowly died; the only sound was the sound of someone crying. Was it himself?

His office reappeared. He focused. There was the hated Picasso on the wall where it had always been. There was his laptop on his desk, his pen and pencil set, the shallow leather file tray, the telephone. He slowly got a grip on himself. He was sweating profusely, his undershirt wet, his palms coldly damp, his breathing restricted. He came from behind his desk, almost too weak to stand and fighting back dizziness. In his private bathroom, he splashed cold water on his face. When he came back out he went to a closet and punched five numbers on the little electronic keypad that would unlock it. The door clicked open. In the closet there was an overcoat in case he got caught short by sudden cold weather and a complete change of clothes: underwear, socks, shirts, a tie rack, his gym pants and sweat shirt, and running shoes for when he went to the health club. There was also a small office-style refrigerator where he kept vodka and cold drinks.

On a shelf there was a sizeable cardboard suit box from Barney's, New York's most expensive men's clothing store. It was still there. Good. He got it down, opened it to check its contents. He had to be sure. If they tapped his phone, they could also somehow have had access to his closet. But it was okay. The picture frame was safely there. He could tell from feeling it through the paper it was wrapped in.

He came back out and glanced again at the Picasso that he'd ordered maintenance to take down before the day was over. But he shouldn't hate it, he thought. Returning to his desk, he gave it a mock salute.

That awful morning when he'd got the bad news from Horst Von Ludlow, when he'd sat feeling his whole world splintering around him, and when Selma had left after announcing a meeting with DeWitt, he'd become aware that he'd been staring blankly for some time at the Picasso painting he so loathed. That was when an idea slowly began to formulate, first only vaguely, then so clearly that it jarred him into a burst of involuntary laughter. He'd let the thought crystallize, had begun to feel a flood of relief so strong that weakness no longer pinned him to his chair. Several times, talking to Bracer the next morning after his rush to New York, he'd been tempted to reveal it. But he hadn't. Bracer had shut the door on any further sharing or trust.

The thought, nurtured carefully, a lifeboat sometimes

forgotten but always still there, had saved him. Even before the funeral he'd turned it into action.

The day after the Fourth, on Tuesday and with Darwin's funeral arrangements completed, he'd found an excuse to fly to New York and had done two things. First, he'd looked for a specific-size painting that had come into Carlyle for auction, and had come across the one titled *Cape Cod Blue*. To his delight, it was part of an estate, one of a dozen other paintings and some relatively interesting furniture. It was a presentable work he was certain he could buy for its reserve, or even less, without arousing much interest. It was due for auction in two weeks' time among secondary nineteenth-century works of lesser importance and to be pre-auction exhibited in ten days. It had not yet been cataloged. Any question as to why he wanted it could be fobbed off with, "My wife's birthday. She loves impressionists." Indeed, he'd thought, besides being unsigned, it was just the sort of painting that Felicity would like. He'd use it to replace the hated battling men-o'-war that Darwin had hung above the living room mantelpiece.

He'd let the auction department know he was planning to buy the painting and was taking it home and had simply walked out with it under his arm. As he'd anticipated, he wasn't questioned by a deferential security guard. It wasn't an important piece, it had come in as part of an extensive estate, and he was the boss. The problem had been the frame. Something far more suitable, an antique one, would have to be found.

Carlyle kept a considerable supply of frames, both antique and modern, for those paintings that came in without them or with frames that were damaged. Chase had gone to the storeroom where they were kept and looked for one with some depth to it, one the painting's wooden stretcher could readily recess into. To his annoyance, he'd found nothing, and it would have been dangerous to ask one of the shop workers to custom-make a frame. That would have called far too much attention to the painting.

That same day, he had gone to a junk dealer on the lower east side, a shoddy little antiquarian with whom he knew Jason Olenski often did business. The man specialized in discarded posters and pictures and picture frames. Among the many stacks of them, he'd had the good luck to find a suitable period frame and had paid the dealer extra to tailor it down to fit the *Cape Cod Blue*'s stretcher with a quarter of an inch to spare on each side.

Satisfied with the preliminaries of his plan, Chase called Jason to advise he was coming later, settled into hated but necessary work, and at the end of the day carefully locked the closet and left his office. It was late, he'd realized, the building virtually empty. He decided against calling Nantucket to say he was staying in town. They'd figure that one out themselves. He'd go to his Seventy-Fifth Street apartment. He needed a drink and company. He'd check in with an escort service. What he planned to do was dangerous. And at the same time exhilarating. If all went well, he was going to recoup the money he and Bracer had extorted from Carlyle. And that was just the beginning.

With Darwin dead, he could do a lot more than his planned return of the eighty million to the pension fund. Much, much more.

Eventually, when Darwin's estate was completely settled, perhaps within a year or so, he could sell his share in the Carlyle Foundation, which he would have the right to do. Let somebody else worry about young artists and promising talent, all that stupidity. Worth nearly half a billion, the shares of the foundation were now split equally among Darwin's estate, Haydn, and himself. By the sale he would realize at least a hundred and fifty million, enough and then some to buy a partnership in Kleinmann-Roth or some other prestigious investment banking firm and bask in the glory of being able to laugh at those who had laughed at him.

Meanwhile, however, to avoid trouble sure to arise from

an audit of all the company books that would be forthcoming in settling the estate, he had to cover the pension fund loss as quickly as possible. Inwardly he heaved a congratulatory sigh of relief that he had already laid plans to do so before Darwin had died.

Leaving the Carlyle building, Chase found it far easier than usual to extend a polite nod or send a pleasant hello with their name to those employees who remained and saluted him on his way.

FIFTEEN

Aaron Klein was finishing off a mid-afternoon slice of pizza, trying to keep it away from the pile of paperwork that littered his desk on the top floor of the unit's office in an East Side precinct. The air conditioner had broken down and the room felt like a Turkish bath. His shirt was sticking to his back with sweat, and it was hard not to think of his wife and the boys and the lake. He missed them. Especially her. Although after twenty years of marriage some of the fire had dimmed, there was enough romance left so that whenever she was absent he felt a little lost and vaguely jealous, as though she had to be flirting it up with someone or perhaps worse, even though he kept telling himself that was an impossibility. Last night in their small apartment in Queens, where every object was somehow "her," had been especially rough going. He'd microwaved a pizza and watched a ball game on television until the mindless chatter of the sports commentators forced him to turn it off. He'd tried to keep from talking to himself and hadn't got to sleep until past midnight. He had promised to join his family on the weekend, but with the worn-out-by-the-heat way he felt at the moment, he doubted he'd make it. It was a six-hour drive up to the lake, then six hours back. It didn't seem worth it just for one night.

Klein's desk was one of two facing each other in a small room cluttered with computer monitors, file cases, a television, and a police radio; on one wall there was a Mercator projection of the world, a map of the United States, an even bigger one of greater New York; on the opposite wall there was a crime board where daily progress on a number of cases was graphically noted with colored pins. The second desk was Georgie's.

The office, like that of his boss, Lieutenant Clinton Crandall, who headed the unit, overlooked, through one partially glass wall, the unit's bull pen, where a dozen desks were occupied by clerks and lesser detectives. The noise level there was such as to make Klein grateful that at least in his cramped surroundings there was relative quiet.

Stuffing the remains of his pizza box into his scrap basket, he donned one of several pair of drugstore glasses on his desk and returned to his computer to read a detailed report on the recovery of a hundred and twenty thousand dollars' worth of diamonds stolen from a Madison Avenue jewelry shop.

He hardly looked up when Georgie came in, kicked the door shut against the momentary wave of office sound that accompanied her entrance, dumped her shoulder bag on her desk, plopped a cold can of Coke on Klein's, and dropped wearily into her desk chair. She was wearing an above-the-knee skirt and a light tank-top blouse. "I've got a real one," she said. "This goddamned heat. The thermometer under the awning at Dunkin Donuts said ninety-six."

Beads of sweat pearled her forehead, glistening against her smooth dark skin, and little rivulets of it ran down her neck into the cleavage behind the scoop front of her tank top. She shifted an uncomfortable bra strap, yanked open her desk drawer, and retrieved a bottle of Tylenol. "Still on the diamonds?"

"Yeah."

"Well, don't forget we've also still got the illuminated manuscripts. That guy Bracer."

"I haven't." Klein's voice was as sour as his expression.

Georgie ignored it. She felt the same way, but she wasn't going to let him know it. No point making his mood worse by agreeing with it. "Aaron, remember that guy Morse? The one who came and went when we were on the Bracer stakeout?"

"What about him?"

"His old man got knocked off."

"So that ties him in with illuminated manuscripts?"

"It could."

"Heat's got you, Georgie."

"Maybe."

Klein finally looked up. "Did it ever occur to you that being how Bracer was about to shove off for Europe that Morse, who if I remember correctly is Bracer's CEO at Carlyle, might have needed a last-minute word with him?"

"Some word. What happened to the telephone? Morse flies all the way in from Nantucket and all the way back just for last minute instructions?"

"How do you know that?"

"I checked it."

"Jesus." It was a groan. "When did you do that?"

"Yesterday when I checked on Bracer's phone tap. If it was just a last-minute business powwow, Morse could have telephoned. He didn't. Nothing on the voice mail either."

"Cell?"

"Possibly, but then again, possibly not."

Klein was silent a moment, staring at her. Then he said, "Georgie, you want to know my hunch?"

"Shoot."

"You're barking up a wrong tree." He opened the Coke she'd left on his desk, grunted his thanks, and then said, "What did in the guy's old man?"

"He drowned."

"Oh?"

"They found him in his wheelchair in ten feet of water off the end of the private dock on his property. Could have been an accident, but Booker hasn't ruled out murder."

"Who the hell is Booker?"

"Acting police chief, Nantucket."

"You talked to him?"

"Yesterday."

"And?"

"And nothing, really. I called him about Morse's meeting with Bracer. Thought he might like to know. And about Bracer, too. You can never tell."

A picture came into Klein's head: jigsaw puzzle pieces floating around and trying to connect up correctly. He often had that vision when Georgie started chasing something up: the endless "maybe" and "possibly" that sometimes never connected but also sometimes did. Now it was Bracer's art auction house boss flying in from Nantucket to talk to him for half an hour early on a Sunday morning and then the CEO's old man getting possibly knocked off. Because he knew something about the manuscripts, was that what Georgie was thinking?

He never got a chance to ask. The door to the bullpen opened with a blast of sound and the big ebony-skinned overweight form of Crandall appeared, mopping at his moon face and sweating so much even his ever-present bright-red necktie seemed wet with it.

"Hey, you two. Just got the usual call about the manuscripts. Anything new on them?" Unlike Klein, whose rabbi father had seen Klein's boyhood interest in police work as a lamentable lack of religiosity, or Georgie, who'd come up from a ghetto deprived world where "police" was a dirty word, Crandall had been raised in a police family, the son of a veteran cop. From childhood he had never known anything but the harsh world of law and order.

Georgie tossed Klein a "speaking of the devil" look and threw up her hands in the way of a negative. "Interpol said he's met up with the Dutchman, but all they talked about was Greece dragging down the euro."

"Well, stick with it, will you? I'll tell him you're chasing up a new lead."

Klein laughed. "Georgie is." And ducked when Georgie

slung her empty coke can at him.

Crandall exhaled patience. "Come on, guys, cool it, for Christ sake. The bastard's driving me nuts. Okay?" The bastard to Crandall, as well as to everybody else, was the cadaverous, balding Wolkowski, the lieutenant in charge of the art theft division. Crandall saw him as a noncop, a freak who beat up on lesser ranks and had got to where he was through playing cozy with all the right people and by becoming an institution at the kind of art gallery shows frequented by the superrich and the wives of city hall politicians.

Georgie said, "Sorry, chief. We are giving it our all. We really are."

Klein said, "Yeah. Honest Injun."

Crandall acknowledged with a resigned wave of one huge hand and retreated, closing the door softly behind him.

Klein went back to reviewing what he'd written up on the diamond case. Across from him, Georgie turned to her computer and pulled up a French police report on the disappearance of three priceless manuscripts shipped under guard from a Coptic monastery in Turkey to the National Museum in Paris, the apparent theft coincidental with a business trip Bracer had taken to France the year before. She found it hard to concentrate. Her headache had ebbed, but she kept thinking of Adam and his elation on getting the Texas dollhouse order. Along with a possible promotion for her, if she could crack Bracer, they'd soon have enough to get married and have the baby they both wanted so badly. She'd never seen him as happy, except when she'd told him that she wanted one by him. Her eyes wandered to the two small framed photos she kept on her desk—"Makes you a corporate executive type," Klein had teased. One was of Adam on a California beach with his surfing board, all salty and bronzed and looking like a Nordic god with his hair a lion's tawny mane. The other was a faded photo of two very poor and tired-looking young people in work clothes sitting close together and holding hands on the steps of an old farmhouse someplace in the South. They were her parents, who had died in a fire weeks after her birth, never knowing she'd be sent to remote cousins to grow up mostly on her own in a deprived and often brutal New York City ghetto.

Remembering the report, she forced back the pain of loving and wondering about them that constantly haunted her and got back to work. One of the guards had reported he'd seen an American who answered Bracer's description talking to the museum curator, who was a primary suspect as the possible trafficking mastermind. Georgie noted the fact, reminded herself to tell Klein, then buried her mind in the rest of the report.

SIXTEEN

On Saturday, only three days after the funeral and with all vacation plans shelved, Haydn was obliged to return to New York and relieve his assistant. La Rive Gauche did its greatest volume of business on weekends. With Chase remaining in town, he asked Gabrielle to stay with Felicity and David to help them manage the shock and sorrow they'd experienced and to look after things. "The servants are great, he said, "but it's not right to ask them to assume responsibility for running the place."

His request jolted Gabrielle. Did all the time they'd spent together give him the right to ask her? She immediately felt cornered. She had badly wanted to return with him and to get away from the oppressive atmosphere of death that had settled over The Moorings. She felt hurt, too, by the presumptiveness, that he seemed more worried about the family than about her. Had Haydn forgotten that she was a journalist, not a relative or, ridiculously, a nanny or a housekeeper? More important than any of that, however, were the serious misgivings that had begun to weigh on her about spending any additional time in the role of a household guest who had become virtually accepted as one of the family. Had he forgotten, also, that she was due to return to France? An angry e-mail that day from Bernard Bligny wanted to know why she had not immediately filed a far more human-interest story on the murder as well as a follow-up on the funeral. The veteran editor clearly hinted between the lines that her job was in jeopardy, perhaps even her career as a journalist, if she did not deliver. "Wrap this one up as soon as possible and get back here, and forget facts," he'd written. "I can get those from *Le Monde* or *Le Figaro*. I want the inside story of how the family feels about murder in their midst."

But how could she? Everything in her told her that to do as the editor wished would be to betray the confidence and trust Darwin, then Haydn, had placed in her and to abuse the warm personal friendship of Felicity. And now, to heed Haydn's request would compromise her standing as a journalist even further.

Trying to make up her mind, she found an excuse not to answer Haydn. She took Felicity's station wagon and drove aimlessly around the island for an hour, finding herself for the first time furious with him. Did he have any idea of the position he was putting her in? And if he did, did he care? Worse was her chagrin. She had nobody to blame but herself for her dilemma. She'd come to the Morse family on a job and had allowed herself to be drawn into a fool's paradise that seriously jeopardized her professional future.

She returned to The Moorings defensively angry: hating the place, hating Nantucket, hating the very words *Morse* and *Carlyle*, deciding that she could no longer go on being virtually taken for granted. And hating Bernard Bligny and *France Aujourd'hui*, too, and anything to do with journalism. Maybe she'd take the next plane to New York, type up all her notes in the miserable little West Side apartment, and then head straight back home to the old château.

She found Haydn all packed up and in the hall, ready to go.

She was slightly taken aback at seeing him still there—she'd hoped she wouldn't have to face him. Clearly he had presumed that she would agree to his request. A voice in her screamed, "Stop taking me for granted, dammit." Wanting to have it out with him there and then, she was unable to keep anger from her tone. "Oh. I thought you would have gone by now."

"I wouldn't go without saying good-bye."

"Well, have a good trip back. I'll try to keep an eye on things, although I have a pile of my own work to do. My editor is merciless."

"I'm sure you'll be okay."

She went on, knowing it might hurt him but unable to stop. "After all, Haydn, that's what I came here to do, isn't it? Write stories about all you people. It's what I'm being paid for."

She saw a kind of panic sweep his face. It was just for an instant. Then it was gone, replaced by a stubborn expression of anger. His body language when he hefted his suitcase was stiff and unforgiving.

"You know best," he said, but with his old nervous stammer coming back on him, "Say the word and I'll get someone out here to look after things."

He turned abruptly and headed for the door where he threw back, "Take care," and to her surprise she found herself automatically saying, "You, too," her own voice sounding strange to her, as though someone else were speaking.

The door closed hard behind him, and she was alone in the hall and instantly wishing she wasn't. She hadn't meant to say anything she'd said. She loved him. She loved him even though clearly he didn't love her. He'd stopped making passes at her, and she'd been right to resist right from the beginning. The pain of it was nearly unbearable. She stood in the silence hating herself, hating her coldness and anger, hating the way she'd spoken, what she'd thrown at him, hating her bitter disappointment.

The grandfather clock struck five with its oft muffled boom. Gaugin appeared to nuzzle her hand before he collapsed on the cool floor by her feet with a contented groan. She bit back tears. She wanted to erase it all, to start again, but it was too late. "Imbecile," she whispered after him. "Tu me fait folle."

Perkins appeared. "Is anything wrong, Miss?"

She pulled herself together, managed a smile. "Nothing, thank you, Mr. Perkins."

"At what time did you want dinner, Miss?"

"Seven o'clock will do, Mr. Perkins."

"Very well, Miss."

That night, when Felicity and David had gone to bed, she got out her laptop and worked out her report, trying somehow to inject human interest and finding it nearly impossible. She couldn't say what she actually thought about Chase, that he was an insufferable snob, that he was cold and utterly uncaring and, she thought, totally involved with self while oddly at the same time completely victimized by his father. Or that she even found something strangely frightening about him. Equally difficult was not to say that the legendary Darwin was a bullying tyrant where his family were concerned, except for Haydn, who'd gone off on his own, and that life for everyone was more peaceful in a way with Darwin gone. She walked a thin line, making up family attitudes and dynamics that didn't exist and feeling a cheat and dishonest for doing so. She stressed pleasant things instead of the truth. She didn't mention what was clearly Felicity's unhappy marriage. She complimented Felicity's talent as an artist and ceramist. She lied about DeWitt Bouchard and glowed about his extraordinary, almost hypnotic power over people. She didn't write that he had an unattractively high opinion of himself, was anti-French, and wasn't liked at all by other Carlyle employees. When she described The Moorings, she skipped her opinion of the family's inherited *Social Register* background and glowed about its elitism as though they had all earned it.

The hard part, when she got to it, was to describe Haydn without revealing how prejudiced she was. The words she wrote about him made him seem almost a stranger. Pressing the Send key on her laptop, she thought, *Nobody ever told you love could be hell.*

It was during breakfast the next morning, with Felicity acting in a distracted manner to questions from David about what they could do that day, that she decided, since she was apparently stuck there for a while, that one way to help out was to take David off Felicity's hands as much as possible and keep him entertained. It immediately became apparent, however, that Felicity didn't want this, and that David's presence was keeping her from some sort of breakdown. Always quiet and unobtrusive, which was her nature, something in Felicity seemed to have abruptly changed since the funeral. Within a day of the interment, she began to pass from vacant staring to sudden nervous twisting of her engagement and wedding rings on her finger. Or she would be found by herself, pacing up and down.

Gabrielle tried to get her to talk, but to no avail. Urging Felicity to say what was bothering her produced nothing except, "I can't talk about it, Gabrielle. Please," in a voice shimmering with tension.

During the rest of the weekend and into the following week, Gabrielle tried everything she could think of to ease Felicity's distress. She, arranged a day's sailing on the *South Wind,* courtesy of a kindly neighbor who was highly experienced in boats. She set up a croquet tournament by day and endless Monopoly and chess games in the evenings. She drove mother and son to the movies. She even conned Peter Doyle, the executive jet's pilot, into a sightseeing flight over Martha's Vineyard and the Cape with a promise that he wouldn't tell Chase. It was all to no avail. Several times she found herself nearly losing patience and sympathy. Haydn was managing. He'd gone back to work. Perkins, whom she knew had been terribly shaken by Darwin's death and all the police presence, went stoically about his duties as did the rest of the staff. She wanted to tell Felicity to pull herself together; everyone was shocked and overcome but handling it. One simply had to rough one's way through.

Meanwhile, without a word from Chase, and with only one call Sunday night from Haydn, in which neither managed to find much to say to the other, and with Felicity being uncommunicative, Gabrielle immersed herself in running The Moorings to keep her mind off dwelling on how hopeless her own position seemed to be. The staff accepted her authority without hesitation, and everyone immediately looked to her for everything. Each day, while chafing at her new role, she would discuss the daily menu with Nellie and any special arrangements with Perkins. Each day she'd give Thomas whatever orders were necessary for transport and dealing with tradesmen. Each day she'd go over gardening with Asa, determining what flowers would be needed in the house, and each day she'd formally greet Chief Booker and the state police detective lieutenant and his forensic team.

They would arrive at nine sharp in the mornings to go silently and almost apologetically about their work of delving into every aspect of Darwin's private life as contained in boxes of stored-away files of his private letters. One by one, they once again conducted exhaustive interviews with family and staff in which everyone was asked to try to remember every single incident of the fatal evening as well as several days prior to Darwin's death, even every word spoken.

Profiling Chief Booker for *France D'Aujourd'hui* and Bligny gave her a line on filing other reports that avoided revealing any personal information on the family. She simply outlined in detail, for French readers, the functioning of a wealthy American home: who the servants were, what each one did, when the meals were, and what each was like. Casting herself as the housekeeper, she outlined in detail what her own day was like, and included everything from ordering food to keeping the linen cupboard organized. Always she included a daily weather report, and always she closed with an item on some aspect or other of the island of Nantucket itself.

It was easy work, but worrying. Was there enough about the family itself, Felicity, David, Haydn and Chase, how it affected all four; and about Carlyle, too: Selma and Bouchard and the general mood of all the other employees? She could only cross her fingers and hope so. And to hope that emphasizing the almost British stiff-upper-lip character in the family that caused each to hide, even from each other, personal feelings about nearly everything except the weather, would make up for lack of human interest.

But then, on Tuesday evening, nearly a week after the funeral, something happened that made everything different. Something that, for Gabrielle, changed The Moorings from a place of grief and gloom into one of chilling fear.

SEVENTEEN

The uneventful day had become increasingly humid and hot. "We're going to have a thunderstorm, Miss," Perkins announced at lunch on the terrace. Indeed it looked it, Gabrielle thought. The sky had that heavy, hazy appearance that made you feel that all the moisture in it would quite suddenly metamorphose into menacing black clouds. And at about five o'clock, that's exactly what happened. One moment there was sunlight penetrating the humid haze; the next moment the sky was black. The wind began to rise, sucking moisture upward into the gathering storm. Gabrielle pulled Felicity and David off the lawn where they were playing croquet. With David at once eyeing the sky excitedly but Felicity completely withdrawn into herself, Gabrielle hurried them both back to the house, where they were greeted on the terrace by Perkins waiting to tell them where he had put candles and flashlights in case of a major power cut, as their generator was out or service and being repaired by Thomas.

And there was indeed one. When the storm broke, it was ferocious, with a seemingly endless crash of thunder often muffled by the drumming downpour of rain. It lasted until eight that night when Perkins, ever prepared, brought sandwiches and drinks into the living room where they had waited it out. For David, the storm provided a much wanted distraction. Not in the least frightened, he stood by one of the tall French windows that overlooked the lawn and watched the lightning, reporting on how far away it was or how close by when it struck, and occasionally relating what Asa had taught him: that birds and animals, to protect themselves from so much wind and torrential rain, would abandon high branches to take refuge under the very bottom leaves of bushes and brush, a safe haven even from predators, for predators likewise always sought shelter in their burrows or dens when it stormed.

When finally the rain stopped and the thunder had died away in the distance to an occasional far-off impotent rumble, the power came back on in a blaze of light that for several minutes made everything seem unreal. Gabrielle helped Felicity get a reluctant David upstairs to bed, tuck him in, and kiss him goodnight. Then both women came back downstairs to the living room, where they sat in silence. Gabrielle wanted nothing more than to go to bed herself but was reluctant to abandon Felicity, who, as she had done during most of the storm, continued to sit, silent and uncommunicative.

The silence continued until Gabrielle decided perhaps a drink would help. She had gone to the sideboard, where there were always several decanters, an ice bucket, a crystal siphon of seltzer, and glasses, and had just begun to fix them each a scotch and water when she heard Felicity make a strange mewing sound like a small animal in distress. She turned quickly to see her rocking back and forth, her hands covering her face. She went to her at once.

"Felicity?"

There was no answer. "Felicity, answer me. What's wrong?"

Felicity lowered her hands and turned to face her, tears streaming her cheeks. "Gabrielle. I'm so frightened. I'm so frightened. I can't stand it anymore."

"Frightened of what, Felicity?" Gabrielle sat next to her on the couch. She had become used to Felicity becoming withdrawn, but this? She took both her hands and held them tightly. "What is it? Trust me."

She waited anxiously while Felicity simply stared, her eyes

meeting hers and, through her tears, filled with a pleading look. When she finally spoke, it was in a strangely flat tone, as though stating the obvious that Gabrielle should have known. She said, "I think Chase killed Darwin."

For a moment Gabrielle couldn't find any response. "Chase what?"

"Chase killed him. I'm sure he did."

"Felicity!" Had the woman lost her senses? How could Chase have killed Darwin? Darwin was his father.

"Gabrielle, I'm so frightened."

"Felicity, what are you saying?"

"I saw it."

"You saw it?"

The words began to tumble out, first jerkily, almost incoherent, then in a flood. "Darwin asked me to leave him and Chase together. I knew it was for a private talk, so I went upstairs. I felt exhausted and took a sleeping pill and went straight to bed. When I woke up to go to the bathroom, I think it was almost dawn; it was getting light outside, and I looked out the window and saw a man coming up from the dock alone. I was so drugged, it didn't really register. It was like I was dreaming. I guess I fell back into bed because the next thing I knew it was daytime and David was screaming."

A shadow of dread began to steal through Gabrielle. "And you think it was Chase?"

"Yes."

"You weren't just dreaming?"

"No. I didn't dream it. I didn't. It was real."

"Are you sure it wasn't somebody else?"

"I checked. I thought perhaps the lobsterman, but it wasn't him. It had to be Chase."

Gabrielle tried to make sense of it. Chase had hated Darwin; she'd become more and more certain of that. But murder him? An image of Chase with his always "correct" manners, his social position, and his being now not only titular head of the

Morse family but also head of the world-famed Carlyle auction establishment; it made what Felicity said seem impossible. Besides, if it actually had been Chase crossing the lawn from the dock, it didn't prove him a murderer. He could have risen early and gone for a walk on the beach.

She said that to Felicity and then said, "Have you told anyone else this? The police?"

Felicity shook her head. "I didn't remember it until the funeral. I was so sound asleep. And then it suddenly all came back to me. Ever since then, I've been so frightened."

"Well, no matter whether it was Chase or not, they ought to know. I'll call Chief Booker."

"Gabrielle! No!" It was almost a scream. "Don't you see? He'll start asking Chase questions, and Chase will say I was hallucinating and get away with it because it's so awful nobody would believe me and everybody would believe him. And where would that leave me? With Darwin not here any longer, Chase would come after me then and kill me, too, to shut me up. Ever since the funeral it's all I can think of. Don't tell anyone, Gabrielle. *Please* don't."

Gabrielle took her gently by the shoulders. "Felicity, look at me." And when Felicity did, she said, "You mustn't think that Chase is going to kill you. You mustn't."

Felicity said, "You don't know Chase, Gabrielle. He—he can be so violent. And I can always tell when he's going to be. He gets this strange kind of blank look you see in a dog's eyes if it's getting ready to turn on you. There's no light in them. And there's this muscle in his cheek that starts twitching and he goes sheet white. He was like that when Darwin told him they had things to discuss, and I left the room so they could and went upstairs. Please believe me, Gabrielle. Please. I've got nobody else."

Gabrielle put down her drink and tried to think clearly. Did she believe her? It was hard not to. She'd never known Felicity to fantasize, and she wasn't given to hysterics or overdramatization.

She was a mature woman, a wife and a mother who always seemed rationality itself. She hadn't seen Chase wheel his father down to the dock, only "someone" coming up from the dock at dawn, but if she wasn't right, then who *had* killed Darwin? Someone who just happened to come by the dock in the middle of the night to find Darwin there alone? Then how had he got there? Felicity said she'd left Darwin and Chase in the living room and gone straight to bed. And Chase had also told the police he'd left his father in the living room, as Darwin was capable of getting upstairs by himself. The police had apparently cleared all the servants and anyone like Marie or old friends who lived off the property, and no stranger could have wheeled Darwin across the lawn without Darwin raising a storm that she or Haydn or Chase himself surely would have heard.

Gabrielle began to feel Felicity's fear grip her, too. She shivered and heard Felicity say, "Gabrielle, what am I going to do?"

Not just you, Gabrielle thought. *We.* I'm stuck here like you and David and Haydn when Chase flies up, a free man whom the police at the moment couldn't touch. You couldn't arrest someone for murder with no hard evidence. To indict Chase for murder, someone would have had at least to see him wheeling Darwin down to the dock if not actually pushing him in his chair off the float. And if she told Haydn and he didn't listen and went to the police or confronted Chase himself, he would expose himself as well as Felicity to just what Felicity was scared Chase might do. And if she herself spoke up, Chase would have her out of The Moorings in a flash, and that would leave Felicity totally alone and vulnerable.

She answered Felicity. "I don't know just yet what you should do. Or what I should do either. Except for the moment, we're going to keep our mouths shut until we are absolutely sure; I mean, until we have something definite we can give the police. Can you handle that?"

When Felicity didn't answer, she repeated the question, and when Felicity managed a wan smile and nodded, she rose and said, "Okay. Now, let's both have the drink I was making. I think we need it."

She went back to the sideboard, finished fixing the drinks, and brought them back to the couch. They drank silently. Relieved to have shared the horror she'd been keeping to herself, Felicity seemed to have become her old self again. Gabrielle said, "Can I ask you a personal question?" Felicity nodded, and Gabrielle considered how to put it tactfully before she asked, "I mean, outside of all this, you never seemed to me to be happy with Chase. Am I right?"

It took Felicity by surprise, and it was a moment before she answered. She seemed to be looking back through her marriage, adding things up. Finally she said, "I don't know. I guess not. But my mother always told me you have to deal with what you have."

"Then when did it go wrong? I mean, surely when you first married it must have been okay."

There was reluctance in Felicity's tone. She toyed with her drink. "No." she replied. "It wasn't really."

"But why did you? Marry him, I mean. Were you terribly in love?"

Felicity thought again before she looked at Gabrielle and said, "I've never told anyone this." Gabrielle waited and then Felicity said, "I had to marry him."

"Oh?"

Felicity rose, and went and put more scotch in her glass, and came back, and said, "I'll probably get drunk."

"It wouldn't hurt you."

"I was in love with this boy, see. In college. We dated for a couple of years. I was kind of old-fashioned, and I was a virgin when I met him. I know it sounds silly nowadays, but I was. I held off for a long while, and then he was my first experience." She took a deep breath. "I got pregnant, and the moment I told him he disappeared. I mean, he just up and ran off. I think to California. I never saw him again. He never even called or wrote. It hurt terribly. I loved him so."

"Oh, Felicity, I'm so sorry."

"It's all right. I got over it. But I didn't know what to do about being pregnant. I told my mother, and she promised to help and never tell anybody, but she told my father. I wanted to have the child so I could still have something of him in my life, but they insisted I have an abortion. 'We're not having you disgrace the family with illegitimacy,' my father said. I'll never forget that. He had a friend who was some big doctor and arranged for it in a New York hospital. Okay, but the doctor wouldn't do it unless he had reports from two psychiatrists saying I shouldn't have a child."

"Why? That was true once, but this was after *Roe v. Wade*. An abortion wasn't illegal anymore."

"I know, and I did ask why. My father said that the doctor needed to protect himself from looking like an abortionist to his colleagues and in case for any reason I got it into my head to sue him."

"But, Felicity, that's nonsense."

"I know that now. Back then I was too upset and frightened to question it. And try to understand, Gabrielle, I was terribly sheltered. I really didn't know anything about anything."

"Okay, and so then you married Chase?"

"A year later. My father and Darwin were good friends. They'd been college classmates and they decided it was a good thing, and so they conspired to push me into it. Chase was brought into my life. My father saw a chance to get rid of me, Darwin saw a good business deal with my father in the offing, and also, I learned later, saw it as a way to get closer to my mother, whom he had his eye on. So I was told endlessly what a great husband Chase would be, how I needed to be married. All that."

"You were just pressured into the marriage? Like some poor woman in India?"

"I guess."

"And you went along with it?"

"I didn't know at first that it was a put-up job, and I was so tired, Gabrielle. And Chase, you know, he can be very attractive when he wants to be. Everybody seemed to like him, and he was very nice to me."

"But you didn't love him."

"Thinking back, no, although I think at the time I persuaded myself I did. I needed to in order to forget being ditched when I really did love. It wasn't until after we'd announced our engagement that I suddenly came out of it and tried to back out. But it was too late. All the wedding announcements had gone out, and I was swamped with wedding presents. My father was furious."

Felicity paused and laughed. "I can laugh at it now; he was so damned awful it was like something in a corny Victorian novel. But I didn't laugh at it then. He said I had to get married, like it or not. He said nobody else would ask me when they found out I'd already got pregnant from somebody else and had an abortion. Again, like a fool, I believed him. And when I asked him how anyone could find out, he said—can you imagine?—he said, and my mother sided with him when he said it, he said, 'If you don't marry Chase Morse, don't count on me to hide your disgrace. Or for me to keep a roof over your head.'"

"Oh, my God! Felicity!"

"It's true, but it's all right. That was years ago, and other people have been through much worse. After that, though, I just didn't have the strength to say no. So I got married, and I tried to love Chase, but I just couldn't."

"And now this. But how did Chase feel about your being made to marry him? Did he know?"

"I think he did, but I've never been sure."

"Do you think he loved you?"

"Oh, I don't think he loved me at all. In fact I'm sure he didn't."

"Then why …?" Further words failed Gabrielle.

Felicity laughed again, as though Gabrielle ought to know, or at least have guessed because it was so obvious. "Because Darwin ordered him to," she said.

"He what?"

"He married me because Darwin made him. Just the way Darwin made him leave investment banking and run Carlyle. Darwin wanted to be sure there was an heir to take over Carlyle, and Chase has always done what Darwin ordered. The only way he could ever say no was behind Darwin's back. But just to make sure, Darwin said he'd disinherit him if he didn't."

Now Gabrielle laughed. "I don't believe this." Meaning, of course, that she did, and that it was just as Felicity had said. It was out of a Victorian novel. So much for the *Social Register* crowd's inviolate code of behavior, and perfect manners, and disapproval of anyone who didn't fit. She wondered what the impeccable Mrs. Rhinelander, with her horrid little Corgi dogs, would say if she knew what sort of scandal was hidden in the Morse family.

"And I wasn't so plain then, and my figure was better," she heard Felicity say. "And I came from a good family. So why not? He just saw me as a way to placate Darwin, and it didn't cost him anything. Besides, he was getting to an age when all his friends were married or getting married. He was beginning to look silly as a bachelor. Business-wise."

She rose, went to the sideboard, poured herself a straight scotch and turned and said, "And guess what, Gabrielle. As long as we're into the sordid details. He cheated on me during our honeymoon."

"He what?"

"Some girl he picked up at the bar in the hotel we were staying at. I don't know who. The third night. When he came back to our room after he'd had her, he wanted sex with me, too."

"You can't mean it."

"I told him to go to hell. I'm not a complete mouse." Felicity knocked back some of the scotch. "Well, to be honest, that's what I wanted to say, and didn't quite dare. Actually I told him I felt sick. And was getting my period."

"What did he do?"

"Went back downstairs again to whomever she was, of course. I think that was the end of our sex life. Except when he absolutely demanded, which wasn't often, thank God. Well, enough to get me pregnant with David. And a few times since because Darwin insisted we have another child."

"Do you still?" Gabrielle thought it was the last question she dared ask. She'd let curiosity get the better of her, and she'd pried enough.

But Felicity didn't seem to have any problem answering. "Good heavens, no. Not for a couple of years. Chase is like Darwin. You don't say no to him. But finally I did. I got up enough nerve to. All I could think of was who else he'd had sex with. Maybe even that day. He stopped demanding then, and I'm sure he's had no trouble finding others to take my place. Before me, he was having an affair with one of those super Wall Street dynamos, Courtney Sherwood. She's a partner now at Kleinmann-Roth. I read that in the paper the other day. He may still be seeing her. Or the other way around. I always suspected her of calling the shots and seeing him when she felt like it. She looks that hard. And then I'm sure there are lesser ladies. Carlyle keeps an apartment on Seventy-Fifth Street and York for business entertainment. I was in town one day, maybe a year and a half ago. It was after I drew the line against further sex. I had lost my ATM card and needed money. I thought Chase might be there; he wasn't at the office, and when I asked the doorman if he was in, the man grinned and said he'd gone out, but if I was from the escort agency, to come back in an hour."

It took a few moments for Gabrielle to absorb the misery Felicity must have suffered. She thought of her own life—her work as a journalist, her loving parents, the exciting abandoned moments with partners who had cared, and if they hadn't, she'd walked them off fast.

After a while Felicity went to the French doors and looked out at the night, and came back and said it was beautiful outside and the sky filled with stars. Gabrielle said, "Felicity, didn't you ever think of divorce?"

"Yes, of course, but where would I go? And what would happen to David?"

"Go? You could go anywhere you wanted. Chase would have to provide for you."

"I had always thought so, but a couple of years back when I asked the family doctor about it, he insisted I see a lawyer friend of his. The lawyer told me Darwin would fight it. He said the first thing Darwin would do, he and Chase, would be to take David away, so I would have to sue to get him back, and that I probably wouldn't stand a chance because of the psychiatrists' reports when I was aborted that I wasn't fit to have children. And he said they'd find a dozen witnesses, people they could pay to say what they wanted—they've got so much money—and who would testify that I was a lousy mother."

"But Darwin is dead."

"Chase isn't."

"But does Chase care that much about David?"

"No. But he'd fight me just to show his superiority." Felicity was silent a moment, remembering, and then went back to Darwin asking her to leave the room so he and Chase could have a talk. She wondered aloud what Darwin had wanted to discuss privately. "It had to have been something to do with Carlyle," she said, "but I can't think what. Chase never tells me anything that goes on there. That call from Kurt Bracer, maybe. He's never called before."

Felicity's remark struck a chord. Gabrielle remembered only too well Chase's reaction to Bracer's call and to her reporting it to Haydn. After a while she persuaded Felicity to go to bed and went upstairs with her, Felicity's fear of Chase, and now her own, following them from the living room like some ghastly menace about to strike. When they'd checked on David, and Felicity had pulled the covers up around his shoulders and gently kissed his sleeping face good night again, and they stopped outside their rooms to say good night to each other, Felicity said, "Gabrielle, thank you for being here. Could I ask you one thing?"

"Sure."

"Would you promise me, please, that you won't say anything to anyone about my possibly seeing Chase, and everything else I told you."

"Felicity, I'd die first."

In the Blue guest room, getting ready for bed, Gabrielle felt overwhelmed by everything she'd heard. She wondered where Chase was and if he would come home for the night. She wondered, too, if she shouldn't go and sleep with Felicity, even though Felicity seemed to be completely in charge of herself again, her crisis of nerves over. There was easily room in her big bed for two.

She decided against it. Doing that might alarm Felicity even more and undo all the good she'd achieved listening to her. Besides, she'd seen that evening that Felicity was a much stronger woman than she'd thought, perhaps far stronger than Felicity herself realized. There were people like that, she'd learned. Others saw them as weak because they were gentle and unassuming. Look at Haydn. Behind the shyness, the slight stammer, the self-effacing consideration of others, she had discovered a lion. Though never radiant or exuberant, Felicity had always seemed happy enough. Gabrielle realized now, however, that it was an act, the cover-up of a brave woman for the harsh circumstances life had dealt her, for which she bore little guilt except the innocence of sheltered youth, and the trap she couldn't free herself from because of her child.

She checked the bedside clock. It was late, past eleven. She didn't think that Chase would come all the way up from New York at this hour. Not when he could stay in town. Just to be sure, she called Peter Doyle to find out if he'd filed any flight plans. He hadn't, and she felt more secure for having checked.

Before she turned in, she went into Chase's room and looked around. She saw the pictures of the farewell party—Chase surrounded by male friends, and then Chase with two men, one with his arm around a celebrity-looking blond, probably the investment banker Felicity suspected. She looked the type. She had that sort of confident and brittle hardness about her. And opening one of the top drawers in his dresser, she saw, with a wave of repugnance and anger, a package of condoms with half of them missing. But she saw nothing that would have told the truth about what happened between Chase and Darwin.

She went to bed and turned out her bedside light. Unable to sleep, she was lying in the dark thinking about Felicity, how desperate she had seemed, all that strange silence, and then the outburst of accusation and revelation, then finally back to her old self again. Could Felicity really be that resigned to all that had happened? Because she wondered that, Gabrielle suddenly found herself doubting. Suppose Felicity is just imagining half of what she told me. Suppose she's been so abused by Chase over the years that she's finally cracked and is creating a fiction about his killing Darwin out of fear or even seeing a chance for revenge. If that's true, then I'm wrong about her having inner strength. She desperately needs psychiatric help.

Gabrielle got up and went to her window that overlooked the darkened lawn and tried to imagine that there was someone out there. Maybe, she decided, she would be able to see someone if there were more light, but she wasn't sure. She went back to bed and tried to think. She would soon have to e-mail another report to Bernard Bligny, and she could hardly mention any of what Felicity had told her. Besides it being personal family business, she'd promised Felicity never to mention a word of it.

But as a journalist, she more and more saw a real story about the Morse family. Shouldn't she follow up on Felicity's revelations about Chase and be alert for anything new that might develop there, try to find out more? Now quite certain about having no future where Haydn was concerned, there might come a day when she would have license as well as justifiable reason to break her self-imposed restriction on revealing personal matters entrusted to her.

Thinking that way, the whole horror of what was going on, and to which she was witness, finally struck home. In a family like this, parricide? A man killing his father? It was the sort of thing you read about in the tabloids. Something that happened to other people. Degenerates or criminals. With people like the Morses, it just couldn't happen. But it had. Darwin being murdered was real. And if not Chase, who else? The police had not come up with a single suspect or apparently even a clue.

It all suddenly became too much. She wanted only to bury her face in the pillow and not think, just forget all of it and sleep, and in the morning get up and flee back to France and the sanity of *France Aujourd'hui* and her own family.

But in her heart she knew couldn't. Journalism or no, she had come to care deeply about the Morse family, all of them, the servants included. After a few minutes, she got a grip on herself. She was no good to anyone, not the family, not Bernard Bligny, and certainly not to herself if she couldn't face it. And she *could* possibly be helpful, she thought, for unlike the police, she was embedded in the Morse family and privy to far more than they. Her mind tumbled back through all she had heard and seen and, once again remembering Chase's reaction to the call from Karl Bracer, it occurred to her that she ought to try to find out if something had happened at Carlyle that might have led to a serious confrontation between father and son. That would at least be a start. It would lend support to Felicity's accusation and be something the police could get hold of. If she were to contact Karl Bracer, could he perhaps tell her if there had been some problem at the auction house that he'd wanted to tell Darwin about?

Even as she had the thought, she dismissed it as impossible.

She didn't know Bracer, he didn't know her. He would hardly discuss Carlyle matters with her. Besides, Haydn had said he was not someone he wanted anything to do with. Her mind struggled helplessly; ideas came and went. One thought after another spun around and around. Then suddenly, just before she finally fell into an exhausted but troubled sleep, she remembered someone who might help: that wonderful gray-haired older woman, Selma Freedman, who, Haydn had said, really ran Carlyle, and whom she'd liked so much when they met again at Darwin's funeral. Selma, of course. There was something about her Gabrielle felt she could trust, and who could possibly know more about what, if anything, had happened at Carlyle to cause a row between Darwin and Chase? She would try to see her before she went to Canada and dropped out of Morse family affairs. It might amount to nothing, but one could never tell.

EIGHTEEN

In the morning, when she'd seen David and Felicity through breakfast, Gabrielle called Selma from the phone in Darwin's study. Looking around as she waited for Selma to answer, she realized how much of what people did or were in life they took with them when they died. None of the books or the desk mementos or pictures of friends that Darwin had guarded so jealously would mean anything to anyone in a few years' time. They would be as forgotten as Darwin himself, as though put in his coffin with him. For he, someday, like everyone else, would be simply a fading name and dates on a weathered lichen-covered tombstone that meant nothing to anybody except a reminder that they too would one day die and be forgotten.

Selma answered. Gabrielle snapped out of her reverie, identified herself and asked her if she'd like to have lunch with her the next day.

"Lunch? I'd be delighted. You can give me all the news. You're in New York? I thought you said you were planning to stay at The Moorings for several weeks more to finish up your story."

"I'm at The Moorings now, but I have to come in."

"I see. Well, you've only just caught me. You know I've left Carlyle, and I'm off to Vancouver shortly?"

"Yes. Haydn told me."

"Where would you want to meet?"

Gabrielle said wherever Selma would like, and Selma

named a restaurant where she had often lunched with important clients. It was in a small Upper East Side hotel, The Mark,
where the food was excellent and the service impeccable. Most
importantly, it was quiet, for Selma guessed that Gabrielle had
more in mind than a pleasurable lunch, and she wanted her to
feel at ease to say whatever it was without someone listening in.

She arranged to meet at one thirty and asked how Gabrielle
planned to come in.

"I'll fly. There's a plane out of here that goes direct to New
York. Thomas can take me to the airport"

"You can't use the jet?"

"I don't like to ask."

Selma caught the unspoken words: Ask and be subjected
to Chase refusing, his saying with a superior smile that she had
no right since she wasn't family or a Carlyle employee. She said,
"When do you go back?"

"There's a return flight at four-thirty."

"Down and back in one day?"

"Yes."

"That's utterly mad, dear child."

"I don't like leaving David and Felicity too long. Felicity is
still pretty fragile."

There was a faint sound of sympathy from Selma, and then,
"Would Haydn be joining us?"

A moment's silence before Gabrielle answered, "No. Selma,
I hate to ask this, but if you should see or talk to him, would
you not tell him I'm coming into town?"

"Goodness. Well, of course, if you don't want me to. There's
nothing wrong, I hope."

Gabrielle laughed. "No, no. Not at all." But she felt a sinking sensation in her heart remembering Haydn stomping off to
Thomas waiting with the Jaguar to take him to the airport; her
anger at his not seeming to care about the position she was in
by asking her to look after things, and, above all, the pain she
felt at being in love.

When they had hung up, Selma's mind buzzed with speculation as to what it was that Gabrielle might want to talk to her about that would make her endure such a grueling round trip. Her intuition that it must be important was reinforced, since she was leaving the East permanently, that Gabrielle could not be looking to establish a social relationship through a once-only lunch.

She knew when they met, however, and were shown to a quiet table in the dining room, that whatever it was wouldn't be forthcoming immediately. They ordered drinks, Selma deferring to Gabrielle's choice of a light French Chardonnay. She usually forbade herself a drink at lunch. While she waited, hiding her intense curiosity, they made small talk; about Gabrielle's plans to try to renew her journalistic career, her impressions of America and her life at home in France, and about how things were going at The Moorings.

They had been served their entrée before Selma's curiosity was finally satisfied. Gabrielle put down her fork after declaring that the sole meunière was absolutely delicious, looked up from her plate and said, "You must wonder why I wanted so badly to see you."

Selma smiled, confessed her curiosity, and waited again while their waiter refreshed their wine.

Then Gabrielle said, "I want to ask you something. I need information that I don't think I can get from anyone else. And if you are worried because I am a journalist, please believe me that anything said here would only ever be seen in print with your and the Morse family's permission."

"Do any of the family know you are seeing me? Felicity, or Chase?"

"No. Neither even know I came down to New York. I haven't seen Chase, and Felicity thinks I have a business appointment in Boston." Gabrielle toyed with her fork a moment longer, then said, "What I wanted to know, Selma—please feel free to tell me is none of my business. I won't feel in the least offended.

Or that I'd wasted my time coming down to New York." She smiled. "I would have had a wonderful lunch with you."

"Thank you, my dear. I feel the same."

"What I wanted to know is this. Has Chase been in any trouble of any sort, personal trouble or trouble at Carlyle?"

For all her acumen, it caught Selma by surprise. Obviously the young woman suspected something had gone wrong, otherwise she wouldn't have asked But why would she have suspected? What would have led her to? And did she actually know more than she was letting on and was playing innocent as a way of helping to obtain answers? After all, as she said herself, she was a reporter and she had to be a good one if her paper had sent her to America for a job.

It took time for Selma to answer. She found herself staring at Gabrielle and trying to fathom what she might be thinking—or hiding. Lost for a moment in wondering how to answer, she heard Gabrielle say, "Have I offended you, Selma? I'm so sorry if I have."

Selma came to her senses. "Of course you haven't. On the contrary, I feel flattered at your confidence. Let me answer with a question of my own. What makes you think Chase might have been in some sort of trouble?"

"Two things," Gabrielle replied. "Well, three, really. Shortly before Darwin died, actually the night before David's birthday, Darwin told Chase that Karl Bracer had called and wanted to know why. It was at dinner and I had the impression Chase was caught off guard and only barely able to hide it. Haydn thought so, too. The second thing, and quite separate from that, is that Felicity feels something serious is upsetting him."

'Felicity said this?"

"Yes. And, well, so do I. It's the only reason I can see for his not having been at home at all since the funeral."

"Not at all?"

"Only once."

"You're sure?

"It was just for an hour or so."

"Do you know if he's been going to his office?"

"Yes. Because Perkins had to call him about something, I don't know what. But that brings me to the third thing. A few evenings ago, I had to call him, and the maid at Gracie Square said she hadn't seen him at all since the funeral. She thought he was at The Moorings. So then I tried calling the business apartment on Seventy-Fifth street. There was no answer. I left a message on the machine, but he didn't call back. And when I tried both the apartments a couple of times more, I still couldn't reach him."

"I see." Selma closed her eyes and put one hand to her forehead. Oh, God, she thought. Now what? The biggest auction sale of a painting ever for Carlyle with the famous Millet about to go on the block and Carlyle's jackass president and CEO more likely than not up to some sort of nonsense. First Felicity, who she was sure could read her husband's moods and sense something wrong, and now this girl. And it had to be more than Tundra Oil and his unquestionably having filched the money from Carlyle. She'd been around Chase long enough to know how well he could cover that sort of disaster.

She studied Gabrielle, taking in the firm Gallic lines of her face and her expression that was utterly without guile. Then she made up her mind. This girl could handle it as well as keep it confidential. "You're right, my dear. Chase has been in trouble. I might say very serious trouble."

She told Gabrielle about Chase's loss in his Russian gamble.

"Do you think that's why Karl Bracer called?"

"Perhaps. Your guess would be as good as mine. But he could have called for a dozen other reasons. Chase's hand at the Carlyle helm is not exactly a steady one. I personally had to make a lot of decisions because he wasn't there to make them, and I know Bracer did too on occasion. There's more, however, and I might as well tell you all of it. But you will have to be careful. If you should repeat it to Felicity, it could get back to Chase, and I'm not sure what he would do."

Gabrielle assured her she wouldn't.

"Darwin," Selma continued, "didn't trust Chase from the day Chase took over. He was on to me constantly to keep him informed of everything Chase did. Then, fairly recently, about a month or so ago, he became alarmed by something Chase had said, and insisted I have his phone tapped."

"And you did?"

"As far as I was concerned, Darwin was still the boss."

"You think he heard Chase talking to someone about what happened?"

"I know he did. The whole kit and caboodle. Chase got the news from his investment broker in Germany over the phone. I had it on a special line. And it was all on the tape also."

A lot was fitting together. Gabrielle asked Selma how much money was involved.

"He lost eighty million."

"Eighty million?" Gabrielle didn't try to hide her shock. Nor, to an extent, her distaste. Every day she read about corporate presidents getting equal golden handshakes, but it had never seemed personal to her. This did. This involved someone she knew, and to her own family that much money was an unheard-of fortune. She thought of her elderly and retired father up on the roof of their broken-down château replacing broken tiles, and took a breath and shuddered. "I can't believe it," she said. "But he doesn't really have that much, does he? I mean Haydn told me he didn't. Haydn said that Darwin kept both him and Chase on a short leash. Wanted them to prove they could make it on their own and not lie around like idle playboys. Having to work for a living is why Haydn hasn't just up and left for France. He can't work there. He's not French or an EU member."

Selma was silent, and suddenly Gabrielle knew. It was so obvious. "Oh, no. Carlyle?"

"Darwin thought so."

"It's such a lot of money. Could it put Carlyle under?"

"Yes, possibly, although I don't think so. Not the loss itself. It's possibly only the pension fund, but it could create such a scandal if discovered that Carlyle might lose half their employees or so much business that it would go under. Unless, of course, Darwin bailed Carlyle out privately. And secretly. Which, of course, he would have done."

Gabrielle remembered Darwin's virtual command to Felicity to leave him and Chase by themselves, as they had things to talk about, and Felicity telling her about the danger signs she'd seen then on Chase's face. So there it was, she thought. A worst case scenario. Felicity's fright was almost certainly valid. Darwin would have savaged Chase, and Chase might well have reacted with the kind of uncontrolled violence that Felicity had described to her whenever he felt crossed or challenged.

She hoped Selma couldn't read in her face the shock she felt, and made an effort to keep her voice matter-of- fact. "There's something I don't understand," she said. "Why on earth would Chase want to risk using Carlyle money for personal reasons when he'd have so much to lose if he got caught? I mean he's getting a large percentage of Carlyle profits now and a huge salary as CEO."

"Well over a million. And five times that in profit." Selma reflected and said, "I don't think, actually, that it has any-thing to do with money. With Chase, like a lot of other men, it's an alpha-male thing. In the money game, how much you make is only symbolic of success in beating out the competi-tion. Fifty million or a hundred million—what's the difference when it comes to standard of living? Palaces, Rolls-Royces, private jets—big money gets all of that. But fifty million puts you higher up on the totem pole of success, makes you more powerful than the competition. And a hundred even higher. Tundra would have given Chase not just confidence to resist Darwin and to chuck Carlyle, but more important to him, to be back in the running and then some with Kleinmann-Roth, where he was before Darwin bullied him into auctioning. He would have become an alpha male in spades and then some. Most likely he could have bought a partnership at Kleinmann or elsewhere and been able to lord it over everyone."

She was thoughtful a moment again and then said, "That's part of it. I suspect the other part, of course, is that he saw a chance to find enough courage to rebel against Darwin. In his teens his defense against Darwin was to be socially correct in every way while his revenge on his mother was to turn his back on her completely when she wasn't. I'd been at Carlyle for five or six years already before either brother was born, and Darwin often invited me to The Moorings, so I had a chance to watch it all unfold."

"Oh, gosh, of course," Gabrielle interjected. "Then you knew Ariel."

"And very well," Selma said, smiling at the obvious sudden and acute interest.

"Oh, Selma, I've wanted so much to learn something about her. Nobody seems to want to talk about her much, I mean in the family, and I have the impression that other people didn't really know her. For example, Haydn said that she bullied Chase perhaps even more than Darwin did. But is that true? She was supposed to be so liberal and artistic. And he said Chase started off being very creative, and that of the two of them, it was Chase, really, who had inherited his mother's s creative talent."

"Haydn's right. Ariel was brilliant, extraordinarily talented and beautiful, all of that. And she could charm the birds down from the trees. But there was another side of her, the horse-woman side, the woman who could force a balking and difficult animal over a five foot fence. Any child likes to have a mind of his own, develop a sense of independence, and looking back I think Chase especially so. But Ariel wasn't having that. It was do it her way or else. Any failure by Chase to do so, any resistance, brought absolutely heartless insistence down on his poor head.

Golly, I remember once she was having him read to her from a children's book to see how well he could. When he came to a word he couldn't pronounce, she kept him on the couch until he did, and that was most of a lovely summer afternoon, from lunch until dinner, when he was supposed to go out sailing with his uncle. The poor kid, I really felt sorry for him. At the same time, and I guess as result, he was dreadfully spoiled in a way that Haydn never was. By spoiled I don't mean in the usual sense—books, toys, etcetera. No, I mean demanding. If he was denied something he wanted and given something else instead, he'd do anything to get his way: lie, cheat, steal, whatever. It was reaction, obviously, first to his mother then to his father. Of course he almost always got caught and severely punished, usually by Darwin, and he'd get no sympathy from Ariel regardless of what the punishment was. The one thing Darwin couldn't stand in his children was any sort of dishonesty, so there'd be standing in a corner for hours, or going without dinner, or being made to circle the lawn fifty times, or write 'I'm a thief' until his fingers couldn't hold a pencil any longer. And Chase never seemed to learn. He'd go right on doing what he knew he shouldn't, behind his parents' backs, of course, and always getting caught. He almost seemed compelled to be defeated. In a way, Tundra is the same thing all over again."

Gabrielle was fascinated. "Maybe defeated has become what he is so used to that he can't give it up. Psychologically, I mean. People tend to cling to the familiar no matter how bad it is for them."

"Yes, perhaps. I also always saw his behavior as deliberately painting himself into a corner. And that was my one big worry about Chase and Carlyle. I didn't give a damn, frankly, and don't think I ever would, what Chase might do to himself. Chase is often charming, he has impeccable manners, he has social credentials that most would envy, although I don't. But he has another side to him that I think is plain rotten."

"Jekyll and Hyde?" Gabrielle ventured.

"Yes. Pretty much so. And I think he might well end up a suicide when Hyde becomes fully aware of what Jekyll is like, or if Jekyll takes over completely. That or because people who paint themselves into corners usually do. Death is their only way out. It was just that I was constantly scared stiff he'd paint Carlyle into a corner with him. I think that's what had got to Darwin, too. I mean why he had me put a tap on Chase's telephone. He felt he was safeguarding Carlyle, and you've got to remember that Carlyle was his whole life. If you defied him or even just disagreed when it had anything to do with Carlyle, he crushed you. It was his way or else."

"And yet he could be very likeable."

"He thought the world of you."

"Did he? I'm glad. I thought probably just the opposite. But then I wasn't any challenge to him, was I? How did Haydn escape?"

Selma thought a moment before answering. "Escape," she said finally. "Yes, that would seem to be the right word, but I don't think it really is. Do you? I mean, you've got to know Haydn quite well by now, if I can judge a young woman's emotions at all."

When Gabrielle immediately looked uncomfortable, Selma put her hand over hers and went on quickly. "Don't let me distress you, my dear. Haydn is a most extraordinary young man, and where he's concerned, I'll be in your corner all the way."

Feeling herself blush, Gabrielle wondered if Selma could possibly realize the nights she'd lain awake, torturing herself with thoughts of Haydn, knowing she would have wrapped up her reporting job already and returned to France if she hadn't been holding onto a dim hope where he was concerned.

She snapped out of her brief reverie and heard Selma say, "What I wanted to tell you was this: escape means fleeing from something, and I don't think Haydn is a man to flee from anything. I saw him stand up to both his parents when he was only five or six, and in such a quiet and determined way as to make them back off. His virtually divorcing himself from Chase and his father now is because he has his own ideas about the sort of life he wants and always has had from a very early age. And it's not theirs." She paused and added, "But you know, in a funny way Haydn is very much like his father, but without any of Darwin's bad sides. He seems to have inherited the best part of both parents."

"And Chase the worst?" Gabrielle ventured.

Selma laughed. "Shrewd young lady. Yes, exactly. It's a case of like father, like son, a mirror image in many ways, except with Chase those ways being only the bad ones. I think Darwin has always seen Chase as a serious threat to his dominance and never wanted him to get an upper hand."

"But why, then, did he turn Carlyle over to him?"

"In his view, he had no choice. It was Chase or lose family control over it, and Carlyle had always been a family firm. He once said to me he was going to hold his breath until David grew up and took over."

"Haydn says Chase hates the job."

"That's quite true. Chase has only stuck it because of Darwin. Now Darwin's gone, who knows? I, for one, can only hope he finds a way out of this mess, and if indeed he's taken the money from Carlyle to invest, then to manage to replace it somehow and as soon as possible. I would hate for it to become public—for everyone's sake. The family as well as Carlyle. It's why I haven't said anything about it except to you. Whatever happens, one thing is certain. I wouldn't want to be in Chase's shoes."

Gabrielle said, "One almost has to feel sorry for him."

"Well, you know, to be fair, I always did feel a little sorry for Chase, when he wasn't being so overbearing that you could only hate him. Mostly, I found him pathetic."

On the way home, Gabrielle thought of her own family, so loving, so undemanding, so loyal to each other, so without pretensions. She couldn't help but compare them to the Morses. Except for Haydn, everything about the Morse family was sad: Felicity, Chase, Darwin—Felicity living in fear, Chase hating his mother, Darwin bullying Chase and what Selma had said about Chase painting himself into a corner. Small wonder Haydn had turned his back on both of them and gone off on his own. The story she had come to do about the Morse family was getting bigger and bigger by the day, she realized, and it was going to become more and more difficult to keep it all to herself. She now knew enough about the Morses to give Bernard Bligny, if she chose to, enough material for an article that could be serialized in a dozen issues and even get herself a promotion to editor. What would be next?

When her return flight touched down on Nantucket, she found Thomas with a warm, welcoming smile waiting for her with Felicity's station wagon, the much appreciated air-conditioning on full blast. It was nice being rich, she thought, even if just for a short while. The drive to The Moorings only took a few minutes, but the stress of meeting with Selma, hiding her feelings about Haydn, and never revealing Felicity's certainty that Chase had murdered his father, or the misery of her "arranged" marriage, had left her feeling exhausted. Her mind shut down; she couldn't think of any of it any longer. Before she knew it, there was the crunch of gravel on the station wagon's tires as they passed between the two big stone gateposts with their grinning gargoyles that was the beginning of The Moorings' driveway through its avenue of gnarled old apple trees.

It was then that she realized that for all the family problems and the horror that had descended on it, how very attached to the place she'd become. Coming there was like coming home.

NINETEEN

While Gabrielle was meeting Selma for lunch, Jason Curtiss-Pelham, alias Olenski, appeared in the shaded courtyard of Carlyle House. The day had turned mercilessly hot, giving the air of the city a feeling of heaviness that pressed in on all sides, and before entering the building with its two great bronze doors and flawless glass facade, he stopped by the Hiram Rosencranz fountain to breathe in the garden's relative coolness. His expression, as he looked around him and at the famed La Chaise statuary, was bleak. The great art he saw, as well as what he knew lay behind the mirrored surface of the building, painfully reminded him that his dreams of success and future renown as an important artist had somehow slipped away. In his heart he felt torn between reverence for all the great ones, past and present, and angry resentment against them for the talent and genius he didn't have himself.

Only those who knew Jason well would have recognized him, and then only from his prominent profile, for his appearance had undergone a considerable change. He looked for all the world what he wasn't—which was a successful artist. The tangled brown hair, while still nearly reaching his shoulder, had been trimmed, combed relatively straight, and was several shades lighter. Gone, along with his perpetual three to five days' growth of beard, were the paint-stained chino pants and tattered T-shirt. These had been replaced by the sort of slightly ill-fitting suit a truly poor artist would take from his closet to wear for funerals, weddings, or some other equally important occasion. His dark blue work shirt was highlighted rather than disguised by a slightly garish yellow necktie. To complete the startling metamorphosis, his formerly sandaled feet were shod in proper sneakers, and he carried a rather battered art portfolio case.

Jason was hardly happy with his appearance; certainly the sourness of his expression was partly due to that. His ears still rang with Renata's laughter when he'd first tried on the ill-fitting suit Chase had forced on him. Cursing Chase, he'd finally lost his temper. "Shut the fuck up, Renata." She'd retaliated with an icy refusal to speak to him for the whole time it took him to copy the painting, which made it all even worse. When she'd taken on Jason as a lover and cotenant, both he and she had tacitly agreed that other than share bed, bodies, and work space, neither would interfere in the outside lives of the other. A suit was one thing, but when Renata found Jason dyeing his hair, and he could only tell her there was a possible good job up at Carlyle, and that Chase didn't want him seen there the way he normally looked, she kept to herself her nagging misgivings that he might be up to something that spelled the kind of trouble that might seriously reflect on her.

Carlyle House was almost cold in contrast to the ninety-degree reality of the city outside. Jason presented the business card stating that he was Ari Pindar to one of the pretty front-hall receptionists She verified his appointment with Chase and noted the time in her log book as eleven fifty-five; he then headed for an elevator which would take him to the top-floor executive suite, pausing briefly to allow a security guard to glimpse into the art portfolio case and note in a log book that it contained an unframed full-frontal nude of a woman.

At the executive suite, the receptionist escorted him promptly to Chase's office. They passed by the room once occupied by Selma but now by a far younger, impeccably groomed and brittle-looking blond woman who was clearly just moving in. This was obvious from the stacks of files dumped on her desk as well as the open drawers of file cases, along with an efficient-looking bearded person busy checking out her computer. A desk sign identified her as Alice Marks.

Chase met Jason and the receptionist at the door and curtly told the girl, "I don't want to be disturbed for half an hour. Understand?"

"Yes, sir."

"Nobody."

"Yes, Mr. Morse."

The young woman retired. Chase closed the door firmly behind her, punched in four numbers on a keypad to lock it, and, studying Jason, managed a smile at his appearance. Jason ignored it, put his portfolio case on the sofa, and extracted the oil painting from it.

Chase took one look at it and swore. "Jesus Christ, Jason! Thanks a lot."

"What's the problem? You said to cover the canvas I'm going to use with a painting."

The nude was of Renata, who stood, hands on her ample hips, her shoulders thrown back to emphasize her magnificent breasts, and her expression as proudly defiant as the thick darkness of her pubic triangle.

"I didn't mean you to come in here with one of that bloated bitch."

Jason managed to hold his tongue. "Okay. Where's the job?"

In answer, Chase went to his closet, punched in the code to open it, and retrieved two things. One was the Barney's box containing the frame he'd purchased from the sleazy antiquarian dealer. The other was a painting wrapped in protective quilt. He stood it up on the couch and unwrapped it. "Okay, get busy. Take it out of its frame. I already loosened the screws holding it in while I waited for you. Cover it with the copy of the beach scene you've got behind your nude there, and fit it into this frame that I bought. It will just go. Then put the nude by itself back on the stretcher you brought it in on."

He went to his desk, opened a drawer, and fished out a small roll of old burlap and a tube of glue. He put them on the couch next to the Barney's box. "This came from the real *Cape Cod Blue* painting. I took it off to see if there was anything on the back of the stretcher indicating its origin or the artist. There wasn't. Paste it on the back of the covered painting to hide its age and authenticate the covering beach scene. All finished, and you can go."

He looked at his watch. "It's exactly five past twelve. I must have the old empty frame wrapped up and back downstairs by twelve forty-five, preferably sooner. So get busy."

Jason hadn't moved or spoken. He stood, as though in a trance, staring at the painting he was due to cover with a copy of the *Cape Cod Blue*.

Chase's voice was a hiss. "Jason, snap out of it and get to work."

Jason came to life. "Chase, have you lost your goddamned mind?" Shock produced Curtiss-Pelham, not the affectation of Jason Olenski.

Chase didn't answer. He glanced at his watch again. "You've less than forty minutes left."

Jason didn't answer. He continued to stare in transfixed disbelief at the famous Millet.

"Jason! Let's go."

Jason finally found his voice, "That's the Millet, for Christ sake."

"Chase smiled coldly. "Good guess, Jason. And you're going to cover it up temporarily with an unknown impressionist named *Cape Cod Blue*."

Jason eyed the Millet again, then Chase. "Sorry, Chase. Not something this big." He shook his head. "No way. Not me."

"Yes, Jason. You. And if you don't do it right now, in the little time left, I've got enough on you, starting with your drug dealer fronting as a diplomat, and your girlfriend being in the States illegally, that can …"

Jason didn't let him finish. It had taken only seconds for him to see where things stood. He turned on Chase. "Stow it, Chase. Two can play at that game. You having me up here for this for a start. You think I'd keep that to myself? Are you crazy or just plain stupid? You want me for this bit, you double what we agreed on and add ten. Fifty or nothing." He glanced at his watch. "Make up your mind, Chase. You're the one who set the time frame for this."

Chase's eyes reflected his rage at underestimating Jason and being trumped. "Okay. Fifty it is. Now get moving." When Jason nodded and resumed work, he stalked in bitter silence to sit at his desk where, in an attempt to restore his authority, he removed his wrist watch and laid it pointedly on the desk blotter.

Jason got to work. He produced a staple remover with which he quickly pried out the half dozen light staples holding the nude of Renata onto its stretcher and removed it, revealing, also loosely fixed to the stretcher, a copy of the *Cape Cod Blue* which he had so authentically aged that it looked as if it had indeed been painted in the nineteenth century.

Chase checked his watch. About two minutes had passed. Jason quickly fitted the Renata nude back over its stretcher, produced a small staple gun from the pocket of his suit, tacked it once, and dropped it back into his portfolio case. Next, he took the screwdriver Chase handed him and finished removing the screws that held the Millet in its heavy antique frame. Very gently, he removed the Millet, which was mounted on a very old stretcher.

Watching him work, Chase began to feel a euphoria to which he had almost become a stranger. Jason was doing what had to be done, fast and expertly. His easy handling of the Millet and the perfect copy of the *Cape Cod Blue* was deft and sure. So what if he'd screwed thirty thousand for the job. Chase knew it was something he never could have done himself.

His euphoria grew. He was halfway there. Planning and

deciding to do it had almost been the hardest part. Now it was only a question of time before he'd be out of this mess Putin had embroiled him in.

On an impulse, he picked up his telephone and dialed a number.

The phone answered. "Courtney Sherwood."

"Good morning, Courtney."

"Chase."

"One and the same. It's been over a week."

"Does one offer you condolences, commiseration, or congratulations?"

"Your choice."

"Knowing you, I'll avoid all three, thank you." Chase could see, through her tone, the sardonic smile she had to be wearing. It was the smile he was sure she always wore when she'd call him and say she felt like getting laid and where should they meet. She said abruptly, "I saw you the other night."

"That's interesting. Where was that?"

"You were getting into your car outside the Chandelier. I was pulling up in a taxi. Who was she?"

"Nobody you would know."

"A bleached blond like that? How right you are."

Chase laughed. "Competition comes in all forms, Courtney."

"True. But aren't you coming down in the world a little?"

"Women come in all classes, Courtney. A lay is a lay."

"True. It's the same with men. Although occasionally there's someone special. Shall I tell you whom I was with then? Or where we dined magnificently first?"

While they talked, Chase visualized her slender figure, immaculately dressed, her leaning back in her office chair and tapping her perfect teeth with her pencil while her smile became increasingly sardonic at catching him with the escort girl. And trying to lessen him by insinuating the night she'd spent with someone superior. Courtney, as usual, confidently challenging.

Chase spun his own chair around and let his gaze wander sightlessly over the traffic bustle of Second Avenue. For the first time in over a year of Courtney calling all the shots, he felt totally dominant. In her cool, in charge, inimitable way, she could banter all she wished in her sureness that she had the upper hand as usual. Poor Courtney. She didn't know it at the moment, but it wouldn't be long before she would be more than glad of the privileged opportunity to try to prove she was better company than any escort girl.

"Anyone can assuage your culinary appetite, Courtney. To satisfy your other appetites requires talent and finesse."

"Yours?" she said, with a touch of mockery.

"Anytime the fancy strikes you, Courtney."

"You know, Chase, dear boy, there might come a time when I don't fancy such a fancy anymore."

"An idle threat, my dear."

"Is it?"

"Courtney, like any good banker you know your welfare depends on the luster of the marketplace."

"In your case, meaning?"

This time Chase caught a faint disdain in her voice. He laughed again. "Courtney, do you remember when we both joined Kleinmann-Roth, and I came up one week with five million of the best and everyone's congratulations? I'm sure you do. And do you also remember the champagne night we spent together afterwards? I do. And guess what. I remember a little gal named Courtney Sherwood knocking her brains out, along with her body, to prove she was the best goddamned fuck in greater New York, bar none."

There was a moment's dead silence on the phone. Chase waited for her to break it. When she did her voice was like ice. "Are you calling me a whore?"

"The most high priced, east of Las Vegas."

"In whore's language then, Chase, so you'll understand it. Nowadays, I don't fuck losers."

Her phone slammed down.

Chase felt a rare delight flood through his entire being. He'd stung her, and stung her good. But that was only the beginning. No matter what she could say or think of him now would only make sweeter the moment of glory he'd have seeing her swallow her words. Soon enough, when he bought a senior partnership in Kleinmann-Roth, she'd pick up her phone to call him and suggest where they'd get laid that afternoon.

He was suddenly snapped back to reality by the sour sound of Jason Olenski's voice. "Okay, Chase. You got it."

Turning, Chase saw Jason holding up the antique frame he'd bought to fit the Millet and which now showed only the beach scene of the Victorian woman and child under the umbrella.

"So much for Millet," Jason said and laughed. He laid the frame on the couch and finished pasting the burlap Chase had taken from the original *Cape Cod Blue* onto the back of the stretcher. "Just to further authenticate it," he said. "Paste will be dry in ten minutes or so."

Chase rose and came from behind his desk to eye the painting. "Not bad, Jason, not bad."

"Fuck you, Chase. If you can disguise the Millet better, I'll give you your folding green shit back. And while we're at it, you'll be lucky if I don't charge you another thirty for involving me in a felony."

Chase forced a laugh. "Fair enough." He eyed his watch. It was twelve forty exactly. Reality returned in force. Jason had finished quickly, but he still only had minutes in which to act. "Okay, now get the hell out of here. Fast. I'll see you at your place. And get something in to drink. I'll need one."

Jason grabbed up his portfolio, started for the door and stopped. "Oh, one more thing, Chase. Don't even think of taking the beach scene off the masterpiece yourself. Okay?"

Chase bristled, sensing trouble. "What do you mean? Why not?"

Jason managed patience. "Because the fit in the new frame

is so tight that I had to protect the Millet's old varnish from being scratched by the canvas back of the beach scene." He held up a small spray can. "I coated it with this. A special plastic. The rush you're in, there's not been enough time for it to dry, so the two paintings are stuck together."

Alarm and fury raced instantly into Chase's face. Jason quickly raised a forestalling hand. "Don't panic, for Christ's sake. Any competent art restorer can separate them. Doesn't take long; they do it every day. They'll use a plastic solvent that won't damage the Millet and which can be wiped off in minutes with a damp cloth. Guaranteed. Running this fancy art factory, you didn't know that?"

Punctuating his last words with a slightly sneering laugh, he went to the door. Silenced, Chase swallowed his contemptuous dislike of him, unlocked the door, and Jason left.

Downstairs, the security guard cast a quick glance at the Renata nude Jason had brought in, checked it with the note in his log book and nodded him on his way.

The instant Jason had gone, Chase relocked his door, unlocked the door to his closet, and from the little cold drinks refrigerator produced a small bottle of vodka. Not bothering with a glass, he drank directly from the bottle. Emptying it, he hurriedly fetched the Millet frame, now devoid of its painting and wrapped again by Jason in its quilt. Unlocking his office door, he looked carefully out into the foyer of the two offices, his and Alice Marks's, and the conference room. Seeing the way clear, he ducked out through a side fire door and into a service corridor, thence to a service elevator at the corridor's far end. He rang for the elevator. When it came, he got in, punching the fifth-floor button. The moment the doors closed he pulled a pair of surgical gloves from a pocket and slipped them on, then waited tensely until the elevator jolted to a stop and the doors slowly opened. Directly opposite there was another service corridor which took him to fire stairs to the third floor, a route that he had carefully conned as being rarely used except by the cleaning squad that came at night, and only otherwise by three clerical workers from the building maintenance department who always went as a group to lunch in the Carlyle cafeteria at twelve fifteen sharp. He had used the same route to bring the Millet up to his office an hour earlier, choosing a time when he was certain everyone would be occupied with work in their various offices.

Cautiously scanning the carpeted hall outside the service area, he saw the way clear, took a deep breath, reached the fine art vault room, and stabbed in the five-digit door-open code on the chrome pad, with its black numbers in two neat rows of buttons on the wall, three inches from the right door frame. When the door responded and swung inward, he entered to return the frame to its slotted position on the shelf alongside the Degas, the Chavannes, and the Corot. It had been out of the vault less than an hour. Leaving, he pulled the door closed behind him, making sure that it had locked automatically.

Done. Almost dizzy with relief, he pocketed the gloves and walked casually to the nearby elevator lobby. He didn't care now who saw him. He nodded at one or two employees he passed on the way and rode back up to the top floor and his office. There he locked the door again. He had one more job, and that was to pack his antique frame with the Millet, but showing only the *Cape Cod Blue* copy, into the Barney's box. The frame was deep enough and the box strong enough so that the painting would be protected from any damaging blow.

Two hours later, he left his office.

On his way out of the building, he stopped by the scheduling department to have a word with the gray-haired woman in charge. It was her job to check and catalog every painting that came in for auction, then to see each was turned over to the head porter and his crew to be first stored, then hung for viewing several days before each was due to be auctioned, and finally, on auction day, brought in correct order out onto the auction room floor.

Chase opened a catalog on her desk, flipped pages until he came to one with a small photograph of the *Cape Cod Blue*. "This one, Mrs. Henry. I have it out on trial. It's in that estate that came in from Chicago. I'd like you to have someone get hold of the estate lawyer and tell him we have a private buyer. Safer for them. You can say DeWitt's pretty sure bidding won't reach the reserve, but we'll pay that, plus the commission."

She smiled knowingly. "I take it you're the buyer, sir."

"Birthday present for my wife. She's keen on American impressionists, especially ones by women, and we're pretty sure a woman painted this one, even though it's unsigned."

"I'll take care of it first thing, Mr. Morse. I'm sure she'll love it. It's an especially charming painting, sir."

Chase left the woman reaching for her telephone, went to the basement garage, and got in his BMW convertible. Out on the street, he started to let the top down but changed his mind. If he was caught in any kind of a gridlock, both the *Cape Cod Blue* and the Millet would cook; the hazy sun still beating down on Manhattan felt that hot. He left the top up and turned on the air conditioner. The traffic turned out to be light, however, and he easily accessed the FDR Drive. In minutes, he was at the Willis Avenue bridge that crossed the Harlem River. Coming off the bridge into the Bronx, he turned down onto Bruckner Boulevard. Three blocks farther on, he crept around a big moving van off-loading furniture in the bay of a furniture storage building, and in a minute parked in front of the derelict warehouse that housed Jason's studio. Given the rough character of the neighborhood, he decided it unwise to leave the Barney's box in the car. To lose the Millet and his potential salvation after all he'd been through was unthinkable. He took the box with him.

When the bell over the steel door jangled, Renata was hard at work rushing to complete the giant statue that dominated her work room. Her hair was only partially covered with a beat-up visor hat and she was wearing her usual work apron and nothing else. Her face, as well as the skin of the broad expanse of her bare back and buttocks, was shiny with sweat and splattered wet clay.

"Jason!"

When there was no answer, she cursed under her breath and went to the door. The caller was Chase. Barely hiding her displeasure at seeing him as well as being interrupted at work, she said coldly "Yes? What is it, Chase? I'm working right now."

"I'm here to see Jason."

"He's not really available. Could you come back?"

Chase didn't bother with any further exchange. He strode past her into the room as though she didn't exist, tossed the Barney's box onto Jason's chairs by his easel, and went to the fridge. "I trust you still have some vodka left."

Renata didn't move, and her eyes burned with her dislike of him and at his extraordinary cavalier effrontery. She said, "Help yourself." On her way back to her statue, she stopped to pick up the Barney's box. "Well, well. Barney's Aren't we smart? What did you buy?"

Chase had opened the freezer door of the antiquated fridge and found the vodka. The half empty bottle in his hand, he spun around as though shot. "Get away from that!"

Renata put the Barney's box down, sauntered slowly back to him and, muscular arms folded across her chest, pushed her face very close to his.

"Let's get something very straight, Mr. Morse. This is my home, and I'm not exactly one of your servants. One more uncivil word out of you and you're out on your ear along with whatever crooked nonsense you've got cooked up with Jason."

Chase quickly decided a row with her at this point wasn't worth whatever risk might emerge. He backed off. "Of course." He turned away, poured a straight shot of vodka into a tumbler, and then, avoiding the sight of Renata's expansive nudity as she went back to work, tried to make light of her fury. "Seriously, is Jason actually here?"

The answer was cryptic. "He's in the shower trying to match his head with his tail."

Renata had hardly spoken when Jason appeared naked from the other room, still half wet and rubbing his now crew-cut head ferociously with a towel. "The fucking stuff won't wash off." He saw Chase and wrapped the towel around his waist.

Chase laughed. He produced a small bottle and tossed it to Jason. "Use this a couple of times until it grows back naturally." He held up the vodka glass to the light from the studio windows and examined its contents. "Actually, this isn't such bad stuff, although if you loosened up a bit, you could buy something better."

Jason went to the chair and the ashtray filed with roaches, found the largest one, and lit it up. And then said, "Okay, cut the shit, Chase. You didn't come to talk about vodka."

"That's right," Chase said. "I didn't." Making Jason wait, he knocked back the vodka and put down the glass before extracting a thick envelope from his inner breast pocket. He tossed it casually to Jason, who caught it, tore it open and pulled out a thick sheaf of thousand-dollar bills.

"Go ahead and count it," Chase said. "It's all there. Use some of it to buy an air conditioner. This place is like an oven."

Jason put the ashtray of roaches on the floor, sat down on the chair, and started counting. Nearly overcome by actually having the money in his hand and completely forgetting Renata, he began snapping bills and holding them it up to the light to check their authenticity.

Chase ignored the shocked look on Renata's face as she came over and saw the amount of money and each bill's value. He asked Jason, "What did you do with the suit?"

"Over there."

Chase looked where Jason pointed and saw the suit dumped on the floor in a corner. "Get rid of it. What about the painting?"

"The beach scene original? You said to burn it."

"Did you?"

"Guy down the street has an incinerator."

"Give him the suit, too."

"My pleasure." Rifling through the bills, Jason added, "What the hell am I supposed to do with thousand-dollar bills?"

"I don't care what you do with them."

"I turn these in, they'll think I robbed a bank."

"That's your problem."

Chase collected the Barney's box from the chair. Heading for the door, he found his way blocked by Renata, who had taken a bill from Jason and was holding it up.

"One moment, please, Chase. Precisely what the hell is going on here?"

"Just a little business, Renata. Being Armenian, you ought to appreciate that."

Renata didn't buy it. On seeing the money, her vague misgivings had quickly soared into a solid fear of real trouble. "Jason, what's the money for?"

"Job I did."

"What kind? You never made so much money."

"I told you. Up at Carlyle. Restoration."

"You dye your hair and burn a suit to restore something? Sorry. Whatever's going on here, you're not doing it out of my home. Give him back his money."

For a second, Jason forgot himself. "Are you crazy? No way."

"Jason, you heard me."

"Forget it."

"Then load up your easel and backpack and get the hell out of here."

Chase tried to intervene. "Take it easy, Renata."

"And you with him."

Chase laughed. "Okay," he said. "Now our famous sculptress has expressed her disapproval, it's my turn. If you can leave your overblown nymphs there long enough to listen, think on this one. If you so much as even breathe one word to anyone about Jason dressed like a freak and copying a beach painting for me, or kick him out of here, I'll have a few things to say to friends in Washington about how you got your green card."

He smiled dangerously at her sudden shocked silence and left. When the heavy door thudded behind him, Renata remained motionless a long time, eyes smoldering with hate, before she silently went into the bedroom, returning a moment later with the *Cape Cod Blue*. She hung it back up, studied it a moment, eyes softening, then, ignoring Jason, except for a look of contemptuous disdain, she went back to work.

Getting into his BMW convertible on the street below, Chase reflected that Renata didn't ever need to know how he'd learned that his father, in an expansive moment, had bribed a high-ranking government official to grease the way for her to get a green card illegally. Her fear he could possibly expose her was enough. One more precaution safely buckled up, he thought as he headed for the bridge back to Manhattan.

TWENTY

Friday—July 16th. It continued mercilessly hot over the whole Northeast, even on Nantucket, normally cooled by sea breezes from the Atlantic. In the cloudless afternoon, heat pressed down on the island like a giant fist. Every sort of life seemed momentarily stilled. Not a leaf stirred on the apple trees shading the long driveway of The Moorings. No sound of boat engines or even the occasional shrill call of a gull came from the long wide harbor beyond the grape arbor where the water's surface was silvery in its flat, glassy calm. Lunch, served to David by Perkins, was over, the house silent. Felicity and Gabrielle hadn't yet returned from a neighbor's place, where they'd gone to a garden club buffet. The voices of the servants were stilled as they rested in their rooms or in the little sitting room with its television just off the kitchen where Darwin, who hated air conditioning, had installed the only unit in the house. David was bored. He sat, staring off at nothing, on the bottom of the stone steps to the kitchen at the beginning of the garden path that led to the garage past the laundry stockade. A few feet away, Gauguin had scratched off a patch of shaded grass to reveal slightly cooler earth. He lay on the dirt, stretched out in sleep.

David wondered how long it would be before Mr. Perkins got up from the nap he always took after lunch. Some afternoons if his mother was busy painting or making pots, he'd keep Mr. Perkins company. Mr. Perkins didn't talk much and always looked severe, but he let him help polish the silver and once handed him the keys to the mahogany cigar humidor, so he could bring the box of Havana cigars to the sideboard. With Mr. Perkins, David always felt liked. It was the same with Mary, who let him run the vacuum cleaner when she wasn't in a hurry, and Nellie, who would let him wipe away with his fingers what was left of the chocolate cake mix after she'd poured it out of the bowl and into the pan to be put in the oven. "Now, you be sure you lick that bowl clean, Mister David, so I don't have to bother to wash it," Nellie would say. sending Mary, watching, into a burst of wild Irish laughter.

David reached down to pick up a small stick lying on the path and poke at the gravel with it, making a little ridge to block the path of an ant carrying a shred of leaf ten times larger than itself. The ant had caught his eye as it made a jagged crossing of the path from one side to the other. When it reached the top of the little ridge, David pushed more gravel up into its way. Encountering it, the ant lost momentum and tumbled backward down to the bottom of the ridge where, nothing daunted, it tried again to overcome the gravel mountain, reaching the ridge only to find it higher yet again and to fall back down once more. Persistently it kept trying until David, tired of the game, tossed the stick away and rose.

"Come on, Gauguin."

Careful to avoid stepping on the ant, his hands thrust disconsolately into the pockets of his shorts, David came down off the steps and headed for the garage with the vague hope that Thomas might be sleeping the way he always did in the afternoon. If he was, David thought, he could chance the strictly forbidden and slip unseen behind the steering wheel of the Jaguar and pretend he was driving it. Weary from heat and doing nothing, the dog followed.

Awakened by his mother for breakfast at eight o'clock, and told it was going to be a very hot day, David had worn a T-shirt defiantly emblazoned with a picture of a snow-capped mountain and "Vail—Colorado." His uncle had got it for him during a week of skiing at Easter time. But it hadn't done any good. The only relief he could feel from the heat was in thinking how cool the Jaguar's leather seats would feel on his bare legs.

The wide, overhead garage doors were open. The Jaguar, its top down, crouched enticingly in the garage's shadowy cool. He went in and was leaning over the door on the driver's side, so he could see the instruments and trying to adjust his eyes to the gloom after the brilliant light outside, when Thomas suddenly appeared from a store room in work clothes, his shirtsleeves rolled up and wiping his hands on a greasy rag.

Seeing David, he stopped short. "Well, well, If it isn't Mister NASCAR himself. The young man thought I was upstairs asleep and he could slip into the Jag and go for a drive, eh?" Thomas's lips spread in a smile of triumph.

For a moment too frightened to speak, David managed to babble out, "Gee, Mr. Thomas, I'm sorry. I was just looking. Please don't tell my father. Please. I won't do it again."

The response was an even bigger smile from Thomas, then a burst of laughter, and David found himself lifted up and seized in a hug that smelled of garage and gasoline.

"Now, Mister David, do you really think old Thomas would snitch on you? Why, that's the last thing he would ever do, okay? Now I tell you what. Let's you and me slip into this beauty and go for a spin, yes? Would you like that?"

And an astonished David found himself seated on Thomas's lap behind the steering wheel and doing a turn down the driveway to the front gates and then back, with Mr. Thomas letting him actually steer the car for a while and explaining what all the instruments were.

In the garage, they sat for a moment, and Mr. Thomas said, "Liked that, did you? Thought it might cheer you up a little. Been down in the dumps these past few days, haven't you. I know. It's been real hard losing your grandpa. You and he were special close." He hugged David's shoulder. "We all loved your grandpa, David. He was a wonderful man. And he was real good to me. When he found out I'd been in prison a spell, he said every man deserves a second chance, Mister Thomas— Mister, mind you—and went right ahead and hired me, god bless him. I'm going to miss him real bad, just like you. Last I ever saw of him was the night before he left us. I was already in bed—I'd got up for something, can't remember what—and I looked out the window and saw your Dad wheeling him across the lawn toward the grape arbor. Night or day, that was always your grandpa's favorite place, in the shade just where there's the opening for the dock. I almost went down to help out when it would come time to wheel him back because pushing a chair through the grass isn't easy; wheels get stuck all the time. But I didn't. I was tired and went to bed. Wish I had, though."

Thomas had to get back to work then. He was repairing the emergency generator used for power when a bad storm cut off their electricity. David stood in the garage door a while, not knowing what to do next and wondering when his mother and Gabrielle would be coming home. Because of what Thomas had said, he thought about his grandfather. Nothing was any fun anymore since he was no longer there. His mother told him not to think all the time of Grandfather not being with them because in a way he still was, but that didn't make any sense because Grandfather Darwin was in a coffin under the ground in the family cemetery—he'd seen that with his own eyes—and you couldn't be two places at once, not even Grandfather.

Once when he asked her how Grandfather Darwin had died, she'd gone all silent and asked him if he didn't remember. When he said he didn't, when he said he only knew they'd all had dinner and it was his birthday, and Grandfather had told him he could go fishing now that he was seven, and the next thing he knew they were burying Grandfather, she'd explained that during the night after dinner Grandfather had just become so tired he only wanted to sleep forever, so God had told him he could and let him climb up to heaven to rest. But Thomas had just said he'd seen Grandfather being wheeled down to the grape arbor by his father.

Earlier today, he had thought to go fishing just to feel the coolness of the water on his hands and feet if he sat down on the float, but for some reason, he didn't know why, every time he thought of fishing since Grandfather had told him he could, fishing seemed horrible.

He was still standing by the open garage doors, seeing Grandfather's big reddish face and white hair in his mind and hearing his booming voice, when he became aware of a familiar sound. It was the scraping metal sound of a whetstone on a scythe blade, back and forth, back and forth. Gauguin heard it, too. The dog's ears pricked up, and he came to life and trotted for the cluttered garden tool room at the end of the potting shed the other side of the green house. David followed. Asa would be getting ready to cut some of the tall grass that fringed the croquet lawn just before it came to an end at the high privet hedge that ringed the whole property.

"Durned stuff is so long it fouls up the lawn mower," Asa always said. When David wondered why he didn't use the mower on it when it was shorter and wouldn't foul, Asa said he couldn't because his mother had asked his Grandfather not to let him cut down the wild flowers. That meant the Queen Ann's lace and Michaelmas-daisies along with occasional tiger lilies and black-eyed Susans which grew here and there in clumps. She liked to collect and dry them and put them in vases in her room as decoration during the wintertime. The spaces between the flowers that needed cutting weren't big enough to bother getting out the lawnmower, Asa said. But Grandfather had laughed at that, and said he thought the real reason was that Asa still liked doing things the old-fashioned way.

David found Asa just inside the door to the tool room expertly quick-running the foot long whetstone back and forth over both sides of the scythe, which he held upright so that the long curved blade was chest high and faced away from him.

Seeing David in the doorway, he stopped and wiped the whetstone against his worn, workman's trousers, the seat of which was all shiny from sitting down and which were held up by a wide black leather belt which was all scratched and stained and which Asa said had once belonged to his father.

"Yup. Thought you'd come running when you heard me sharpen up." Asa knew David loved to watch him cut grass with the scythe and once, to prove how good the scythe was, had showed David that he could use it to cut grass shorter than the lawn mower, almost as short as the grass on the putting greens of the golf course. The blade was so sharp, Asa said, that he could shave with it, and Uncle Haydn said that was probably true because the steel in it was better than what the Romans had back in Roman days, and the Romans had shaved sometimes with their swords.

Asa lifted his worn squire's cap and wiped sweat from his balding head with the handkerchief that always hung half out of his hip pocket. Then putting both items back where they belonged, he resumed his work on the scythe blade with the whetstone, first dunking it in a half-filled pail of water that stood on a work bench cluttered with cans of motor oil, brass hose connectors, cans of insect spray, boxes of rose fertilizer, and sundry clay flowerpots of varying sizes. David pushed some of the clutter to one side and hopped up on the bench to perch there, legs dangling.

He was still sitting like that, with Asa rhythmically sharpening the scythe blade, when he became aware of Gauguin sniffing at something in a corner. He hopped down off the tool bench to see what the dog was after and found a pair of his father's expensive tasseled town shoes resting on a large overturned flowerpot. David picked them up. "Asa, what are these doing here?"

Asa turned to look. "Them's your father's shoes."

"I know that." David briefly examined the shoes. The leather sides and tops were gashed and scratched, and there was a strand of seaweed jammed under the laces of one. "How did they get all beat up?"

"The beach."

"The beach?"

"That's where I found 'em. On some flotsam down the beach a ways. Must be your Dad left them by the sea wall and forgot 'em, an' the tide washed them down shore a bit."

"Jeepers. What are you going to do with them, Asa?"

"Incinerator, I guess. Ain't no good to your dad anymore. Not the way they is."

David studied the shoes. If he cleaned them up and put some polish on them, he could give them to Thomas to wear on his days off when he went all the way to New Jersey. "Can I have them?"

Asa laughed. "Now what are you going to do with them shoes, all beat up like they is?"

"Keep them."

"You don't think they's maybe a little big for you?"

David thought Asa might not like his giving the shoes to Thomas instead of him, so he said, "I wasn't planning to wear them. Just keep them."

Asa laughed again. "You is something, you know that, don't you? Okay, then. They's all yours. Let's go scythin.'"

David with his father's shoes followed the old gardener out the door and to the south side of the property where there was a small goldfish pond separated from the privet hedge by a thicket of oleander and flowering hydrangea. The swath of tall grass that ran along the wall to the grape arbor and the beach wall was about two feet wide. Asa spat on his hands, seized both handles of the scythe's long shaft, and began a slow, rhythmical cadence of sweeping the razor-sharp blade low across the unmowed grass. David checked the fish pond to see if he could spot any of the goldfish in it, kneeling down and pushing lily pads to one side to look, but there was no sign of any fish, and Asa had once told him that the heat drove them down to the bottom where the water was still cool.

Looking into the water, he remembered the day when he was very small and had fallen in. The whole world for a moment had turned dark and had tasted like old lily pads, and then he found himself at the edge of the pond, his head back out of the water and holding on to grass. He'd been sitting with a nurse and Nellie on a blanket on the lawn. As he looked back at them, Nellie screamed and leapt feetfirst into the pond to rescue him. He could remember as though yesterday her skirts flying up over her and her pink bloomers and his wondering if she was going to land on him because the pool wasn't much bigger than her. There was a tremendous splash that almost lifted him out of the water, and he remembered Grandfather Darwin laughing and laughing about it later.

After a while, he left the pond and sat on the lawn near Asa. He was hoping Asa would let him try scything just once, when Gauguin, who'd found shade nearby, barked, and David saw Chief Booker's car coming slowly up the driveway toward the house. He wondered if Chief Booker had found the robber yet. After Grandfather died, he'd asked why there were police at the house all the time, and Uncle Haydn had told him somebody had robbed some very valuable papers from Grandfather's study, and they were trying to find out who did it. His mother and the servants said the same thing. He wished the police would hurry up and find out who the robber was, so they would go away and leave the family in peace.

Asa looked up and saw Booker's car, too, but never stopped his rhythmical scything.

David said. "That's Chief Booker."

"Likely."

"Maybe he's found the robber."

"Not likely," Asa lifted his hat to wipe away sweat before he went back to scything.

Booker parked and emerged from the driver's seat of the police car, a briefcase in hand. Greeted by Gauguin, he ruffed up the fur on the dog's back, and gave it a friendly pat or two before going to the front door where he rang the bell and used the heavy lion's head brass knocker for emphasis.

Mr. Perkins appeared in his shirtsleeves. David guessed he'd been polishing silver or maybe setting the table for dinner, even if dinner was a long time away. Mr. Perkins always said he liked to do that early and not leave it to late in the afternoon when he had other chores. He couldn't hear either Chief Booker or Mr. Perkins when they exchanged a few words, but Chief Booker opened his briefcase and gave some sheets of paper to Mr. Perkins and then headed back to the police car. David remembered then that Chief Booker had promised one day to bring him a couple of cartridges from the police firing range to use as cannon for his toy soldiers. Hoping the Chief had remembered, he jumped down off the wall and ran across the lawn to the car.

"Hello there, big guy. How are we doing today?"

David grinned. He liked Chief Booker. The day after Grandpa Darwin's funeral Chief Booker had taken him for a ride in his police car and had turned on the siren and the car's flashing red and blue lights for him. Now he said he was hot and asked Chief Booker why he'd come out.

"Nothing important. Had some papers for your mom to sign, but your Mr. Perkins said she'd gone out, so I left them with him."

"Chief Booker, did you remember the cartridges?"

Booker put on a suitably stricken expression. "Oh, my goodness, David, I forgot. But I promise I won't forget again." He took a small leather notebook and a pencil from his pocket and wrote "Handful of spent cartridges for Mr. David Morse." He put the notebook away. "There you are. I don't forget anything I write down, David. Not ever. Makes it official. So next time I come out, you'll have your cartridges."

'Gee, thanks, Chief Booker."

"My pleasure, young man. My pleasure." Booker gave

David's shoulder a friendly grip and, looking down, saw the shoes David was carrying. "What are you going to do with those? Bit big for you, aren't they?"

"They're my father's. Asa found them on the beach."

"On the beach? I see."

"Yesterday. They're no good any more. They're all scratched up."

"Could I have a look?"

"Sure." David handed the police chief the shoes. Booker studied them, gently touching the strand of sea weed trapped under the laces, then brought them up to his nose and sniffed. He smiled at David. "Smell of sea water. He must have gone wading in them." He thrust a hand deep into one of the shoes and pulled it out with sand and seaweed clinging to it. "Sure. Still damp inside. Asa found them, did he?"

"He was going to put them in the incinerator because he said my father would never wear them again."

"I don't guess he would." Booker was thoughtful a moment and then said, "Tell you what, David. Would you let me borrow these for a day or so?" When David looked crestfallen, he added, "I said just borrow. Do me that favor, and when I bring out the cartridges. I'll bring you an old police badge that's been gathering dust at the bottom of my desk drawer. Would you like that?"

"A real badge?"

"Always looked real to me."

"Gee, thanks a zillion, Chief Booker."

"Can you wait a couple of days, David?"

"Yes, sir."

"Good man."

Booker got back into his car with the shoes. He punched the siren button, letting it rise for a second or two before turning it off. Then, smiling at David's delight, he started up the car's motor and drove off, the car's police lights flashing blue and red. Halfway down the drive, he met Felicity's station wagon coming back to The Moorings. The two cars stopped side by side, and David saw Chief Booker talking to his mother and gesture back at the house before both cars continued on.

When the station wagon pulled up by David, he burst out with his news. "Mom, guess what Chief Booker promised me. I gave him a pair of Dad's city shoes, and he promised me a police officer's badge. A real one, Mom."

"That's wonderful, darling. But whatever shoes are you talking about?"

"A city pair Asa found on the beach someplace. They were all wet and full of sand and seaweed. Dad must have been walking along the beach with them. It's okay, Mom, he couldn't have wanted to wear them anymore. But you won't tell him just in case, will you? Mom?

"Of course not, darling."

Dancing along beside her and Gabrielle as they went into the house, David missed the look that passed between the two women.

In bed that night, after his mother had kissed him and turned out the light, David thought again of how neat it had been to ride in the Jaguar, and then what Thomas had said about his father wheeling Grandfather Darwin down to the grape arbor before he went to sleep forever. His grandfather loved the sea and everything about it almost as much as his auction house, and David was glad that before he died, he had a chance to sit in the cool at his favorite place and listen to the distant horn of the lighthouse and the rustle of waves on the shore.

TWENTY-ONE

The theft of something as important as the Millet portrait could not remain unknown forever, and its loss was to involve Chase Morse in a world far different from his Carlyle executive suite, The Moorings, or the escape offered by his BMW convertible and the Dassault Falcon executive jet. It was to divorce him from Carlyle's obsequious employees and introduce him to a world where, without the inherited privilege that was his, people desperately struggled to make ends meet and to keep body and soul together while striving to achieve the most modest of dreams.

The day after David loaned Chase's scratched up business shoes to Chief Booker in exchange for a police officer's badge, and while Chase, almost numb with anticipation, waited for the theft of the Millet to be discovered, it fell to the young auctioneer, Brian Grey, to break the news that the greatest jewel in the Carlyle crown had been stolen.

Brian was a BFA graduate of the School of the Museum of Fine Arts in Boston and of the Christie's Fine Arts course in London. At Carlyle house, DeWitt was nurturing him as an assistant to take care of some of the minor auctions he felt beneath him. Meanwhile Brian's principal job was writing up for potential buyers the history of paintings due for auction along with the each painting's condition and the condition of its frame as well. For this he had access to the fine arts vault by code-number keypad.

Around lunchtime, Brian, who was researching an early Titian, received a call from a young woman specializing in medieval art. Only recently employed and working in the office of Carlyle's expert on authenticity, she had received an e-mail from her boss, currently in Berlin, asking her to verify if a Pre-Raphaelite work by Edward Burne-Jones that was up for auction was the original and not a nearly precise copy made by the artist of his own painting made several years later. If a copy, there would be a small bird pecking a seed in the lower right foreground that would not be found in the original. The painting was in the vault. The young woman did not have vault access. Could Brian help?

The young man was only too glad to oblige. The caller was extremely attractive, and he'd had his eye on her ever since she'd joined Carlyle. The request gave him a chance to line up a date and score extra points by showing her the Millet. Ten minutes later, he met her at the door to the vault lobby.

Once in the vault itself, the Burne-Jones was quickly found and its protective quilting carefully removed to reveal, in the absence of the small bird, that it was indeed the original. Putting it away again, Brian said, "Want a peek at the Millet?"

She didn't have to be asked twice. At her expression of delight, he took down the Millet and carefully removed its protective quilt only to find himself looking at an empty frame.

The young woman laughed and said, "Wrong one."

Brian checked the identification tag and felt something well up inside him—shock. His mouth went dry with it. "No," he said, "I checked this a couple of days ago."

DeWitt Bouchard was on the telephone in his opulent office, negotiating with a gallery owner the price of a Georges Michel painting, one of the many the artist had done of a windmill on a high bluff in Holland, when his administrative assistant abruptly appeared before his Louis XIV desk.

At the interruption, DeWitt angrily cupped the telephone's mouthpiece. "Well?" Nobody was allowed in his office when he was on the phone.

"Mr. Grey has to see you, sir. Immediately."

"Grey? Brian Grey?"

"Yes, sir."

"Tell him to wait someplace." The auctioneer turned away to continue his conversation.

"Sir, he says it's extremely urgent."

DeWitt swung back hard, his mouth a thin line. "Now look here—" He broke off as Brian himself burst in.

"Sir!"

DeWitt expression turned to one of resigned incomprehension. "It better be good, Brian." He excused himself to his caller and hung up.

"It's the Millet, sir. I had to go down to the vault a few minutes ago. It's not in its frame."

DeWitt's mind froze. Had he heard correctly? He looked from Grey to his administrative assistant and back again. They were statue still, waiting. The room fell into dead silence.

"The Millet is not in its frame," he repeated stupidly.

Brian had begun to realize he was witness to something momentous. Excitement began to dominate his fear. "I spoke with the head porter, sir. Nothing. And the registry book showed the last person in the vault was yourself, sir."

Another silence. The auctioneer came to life. "Security?"

"No, sir. I came straight to you."

DeWitt picked up his telephone, punched in a button. "Chase? Don't go anywhere. We have a problem." He dropped down the receiver and rose. "You two. Discuss this with no one, understand? No one." And to his assistant, "Get hold of security and tell them to shut the building down. Nobody leaves for any reason. Nobody. My order. Right this minute." Without another word, he left the room.

TWENTY-TWO

Georgie was in the glass stall shower of the tiny Brooklyn Heights apartment she shared with Adam Skye when Adam rushed into the bathroom and yanked the shower door open.

"Hey, love-boat, your beeper's gone crazy."

"My beeper? Are you sure?"

Adam eyed her quickly. She was head to foot with lather from washing her hair. She and Adam were going to a party at his brother's. "Rinse off. I'll bring it in." He dashed back out.

Georgie had got the worst of the soap off and stepped out before he reappeared with her police pager.

"White speaking."

The voice on the other end was Crandall. "Georgie, get your pretty butt over to the precinct, and double time, okay? We've got an emergency."

"What? Boss? Are you there? What, what?" she clicked off and reached for a towel. "Jesus. It never fails when I have time off."

"What's happened?"

"Who knows. That was Crandall working up a sweat. I'm on deck like right now."

"Damn. What about the party?"

"I'm sorry, honey. Know it as gospel—never love an emergency medic or a cop."

She pressed her still-wet body up against him, and giving

her mouth warmly to his, felt the heaven of his instant response, and wanted to be locked in his arms forever.

She forced herself to break free. "You go to Charley's without me. I'll make it up to you tonight. Promise."

She ruffled his thick hair, and ten minutes later, in a tank top and miniskirt, she was first in a cab going over the Brooklyn Bridge, then getting dropped off at the IRT and holding tight to her shoulder bag to keep her Beretta handgun from flying out, dashing down the stairs two steps at a time to dive through the closing doors of a waiting uptown express.

Klein got the same call. He'd decided to paint his apartment as a surprise for his wife and was up on a ladder doing the molding where the walls met the ceiling. He had just dipped his brush into the paint can to load it up again when his beeper sounded. He scraped most of the paint back into the can, laid the brush on the can's lid and unclipped his pager from his belt. "Klein speaking."

He heard the same urgent order from Crandall, cursed, got down off the ladder, knocking over a half empty can of beer as he did. He left it dribbling its contents over the floor, changed out of his paint clothes into something more presentable, and raced out to catch a train headed for the Queensboro Bridge and Midtown Manhattan.

He and Georgie nearly collided going into the precinct building.

"What's up? Did Crandall tell you?"

"Haven't the faintest."

Upstairs they threaded their way between the cramped desks in the bullpen and burst into Crandall's office, only to find it empty.

"Oh, for Christ's sake," Klein said. "Double time. This is an emergency.' Balls!"

Georgie muttered "shit" under her breath and said, "Where were you?"

"Up a ladder painting the ceiling."

"I was in the shower covered with shampoo. Adam and I were going to a neat party at his brother's."

She'd hardly plunked down on the corner of Crandall's desk when Crandall appeared, puffing like a walrus and drenched in sweat. He pushed Georgie out of the way, circled his desk and collapsed into his chair, mopping his big moon face with a towel he yanked from a desk drawer. He stopped only long enough to look at Klein and Georgie and say, "Running."

"Were you chasing her? Or the other way around?"

"Not funny, Klein." Crandall stowed the towel and said, "the deputy commissioner hot-lined the captain, and he nailed me on my cell phone on Central Park West and Seventy-Seventh Street. I got in a cab and rolled into gridlock halfway across the park. Accident or something. Had to hoof it."

Georgie was at the water cooler getting him a drink. "That's not good for you, Boss. In all this heat."

"Thanks for the kind words." She brought the paper cup of water to him, and he said, "Okay, here it is. Give me two minutes to get my act together, and then we're all going over to Carlyle House. That famous painting, the one's been in all the papers and coming up for auction? Worth eighty million or so? We've had a robbery report."

"Kee-rist," Klein said. "You're kidding."

"I kid thee not. Head honcho there skipped 911. Got pull with the deputy. Wanted to keep it quiet for the moment. So that means just that. No press, guys. Georgie, if he shows, tell that *Daily News* creep to drop dead. Okay? I'm talking about the idiot who keeps following you around with his lovelorn tongue hanging out all the time."

She smiled wryly at Crandall and said, "My pleasure." To Klein she said, "See? The plot thickens."

"Meaning?"

"Meaning I don't believe in coincidences. The stakeout. Remember?"

"Like an elephant. Beer on me for a month, Georgie, if there's a tie in."

"You go to your church, I'll go to mine."

"Hey! Quit gabbing, you two," Crandall said. "And let's go. Jacket, Aaron. Carlyle is politeville."

He eyed Georgie's short skirt, gave up and heaved his bulk out of the chair, straightened the bright red necktie he was never without, no matter how hot it was, and headed out. Klein pulled his seersucker from a hook on the door of his and Georgie's adjacent office, and he and Georgie followed.

Almost at the same time, another police officer, Angela Rodriguez, left her squad car, notebook in hand, to check out an aged beat-up Volvo station wagon. It was parked askew across the side entrance to a furniture warehouse that occupied most of a narrow dead end just off Bruckner Boulevard in the Bronx. A veteran of twenty-three years' service, Angela had seen three children she'd somehow managed to raise on her police-woman's salary all graduate from college. One was already an advertising executive living in an expensive Connecticut home and the father of her first grandchild; another was doing her residency at St. Luke's Roosevelt hospital. Burdened by a wor-rying weight problem, Angela had a bad knee. As she crossed the street, the knee, after being bent inactive while she drove around for an hour, sent lances of sharp pain up into scar tissue in her left thigh where she'd taken a bullet from a crack-crazed kid in East Harlem eight years ago when she'd walked in on a bodega robbery.

The heat got to her before she was halfway across. She felt weighed down not just by her uniform trousers but by her service revolver, slung low around her ample waist, her pager, handcuffs, night stick, restraining chain, and flashlight. Almost all she could think of was getting home that evening, taking off her clothes, fixing herself an iced tea, turning on the air conditioner, and collapsing in front of the TV, maybe calling the kids to find out how they all were. She might even get a chance to talk to her grandchild, who would very soon be four.

A seedy, thin-faced warehouse employee met her at the car, voice sharp with antagonism and hostile pleasure at seeing someone in trouble. "Boss said, tell you to tow the bastard away. Sonofabitch. Some fuckin' guys think they can park wherever they please."

Angela didn't bother to answer. She lifted her short dark ponytail a little to cool the back of her neck, and, passing an experienced eye over the rusty and battered metal doorway the car was blocking, figured it hadn't been used for years. A sign over it that said "No Parking" was weatherworn almost to non-existence. For the warehouse owner to have called in meant two things: The car belonged to someone he knew, and the someone was a person he had a grudge against and was looking to make miserable. She jerked her notebook at the Volvo and skipped ceremony. "Know who owns it?"

"Yeah. Lives upstairs." The warehouseman waved a hand at the building next door. "Him and some bitch with a foreign accent. Stupid fuckin' artists."

Angela thought a moment. Whoever lived in a hole like this and drove a half-wrecked Volvo hardly had the money to pay the $50 parking fine, the $125 tow away fee, and God only knew how many parking tickets they owed before they could retrieve the car. Without speaking again, she went back to her cruiser, shut down the motor, locked it and went to the door the warehouseman had indicted.

He came to dance excitedly by her side. "Upstairs. Third floor."

Angela said, "We need you, we'll be in touch." Years of being a cop had taught her that the less talk, the better.

She looked for door bells, didn't see one, tried the door. It opened. She went in and closed it behind her, shutting the warehouseman out.

The half-dark coolness inside was a relief. Angela found herself in a large unlit empty space that smelled of damp plaster and where she figured there might have once been an office. Across this wasteland from the door there was a freight elevator, and next to it a dark stairway. She decided on the elevator; her leg hurt too much for stairs. She pressed the call bell and was glad when a rumbling noise above told her that it worked. When it arrived, she levered up the heavy steel door then pulled back the inside grill, which complained screechingly, stepped inside, and jabbed at the button marked "#3."

On the third floor, she went through the same strength-testing, door-opening process to gain access to a foyer lit only by a window in the adjacent stairwell. With but one door apparent, she freed her service revolver from its holster, rapped sharply on the door with the gun's butt and waited, gun reversed and ready. There was the rattle of a chain and the door opened wide enough to let her see a big muscular white woman with nothing on but a neck-to-knees apron and splattered with what looked like wet clay.

Angela said only, "Police." And waited. A moment passed while the woman simply stared, then the chain rattled again, and the door swung open.

Renata said, "What's the matter?" Across the room, Jason, hearing Angela say "Police," had taken the few seconds before Renata opened the door to dump the ashtray with its perpetual roaches into a pocket of his chino pants and resume work on the fourth copy of a corporation president's portrait that was to be distributed to branch offices across the country.

Angela came in, and put her service revolver back in its sagging holster. The first thing she saw was the huge statue of the two nude women Renata was working on and the clutter of tools and buckets of clay around the women's feet. Then she took in the size of the place, with the flood of light coming through floor-to-ceiling windows onto its bare whitewashed walls emphasizing its barrenness and dwarfing the few pieces of furniture she saw: a couch, a couple of chairs, and a table. Compared to her own two-bedroom apartment in the Bronx's huge Co-op City, where the builders had kept space to a minimum, this was like walking into Grand Central Station.

"That your Volvo downstairs?"

Jason seated before his easel decided to answer. "Yeah. Mine."

"We had a complaint from your friends next door. They want us to tow it. We can do that, or you can go down now and move it someplace else."

When Jason didn't move, Renata said sharply, "Jason! Get with it."

Jason heard warning in her tone and resignedly hitching his pants up to his waist and, reaching for the T-shirt he'd taken off, put down his brush and grudgingly rose.

Angela eyed the statue again. She didn't know much about art, but the mere size and the sense of force she felt from the two huge nudes said it was important work. She said to Renata, "That yours?"

Renata smiled and said, "When I get it finished and cast it's going in front of an office building in San Francisco." She added, "Please excuse my appearance. It's hot work."

Angela nodded and said merely, "Yeah. New York." It had struck her that artists were found in the oddest places. As she turned to go, her eye fell on the *Cape Cod Blue* Renata had hung over the sink. She didn't know much about painting, but she thought it was beautiful. All that sea and sand and the mother and child under the parasol looking out at the little boat. In a funny way, it hurt. The best she'd ever been able to do for her kids was a crowded Sunday beach at Coney Island.

"Where'd you get the picture?"

Renata, relieved that the police visit was for nothing more than a warning about the car, nodded at Jason. "He did it."

Somehow, Angela didn't quite believe her. She could fit the woman to the sculpture, but looking at Jason, she couldn't believe he could ever paint anything so pretty.

"Want to sell it?"

Renata laughed. "Sorry. No way."

Angela quickly took in the surprising mirror similarity between the nudes and Renata herself and headed out. At the door, she glanced back at Jason, who was putting on sandals. "I catch you parking across his garage door again, I'll ticket you." And left without another word.

Back at the precinct at the end of the day, she passed by the desk of a young white girlfriend, Mary Hodder. Mary was a rookie who had gone to Fordham, where she studied criminology but had also taken a short credit course in art history and had spent time visiting museums and art galleries to look at paintings. Getting out of the police academy, she was assigned to a unit chasing down jewelry and household items reported lost or stolen, among them artworks. Angela had taken a motherly interest in her. She saw Mary as a bright kid who was going places, possibly all the way to the top, not someone like herself who, with only a high school education, would spend all day in a hot patrol car or pounding a back-alley beat. So she always took a moment to pass on basic information about police work she'd learned the hard way.

Knowing how much Mary liked art, Angela told her about the painting she'd seen and described it the best she could. "It was like a different world, Mary," and finished by saying, "Wish you could have seen it. It was one of those pictures that made you want to walk right into it and stay there. All that quiet sea and sand and blue sky. And seagulls." She laughed. "I didn't want to leave it. I just wanted to be in it, know what I mean? And never come back."

When she'd gone, Mary sat thinking about Angela, her lonely life in her small Co-op City apartment, her husband dead five years now and all her children grown up and leading their own lives, and how the painting had spoken to her. Paintings that did that to people were usually good art. She wished she'd been with Angela, too, and seen the giant statuary. Angela hadn't said who the sculptress was, only that she was imposing, but she guessed from the description of the two women that it was a sculptress named Renata, who had a major work in the lobby of an office building down in Wall Street.

She'd risen to tidy her desk and get ready to go home when Angela's description stirred a memory, but one so elusive that she couldn't make her mind identify it, couldn't focus. It was as though she herself had seen the painting. Had she? Was her mind playing tricks? Had she seen some other painting or a picture of one when she was studying art history that was more or less the same subject? Or was she just imagining that, too?

If there was anything there, she thought, it would surface sooner or later. A white sandy beach, blue, blue sky, a Victorian woman with a child seated beneath a gaily striped parasol watching a little old-fashioned lobster boat offshore. If it was the way Angela described, it was the kind of painting she'd love to own also, and hang in her apartment, and never take her eyes from it.

TWENTY-THREE

Gabrielle knew that Felicity had wanted to spend a few quiet hours painting the lilies on the fish pond, now in flower, their lovely pink and lavender hues in such contrast to their light green pads floating on the dark surface of the still water. She knew David wasn't ready yet to go swimming off the float; she wasn't herself. How could one, without remembering? It would do him good to get away from The Moorings for a day, and for her would be a welcome opportunity to get to know the boy better. So she bundled him into Felicity's station wagon and took off without any real idea of what he would find interesting to do. She knew he had already visited the Great Point and Sankaty lighthouses as well as the rescue museum, which was quite close to The Moorings. He was past the age of playing in the sand on a beach and not old enough to enjoy just lying in the sun and reading a book. He was too young for kite-surfing or waterskiing.

Hard put for ideas, she started off on Main Street in Nantucket Town, where she bought him a T-shirt emblazoned on the front and back with a hairy, scary monster that had caught his fancy, then treated him to a milk shake in one of the town's two pharmacies that had a soda fountain. With no further ideas, she had driven aimlessly down past the boat basin with its marina, steamer docks, and scores of moored sailboats when she was suddenly struck by an idea. Why not take him ocean fishing? Nantucket boasted a number of fast oceangoing cabin cruisers fully equipped for the sport.

Then she remembered. Did she even dare mention fishing to the boy, so traumatized after what had happened the first time he was allowed to fish off the float by himself? Wouldn't just the word *fishing* risk doing him serious psychological damage? She tried to think of what Haydn would do in her place. Would he risk even asking the boy?

Deciding he would, she pulled up on a wharf where half a dozen fishing cruisers were tied up, their bristling display of deep-sea fishing rods and safety chairs inviting.

She took a deep breath and said, "David, how would you like to go out in one of those?"

And waited.

For a moment there was no response. David looked at her, then turned to study the nearest boat, whose captain was busying himself on deck tidying fishing gear.

Gabrielle felt as though her heart would stop in suspense. She thought, *I've blown it. I was right to wonder if I should, and I've gone and hurt him worse than he already was. Oh God, how stupid of me.*

David turned back to her "Today?"

At first it didn't really register. She was too anxious. Get out of it somehow, she was still saying to herself. Any way possible. Get out of it and get him back to The Moorings where he's safe. And do it fast. To David she said, "It was just a thought." She gave his shoulder a quick hug and started to put the car in gear.

"Gee, did you mean it? Go out and fish on one of those?"

Gabrielle took the car out of gear again and slowly found her voice. "Well, yes, but we don't have to if you don't want to."

"Wow. Wait until I tell Mom I went ocean fishing."

Gabrielle followed him out of the car, weak from relief.

Ten minutes later the cheerful, bearded captain of the boat was steering them past the lighthouse at the harbor entrance and opening the boat's throttle as it met the ocean, the cruiser's pennant and flag snapping in the wind, and David ecstatic as he stood by the captain at the wheel.

Then, half an hour later, Gabrielle found herself holding her breath once more. They had reached fishing grounds, the captain had throttled back, letting the boat roll gently in the ocean swells, and was introducing David to the safety chair the boy would be strapped into.

Getting the harness ready, he said, "Fish might give you a good fight, young man. Try to pull you overboard. That's why we strap you in."

When he'd got David into the chair and buckled him in tight and presented him with a rod and showed him how to hold onto it, he said, "And don't let go of this, no matter what. Okay?"

David said, "I won't. I know how to fish. At home I have a drop line."

"There you go."

"I'm allowed to fish by myself. Grandfather said so. Poor Grandfather. The last time I went fishing, you know what? I looked down to see if the fish were after my bait, and saw him lying on the bottom in his wheelchair. He'd gone off the float and drowned."

The captain turned sharply to Gabrielle, and mouthed the word, "Morse?" He hadn't realized who David was. Speechless, she nodded, and he said, "Gosh, I'm sorry, Miss. I didn't know."

She found herself crying and laughing at the same time. "It's all right," she said. "It's okay. Let's go catch a fish."

They did, and in one of the most glorious and happy afternoons Gabrielle could ever remember. The sun blazed out of a cloudless sky, the ocean postcard-blue beneath it. David caught a thirty-pound sea bass and a ten-pound bluefish and almost landed a shark, which slipped away just as the captain was trying to gaff it on board.

Driving back to The Moorings, David, exhausted by excitement, fell asleep. Gabrielle had truly enjoyed his company. He had a wonderfully inquisitive mind, and what she had shared with him had been too important for her to think about not being an aunt, just a friend, and probably one for only a short while.

She had hardly pulled around the gravel oval in front of the house and stopped when Felicity came bounding out to meet them and burst out excitedly, "Gabrielle, you'll never guess what's happened."

"Tell me."

"The Millet that was going to be auctioned next week. It's been stolen."

"You're kidding."

"It's all over the television. They interviewed Chase. He said the painting was worth millions."

"Chase was on television?"

"Just now. Along with what's his name, DeWitt somebody, the auctioneer."

"Bouchard."

Felicity seized Gabrielle by the hand. "They'll be on again! Come on."

Leaving David sprawled in deep sleep across the back seat, the fish he'd caught in the baggage area behind him, Gabrielle allowed herself to be rushed to the library to watch the six o'clock news, wondering as she went what Selma would make of this fresh Carlyle disaster. Much, much later, after David had woken up and proudly shown off his catch to everyone at The Moorings, except for Thomas, who had gone off for the weekend, and had recounted in detail every moment of his fishing expedition, she was to remember a fleeting thought that there was something strangely coincidental in such a theft, Chase's financial disaster, and Darwin's death.

TWENTY-FOUR

Several hours earlier than Georgie being pulled from the shower and Klein being brought down off a ladder, Chase, locked in his office with orders not to be disturbed, waited, as he had the day before, for the discovery that the Millet was missing. Since he'd paid off Jason and taken the disguising *Cape Cod Blue* to his apartment, he had suffered a nightmare of conflicting emotions—the razor sharp realization that there was no turning back mixed with strained attempts to envision what chain of events would unfold when the police were called, as sooner or later they would have to be. And how would the press play it? In his mind, he could see the big black headlines in the tabloids, the endless insidious speculation.

While these thoughts raced and tumbled, he kept desperately reviewing all the steps he'd taken to protect himself, reassuring himself that it would all work out: the anonymous e-mail ransom note, the shell companies he'd set up in Gibraltar and elsewhere to receive the money, the deal with the Malaysian bank for land purchase on Sumatra when the money was transferred, the sale of the land to a dummy Central American consortium in which Carlyle would invest, then finally the money back into Carlyle. It wouldn't be hard to get Bracer to manage that last step. It was all foolproof, and he'd be able to cover his embezzlement without exposure.

But almost simultaneously he was gripped with terror that somewhere, somehow he had indeed made some mistake he was now overlooking, and that he was sure to get caught. His tormented mind flashed pictures of police and courtrooms and lawyers, all the horrible machinery of the law he'd always seen as being for others but never for himself. He kept seeing prisoners brought into court in orange jumpsuits, their legs manacled, their wrists in handcuffs.

While all the voices of his mind warred with each other, he kept coming back to Darwin, whose fault this all was: Darwin who had driven him to taking Carlyle money, Darwin who had forced him to take on the onerous job of running the auction house. It was because of Darwin that he'd had to get the money out of Carlyle in order to escape it. If Darwin had just left well enough alone, he'd be making it big at Kleinmann-Roth, sailing the *South Wind* around resorts in the Caribbean, or living it up in London, Rome, and Paris with Courtney. He wouldn't be stuck with boring, middle-aged Felicity and the suffocating business of family. But Darwin hadn't left well enough alone, had he? Bloody Darwin had to have the last word. Do it his way and do what he said or else. Just as always.

The minutes ticked by. Shouting voices once more invaded his mind—his own voice and Darwin's. The sound of the heavy splash of water repeatedly rolled over him. Desperate for silence, he paced his office, threw himself into the high-backed swivel chair behind his desk, leapt up to pace again, only to seek refuge in the chair once more. All to no avail.

When would it come, when would it happen?

When it finally did, it burst forth as a phone call.

"Chase? DeWitt. We've got big trouble. I'm coming up."

Well, here it is, he thought. His heart began to race. Stay cool. You've got it all planned. It will work. Just stay cool. "I'm a little busy right now, DeWitt."

"Forget it. I'm on my way."

A click as the phone was slammed down.

Chase braced himself. He must not feel cornered, he must pretend to himself that he wasn't guilty so he could act convincingly. He had to feign astonishment, then shock. He would put on a certain degree of frenzy and outrage, order the building shut down if DeWitt hadn't already done so in case the painting was still there. Knowing it wasn't, he was struck by the irony of possibly issuing such an order himself, and found himself almost laughing.

Then DeWitt was suddenly there, bursting in without even bothering to knock, closing the door firmly behind him and coming right out with it. "Chase, the Millet is missing." The auctioneer's normally suave face was like gray putty.

Chase went into his act and found it hard not to smile no matter how his stomach churned. If he'd ever wanted to pull DeWitt down off his pedestal, wanted to see him suffer for all his patronizing and condescension, he'd got his wish.

"DeWitt, calm down. What are you talking about?" He forced a light laugh.

"Chase, get serious. The Millet is gone."

"Oh, come on. Gone how?"

"We've turned the place upside down. Brian Grey went into the vault just now about a Burne-Jones and found an empty picture frame."

"And who is Brian Grey?"

"Brian, Chase, for God's sake. Brian! The boy I'm training as an auctioneer. You know him."

"Ah, yes. Brian. Of course."

He played with DeWitt a moment longer, pretending DeWitt was putting him on, and then when the auctioneer seemed ready to explode with frustration, he forced an expression of final comprehension and shock. "Jesus bloody Christ." He made his voice hoarse. "You're not kidding me, are you? The Millet's been stolen?"

"I've got a security guard on every door," DeWitt said. "Until the police get here." He paused to yank loose his tie and collar button and added, "But we'll want to conduct a major search before we ring them in, I should think. Just in case."

It sounded to Chase as if, outrageously, the auctioneer was putting himself in charge, something he never would have permitted under ordinary circumstances. But the present circumstances were not ordinary, so let him, he thought. It saved him from making a mistake or sounding insincere in his feigned shock. He'd stick to his office as much as possible.

From then on it all seemed a jumbled dream. Time passed at an interminably slow pace while simultaneously seeming to race by. Chase felt he was someone else and looking at himself from afar. None of it felt real. All business in the great auction house came to a halt. Department heads were assembled and briefed on what had happened. Employees in every section of every floor were seen knotted together, whispering. The entire building was searched, every closet and file case opened and examined, every store room ransacked, its contents scrupulously checked. In the locked company garage below, every single car was thoroughly gone over.

Two hours later, a haggard DeWitt Bouchard, no longer the suave, totally confident auctioneer who, with a few smiling words, could sway people's minds, suggested the time had come to ring in the police, and Chase agreed.

Their first presence in view of his call to the Deputy Commissioner, who promised prompt high-level action, was a shock. Three unimpressive plainclothes detectives, two men and a young woman, were shown into his office. He found one of the men, a big, overweight African-American, who said he was a lieutenant and seemed in charge, to be disrespectful. The other man he thought could have been an advertisement for the worst possible taste in clothes. The young woman, who was also black, looked more like a model than a cop. Altogether, he thought all three were better suited for giving out parking tickets than investigating a major theft.

At the same time, he told himself that he should have expected this and prepared for it. Until he recouped the eighty million and quit the cursed place, the officialdom with which he would henceforth be dealing would be for the most part anonymous meaningless bureaucrats.

Almost immediately, he began to clash with the lieutenant, who was clearly unable to distinguish the social gulf between them. When Chase began to interrogate one of his own department heads, the officer had the temerity to say, "If you don't mind, mister, I'll ask the questions."

Mister? The very presumptuousness of it jarred Chase into the dismal realization that he would be obliged, like it or not, to hide how he felt about such people. These three weren't even the Nantucket police chief, Booker or whatever his name was, who clearly knew his place and had taken his hat off when he entered the front hall of The Moorings and, though he'd soon found out Perkins was just a servant, had continued to address the butler respectfully as "sir."

To his relief, the detectives were brief. Their visit was purely preliminary, they said, explaining that they were part of the major crime unit that would be investigating the case but at the moment were only there to gather a few basic facts, to familiarize themselves with the crime scene, to verify what it was that had been stolen, and to let Mr. Morse know that the police would be taking immediate and aggressive action.

Chase patiently answered their few questions, ignoring as best he could the lieutenant's flamboyant red tie and appalling bad-taste socks and the fact that the female one, who didn't look like a cop at all, kept staring at the large blow-up photograph of the *South Wind* which had replaced Picasso on his office wall. Yes, the Millet was probably worth close to eighty million, if not more, and no, nobody at Carlyle had any idea whatsoever what had happened to it, and yes, the theft had only been discovered that afternoon. He told them that every effort possible had been made to locate it; that as far as he knew nobody except one or two leading experts in the field of fine art had ever come to see it.

Eventually they put away their notebooks, thanked him,

and were shepherded away by Alice Marks after informing him that a police officer would be placed at the vault from whence the painting had apparently been stolen pending the arrival, shortly, of forensic experts to dust for fingerprints, and that they themselves would begin serious questioning as soon as they had requisitioned a complete list of employees and been given a tour of the facilities.

Leaving the building, Aaron said to Crandall, "Okay, boss. I guess this lets us off the hook with illuminated manuscripts, right?"

Crandall let loose his deep basso laugh. "Where do you think you're at, Aaron, a retirement home?"

He missed the "I told you so" face Georgie made at Aaron and Aaron's mock threatened blow of revenge.

Around the time they got back to the precinct, Chase had begun to wonder, for all his anxiety and worry, if this low-level, low-key appearance was all a police investigation would amount to. He had begun also to indulge in a slight sense of relief when the New York chief of police was announced and appeared along with the deputy commissioner whom Chase had called. With them was a Lieutenant Wolkowski, a police art expert whom Chase recognized at once.

Middle-aged and balding with a skeletal frame and a narrow gray face that looked as though it had never worn a smile in its entire life, Wolkowski was a fixture at many an important auction, his gaunt form seen also whenever there were important gatherings at major art galleries and museums. Chase inwardly cursed himself for forgetting that of course Wolkowski would show up. The police officer, who for a short while had owned a gallery, had impulsively become a cop when a young cousin was hijacked along with her car, then brutally raped and murdered. Seeing firsthand the power that police work offered, he joined the force and became relentless in tracking down the guilty.

Chase, feeling secure that Wolkowski would grant him a certain reverence and respect because of his stewardship of Carlyle, was caught off guard by Wolkowski's aggressiveness. The officer wasted no time barraging Chase with questions in a flat monotone, among them: describe the painting, oil or watercolor, size, date it was painted, name of the artist. It was as though he'd never read a newspaper in the past month nor had ever heard of Millet, about which he probably knew nearly as much as anybody.

Irritated almost beyond speech by Wolkowski, Chase deliberately demurred, claiming shock had robbed him of any intelligence about the painting and insisting that DeWitt could provide better answers. The auctioneer readily did so, and when Wolkowski had exhausted all possible questions and in a last hope that the painting might somehow show up and not have been stolen at all, requested that the press be held off. For appearances Chase seconded the request, saying that the publicity attendant on such a theft couldn't do the auction house any good. Somebody, however—one of the detectives who had first come in was always suspected—apparently leaked the news to a media contact. The police hadn't been on the job an hour when the press was hammering at Carlyle's door, and the story was breaking news on national television.

It was as Chase had expected and prepared for; the press were no better, if indeed not worse, than the three detectives. This was especially true of the television people. Where the police at least exercised a degree of the protocol that regulations required of them, those who wielded microphones and shoulder held cameras seemed to recognize no restraint whatsoever. It was the press invasion of The Moorings all over again. Like Wolkowski, they failed to defer to him for one moment either as president and CEO of a great auction house or as the titular head of one of America's great families. Not a minute passed but that a microphone was shoved in his face. Camera flashes flared incessantly, half blinding. To move from one place to another was to pass through a gantlet of shoulder-held TV cameras with anonymous voices behind them shouting stupid questions: "What's the value of the Millet?" "When did you first notice it was gone?" "Will there be a reward for it?" until Chase finally found himself virtually pushed before a bank of microphones to tell the world of the painting's importance and with the New York police chief next to him assuring the world that no stone would be left unturned in their effort to recover it.

It seemed forever before the circus slowly came to an end and, thoroughly wrung out by the whole experience, Chase was able to retreat to the quiet safety of the Seventy-Fifth Street apartment. There would be more, he knew, but there would be at least twelve hours of respite before it began again. Interviews had been scheduled for the following morning among the original three detectives, along with half a dozen others, and every employee in an attempt to discover whether the theft was an inside or outside job. There would also be interviews between himself and his department heads with insurance company investigators.

And, of course, there would be more unwanted presence of the persistent press. Even before he had finally left his office, CNN, FOX, MSNBC, and all three major networks had requested live interviews. He had readily agreed. It would be a chance, he thought, for him to add armor against any suspicion as well as to separate himself from the irreverent nonsense to which he'd been subjected all afternoon.

He fixed himself a double shot of vodka on ice, took a shower, and from a dozen photographs of young women from various escort agencies, selected one called Nadine he thought seductively young and whom he hadn't had before. She wasn't immediately available, he was told, but something about her photograph, a kind of challenging sexuality, intrigued him, so he arranged for her to come and spend the next evening with him.

Resigning himself to an evening alone and deciding on the Union Club, he checked the Barney's box before leaving the apartment and saw to his satisfaction that the disguising camouflage of Jason's copy of the *Cape Cod Blue* was firmly in place in the frame he'd bought. He was tempted to pull it out on its stretcher to enjoy a moment or two looking at the Millet behind it but then remembered what Jason had done with a plastic shield. Cursing to himself, he wondered if he shouldn't try to find a restorer immediately to separate the painting, but at the same time realized, given the uproar in all the media, how dangerous that could be. Besides, even if he bribed some restorer with a small fortune, he would leave himself open to whomever he picked blackmailing him for more. Or even betraying him for the reward being offered for the painting. He would have to be content just knowing the Millet was safe the way it was and himself with it. As soon as things calmed a little, and he could move about without the nuisance of the media or the police, he'd be able to take it home and hang it up over the mantelpiece in place of Darwin's cursed sea battle. Only he would know that eighty million dollars graced the wall above the Adams mantel. And, virtually eliminating the last trace of Darwin in the house, there it would remain until he collected the ransom for it. Then he would either find a "safe" restorer, or, it had occurred to him, get some of the necessary solvent and after experimenting with a couple of worthless paintings, see if he couldn't separate the Millet from the Victorian sea-scape himself.

Amused at such final irony, he put the Barney's box back on the shelf in his closet and took himself off to the Union Club.

TWENTY-FIVE

At The Moorings, the day after the theft of the Millet was revealed and now two weeks after Darwin Morse met his tragic end, Gabrielle awoke very early from a terrible dream. The first sign of eventual day was still no more than a darkness on the horizon, but a darkness slightly less profound than the night sky above it, where stars had begun to lose their luster. On the bedside table, the red numbers of her digital clock said 4:05.

The dream clung to her whole being, an enveloping and cloying fog that obliterated any other thought and refused to let go. She dreamed she and Haydn had been sleeping in some strange empty house, one devoid of any furniture except for their bed and where there were seemingly endless corridors. In the dream they had both woken when sensing some menacing presence, something dead and horrible that was seeking them. Haydn rose to try to flush it out from wherever it was, and Gabrielle followed him. They became separated, and she found herself alone in a large, empty hall with whatever it was suddenly close behind her. She fled on legs turned to lead, screaming soundlessly for Haydn. As she rushed blindly down corridors and through rooms, the building slowly crumbled behind her with the advance of the awful unknown until there was no further place to which she could flee. She stood naked and trapped in a dead end narrow space with terror gripping her heart. As the nameless horror finally caught up to her, she awoke.

For a while she lay staring into the darkness, still gripped by fear, and since she and Felicity had gone to bed so early, even slightly before nine o'clock, she knew she was not fatigued enough to override the dream and sleep again. Rising and slipping her light summer bathrobe over the coolness of her bare skin, she left the room and went downstairs.

As she reached the hall, the old grandfather clock resonantly struck the half hour, 4:30. Through the open door of Darwin's study, where Gauguin slept on his dog bed, she could hear his heavy, sonorous breathing. For a moment her heart nearly stopped. It was as if the breathing were Darwin's and the old patriarch himself was in there. Shrugging off the illusion, she felt her way through the dark to the living room as silently as possible so as not to wake the dog.

Finding the couch, she sank into its cushions, her whole being still divided between the reality of being awake and the terror of her sleep. In the dark silence, she began after a while to discern the outlines of furniture, irregular gray shapes against the lighter gray of the surrounding room. Dawn had finally come. Through the tall French window, she could see a crack of light on the Atlantic horizon.

She rose and went outside onto the terrace, then stepped down onto the lawn with its symmetrical pattern of croquet wickets, letting the wetness of the night dew on the grass chill her feet. Looking back at the old house, which was no longer a black, shapeless mass but now visible with its roof line etched against the lightening sky, she suddenly felt—even more than she had on returning from her lunch with Selma—an overwhelming sense of belonging to everything that was The Moorings: the lawns and walks and trees and shrubbery. And yet, she knew she didn't belong. Soon, when Bernard Bligny had had enough of the Morse family, she would be leaving and all, especially Haydn, might be only a painful memory.

She turned to face the harbor. Below its mast-head riding light, the sleek hull of the *South Wind* was now visible at anchor over by the Coatue bar. And, under a smaller lower light a good distance beyond, she made out the form of a dory then heard its motor as it came up the harbor with several men in fishing clothes and with rods. They would disembark, she knew, far up at the head of the harbor to cross the bar to surf fish.

Watching the dory go by, her dream suddenly merged with reality, and she understood it. In spite of herself, she had so closely come to identifying with the Morse family—with Felicity, Haydn, and David, at least—that in her dream she had become them. It was they, represented by herself, who were pursued by some terrible unknown thing, and it was they, not her, who were in danger of being destroyed while The Moorings and the great auction house of Carlyle, even Haydn's La Rive Gauche, crumbled behind them.

How long she stood on the lawn she didn't know; time seemed to have stopped, but when the gray sliver of dawn to the east had begun to redden, when the stars had disappeared and given way to a far lighter blue heralding a daytime sky, she went back into the silent house and made coffee in Mr. Perkins's pantry and took it to the living room. And added things up.

Three things had happened. Chase had lost a huge sum of money in Russia; Darwin had been murdered; and the priceless Millet had been stolen. The connection among all three, she was convinced, was Chase himself. It made her flesh crawl. If Chase had indeed robbed Carlyle to make a killing in Russia, and if Darwin had faced him up to his crime with threats of exposure and ruin, inciting Chase to murder him, didn't it stand to reason that he'd stolen the Millet as well? An inside job, the papers said. Indeed, why not? Who had a better motive than Chase, faced with the need to make good his embezzlement? Who, also, was in a better position than Chase, with free access to the Millet whenever he wished? Surely, in spite of all the security around the painting, he could have devised some scheme to walk out with it.

Gabrielle shivered and tightened her robe around her. Her

unfinished coffee grew cold in her hand. She again relived the terrifying nightmare with all the feelings of helpless vulnerability she'd felt. The destiny of Carlyle, The Moorings, and the Morse family was in the hands of a thief and a murderer—the dream horror that had stalked in her restless sleep.

Relief only came when she heard Mr. Perkins at the door to the hall saying, "Good Morning, Miss Gabrielle. You are up early. May I get you more coffee?"

Something about the butler's steady presence, his forever reassuring calm, gave her sudden and stubborn determination not to allow the future to be written by Chase, even if the only thing she could do was to stop being frightened. She owed that to Felicity and Haydn and David, if nothing else. She thanked Mr. Perkins, and when he returned shortly with fresh coffee, took it upstairs to her bedroom, showered, and got dressed.

She was coming back downstairs when the phone rang. Perkins, who was near the hall telephone, answered.

"The Morse residence. Good morning."

And then, "Oh, yes? Very well, thank you. And yourself? Yes, she's just coming down." He cupped the receiver. "It's for you, Miss Gabrielle."

"Who is it?"

"Miss Selma, Miss."

"Selma Freedman?"

"Yes, Miss."

Gabrielle rushed to take the receiver from his hand. "Selma?"

"Gabrielle. Yes, it's me. My trip west has been delayed, and I'm still in New York and would love to see you again."

"What's happened? Why didn't you go?"

There was a moment's silence as though the older woman was hesitant to give the reason. Then Selma said, "The robbery. The New York police want to interview me."

"But why you? You weren't at Carlyle when it happened."

Selma laughed. "Maybe that's why." Then she said. "Gabrielle, I've been wondering if I shouldn't reveal the trouble Chase got into in Russia. I wouldn't want it coming out later and being asked why I'd said nothing. What do you think?"

"Do you think there's a connection? With the robbery, I mean?"

"Don't you?"

Although she'd been sure of Selma's answer even before she asked the question, the abruptness of the response, as a question in return, surprised Gabrielle. She hesitated before she said, "Yes. Yes I do, Selma."

Her caution fled then, as the need to confide burst in her. "Selma, I think there's much more." Unable to hold back and hoping Felicity would understand and forgive her, she rushed on to reveal Felicity's fears and what Felicity had seen.

There was a silence before Selma answered with surprisingly matter-of-fact calm, "Yes. You know, I think I had my suspicions, too, but I buried them as almost too horrible to think of, even for one moment."

"How long do you think you'll be staying?"

"I don't know yet. Depends on what I can wangle for hotel reservations. I'm out of my apartment tomorrow. There's a small hotel close to where I lived."

"Selma, you're not staying at a hotel. You're staying here. Fly to Boston. There's a plane from there to here. I'll meet you at the airport."

"Oh, I couldn't do that."

"You can, Selma and will. You're family and we're in a jam. Do you think we should tell the police what Felicity said?"

"Candidly, yes, I do. And why not? They're not stupid. They'll find out sooner or later. And sooner means maybe there'll be an end to all of this." She added, "That poor little kid. And his mother. Don't leave either alone, Gabrielle."

TWENTY-SIX

That same morning, at the Midtown Manhattan major crime unit, Detective Sergeant Klein hunched his lean form forward in his chair, his knees thrust up against the bottom of his desk drawer, and stared thoughtfully at his open notebook lying next to his keyboard. He kept coming back to Georgie's theory that Morse was tied into what Bracer was suspected of, trafficking in priceless manuscripts. Otherwise why the early morning meeting? It seemed to him, however, that somehow the very thought of a Morse-Bracer alliance was a block on thinking differently. Unless—*unless*. During the night he'd come up with a fresh slant on the theory.

"Georgie." He looked across his desk at her. She was shuffling pages of notes, a puzzled frown on her face, and looking miserable. The air-conditioning had broken down again and it was fetid hot in their crowded little office.

She looked up. "What?"

"Your idea. Morse and Bracer in cahoots."

"What about it?"

"Don't go all defensive on me. I concede you might be right. Except I think you might have the accent on the wrong syllable."

"Meaning?"

"Meaning they're in cahoots about something that has nothing to do with manuscripts."

Georgie's irritated frown had disappeared. She immediately

looked thoughtful. "Like what, Aaron?"

"I'm not sure. We know Bracer is a crook. We don't like Morse but we have no evidence that he is one except 'birds of a feather' and all that. But when we were asking about other employees and brought up Bracer, he made Bracer sound too good."

"He was being protective?"

"He came across that way, yes. Especially since, from what I've gathered about him, he doesn't like anyone at Carlyle and hates being there. I think we ought to ask for an audit of the book."

Georgie silently examined her fingernails. Aaron waited. When she looked up, she said, "Do you think the robbery is connected?"

"What do you think?"

She didn't answer him directly. "Well, you and I both think it's an inside job, right? And who better than Morse?"

"Except he's a goddamned zillionaire. He needs to face jail for theft like we need more hot weather."

Georgie shrugged. "Money's not the root of all evil."

"Come again?" Klein locked eyes with her, trying to read her thoughts.

She ducked explanation. "I'll say one thing about our zillionaire. He's hiding something. Or else he just didn't like answering questions from me. Bad enough coming from an N-word—me in his vocabulary. But a female on top of it? Wow!"

She laughed, adjusted the always bothersome bra strap on her left shoulder, and pulled her damp tank top away from her body a moment, letting her skin breathe. She said, "Crandall thinks maybe it's not an inside job. Him and Wolkowski both. Their slant—so officially ours, too: Bouchard wouldn't jeopardize a career that's bringing him fame and fortune; Brian Grey hasn't the chutzpah. Ditto Selma Freedman, Morse's assistant, the one who just retired. I'm writing her off before I even see her. A woman her age? Do me a favor. That bitch who took her place, Alice Marks?" Georgie shook her head. "Not enough imagination." Interviewing Marks, she'd found herself face-to-face with an arrogant uptight woman who, behind a surface of perfect makeup, clothing, jewelry, and hair, was condescension itself. But a thief? No way.

Klein said, "You're right, and Crandall and Wolkowski are full of shit. It has to be an inside job. The joint is a fucking fortress. You'd need a tank and a bunch of marines to get into it when it's shut down. And whoever did this, Georgie, has to be someone who knows the place inside and out, someone who could get into the vault and back out with the painting without being seen. Timing. That had to be all important. Picking a moment when they knew everyone would be occupied elsewhere—maybe lunch. All they had to do was get it out of the building, and they must have because, God knows, we've scoured the place. That's the one bugging me the most. If I'm right, how the hell did they pull it off? The guards check everything that goes out."

Georgie looked at him thoughtfully then rose and stared out the window at the street below. "Disguised it?"

"Disguised it?"

"Yeah. Disguised it somehow. It could still be there right under our noses. Waiting for a safe day. Ever think of that?"

"Oh, come on—how the hell do you disguise a painting?"

"I don't know. Maybe make it look like another painting? Paint another painting over it?"

"Sure. Paint a mustache or a beard on an eighty million dollar laundress. Right? Or maybe slap an election campaign sticker on her." Klein laughed. "You've got subway graffiti on the brain."

"Just a thought." Georgie turned away from the window. She said, "Okay, I'll surrender on Morse being tied into illuminated manuscripts. And to your idea they're in cahoots about something else. But like what? Cooked books, maybe?

Let's get that audit request in pronto."

"I'll bring it up when we to meet with Crandall and Wolkowski this afternoon."

"And one more thing. The old man getting dumped in the bay. Morse and Bracer meet urgently, the painting gets stolen, the old man's a homicide. It's all too cute for words, right? There's a connection there, Aaron, I swear there is. I'm going to hike up to Nantucket on the sly, have a talk with Booker and take a look at the family set up for myself."

"If there's a squawk, I'll back you," Klein said. "Who knows what could turn up?" He watched her at the water cooler as she filled up a cup, pulling her tank top away from herself again and found himself wishing she wasn't so attractive. Christ, what a woman. Million-dollar legs and body and a face and personality to go with it. She'd been gorgeous even when on the beat and dressed up like something in the circus in the stupid men's uniform they made women cops wear, all weighed down with a gun and radio and the rest of the crap. How the hell was one supposed not to occasionally have stray thoughts in such close quarters with a female who was one hundred percent desirable even when in a bad mood? And it was even worse when you were a bachelor all summer.

That made him think again of his wife and kids at the lake, and he felt a little ashamed of himself, as though he'd actually been unfaithful, and especially that he'd had such thoughts about Georgie, of all people.

Then he thought again of this case. Maybe more than eighty million bucks, the auctioneer had said, if the crowd was right and he really got things going. Christ, it was frustrating. A week and they were no place. They needed to crack the case. He'd get a promotion if they did, and more pay. He had to do it for his family.

He put his notebook away. It was a waste of time looking at it. What they needed was a whole new slant on things. Start off fresh. Forget all the interviews, all the routine police work, fingerprints, DNA, none of which had turned up any-thing. This wasn't a routine case. Thinking that, he suddenly thought, suppose Georgie was right. Suppose the painting was still there, disguised somehow. Or that's how it got out past the guards. It needed some serious exploring. Forensic ought to look around in the art restoration section where they repaired and framed paintings. He rose abruptly. "Georgie kid," he said. "C'mon. I'll buy you lunch." He'd tell her maybe she was right about disguise while they ate.

She dropped her cup into the wastebasket. "Man, what got into you?"

He had a fleeting vision of himself and his wife in bed in an air-conditioned room someplace, and then it vanished. "Hun-ger," he said.

Detective White grabbed her shoulder bag and followed him out.

TWENTY-SEVEN

That night, watching the movement of the small blond head, the fine platinum hair spread out over his thighs like a fan and as waves of pleasure radiated up through his body, Chase was beginning to find it hard to think of anything else. He'd had her pinned down on the bed, thrusting hard and deep into her until, laughing, she'd suddenly wriggled free twisted around, and begun giving him head. With most girls their oral effort never produced pleasure that was particularly out of the ordinary. The excitement for him lay in knowing that at any time, when tired of their efforts, he could shatter whatever illusions or hopes they held that they would be rewarded in some way other than the fee they'd share with the escort agency for their evening's work.

This girl was different. This one had none of the anxious-to-please subservience about her that most of the others did. She was just like her picture—challenging. The way she'd stopped several times to look up and laugh before continuing, she made him think of Courtney. From the moment she'd walked in the door, too, in the way she had ignored him. She'd looked around the room, glanced over some erotic photographs he hung up whenever he had a date and said, "You maybe need this for fun. I need food. Where are you taking me to dinner first? The Spotted Calf, maybe, okay?" That's the way Courtney was.

To his chagrin he'd found himself going along with it. Maybe it was because she didn't give him time to think. She simply marched back to the front door and said, "Okay, handsome, let's go," and had run one hand provocatively up the front of his trousers right then and there before exiting into the hall.

What was her name again? Nadine? Said she was Lithuanian and had come to the States on a student visa and decided to stay. At dinner, she'd given him a story about her father and mother, she said were both doctors, and a brother who she said was a colonel in the Lithuanian army, and how they had got the family estates back after the Russians had finally left—a château and several hundred acres of farmland. What nonsense. She's probably a secretary, he thought, conned into the escort business.

Listening to her, his thoughts had drifted back over the day. For the first time, he'd begun to feel totally confident. The stupid police could come and go as they pleased with whatever suspicions they might grasp onto to make themselves feel they were doing their job. They might even come to the conclusion that he had stolen the Millet, but in the absence of the painting, how could they prove it? Any doubt he wouldn't get away with it had fled. He'd pulled it off. All he had to do now was be patient. In ten days' time, he'd spring the ransom note on them, addressing it to himself.

It was his last thought for the moment. The sexual pleasure she'd created suddenly became climactic. A darkness and a violence filled his whole body, sweeping him helplessly up in its embrace before it slowly died away, and he found himself looking at her smiling face, her slender hands still quietly caressing. And then her standing up, beautifully slender and naked, right there before him.

In the shower she'd insisted on, she soaped him down, and her rippling laugh burst forth at how small and unimportant he'd become. "We can't have that," she said and kissed it provocatively and got out. He stayed a while under the soothing water, trying to get himself back together. Christ, this girl had really made others seem a waste of time. If only she wasn't so goddamned bossy, doing whatever she wanted. And just now, laughing at his sexual collapse.

He got out and slung a towel over one shoulder and headed for the living room. He'd fix another drink for both of them. In his mind he saw himself naked and virile and drinking with a beautiful young, naked woman between walls decorated with erotica. He wouldn't bother with the bedroom again, he'd take her standing up this time right here, her back against a wall and her legs wrapped around him.

In the doorway, he stopped dead. The fantasy vanished. Something in him exploded. A redness half curtained his sight, his eyes disbelieving at what they saw. The Barney's box lay open and propped up on the couch, a layer of protective tissue paper removed so that the *Cape Cod Blue* was plainly visible. And she, incongruously naked, was standing in the middle of the room studying it.

"What a gorgeous painting. Why are you keeping it in a box in your closet? Let's hang it up. Unless you got it for me, did you?" She pointed a slender finger at him. "Hey, maybe you stole it like the one in all the papers. Did you? I won't tell."

His blow sent her flying half across the room, bringing down the drink table with its glasses and bottles and bowl of ice and her on top of it all. Looking up, dazed, she in turn saw rage-maddened eyes, clenched fists, the limp, impotent penis she had just subjugated now an instrument of male terror and hatred. The whiteness of the man's face, the whole left side of it twitching, like a wild animal's. And the voice: "Get out of here, you dirty little whore! Out!"

Yanked to her feet, she felt a terrible blow in her side just below her ribs. Then in one violent move, she was spun out of the living room to collapse in the foyer. She was kicked to her feet, more blows rained, the door was flung open, and she was thrust violently into the elevator hall.

She painfully rose to her knees, bewildered. It had happened in seconds. Why? What had she done? Her clothes and hand bag landed next to her. Then her shoes, one striking her in the eye.

"Fucking bitch."

The door slammed. She was alone. She rose in clumsy paralyzing terror, a sudden sharp stabbing pain in her side. She tried to think. She was naked. Someone could come out of another apartment or from the elevator. Panicked, she pulled on her dress, frantically stuffed her panties and bra into her hand bag.

She couldn't take the elevator. Suppose someone else was on it? She went down the fire stairs, floor by floor. It seemed to take forever, the pain in her side made her want to scream. At the bottom, she managed to open a heavy fire door into an alleyway that led to the street. Outside, she slipped on her shoes and stumbled the few yards to York Avenue, then turned uptown and at the end of the block turned west toward First Avenue.

Mid-block, she stopped to catch her breath and sank down on the steps of a brownstone. Looking back, she saw nobody. The street, all the way up to First Avenue, was empty and nighttime silent. She got out her cell phone and punched in numbers, calling Anik, with whom she shared a room. Anik was Finnish, tall, slender, and beautiful. She'd fallen into the same American trap, and swore someday she'd kill to get back home.

A young woman's voice said, "Nadine? What's up?"

"I just got beat up."

"Oh, shit. Who?"

"My date."

"But why?"

"I don't know. I was looking at some painting he had in a Barney's box. I started teasing him and asked if maybe he stole it like the one that's been in all the papers and on television."

"He got mad at you for that?"

"He was like crazy."

"What kind of picture?"

"I don't know. A lady and a kid sitting on a beach under an umbrella."

"Are you hurt bad? Do you want me to come?"

"It hurts so where he hit me."

"Where?"

She tried to answer, for a moment couldn't. The pain seemed everything. And now she was swept with nausea.

"Nadine?"

"Yes."

"Where are you?"

"East something. Seventies."

"Shit. Well, come on. Grab a cab home."

"Okay."

"And don't worry about the date. Vinnie will take care of him but good."

"Yeah. Vinnie. Okay. See you."

Nadine put her cell phone back in her handbag and thought of Vinnie Borodino. Heavyset, hair slicked down with Vaseline. He provided girls for the escort service who would do more than just look pretty for an evening. Vinnie would maybe send around a couple of his guys to beat the shit out of this bastard.

She huddled for a long time on the brownstone's steps, thinking about home, wanting to cry and knowing crying wouldn't help. She thought about her mother, who'd come to live in Vilnius from their village and had taken a night cleaning job in one of the government buildings to make ends meet after the police had shot her father. And about her brother who said he was going to South America and whom they'd never seen or heard from again. What was she doing here? Why, why? New York sucked. She hated it. It was dirty and smelled, and nobody had time for anybody else. People rushed along in the streets with their heads down, in their own world. She'd come here promised an office job and ended up pleasuring rich slobs who couldn't get it from their wives or from anyone else either. Except from someone like herself who'd been stupid enough to think that the ad from an employment agency was anything but a trap.

Home was West Ninety-Third. She rose slowly to her feet

and almost couldn't. The pain—she felt as if she were being cut in half. She tried to figure out where she was. Maybe Anik could come and get her. She remembered now that the guy lived on York and Seventy-Fifth. She had made it up a block and was on Seventy-Sixth. She headed west, fumbling once more in her hand bag for her cell phone. She got it out and called Anik again. The line was busy.

She'd got half way up the block to a dark stretch between two street lights and had to stop. The pain in her side was everything. The street in front of her blurred and swam. She fumbled for a tree close by, held onto it. Everything got dark, and she felt she was falling, falling into darkness.

A couple who lived on the block and were returning from late dinner after the theater found her ten minutes later. She was sprawled across the low wire guard around the bottom of the tree to keep dogs from it. They called the police and an ambulance, but when the ambulance finally got there, it was too late.

While she'd been talking to Anik, Chase slowly came to his senses. The roaring sound in his head had ebbed, the side of his face had stopped jumping. He fixed himself another drink. Sitting with it on the couch next to the Barney's box, he felt a vague anxiety. It could be awkward if she caused trouble. He would have to claim she'd been mugged out on the street someplace. He could probably count on the night doorman not having seen the way she must have looked when she got down to the lobby. Probably the man had either been asleep or in one of the back rooms having a drink because if he had seen her he would have phoned up. Anyway, if she made trouble, she'd get nowhere. Why on earth would someone of his position, weighed down with all the sadness of his father's recent death, beat up on some stupid little escort girl? The tabloids could make all they wanted to of it. And Felicity wouldn't dare cause problems at home. He only had to threaten to take David away to shut her up.

He carefully put the protective tissue paper back over the *Cape Cod Blue* and the top back on the Barney's box, the box back on a top shelf in his bedroom closet. Then took another shower.

Under the rushing water, he tried to remember her name. What was it again? Nad something. Nadine? It didn't make any difference. Stupid little cunt. Anger stirred in him again. Saying what a pretty painting it was. And why did he have it in a box? Damned lowlife whore. Dirt. Walking into his apartment as though she owned the place. Laughing at his art work. Ordering him to feed her. And at the Spotted Calf, too.

His cheek began to twitch again, and with it, one eye. The bathroom darkened. Again there was a roaring sound in his head, the same, almost deafening noise as when he'd caught her with the painting.

He turned off the shower, got out, toweled, fixed himself another drink. The roaring slowly quieted. He turned on the television. When some talking head started mouthing "expert" opinions on the theft of the famous Millet, he switched it off and headed for bed. There'd be the stupid police again tomorrow, and he needed a good night's sleep.

TWENTY-EIGHT

The police came to Carlyle only minutes after Chase himself arrived. When the receptionist announced them, he was tempted to tell her to ask them to wait. He wasn't in the mood for coping with anyone in the common herd, let alone cops, but he decided against it.

"Which ones?"

"Detectives Klein and White, sir."

Chase thought, *That pair again.* He took a deep breath and exhaled. "Okay, I'll see them."

He settled himself behind his desk, prepared to seem as relaxed as possible, and was surprised by their appearance when the receptionist showed them in. They had dressed, he thought probably ordered to by the deputy commissioner, in what was more appropriate for the executive suite of Carlyle than their previous attire. Klein wore a lightweight gray suit, sported a relatively inoffensive necktie, and wore dark brown oxfords. White wore a trim navy suit with no embellishment save for a gold chain visible at her neckline. She had on high heels that matched the suit.

Chase rose and greeted them with affability and asked them to be seated. He had difficulty in not looking too directly at Detective White, whose slender figure was shown to almost perfect advantage by her suit and whose wide dark eyes were set off from her darker skin by subtle make up.

"Can we get you some coffee?" When they politely declined,

he said, "Now, tell me how you're making out. And what can I do today to help?"

If he'd expected an equally affable answer, he was wrong. Klein was suddenly all business. "Thank you, Mr. Morse. We need to ask you a couple of questions, if you don't mind."

Chase felt a stab deep in his stomach. He forced his smile to stay on his face. "By all means."

Detective White, her dark face unsmiling, produced a notebook from her shoulder bag.

Klein said. "We've had a communication from the police chief on Nantucket. I believe you know him."

"Of course. He's investigating my father's murder."

"He's come across a pair of your shoes in rather unusual condition and asked our help in seeing if you possibly could shed some light on them."

Chase didn't have to play dumb. He couldn't imagine what they were talking about. He had an instant sense of dread at what they might spring on him. Unless Booker had been sidetracked by some ridiculous nothing, it could possibly be something incriminating. Why else would he have communicated it to New York? His mind raced; shoes, shoes—what shoes?

"A pair identified as yours were found on the beach several days after your father's demise. They had obviously been in the water, had sand and seaweed in them, and were badly scratched up."

Chase forced a laugh. "Oh, so that's it. You know, I frequently walk on the shore, especially if we've dropped something overboard from the *South Wind*. That's my sailboat. Things that float wash up and get caught and don't wash out again. We quite often recover seat cushions that way."

"I see. When you go on the beach, Mr. Morse, I take it you don't go barefoot."

"No, no. Not to walk, anyway. The occasional broken shells and flotsam. You risk cutting your feet. For beachcombing you wear old running shoes or work boots."

"The shoes found were expensive dress shoes, Mr. Morse. Probably four or five hundred dollars when new."

The stab he'd felt suddenly spread through his whole body. The room darkened before him. None of this made any sense. Were they making all this up? Was it some kind of a trick? And if it was, why?

"Mr. Morse?"

He was aware of a heavy silence. How long had it been? He broke it. "I wouldn't know how shoes like that could get on the beach. Unless, of course, and that's probably it, they went overboard, perhaps early in the summer when we first readied the boat for the season's sailing. That was some time ago. I wouldn't remember whether I'd gone out to the boat in good shoes right after getting home on Friday. But I must have."

"Chief Booker reports that Falmouth forensic said the shoes couldn't have been in the water more than a minute or so."

Now what? Chase wondered. Damned shoes. "Really," he said. He glanced at Detective White. She was making notes.

It came back to him, then. Suddenly. The awful splash, the bubbling sound coming up from the dark water, the chair surfacing and his almost standing on it to force it back down. Then silence and the faint sound of the *South Wind*'s rigging rattling slightly in the evening offshore breeze as the quicker-to-cool land air of late night flowed gently back out over the warmer sea. And his terror, his desperate need to get away from the dock. Anywhere but there. Anywhere. And finding himself walking along the beach. Not walking, really, but stumbling and falling and slipping, but going, going. Until he'd finally stopped and sunk onto some seaweed.

After that, he couldn't remember anything, except that he was chilled to the bone, that the sky had begun to lighten, and he knew he had to get back to the house as quickly as possible. His feet tortured him in his business shoes, reminding him that he shouldn't wear them up to the house. They'd make a noise on the terrace and especially inside on the hardwood floors. He'd go barefoot. He'd left them on the beach, thinking he'd collect them the next day when no one was around. And had forgotten.

He was aware of the silence again and the two detectives staring at him, expressionless. Bloody vultures. Thought they were going to trip him up, did they? Well, they're weren't going to succeed. All he had to do was put on an act. He'd learned how to do that fending off Darwin: learned to brace himself against the big red face, to suddenly look bright and no longer cowed, not the way he really felt, to act as though some misdemeanor he'd been unjustly accused of had suddenly been remembered.

He did that now. He stiffened abruptly in his chair and leaned forward over his desk, putting on a sincere, contrite smile and a tone of voice to match. "Ah, of course. Stupid of me not to remember right away. After Dad ..." he let his voice break slightly, "After that terrible morning, I think it was that afternoon, I had to get away from all the circus at the house. Police. The media. I don't know if you've ever lost anyone, a parent, but it's a terrible shock even under ordinary circumstances. You feel utterly rolled under. But the way Dad went." He paused and shook his head as if trying to erase the awful circumstances from his mind.

Then he said, "That afternoon, I took a walk on the beach trying to pull myself together. I remember thinking that I had to set a standard for my wife and child, be someone they could hold on to, know what I mean? I didn't think of anything else. I was too upset to worry about my shoes. I just went down on the beach in the clothes I'd had on. I think I walked quite a ways, I can't remember exactly how far, but when I finally caught my breath and came back, my feet hurt too much from all the sand in the shoes, I couldn't walk in them any longer. So I took them off and left them someplace. I figured to pick them up later and forgot. Dad's leaving us, all the tears, and then his funeral. You understand?"

Chase waited. The two detectives said nothing. Detective White looked at her notes.

Then Klein finally said, "I guess that buries that one. I'll let Chief Booker know what you said." He rose. "Thank you for your time, Mr. Morse."

"I'm here whenever you want me."

The two detectives headed for the door. Detective White suddenly stopped and turned. "Oh, Mr. Morse. There is one more little thing." She'd pulled her notebook out of her shoulder bag and glanced at it. "Your Nantucket home is your primary residence, but you also keep an apartment in New York, is that right?"

"Yes. We have one on East End Avenue, just by Gracie Square." He forced a laugh. "Keeping an eye on the mayor."

"That's where your family spends some of the winter, you, your wife and son? And before he died, your father?"

"That's right."

Detective White glanced at her notes again. "Actually, I didn't mean that one, Mr. Morse. I meant the one on Seventy-Fifth Street and York. Condos. There's one in Carlyle's name."

The stab in the stomach again. "Yes. That's correct."

"What's that for?"

Chase fumbled. "What's it for? It's for business. Nothing unusual. A lot of corporate heads have two apartments, one for living, one for business entertainment. If you can avoid it, you don't like to let a horde of business people swarm into your home and inconvenience your family. Dad used the Seventy-Fifth Street apartment all the time."

"But your family's not in New York in the summer, Mr. Morse."

"Well, we—we pretty much shut East End up all summer just because they're not. The condo apartment is more suited to someone on their own. East End is pretty big. I always felt uncomfortable all by myself in all those rooms. Seventy-Fifth Street is just two bedrooms, living room, kitchenette, and bath.

And closer to the office here. More convenient."

"I see. Thank you, Mr. Morse." She put away her note book and went out, closing the door behind her.

Down on the street, she and Klein, once again confronted by the stifling New York heat, headed back to their own office. They stopped at a favorite bar on Third Avenue, empty at that time of day, took a booth, and ordered a beer each. Before either spoke Georgie removed her tailored jacket, revealing a very feminine lace-trimmed camisole. Klein took off his jacket as well, along with his tie. He said, "Your idea."

"You bought it."

She'd suggested that if they didn't look like cops it might put Morse off his guard.

Klein said. "It was worth it. You looked good."

"Thank you, Aaron. You looked the proper preppie yourself." She laughed and reached out for a quick high five, letting him know that she cared. She often thought how lonely he had to be, on his own all summer, and what a good faithful husband he was. She knew too many cops who got hot tips from the vice squad on where to go for action. His wife was a lucky woman.

When their beer came, Klein said, "So, what do you think, Georgie?"

"I think he's bad news. Maybe even the guy we want. But pinning anything on him will be a job."

"How bad?"

"Not sure. But he was lying his head off."

"About the shoes?" Klein toyed with his beer glass, making a wet pattern of overlapping circles with the glass's bottom on the booth table between them.

"What else? It was written all over him."

"How about the apartment?"

"We'll check it out, but why he uses it when the place at

East End has a housekeeper to look after him is pretty obvious."

"Girls?"

"Sure."

Klein was silent again. He thought of Chase's wife, trying to envision what she looked like; probably in her forties, he decided, typical socialite type, probably getting dowdy. He wondered if she knew about the apartment and suspected her husband might be unfaithful. They'd check that out, too. The Nantucket police might have a line on it.

Georgie said, "Let's get a warrant and have a look at the place."

"Why not?"

"I get in there, I can tell you quick enough if he's had girls up or not." Then she said, "What do you make of Chief Booker?"

"Career cop who had all this dumped on him. The actual chief is ill. But from what I gather he's faced up to it and he's good. Local guy. Popular in town. Has a wife and kids, was quarterback on his high school team. Top marks in police academy. Runs a tight ship because he has to but is no stickler for rules. Before police work he was into ocean navigational equipment. That's tricky stuff."

"Just the same, you don't think he's maybe in over his head with the murder?"

Klein laughed. "He told me that's what his wife said, but he said he didn't think so, and neither do I. Not at all. When I phoned him he was playing a little cagey, like he didn't want to make himself look stupid with a misjudgment, but I got the impression just the same that he thinks our friend over at Carlyle could possibly be implicated in some way, hard as it is to believe. After all, we're talking about theoretically civilized society people, not some drugged-out gangster types in Brooklyn."

"Implicated, meaning murdered his own father? Parricide? I wouldn't doubt it."

"You've really got it in for the guy, haven't you."

"Yeah, and it's not because he's a stupid racist either, believe me. It's the woman in me. Let's put it this way, Aaron. I'd sure hate to be his wife. Or for that matter any of his girlfriends."

"If he's playing around, Georgie, who do you think it's with?"

"Guy like Morse? Certainly not with anybody in his own social set: probably bar pickups, one night stands. Or something more certain that wouldn't cause him problems. Escort service girls, probably. I'm going to check that out, too."

On the way back to the precinct, Klein said, "That woman you're seeing Monday. What's her name again? Freedman?"

"Yeah. Selma Freedman."

"Incidentally, she called. Crandall picked it up when we were out, said she was at the Morse home in Nantucket for the weekend."

"Really? She's closer than just business, then. I might have a few words with her when I go up there. My hunch is that whatever she has to tell us could be interesting. All the employees at Carlyle I talked to tell me she ran the place ever since the old man retired. And even when he was still there."

"You think she'll point a finger?"

"At Morse? I hope so. And maybe more than just about the painting."

"You mean about the murder?

"What else?"

"You see them connected?"

"Don't you?"

"As a matter of fact," Aaron said, "Yes." They stopped for a light on Lexington. "Being capable of both is written all over the bastard," he added.

Georgie laughed. "No argument." And took his arm to cross the street.

In his office, Chase cursed them silently, especially the woman. He might have known she'd be the one to come up with something. How the hell had they got onto the apartment? City property registry, probably. Had to be. Or looking into his taxes. Well, let them wonder. There wasn't any law about having two apartments in New York. He wasn't the only man who had a second place for business, or that he used for fun his wife didn't know about. But any girls up there for the moment now was out. Bloody cops. They'd probably stake the place. Maybe he ought to sleep at Gracie Square for a while. One thing was certain; the painting was going out of New York City in case the bitch got out a search warrant, and even if he had to make a special flight to Nantucket. He'd call Doyle and have him file a flight plan for that afternoon.

He returned to his desk and fell into his big high-backed chair. He was sweating. His underarms were wet with it and his chest felt tight. He closed his eyes and tried to review every step he'd taken with the Millet. Had he faulted anywhere? No matter how many times he went through it, he couldn't find that he had. He began to feel better and told himself he shouldn't let himself get so rocked off balance by the police. He'd expected an investigation and questions out of the blue, and they hadn't got anything out of him. How could they hope to disprove his story about taking a walk on the beach to get control of his grief?

His phone rang. He picked up the receiver. "Yes?"

"Sir, it's Brian Grey, sir."

"Yes?"

"That painting that was up for auction that you are buying and took home. The one called *Cape Cod Blue*?"

"What about it, Brian? I'm quite busy right now."

"Yes, sir. I'm sorry, Mr. Morse. But we just had a phone call from the lawyer for the estate that sent it in for auction."

"They want their money, I take it. Call them back and tell them the check's on the way. If the stupid idiot read the newspapers, he'd know we've been having a big headache this past few days."

"Yes, sir. But it's not about payment, sir. He says he doesn't want it sold. It has to be auctioned."

"He what?"

"Wants it auctioned, sir."

"Did you tell him Bouchard thinks it might never reach its reserve?"

"Yes, sir. But he says that doesn't matter. The lady whose estate it belonged to specifically ordered that all her personal jewelry and artwork be auctioned. The lawyer said he can't disobey the wording of her will. He said if you can't comply, he'll be obliged to withdraw it from Carlyle and give it to Christies or Sotheby's. I spoke to Mr. Bouchard, sir, and he said you'll have to bring the painting back. It's due to be auctioned the day after tomorrow."

TWENTY-NINE

Thursday July 21st. Police Detective Georgina White felt embarrassingly overdressed. From movies and television, she'd expected the afternoon auction of nineteenth-century paintings at Carlyle to be a glamorous red-carpet affair with celebrities abounding, the way she'd always seen them at auctions in the movies. She'd visualized eager fans crowding the entrance to Carlyle House and clamoring for autographs while inside uniformed flunkies served tulip glasses of expensive French champagne. She'd worn an attractive scoop-necked cocktail frock she'd stitched up herself from a *Vogue* pattern book, put on some gold and cut-glass jewelry which looked expensive and wasn't, and had been especially careful with her makeup and hair. One for our side, she thought, smiling at the dark face which smiled back at her from her mirror, and at the stunning figure shown to best advantage by the frock.

When she'd told Klein the night before that she was planning to attend the auction, he'd assumed the expression of mock incredulity he always managed when she came up with the unusual and said, "So nice to hear you in a jocular mood, Georgie."

He was enjoying his usual hunched-over-his-notes position at his desk, his knees pressed up under its center drawer, and she'd given him her most practiced scathing look before she turned her back in a manner calculated to depreciate him and elevate herself, and to reply, laughing, "Aaron, we're not all slobs who trash the better things in life."

He'd snorted in response. "Be sure you let me know how you make out bidding for hot clues, if any."

"You'll be the first to hear."

She didn't tell him that she hadn't planned to attend the auction as a cop, but as a private person. Finding out that there was one at Carlyle that afternoon, she'd seized on the chance to satisfy an unrequited curiosity she'd always had about how the auction process worked.

Now she wished she never had. There weren't any celebrities, just very ordinary-looking people, almost all of them white and of differing ages and dressed in the most ordinary of clothes, making the only dressed-up person herself. There were no eager demanding fans with thrust-out autograph books, only a bored looking gardener watering some of the flowers at the foot of the La Chaise statue. And once she was inside, she saw no uniformed flunkies serving champagne.

In the spacious front lobby, she went to the long counter and found a catalog for the auction she would be attending. It listed all the paintings to be auctioned and with those considered most important favored with pictures, the very best ones in color. Glancing through it, she went to the wide central reception desk and asked one of the receptionists where the auction was being held. Clearly not being recognized from her previous visits to Carlyle House with Klein—*I'm out of context*, Georgie thought—she was given a condescending look and referred to a sign on the counter that said "19th Century Paintings, Rm 3, 2nd Floor."

Heading for the escalator, she followed two frumpy-looking middle-aged women whose very appearance, she decided, labeled them as antique dealers.

Going up, she realized Room 3 couldn't be the main auction room. She'd been in that place with Klein and had been duly impressed with its palatial size, its high sculpted ceiling, its paneled walls frescoed with representations of the many different epochs of art from the medieval through the renaissance, the romantic, the impressionists, and the moderns. She'd even made a quick sketch of the room, noting the ornate gold-embossed columns flanking the podium where the polished mahogany lectern was emblazoned with the Carlyle coat of arms and which looked down at rows of red velvet theater seats set on deep pile carpeting.

She was right. Arriving at the second floor, she followed the two women, who obeyed a second standing sign saying "Auction" over a black arrow pointing down the wide hall. Just outside double doors, which opened onto a large bare room where a dozen rows of folding chairs faced a slightly raised podium with a quite ordinary undecorated oak lectern, there was a table behind which were seated two unglamorous-looking people, a man and a woman wearing business suits. Before them was a registration book, the open pages of which were already filled with names and addresses. On the desk also was a stack of book-size white cards, each with a big red block number.

Georgie took the lead of the two frumpy ladies who registered and were given cards, one with the number 152, the other getting number 153. Presented with number 154, Georgie gave her name and home address and then went through the double doors into the auction room, where she found an aisle seat about halfway to the podium.

Waiting for the auction to begin and as the room began to slowly fill up, she picked up from the conversation of others that this was indeed, as she had quickly guessed, a relatively minor affair. The auction room in which she sat was reserved for secondary works of limited importance. The principal auction room was for more glamorous events, such as she had imagined, and entrance was usually only by invitation. In it were auctioned great, near priceless paintings by renowned masters such as Picasso, or Monet, Rembrandt, and Van Gogh, which sometimes sold for anywhere from twenty-five to over a hundred million dollars. The auction today was to be presided over by young Brian Grey and not by DeWitt Bouchard, who must, she considered, have decided it was below his exalted level, as the reserves of most of the items in the catalog were in the two- to six-thousand-dollar range. This was because they were either the work of relatively unimportant artists, the entire collection of a minor estate, works attributed to someone better known while not assured to be, or simply works that were unsigned and unidentified.

She had missed seeing everything to be auctioned. They had been on display in an adjoining room for much of the previous week but were now unceremoniously stacked for bidding in a small anteroom, to be brought out one by one in their catalog order by porters. There were some one hundred and fifty items in all to be auctioned—oil paintings, watercolors, and lithographs—and Georgie thumbed through the catalog slowly, deciding which ones she would buy if she'd come here for that and if she could afford it, which of course she couldn't.

A bustle on the podium made her look up. Brian Grey had appeared and was talking to the head porter. A young woman with an open ledger book and a file had seated herself at a small table to one side. Two other people wearing headsets and with notebooks and pens had entered to stand just off the podium at the end of the first row of folding chairs. A technician appeared at the lectern to adjust a mike and a reading light. There was suddenly sound from the podium microphone as Brian Grey stepped up and tapped it with a pencil and then, looking very much in charge and quite a different person than when Georgie and Klein had interviewed him, began to speak.

"Good afternoon, ladies and gentlemen. Welcome to Carlyle House and today's auction of intermediate-range nineteenth-century paintings and lithographs—a very lovely collection I might add. My name is Brian Grey, and I am your auctioneer. I'm sure you will want to get started without further ado, so here we go."

He nodded at the head porter. Almost immediately another

porter appeared carrying a landscape, which he held up for all to see. Simultaneously, Brian clicked on a power-point presentation and a large blowup of the painting appeared on a wall screen behind him.

"A landscape by the Pre-Raphaelite John Everett Millais. A lovely work, mildly crackled and only slightly damaged in the extreme lower right corner. We'll start, please, with a thousand. Do I hear a thousand? One thousand dollars?"

A hand in the audience held up a card, its numbers facing him. He nodded and said, "I hear a thousand, do I hear twelve hundred?" Another card went up. "I have twelve hundred here. Twelve hundred. It's worth twice that. Come, come. Do I hear thirteen? Thirteen?"

From there it went rapidly to twenty-nine hundred. "Do I hear three thousand?" Brian looked from one bidder to another. "No? Three thousand? No? To this gentleman, then, at twenty-nine hundred."

He struck the lectern with his gavel. The woman at the desk on the podium noted the sale in her ledger book. The man who had won the bidding rose from his seat and began to exit the room. Almost simultaneously, a porter appeared carrying another painting which was also projected onto the screen behind Brian. "Number 2 in the catalog, ladies and gentlemen. This lovely eighteenth-century English landscape by Thomas Girtin. Only slightly damaged. I want fifteen hundred for it to start. Fifteen hundred. Yes, sir. Two thousand?"

Cards went up rapidly. When the gavel struck the lectern, the painting sold for four thousand five hundred.

Georgie was fascinated. Time flew. Before she knew it, thirty-nine works of art had been auctioned, and bidding had started on number 40. She looked in her catalog. Number 41 was a painting in an antique frame that showed a woman and child in a Victorian beach scene and was called *Cape Cod Blue*. The catalog said it was unsigned, but that its artist was thought to be an American woman. Georgie, who thought it especially lovely, also noted that the reserve price on the painting was three thousand dollars.

Nine flights above Georgie, Chase sat in his office, telephone in hand, also looking at the catalog. Via a wall speaker of the sound system connected to the auction room below, he could hear every word spoken by Brian Grey. Try as he could, he was finding it nearly impossible not to let his nerves get the better of him. In the two days since the call from Brian, he had hardly slept. The thought that the Millet and all it represented to him could be put at possible risk by being publicly auctioned was an almost inconceivable nightmare. At one point he had almost decided to see if he himself couldn't separate the two paintings. He'd even taken from the Barney's Box the bulky frame he'd purchased to accommodate both. But at the last moment sanity had prevailed. He had no expertise and could ruin everything by trying to. He'd put the frame back in the box and the box back on its closet shelf. In desperation he'd started to call an independent art restorer to find out what the solvent was that could dissolve the plastic shield protecting the Millet from the *Cape Cod Blue*'s canvas, and where he could buy some, but caution and sanity prevailed and he'd desisted. But again, there were too many chances he might do the Millet serious damage if he didn't use the solvent correctly. Tormented almost beyond reason, he'd been forced to accept the nasty turn of fate the auction represented.

Resignation had brought to him a certain degree of calm. He'd begun to ask himself why he was so nervous. Nothing could go wrong. Someone else would be bound to want the *Cape Cod Blue*—that was natural—and would bid on it, but everyone had their limit and he'd simply outbid whomever it was. The reserve was three thousand. There was virtually no possibility that the bidding would exceed that amount by more than a thousand dollars.

Now, however, with the auction actually in process and the *Cape Cod Blue* about to appear for bidding, and no matter with what rational assurance he applied to his thinking, his nerves had erupted again, and once more fear knotted his stomach.

Downstairs, Lindsey, the young woman who had accompanied Brian Grey when he discovered the Millet missing, was acting as Chase's surrogate. She spoke into the mike of her headset. "It's coming up now, sir."

Brian Grey brought the gavel down on number 40, and a porter appeared with the copy of the *Cape Cod Blue* painted by Jason Olenski in the frame Chase had bought as Chase, upstairs, smiled to himself wondering what the audience would think if they knew it was covering the world famous Millet.

Georgie felt a little thrill run through her. The beach scene painting in actuality was far more appealing than its picture. It had a kind of magnetism that made it hard to look away from it. She didn't know why. It just did. She thought how wonderful it would be to own it.

"Here's a lovely painting by an unknown. We believe the artist was a woman. No, it's not a Cassat, but it slightly has her style and magnetism. I'm starting at fifteen hundred, do I hear fifteen hundred? Thank you, Madam, do I hear two thousand?"

A sharp-faced, middle-aged woman, wearing a wide sun hat guaranteed to block the view of the auctioneer by anyone behind her, raised her card. She was seated three seats away from Georgie.

"Two thousand. Do I hear three? Three thousand?"

Upstairs, Chase frowned. He'd play it safe and stop the bidding right now. He barked into his phone. "Bid thirty-five."

Lindsey, nodded at Brian who called out the bid, then deliberately jacked it a thousand higher.

"Thirty-five, then. Thirty-five hundred. Do I hear forty-five? Forty-five, please."

Brian looked around complacently. It was a good price for the painting. It was an exceptionally nice piece of work, too.

But it was unsigned. There was little chance anyone would want to top that bid.

The lady with the hat raised her card again. Number 167.

Brian tried to hide his surprise. "Forty-five hundred here. Forty-five. Do I hear fifty-five?"

Above, Chase sat bolt upright in his chair. "Fifty-five."

In the auction room, Lindsey nodded at Brian Grey.

Seriously puzzled now, the auctioneer said, "I have fifty-five. Do I hear Six? Six thousand?"

The lady with the hat raised her card again.

"Six thousand, six".

Incredulous, Chase said, "Go to seven."

"Seven thousand. I have seven thousand. Madam? Eight thousand? Yes? I have eight, thousand. Eight thousand."

Chase snarled at his phone. "Who the hell is bidding against me?" It was beyond his comprehension.

"I don't know, sir," Lindsey said. "Some lady with a big hat."

"Jesus fucking Christ. Go to nine."

"Yes, sir."

Lindsey nodded at Grey. "Nine thousand."

"I have nine thousand. Nine. Do I hear ten?"

Number 167 went up again.

Chase had begun to sweat. Something was very wrong. The worst scenario imaginable had happened. He should have had the painting for four or at the most five thousand. Was he being set up? He couldn't imagine how or why, or by whom. Or was the woman crazy? It was unthinkable that she might go any higher. His outbidding her could raise embarrassing questions as to why he had. Voice hoarse with anger, he told Lindsey to keep bidding.

At the lectern Brian also struggled to comprehend. Who on earth was this woman? And why was Chase bothering with the damn thing? Surely he could find something else for his wife's birthday because that's what he'd let out he was going to do with it. And a new fear struck him. Was he himself going to be blamed by Chase for this?

The room, also sensing something odd in the bidding, was beginning to murmur its excitement.

"I'm bid ten thousand five. Am I bid eleven? Yes? Eleven it is. Am I bid twelve? Twelve thousand, yes? Thank you." And getting the nod from a wide-eyed Lindsey, "Thirteen thousand. Thirteen I'm bid thirteen."

Brian looked down at Chase's tormentor. For a moment her head was bent forward. All he could see was her hat. Then she raised her sharp face. She had eyes like a weasel, he thought. Her card shot up, clutched at the bottom by heavily jeweled fingers. A vulgarly large diamond on one flashed in the light. So that was it, he thought. A rich kook. Reeking of money and not to be outbid by anyone. DeWitt had always warned him that there were people like that. If she'd seen the painting in an antique store, she probably never would have given it a second glance. She was bidding only because challenged. He remembered now the way she'd raised her card on the first bid. She had barely lifted it and without even looking up, bidding simply for the sake of bidding. Bad luck for Chase. For the first and only time ever, he felt sorry for his boss. The feeling quickly disappeared, however, when he reminded himself that auctioning was gambling. Chase must have been prepared for something like this. Besides, Chase probably had more money by far than his unexpected adversary in the ridiculous hat.

The bidding continued. "I have fourteen. Fourteen thousand."

And went on upward. The room fell into a dead silence. People held their breath.

Then, when it reached seventeen thousand five hundred dollars, it stopped abruptly. Without a glance at the podium and Brian Grey, the woman suddenly rose and stalked out of the room, her face a pinched mask of hate and her body rigid with anger at having been outdone.

With a nearly audible sigh of relief, Brian banged down his gavel and Lindsey reported success to Chase over her phone.

Slowly the talk that had exploded the moment the woman in the hat left the room died away. A porter brought out another painting.

"Lot 42. I'm starting at fifteen hundred. Do I have sixteen. Thank you. Seventeen?"

Upstairs Chase sagged back in his chair. Cold sweat bathed his drawn face and trickled from his underarms down over his sides. His heart was pounding and he felt sick. He signaled Lindsey. No answer. Strung out by stress and frightened by the fury in Chase's voice, his cursing at the woman in the hat and at her and Brian and at everyone else, she'd taken off her headset and fled the auction room to her own small office to wonder if she'd still be employed the next day.

Chase leaned across his desk and rasped into his speaker phone, "Alice!" When her brittle voice answered, he said. "Get hold of Brian Grey. I want the name and address of that bitch who decided to see how far she could work me overbidding for a small painting I wanted."

Without waiting for an answer, he slammed down the phone. Who she was didn't matter. He'd make her pay for it if it was the last thing he ever did. She'd pay, but good. Sound roared in his head, and the whole side of his face felt like it was jumping loose from his skull. He went to his side table and poured himself a stiff vodka and took it back to his desk, steadying one hand with his other so he could get the glass to his lips.

Cursing the woman, cursing Darwin, who had got him into such a mess, he sat silently letting the vodka begin to take hold. Slowly his face stopped jumping, the noise in his head ebbed to a murmur, his sweat dried. Well, he'd done it, hadn't he? He had the goddamned Millet and he was going to ransom it for eighty million, and what's more, get it. He'd square with Carlyle so nobody would ever know he'd borrowed that amount from the stupid place and come after him. Then he'd walk out the door and never come back.

Meanwhile he also had the silly little painting over the

Millet. In his mind he saw himself hanging it up over the mantel in place of Darwin's hated men-o'-war and saying, "Here, Felicity. Present for you."

He laughed out loud at that. He couldn't help it and couldn't stop. Telling Felicity he'd paid seventeen thousand five hundred bucks for a present for her when she would have been lucky if he spent seventeen.

In her office just past the conference room, Alice Marks heard his laughter and wondered.

Leaving the auction, Georgie also wondered. In spite of her exterior—the smart frock, jewelry, and makeup—inside, she was still Detective Georgina White. Something had come unglued during the auction, she was sure of it. Once, briefly, she'd caught a look of near panic on the face of the auctioneer. And the girl with the headset seemed beside herself with stress, almost near tears.

Who was she bidding for who could do that to her? And to the auctioneer? Could it have been her boss, Chase Morse? The thought came to her quite suddenly. Who else, she asked herself, would have instilled such anxiety? And, if so, why was he bidding so high on a painting that in the catalog only had a reserve price of three thousand? Time would tell, she thought. Things had a way of surfacing.

She went to the Ninety-Second Street Y to save herself the long trip home and changed her clothes so Klein wouldn't see her dressed up and rag her about it for the next six months. Then she headed back to the office. On the way she passed an expensive art gallery that specialized in premodern painting. Looking at two eighteenth-century landscapes in the window, she saw beyond them in the gallery itself a gray-bearded scholarly-looking older man who was just seeing a client to the door.

On a sudden impulse and wishing she hadn't changed clothes, she entered the gallery, and when he returned she asked if he might have a moment to answer a question or two.

"Of course, madam. My pleasure."

Almost thirty minutes later she left the gallery, seen to the door by the proprietor, who bade her good-bye warmly. She went directly back to the office. Klein was still there, at his computer in his shirtsleeves.

"Well?" Klein said.

"It was interesting."

"Learn anything?"

"Maybe."

Klein groaned inwardly. That damn "maybe" again. But he knew better than to pursue it. Georgie was like that, he reminded himself, keeping things under wraps until she was sure they were worth bringing out. He only had to be patient.

While Georgie was settling back to police work at her own desk, Angela Rodriguez, across the East River in the Bronx, was just starting night duty. She left the women's locker room at precinct headquarters where she'd donned her uniform and all the gear she carried, stopped by the desk sergeant to see what car she was assigned, and headed out to the parking lot. On the way, she paused to say hello to Mary Hodder, who was studying a report.

"Okay sweetheart, don't go breaking your brains. They only robbed Fort Knox, right?"

Mary put down the report and said, "A pushcart, actually. And for all of three bucks fifty."

"The world's full of the poor robbing the poor."

"Angela, I've got a problem."

"Caught between two lovers again?"

Mary laughed. "No way. Seriously, it's that painting you described to me the other day, remember? The one of the beach with a woman and a child under a parasol."

"Sure. And?"

"Angela, I can't get it out of my mind. It's like some old song that you keep humming to yourself over and over again and just can't let go. I know that sometime or other I either saw that painting or a picture of it, but I can't remember when or where. It's driving me bonkers."

Angela slid her rump, gun and all, onto the corner of Mary's desk. "Have you tried looking for it?"

"You mean like museums?"

"Museums, art books. Maybe poster shops."

"As a matter of fact, I have. From what you said, it was a good painting, so I checked out the Met and a couple of galleries. And I must have looked at a dozen books on art."

"And nothing?"

"Zero."

"Do you get a feeling, Mary, somewhere back in here, maybe," Angela laid one hand against the pony tail that stuck out from under her uniform cap, "that you saw it fairly recently? Or was it way back?"

Mary thought hard a moment. "I'm not sure. But I don't think it was way back."

Angela was silent a moment, staring off into space. Then she said, "You came here about a year ago, right?"

"Yes." Mary waited again. One of the things she'd learned about Angela was that she had a mind where every thought seemed to have a separate compartment. When Angela needed to go over something and make sense of it, she had to proceed item by item, discarding one completely before starting in on the next.

"Well," Angela finally said, "Here's a thought. When you first were assigned to this unit, what did they have you doing?"

"I had to go through all the files and look at pictures of stolen items they were trying to track down and ..." Mary broke off abruptly and stared hard at Angela as realization hit. "Oh, jeepers. Of course."

Without another word, she leapt up from her desk and

ran to one of several tall file cases. Yanking open a drawer, she finger-raced through a score of files, then tackled another drawer. Again no luck. Almost feverishly, she stopped, thought a moment, then went to an adjacent file case, pulled open its middle drawer and began to search again. Angela joined her just as Mary stopped her search and pulled out a file, flipped back a couple of photos and revealed what she was looking for: an eight-by-ten color photo of a Victorian woman and child seated on a white sandy beach under a blue-and-white striped parasol, and looking at a little fishing boat out on the unruffled blue waters of a summer sea.

An attached identity slip said that the name of the painting was *Cape Cod Blue,* artist unknown. It was valued at three thousand dollars and had been stolen from an art gallery in Chicago ten years previous.

THIRTY

On Nantucket in the evening of that same day, Bill Booker sat at the kitchen table over an unfinished after-dinner coffee in his house on Macomet Avenue in Nantucket Town while Ellen and the oldest of his sons loaded the dishwasher. The sun was sinking low over the ocean behind Sankaty Point lighthouse at the eastern tip of the island. From the adjacent living room, there was the muted sound of television being watched by the two younger boys. On the table next to Booker's coffee cup were the several pages of the forensic report on Chase's sea-damaged expensive tasseled shoes along with a half dozen color photos of them. The shoes themselves were locked up as prime evidence in the safe at the police station. The moment Booker had finished eating, he'd taken the papers from his briefcase to study the pictures for the hundredth time.

"You're going to drive yourself nuts," Ellen said, passing behind him with the remains of a risotto-and-scallops mix in a heavy iron casserole, which she put in the fridge for lunch the next day. "I wish you'd call a halt to all that stuff come dinnertime and you're home. Give yourself a break."

She refrained from saying give her a break, too. Since the day Darwin Morse was reported drowned off the end of his dock in the upper harbor, her husband had become so totally absorbed in every aspect of police work involved in a possible homicide that he'd had almost no time for her or his boys.

It was so unlike him. She found herself going to bed alone at night and instead of making love or just side by side reading until it was finally lights out, he'd still be at the kitchen table or in his so-called study, brooding into the small hours and then passing out the moment he hit the sheets. The boys missed him, too. Always, he was such an integral part of their lives, joining them in everything they did the moment his day at the police station was over, but always aiming for her first with the kind of kiss and words he'd never stopped giving her since they were first married, and with all sorts of questions about her day—what she had done, where she had been?—with never a mention of what he himself had been up to.

She came and sat down, had a sip of his coffee, and looked at one of the pictures of the shoes. "Six hundred dollars if they're worth a cent. Gosh. Rich people. Can you imagine yourself buying a pair of shoes for six hundred dollars?"

"You're damned right. Shoes worth six hundred, a convertible Jaguar, a BMW, and a Dassault jet, why not?"

There was a distinctly hollow note to his facetious laughter before he grabbed the coffee cup back from her, and Ellen realized it was the first time she'd ever heard him take a shot at those who were better off than himself and everyone they knew. This Morse guy had really got his goat.

"Seriously, love, are you getting anywhere with them? Or are they a dead end?"

"In this case, nothing is a dead end. I got a call about them again from the New York people."

"And?"

"The detective named White. She's on the Millet robbery. She wanted anything I could give her on Chase Morse's character."

"She thinks he's involved in *that?*"

"The robbery? She certainly does. Then we got onto the shoes. I gave her all the latest on them, the Woods Hole Oceanographic forensic report, the sand and weed in them matching the beach near the Morse home along with the water. All that and the fact that the shoes had only been in the water a short time. She'd questioned Morse herself about them. He'd told her that he'd walked on the beach trying to pull himself together after his old man's death and was so upset he'd forgot they weren't the sneakers he normally would wear. That's pretty much what he told me."

Ellen said. "Sounds phony to me. How do you get your shoes soaked in water when you're walking a beach?"

"Exactly. The New York cop is one bright lady, and she didn't buy it either. But it's a hard one to get around." Booker sighed. "Bloody shoes. Times I wish to God old Asa had left them on the beach where he told the little Morse boy he'd found them. But they're saying something to me I can't quite put my finger on."

"Keep at it," Ellen said. "You will." She rose and kissed the thick dark hair on the top of his head and went into the living room, closing the door behind her to lessen the noise from the TV for him.

Booker poured himself some more coffee and mentally reviewed the interview he'd had with Chase Morse in his father's book-lined study on the ground floor of The Moorings. The evening before Darwin Morse died, Chase Morse said he'd come home too late to see his son on the boy's birthday. The rest of the family, his brother, Haydn, and the two women, the young French girl and his wife, had gone up to bed, leaving Chase alone at the father's request. Chase had been candid. He'd said he and his father had talked about problems at Carlyle and then he'd gone up to bed himself and left his father having a nightcap.

"What sort of problems, Mr. Morse?"

"One with our chief auctioneer, Mr. Bouchard."

"It was a nice night. You didn't go out onto the terrace to talk?"

"Right under the bedroom windows so all could hear? Hardly."

"I understand he loved being down by the grape arbor. You didn't go there?"

"Good heavens, no. At that hour?"

"Of course. I understand, given his health. Tell me, Mr. Morse, I understand you were never very happy about being at Carlyle. You didn't have any sort of dispute over it that evening, any argument?"

"You didn't argue with my father."

"No harsh words you or he didn't want overheard?"

"You didn't raise your voice to him, either."

"You said you didn't see him to bed. Was he capable of doing that himself?"

"Oh, yes. And often does. You've seen the elevator we had installed that took him up from his study to the hall outside his bedroom. And he has a special bathroom enabling him to use the facilities himself."

Booker took the summary of his notes he'd made at the office from his briefcase. In interviewing everyone at The Moorings, he had managed to assemble a picture of a side of Chase Morse quite at odds with the mannered standards and rules of polite behavior in the social world the man championed. From the servants, from Chase's brother, and from his wife, he had gathered that as a child Morse had been indulged beyond reason. But at the same time, if not getting something he wanted, he had often resorted to lying and stealing, for which he was then severely punished by his father. One person after another had also mentioned his almost uncontrollable temper.

"Oh, he always did have a terrible one, Mr. Chase, sir, and still does." That was Perkins, the butler. "Cross him in any way and he goes up the wall with it, Mr. Chase does. Hardly knows what he's about."

The maid Mary and Thomas the chauffeur had virtually said the same thing.

Morse was a man, too, Booker had observed, who was vanity plus. He was meticulous in his dress and grooming and inordinately possessive about any possession, whether his yacht or a key ring; he was a person, also, who didn't seem to care about anyone except himself. It was obvious he had no relationship whatsoever with his wife. According to the New York detective, he habitually consorted with escort service girls. Nor, Booker reflected, had he seen any evidence of affection in the man toward his little boy. The child spoke with great warmth about his uncle but rarely mentioned his father. The heavily lipsticked social lioness, Mrs. Rhinelander, whom Booker found even more arrogant than Morse, had been candid in saying there had been little if any bond at all between Morse and the deceased Darwin. She'd also said that in his childhood, Chase Morse was known to lie constantly to avoid parental wrath and to outwardly maintain an appearance of obedience to his father's wishes no matter how contrary they might have been to his own.

Booker studied the pictures of the shoes again. Walking the beach when distraught and grieving over his father's death simply didn't ring true. There was a lie here, somewhere. But where? And why? He tried to think outside forensic evidence, to force his thinking onto mental attitudes, in a way to become Morse himself. Does a man, who cares little for anyone, grieve to the extent that he hardly knows what he is doing? Does the same man, if not grieving, and meticulously caring of his appearance and clothes, go walking a rocky beach in expensive city shoes?

The answers began to nag insistently—answers, Booker realized, that he'd dismissed on previous evenings of reflection, and it now seemed inexplicable to him as to why he had. Perhaps it was because they were so simple and he'd been searching for complexities.

A grieving man doesn't become enraged. But a man hopelessly suppressed by a tyrannical Darwin Morse might very well do so. *You didn't argue with my father. You didn't raise your voice to him either.*

No, Booker thought. You just silently rage at him the way you rage openly at servants who you feel have crossed you. Until finally the rage boils over and you stumble away along a beach, heedless. Not the next day, when supposedly grieving, but then, and in the darkness of night. Stumbling, running away. But from a verbal row? Hardly. A child, perhaps, but not a grown man: married, a father, and in charge of a major business.

When Ellen came back in, she found Booker once again studying the picture of the shoes. "Oh, good heavens, darling man, still at it?"

"No," Booker said. "It's all over."

"Oh?" Surprised, she sat down. "Meaning?"

Booker smiled at her. "You said it once yourself. *Crime passionelle*. I've got a case of parricide on my hands."

For an instant Ellen Booker simply stared, almost open-mouthed. When she found her voice, she said, "Christ Almighty, Bill! Are you kidding? You're saying Chase Morse murdered his father?"

"Head of the class. I know he did. Except now, all I have to do is prove it."

Four miles away at The Moorings, and an hour later, it was David's bedtime. Felicity always read to him before turning out the light, and she had closed *The Wizard of Oz*, in which Dorothy had just got the Scarecrow down from the pole he was stuck on, when he said suddenly, "Mom, I need to know something."

"Sure. What?" Felicity waited, wondering. From experience she knew that when David said he needed to know something, it was because something quite important had been troubling him, and he usually took some time in getting it out.

David indeed was silent a few moments. That afternoon after lunch, he'd wandered down to the grape arbor where the dock began and where his grandfather had always liked to sit.

There was garden furniture there under the shade of the grape leaves, and he sat in the chair his grandfather had always used before he'd needed a wheelchair and had thought about his drowning the way he did. He hadn't thought about any of that until he'd remembered seeing Grandfather Darwin lying under the water because everyone had told him Grandfather had quietly gone to sleep forever. Now he understood why Chief Booker kept coming around, and the state police, too, and the lady policeman from New York. There wasn't any robber. They all wanted to know what he wanted to know himself—how had grandfather got there?

The question tumbled around in his mind over and over. Grandfather might have wheeled himself across the lawn, but down onto the float? Somebody would have had to help him. And then he remembered that someone had told him they'd seen his father push Grandfather across the lawn the night before he drowned. He tried to remember who and suddenly did. It was Thomas. Thomas said he'd looked out the window when he was going to bed and seen them. So maybe his father pushed Grandfather Darwin down the dock, too, and accidentally Grandfather Darwin had gone off the float. Thinking that, David remembered the time when he had knocked the big crystal vase on the living room table to the floor when he was bouncing a ball off the wall, which wasn't allowed. The vase, which was one of Grandfather Darwin's favorites, had broken to smithereens, and he'd been scared to tell anyone that he'd done it. Maybe that's what had happened on the float. Grandfather Darwin had gone off accidentally and it was his father's fault because he wasn't paying attention and careful enough with the wheelchair and was scared to tell anyone.

Then the thought had come to him that if someone found out, or if his father finally decided to tell that it had been his fault, then Thomas might get in trouble with Chief Booker and the New York police lady for not having said he saw Grandfather going down to the dock with his father. That would have been telling on his father but would have saved them a lot of trouble. And maybe he could keep Thomas out of trouble now by telling his mother or Uncle Haydn what Thomas had said. Except wouldn't that be snitching? And not just on Thomas but on his father as well?

Felicity had nearly dozed off waiting for David, when he suddenly spoke. "Mom, if someone was found lying in the street and someone told you that they had seen a car accidentally knock him over, would it be snitching on the person if you let the police know what they said?"

"No. I don't think so, darling. Why?"

He was silent a moment again. Then he said, "Because Thomas told me something that maybe he didn't want me to tell anyone else."

"And Thomas would be mad at you if you did?"

"Well, yes, because that would be snitching, wouldn't it? And Thomas is my friend. He let me sit in the Jaguar one day with him."

Felicity thought a moment. What on earth was he getting at? It couldn't be all that serious. Boys David's age had different ideas than grownups about what was serious. She said, "David, do you trust me enough to tell me and let me judge whether or not it should go any further?"

"You mean let you decide whether what Thomas said he saw should stay a secret?"

"Yes."

"Well, okay."

"So what did he see?"

"Well, he was going to bed the night before Grandpa drowned. And he saw Daddy pushing Grandpa Darwin down across the lawn to the grape arbor."

Something in Felicity froze. "When did Thomas tell you this?"

"Last week."

"Did he see Daddy bring Grandfather Darwin back again?"

"No. He didn't wait. But I began to think that maybe Daddy took Grandfather onto the dock, too, and was careless and accidentally let Grandpa roll off the float, and when he couldn't get him back up was scared to tell anyone. And if Chief Booker and the lady policewoman from New York knew what Thomas had seen and hadn't told anyone because he was scared of snitching on Daddy, they might get really mad at him."

Felicity would never know how she had got through the next few minutes reassuring David and trying to keep her own terror from showing. She had seen Chase coming up from the dock at dawn, and Thomas had seen him wheeling Darwin down late at night, but never dreaming of what she knew Chase had done and saying nothing to the police for fear of Chase and losing his job. There had been no report of anyone else around the property or in the harbor at that time, and David had changed her, not daring to tell anybody except Gabrielle. What he said, along with what she could, was enough for the police to arrest her husband. Chase had lied; he'd told the police that he'd left his father in the living room to put himself to bed.

After she'd kissed David good night and turned out the lights, she went directly to her room. She didn't like to break faith with her son, but he didn't ever have to know. In her handbag, she found Chief Booker's card on which he'd written his cell phone number.

She sat for a long time with the bedside phone in her hand, just staring at it. If she called, she might be putting David and herself at a terrible risk if Chase could somehow prove innocence. If she didn't call, and Chase wasn't arrested, wouldn't both she and David still be at risk? If Chase could murder his father, what about his wife and child? But was that foolish? They weren't the same threat as Darwin to Chase. Or were they?

She thought hard about Chase: the enormously wealthy head of a great corporation, his business life, his connections everywhere, even in politics. And she thought about him as lord and master of The Moorings. With Darwin gone, everything in the future, when it came to herself and David, would be Chase. She thought about Chase's eyes, and the twitching muscle in his cheek that day on the *South Wind* just before he hit her, and then the night before Darwin had died.

She dialed Chief Booker's number.

THIRTY-ONE

In the small back-room office of his shop, Haydn put his telephone down on his desk amidst a clutter of family photos and mementos. It took a minute or two for him to calm himself. Chase did that to him, almost always: the patronizing words and condescending tone of voice, the refusal to compromise or see the other side of things even with the most minor of issues, the vision, if you were on the phone, that his voice conjured up of the smug, always-right half-smile, as though you were a child unaware of adult realities. Except for the fact that Chase was family, he wouldn't have bothered to speak a single word to him for the past two years. And he wouldn't now if it weren't for David and Felicity.

He had put off calling him for several days. But family affairs could not always be ignored. A decision had to be made about what to put on Darwin's headstone. The stonecutter had called twice about it, saying he needed to get it done right away or else he would have to postpone the job for probably three or four months. He had other pressing orders. Darwin, who had left no instructions, had often said he wanted only his name, date of birth and death, and a brief quote that would summarize his life. Haydn had wrestled endlessly with one quote after another and, when none suited Chase, had hoped to find some clue as to what Darwin might like among the mass of papers in his study. But Chase had arbitrarily taken all that the police had finished with, without consulting anyone.

Haydn berated himself for having called. He should have known that he'd get nowhere. Chase's response had been that nothing would be forthcoming until he had been through all the papers himself, and up to now he hadn't had time. If the stonecutter couldn't wait, they would find someone who would. Halfway through the conversation, he had given up. He'd find a quote somehow, order it up without consulting Chase and let the chips fall where they would.

While Haydn had been getting La Rive Gauche together and turning it from just another bookshop that would be bound to go under in the face of Amazon or Barnes and Noble, he had reluctantly worked part-time as a fine-art appraiser at Carlyle when Darwin made that available to him. When Darwin turned Carlyle over to Chase, he'd continued the job, against his better judgment, and no matter how galling it was, but he'd only been able to stick to it a month. Chase had immediately begun using his CEO position to openly express sibling resentments he should have abandoned when both left their childhood behind, and Haydn found himself thrust back into a past he'd abandoned when he'd chosen a different life. It made even being in the same building with Chase intolerable. Worse, it made him feel he'd betrayed himself.

Now, over the phone, when Chase asked him when he was going up to The Moorings next, and he told him he planned to leave that evening, he carefully refrained from telling Chase why he was going. This time it wasn't to see David or Felicity, but to see Selma—sadly perhaps for the last time because she was moving to Vancouver and was paying The Moorings a final visit. When she had called him yesterday, she had begged him to come out and had mysteriously said she had some vital information about his father that she didn't want to share on the telephone.

It was Friday, and Haydn dreaded the long drive in summer weekend traffic. He'd not asked for a ride in the jet, and his reluctance was justified when Chase had told him, "I'd say come along with me, but I'm not going up this weekend, and I've given the crew time off." Then, before hanging up, he had said, "I understand your little French girl is still around, Haydn. Sexy little number. Bet she can really put out, you lucky dog. Maybe you'd like to be generous and suggest to her she'd enjoy having dinner with me sometime."

"I don't think so, Chase. Anyway, she's at The Moorings."

"Oh?" Chase laughed. "Without you? That's a little forward of her, isn't it? What's she doing up there, anyway? Thought her story or whatever she was doing was finished?"

"She's helping out."

"Really. Earning her keep, is she? I would have thought Felicity could have managed, but I suppose not, being what she is."

Haydn had ended the call as quickly as possible.

But it wasn't easy to calm himself. His brother's insulting comments about Gabrielle surpassed all decency in their vulgarity. To speak that way of any woman was disgraceful, but about Gabrielle, of all people, the loveliest of women due only the greatest respect, it was inconceivable. For a while he sat numbly staring first at the telephone, then at nothing, then seeing Gabrielle in his mind: her hair, the lovely lines of her face, the warmth in her eyes, her softly accented voice, the clothes she wore, her mildly fragrant perfume, the narrow silver bracelets on her right arm, her slender artistic hands, always so expressive when she spoke.

Then, remembrance of something suddenly surfaced from the back of his mind, and guilt struck him so quickly that it suffused his limbs, making them feel like water. What could he ever do to make up for the insult that he himself had given her? After the funeral, when he'd had to rush back to New York, he had completely ignored that she was a journalist representing one of France's great weeklies, and had forced her into the uncomfortable position of having to choose between her profession and all the sensitive feelings he knew she had about his family. When he'd asked her to look after things in his absence, it hadn't really been a request. It had been a presumption on his part that she'd say yes, and had to have seemed virtually an order, as though she was a poor relative or a servant rather than the woman whom he loved and had thought about every waking hour since they met. Almost worse than his insult was her angry retort. Reminding him that she was there only professionally was the proof he'd feared for so long: that she had none of the same feelings about him that he had about her. Unthinkingly, he had forever closed a door on any hope he might ever have. It made the pain of her going back to France even more unbearable.

Haydn's thoughts were interrupted by his young assistant needing help in the shop. Then, suddenly, it was four o'clock, and he'd decided to fly to Nantucket. The plane left from La Guardia, and if he hoped to make it to The Moorings by dinnertime, then he'd have to leave right away. He grabbed an overnight bag he'd packed that morning and, turning the shop over to the assistant, he fled, realizing as he did how eager he was to get out of the place. He'd made a success of it—buying from him had almost become a cult with important New York intellectuals, and writers—but he was beginning to find the fame and the cachet not enough to compensate for the endless business of being a shopkeeper with every day like every other day. Often, he found himself missing Carlyle, and there were many moments when he envied Chase a job so varied and so frequently filled with suspenseful excitement.

He caught the last commercial flight of the day to Hyannis on the cape. There, he transferred to an Air Island light plane and the twenty-minute flight to Nantucket, finally getting to the island and then to The Moorings a few minutes before eight. The sun had only just set, and the blue of the sky was beginning to darken, the horizon turning mauve and purple.

He'd called ahead. Thomas met him with the Jaguar, and driving through the gates, there was wrenching sadness at Darwin no longer being there, although at the same time he had the feeling of returning to an island of safety and protection against all the anxieties and worries he'd left behind in New York. Along with his many small business problems, the fate of the Millet was a constant nagging worry. It was profoundly upsetting that such a beautiful and important painting was in the hands of Lord only knew who and endlessly exploited by the media, especially the tabloids, which seemed to appreciate it only for its monetary value.

Pulling up before the house, he got out, but instead of going directly inside, he walked across the croquet lawn to his father's favorite spot at the grape arbor, where the dock began. The calm surface of the harbor had turned silver, and eastward, beyond the cranberry bogs between Polpis and Quidnet, the Sankaty lighthouse had begun to flash its red and white warning. Close to the Coatue sand barrier, where the water was deeper, and downharbor a little ways toward the Town of Nantucket, he could see the *South Wind*. The yacht's mooring line was slack at flood tide, and her halyards were drawn tight and silent until the evening breeze would vibrate them against her tall masts to make a humming sound, and wavelets would begin to lap at her hull, rocking her gently.

Maybe he'd take everyone out for a sail. They could run down the bay and then out to sea around Eel Point and Madaket Bay and head for Martha's Vineyard, eat a lobster dinner at Menemsha Bight, and perhaps spend the night on the boat. David would love that.

Reluctantly, he turned away from the view and headed back to house and the terrible sense of rejection and defeat he knew he would feel the moment he laid eyes on Gabrielle.

THIRTY-TWO

He reached the terrace and went into the living room through the French doors. The lights were on now, the room intimate. Perkins was in the hallway door with a bowl of fresh ice and a formal "Good evening, Mr. Morse." David was suddenly there, too, wrapping his thin arms around his legs. "Uncle Hay!" Ecstatic. And then Felicity, her tired face suddenly young with her smile, hugging him close. When she backed off, with laughing questions about his drive up, Haydn, answering, looked beyond her and saw, as she rose from the couch in greeting, the familiar stocky figure in dumpy clothes, the coarse iron-gray hair cut almost like a man's, the ever matriarchal features.

"Selma!" He went to her at once and they embraced. Are you really going to leave us for Vancouver?"

"Afraid so, but not until the cops have done with me."

"Got you sized up, have they?"

Laughter, another embrace. Gabrielle came in from the hall and for an instant, seeing Haydn, just stood in the doorway. She said, "Hi, Haydn," in a forced tone. Haydn had dreaded the moment, and here it was. He felt numb in his whole being and nodded, "Hi. How's journalism?"

"It survives." Gabrielle managed a smile and went to sit in silence next to Felicity.

The tension in the exchange wasn't lost on Selma, who quickly dove in to keep the moment from becoming awkward.

"Well, we have a lot to catch you up on."

She'd hardly spoken when David broke in, too. "Guess what, Uncle Hay. The police came here."

"Chief Booker?"

"No. A lady from the police in New York. She came in a helicopter and landed right on the lawn."

"Detective White," Felicity said. "She was very nice. We gave her lunch. David bombarded her with questions."

"I asked her if she carried a gun," David said. "And she said sometimes."

"She told him lots of police stories."

"Once she had a robber shoot at her, and she said when she went to police school she had to do all the obstacle course things the men did."

"She did better than that," Felicity added. "She persuaded the helicopter pilot to let David sit in his seat."

When David had wound down a little and Felicity had sent him off to wash his hands before dinner, Haydn asked what the New York police expected to find on Nantucket.

"They wanted a statement from me and Gabrielle," Felicity replied.

"About what?"

"Anything either of us might know about Carlyle, which isn't much." She laughed. "It was a little embarrassing She particularly asked me when I had last seen Chase. I had to tell her that he hadn't been home since the funeral, and then she wanted to know if he'd called, or if he'd been acting strangely in any way."

"And what did you say to that?" Haydn's memory flicked back to the two officers who had come to his shop, a graying detective who had seasoned professional written all over him, and a young black woman who was not only very pretty but had struck him as being particularly strong and confident. Both had been extremely courteous as well as intelligent.

"I told her I hadn't noticed," Felicity replied matter-of-factly.

From the moment she had spoken to Chief Booker, she had made up her mind not to tell anyone that she had. If her information and suspicions turned out not to be valid, she would have alarmed everyone for no reason. Chase might hear of it, too and somehow David might also get wind of it. She didn't want that for him. It could frighten him badly. If she were right, they would hear it soon enough from the police anyway. With Chase arrested, the boy would have to feel less vulnerable. It was a bridge crossed and she felt a new woman because of it. What would be, would be.

Felicity's good humor and firmness caught Haydn by surprise. Something in her had changed since he'd last seen her. It was as though a heavy burden had been lifted from her. She was more like the Felicity he remembered years ago when she first came into the family and before his brother's obvious disdain had worn down the charming and innocently open young woman whose presence was always like a breath of fresh air.

Before anyone could talk more, Perkins announced dinner, during which there was David's chatter and, among the grown-ups, Haydn catching up on family news, the others catching up on his. Gabrielle did her best to seem at ease, while on his part Haydn tried hard not to think that this might well be almost the last dinner he would have with her.

Afterward, and when Felicity had got David to bed, there was coffee and liqueur in the living room.

"Okay," Haydn said, "Where were we with this police business?"

"I think, actually," Felicity replied, "the reason the detective came up here was not to talk to me or Gabrielle but to see Selma."

"Felicity's right," the older woman said. I told her, however, that I didn't want to talk to her until I'd talked to you first. So I'm seeing her Tuesday."

"Haydn," Felicity said, "Selma wants your permission to reveal something to them."

"Mine?"

Selma smiled slightly at his puzzlement "Yes. Because what you answer could affect the whole family for a long time. I told Gabrielle what it was when I was still in New York, but before I did I made her give me her word she'd never mention it to a living soul, not even to you. And I'm sure that wasn't easy for her."

Haydn looked at Gabrielle, who met his eyes and said, "I'm sorry, Hay."

Felicity broke in, "We told the policewoman, and she said we'd made her trip up doubly worthwhile."

"Wait a minute," Haydn said. He felt a surge of sudden anger and couldn't hide it. Selma, Gabrielle? Probably Felicity, too. And the cops. What the hell was going on, some sort of conspiracy of women? He had the uncomfortable feeling of being an outsider. "Nice of you to include me," he said. "Never mind. I can read it in *France Aujourd'hui*."

It came out of him before he could stop it, and was the worst thing he could have said. Gabrielle, only barely hanging on in her unhappiness, bristled defensively to hold back tears. "I beg your pardon."

Selma saw an unnecessary storm brewing. "Stop it, both of you," she snapped. "Haydn, please. This is no time for false pride. Or insults. Gabrielle has enough inside information about this family she has never disclosed, nor ever will, to fill the Nantucket Harbor. Gabrielle, don't go French temper on us."

Gabrielle sank back on the couch from which she had partially risen. And with difficulty Haydn forced his mind back onto Selma's needing his permission to say something to the police. Why his? What on earth was it all about? Did she know something about the robbery? How could she? He had a sickening sense that it was bad and forced himself to seem reasonable. He glanced once at Gabrielle, who averted her eyes. He took a breath and said, "All right, go ahead."

"Thank you, Haydn. It's this. We're almost certain your brother had his hand in Carlyle's pension fund. We also think he was probably in it with Karl. He invested what he filched in Russian oil, expecting to clean up. And didn't. Putin seized the oil fields."

"Holy smoke. How much?"

"Eighty million."

There was a dead silence as Haydn absorbed it and grasped at the consequences. Then the unthinkable struck him. He looked hard at Selma. "I see. And are you thinking what I'm thinking?"

"I probably am and wish I wasn't."

"That the Millet would be a way to pay it back?"

"Yes, crazy as it seems. It's hard not to think so, isn't it? Ransoming it could solve all his problems."

"His, maybe. Not ours," Haydn said.

Selma said, "I didn't want to have such an idea, and I'm sure you didn't either. But it shouts, so you can't avoid it. The police will come up with it, I should think, and quickly, too, if I tell them about his embezzlement." She added, "I'm sorry to say this, Haydn. Chase is your brother, but the Chase I know and worked for is more than capable of it."

"I wish you'd told me this before, Selma. Why didn't you? Why did you hide it from me and tell the police and Gabrielle? This is a family matter. Why?"

"I didn't because I thought it so awful. I didn't want to hurt you. I suppose I thought somehow he'd work it out."

There was a stifled sound from Gabrielle who rose suddenly, muttered, "Excuse me," and left the room. Felicity called after her, then followed.

"That was cruel of you, Haydn," Selma said.

"How, what?"

"Insinuating Gabrielle isn't part of all this, not family."

"Well, she's not, is she?"

Selma took a deep breath, "Haydn, do stop it. Please. I can read you like a book. When I sat up there in the ivory tower that was your father's office, I watched you stagger your way through several affairs and if I know one thing in this world that I am dead certain of, I know when Haydn Morse is in love. And Haydn, don't throw love away. It's the most precious quality we humans possess. Since Gabrielle came here, you've been getting *France Aujourd'hui*. Have you ever read anything about Carlyle or this family that revealed anything but what everybody knew anyway? Have you never thought that she might have risked her job by not doing so? Or wondered why she hasn't? And if you think she's still here because she's interested in the Morse millions or social prestige or any such nonsense, think again. She doesn't give a damn about all that, in fact doesn't much like it. So what's she here for? She finished up her story about all of us long ago."

Before she had finished, Haydn began to feel the pain of realizing he'd again bitterly hurt someone he loved and cared about more than anyone or anything. He sat silent, unable to speak.

There was more Selma could have said. But she didn't. There were limits to what you could say without possibly doing serious injury to a person's pride. Especially to Haydn, who, she sensed, had suffered more in growing up with Darwin as a father and Ariel as a mother than anyone ever suspected, yet had never succumbed and had had the guts to strike out on his own.

Instead she said, "And there are other things you ought to know, Haydn. You ought to know that your father saw through Chase. Oh, yes. He certainly did. He saw exactly what sort of a cold, merciless, and utterly selfish person Chase is. Behind all his bluster and hard-nosed authority, Darwin had a decent side he kept from most people. He hated Chase's bigotry and intolerance, Chase's always regarding as nonentities or worse, people less fortunate than himself. He handed Carlyle over to Chase because you had gone off on your own, and he honestly thought you wouldn't want it. And you also ought to know that he appreciated that. A chip off the old block, Haydn, he once said to me. Doing his own thing."

Haydn said, "Did he know about the money?"

"That Chase had filched it? Yes. I told him. The day before he died. I dreaded doing so, but your father and I always had an open and frank relationship. I couldn't hide from him anything that might seriously endanger Carlyle. I knew what he'd think. He'd think what Chase had done was unforgivable, that Chase had betrayed a sacred trust to look after the Carlyle that he himself had held during his whole life. Chase was coming home for Sunday, and he planned to have it out with him."

"And did he?"

Haydn's eyes silently held hers. She finally looked away and with a helpless gesture said, "I don't know, Haydn. I just don't know. Felicity is certain he did."

"And?"

The question hung there. The older woman stared at Haydn. He stared back. Neither could manage to say what they couldn't help but think. Darwin had exposed knowledge of his son's theft to him and the next morning was found dead. Haydn broke first. He sat down and buried his head in his hands, trying to stifle what he felt: pain, now not just because of Gabrielle but also because of Chase. His brother, his own flesh and blood, was a criminal who had given lip service and clichéd platitudes to family and honor and social obligation while all the time he betrayed: betrayed a great family heritage, betrayed the love and respect given him, betrayed his wife with cheap little escort girls, betrayed his mother's memory with bigotry and class hatred, betrayed his father's trust and confidence in him with theft and lying, betrayed the great auction house that had been, and still was, the heart and soul of the Morse family for five generations, and in all that, had betrayed the place that had been home to all of them, the anchor for all their lives, The Moorings.

He tried not to think of the horror that kept thrusting itself into his mind, struggled not to accept the dark vision of Chase and his father having it out: Chase being forced to face up to what he had done, Darwin not letting him lie his way out of something the way he always had because this time the something was too big for lying.

And then what he was certain had happened next.

He finally rose and refreshed both his and Selma's drinks. He felt almost dead inside and he said, "What's going to happen, Selma? If this all comes out. To Carlyle, to all of us?"

"We'll survive. You'll have to take over Carlyle."

"Me?"

"Of course. Who else? Haydn, Carlyle is family. Just like The Moorings here. You can't let Chase destroy either. And what he's done could well do just that. Have faith in yourself. I do. If you can run a small shop, you can run a big one. And you'll do it a sight better than Chase. You love Carlyle. You love art and auctioning. He doesn't. Never has. You'll have department heads who are unbelievably competent and loyal, and I'll stay east for a while to help you get started." She put her drink down. "Now if you will excuse me a moment."

As she turned away Haydn said, "Selma, thanks." She smiled back and when she was gone he rose and stood by one of the French doors, looking at the silent night outside and trying to add it all up.

Upstairs, Selma went down the hall to the Blue Room that had become Gabrielle's and found Gabrielle talking to Felicity. There was a suitcase out on the bed, and Gabrielle was taking things from the dresser and packing it.

Selma said, "Felicity, would you mind if I had a word with Gabrielle for a moment?"

"Of course not." And to Gabrielle, "I'll be in my room."

When she'd gone, it was very silent. Through the open window, there was the distant whisper of the waves in the harbor lapping the shore and the occasional night cry of a loon, and the older woman thought of what a wonderful place The Moorings was. Even if she would never live here herself, how badly she wanted it to stay the way it was.

She turned to Gabrielle, who stood by her suitcase, expectantly, some night things in her hand. She said, "Gabrielle, you once asked me to trust you, and I did. Now it's my turn. I want you to trust me. Life is a lot of steps, dear child. You took a giant one when you left your home in the country and went to work in Paris. You took another when you came here to America to do a story. There's one more you can take—I'm sure you know what I mean—and if you think it's hopeless, I assure you it isn't. We have an old expression in Yiddish, *schoen tszit*. It means roughly—don't sit around, get with it, get a move on."

She gave Gabrielle a hug and went down the hall to see Felicity.

Haydn was still standing by the French window when Gabrielle came into the living room. She went up to him and after a moment said quietly, "France is out there somewhere. Far away. I'd booked a flight to go, but I love you and if you want me to stay, I will."

Haydn slowly put an arm around her and she leaned her head against him. They didn't talk but stood silently close together, looking out into the night.

THIRTY-THREE

Saturday morning. In New York, the investigation into the theft of the Millet had gone into overtime. As Booker was calling headquarters at Barnstable on the Cape, Klein was mulling over notes Georgie had made interviewing Morse's wife when she'd flown up to Nantucket Wednesday. She hadn't got much more than a free ride out of it and a breath of sea air, Klein reflected, except she'd said Morse's wife was obviously keeping back a lot, which had made Georgie more suspicious of Morse than ever. Nor had she got anything from Darwin Morse's former assistant. The Freedman woman had refused to be interviewed until she came in on Monday, raising the question "why not?" unless whatever the older woman might be able to say she had to clear with the family first. Georgie had had to accept the refusal. She was New York police and had no out-of-state jurisdiction to contest the woman. But her conclusion was that the refusal smacked of conspiracy, and conspiracy probably meant information they didn't want anyone to have, which in turn had reinforced her suspicion of Morse.

Klein caught the phone call on its third ring. He flipped up the receiver with his right hand, caught it deftly with his left, cradled it between his shoulder and neck, and leaned back in his chair. "Detective Klein."

The caller was Lieutenant Wolkowski. He started right off by asking Klein if he was familiar with page three of that day's *Daily News.*

"No, sir."

"Your CEO over at Carlyle got in a wrestling match over a painting being auctioned with someone who apparently wanted it as much as he did. The reserve on the painting was three thousand bucks, meaning, for your information, Klein, that's probably all it could go for. Your CEO had to give up seventeen thousand five hundred to nail it."

Klein said, "Yes, sir. I know, sir." He felt like adding, "So what? Money's no object to a big-shit richie like Morse." But didn't.

A silence. Wolkowski didn't like to be one-upped. Then, "How did you know, Klein?"

"My partner was there."

"Your partner?"

"Detective White, sir."

"And since when has Detective White taken to attending sales of expensive art work?" The sarcasm dripped.

"Part of our ongoing investigation, sir. We think everything at Carlyle is important." Klein hoped to God Wolkowski wouldn't find out about Georgie's trip up to Nantucket. Helicopter flights were expensive.

"Correct, Klein. So try this on. The painting the CEO bought: beach scene called *Cape Cod Blue*. Artist unknown. It's stolen goods. Chicago. Ten years back. Or maybe not. Maybe what he got is a copy, and the exact twin we just found, the original. So which did he buy, and why for so much?"

Klein snapped forward and let Wolkowski win the one-upmanship. "Where was the second painting found, sir?"

"Hanging on the wall in the studio of a big-deal sculptress which she shares with a pot-head artist named Jason Curtiss-Pelham, who goes under the alias of Olenski. Ex–society boy and once college classmate of Morse. Earns his keep as a copyist and forger. We've used him occasionally in art identity checks. Do you not see something fishy here, Klein? Your CEO has a multimillion-dollar painting robbed, and a week later bids six times the price for either a stolen painting or a copy of it, when it's known throughout the whole art world that his taste is hookers, not paintings. I'm going over to look at what we found in a half hour. You might consider joining me."

Knowing Wolkowski, Klein took that as an order. When Georgie walked in with sandwiches and Coke for their lunch three minutes later, she found him on his feet, strapping on a shoulder holster with its 9-mm Beretta preparatory to slip into his jacket.

"What's up?"

"What's up is that you were right about something being odd with the bidding at your auction yesterday, and that we ought to pursue it. I'll explain on the way."

"On the way to where?"

"Bruckner Boulevard."

"What about lunch?"

Klein was already out the door. She followed with the sandwiches and Coke.

Five minutes later she was snaking their unmarked black car through heavy traffic, siren on and blue roof and rear window lights flashing, and all the while bolting down a sandwich. Heading up the East River Drive to the Willis Avenue bridge, Klein took a call from Crandall. Georgie, busy forcing drivers out of the way who were so used to sirens and flashing lights that neither registered, had to wait to find out what Crandall wanted until Klein switched the phone off and they'd come down off the bridge onto Bruckner Boulevard.

"So what now?" she demanded. Crandall issuing orders or bringing them up to date on something at the most awkward possible moments never failed to annoy her.

"Morse."

"What about him?

"Our friend Booker up on Nantucket is planning to bring him in on suspicion of murder. The DA up there for the cape and the islands just phoned down."

Georgie barely missed a head-on with a beat-up furniture van pulling out of a storage warehouse. She laughed triumphantly. "You see? I was right about the bastard."

"There's more." They slithered dangerously between a bus and a limo. "Jesus, slow down."

"What? What?"

"That hooker who got it the other night on East Seventy-Sixth Street? The one they autopsied as having a ruptured spleen and other internals? They got a statement from her roommate. She'd been with Morse a half hour before she bought it. He caught her looking at a painting he had in a Barney's suit box, and beat her up and threw her out. She called the roommate on her cell phone just before she died. And yeah, you're right. She told the roommate it was a painting of a woman and child on a beach under an umbrella looking across a bay at a little boat with a sail."

"And?"

"Crandall has a flying squad on the way to Carlyle, and if he's not there, with orders to check out his apartments."

The balding, skeletal Wolkowski was waiting for them with a plainclothes subordinate and a uniformed police driver. Before he condescended to speak, he silently stared down the smile of triumph Georgie was wearing at having figured one case right. Then he began by jerking his head upward toward Jason's studio. "Third floor. Officer on patrol went up to issue a traffic warning. That thing." He pointed to Jason's beat up Volvo parked down where the side street ended. "She described the painting she saw to a friend who found a photo of it in one of her unsolved files. Photo matched the one in the Carlyle auction catalog."

Wolkowski turned his deep socket eyes on Georgie. "You didn't think anything was wrong in the bidding?"

She shrugged. She wasn't going to reveal anything she "thought" to Wolkowski. This was a man who didn't like thinking. He wanted only proven facts. She said, "I'd never been to an auction before."

"Who was bidding against Morse?"

"Don't know. Some lady with a big hat. Scrawny. Middle aged."

"You didn't notice anything odd about Morse himself?"

"I didn't see Morse, sir."

"Then he was probably telephoning his bids from his office."

"There was a young lady relaying orders from someone."

"Check on it."

They went into the warehouse, took the freight elevator upstairs, found Renata's studio door, and knocked. First once. Then repeatedly.

Finally, on the other side, Renata asked who it was.

"Police."

A chain rattled. The door opened slightly to reveal Renata in her sculptor's apron.

Wolkowski thrust his wallet with its pinned on badge at her. "Open up."

Renata saw the badge belong to a ranking officer. She also saw through the slight crack in the open door that it was Wolkowski, whom she knew well by sight. Something in her froze. She said, "We moved the car."

"It's not about the car, lady."

"You'll have to wait a moment while I slip on a robe."

She could be heard walking away. Wolkowski slammed his weight against the door. The chain held. He turned to his subordinate. "Run down and get the bolt cutter."

Klein shot a look at Georgie and rolled his eyes. She stared back expressionless, unwrapped a stick of gum in a way that became an odd gesture of the contempt she felt for Wolkowski.

She got the stick in her mouth, they waited. But when the subordinate appeared at the head of the stairs with a bolt cutter, Renata was already back in her shorts and white shirt. She undid the chain and before she could utter a word Wolkowski barged in past her, followed by Klein and Georgie.

The eyes of all three swept the room, taking in the nearly

finished giant statuary, the pails of wet clay and scattered sculpting tool, and the general litter that working on such a large piece made. Beyond they also saw Jason's nude of Renata on his easel and his two chairs, one with the saucer now empty of roaches which Renata had managed to dump before changing.

Renata said, "Mr. Wolkowski, this is my home and studio, and I am busy at work. Would you mind telling me what this is all about?"

Wolkowski answer was, "Where's Jason?"

A fleeting change in the wary look in Renata's eyes showed a moment's relief that it was Jason they were after and not her. "If you mean Mr. Olenski, he's taking a shower."

Wolkowski spun on Klein. "Go get him."

Klein glanced around, figured the bathroom had to be in the other room through the arched doorway curtained off by the heavy café curtain. He headed for it.

Renata said, "Mr. Wolkowski."

"Lieutenant Wolkowski."

She laughed. "Whatever. Look here, I know you, you know me. Good heavens, we've seen each other enough at art exhibitions and gallery openings. Could we drop all this tiresome officialdom a moment? I can't imagine what Jason has done to warrant this intrusion, Is he under arrest or what? And if he is, why?"

Jason's appearance stopped any answer Wolkowski might have deigned to give. He came in ahead of Klein, dripping wet and with a towel wrapped around his waist.

Wolkowski said, "Hello, Jason. Remember me?"

Jason did. His eyes darted around, trying to size up the situation, knowing at the same time that it had to be bad. Wolkowski wouldn't have been there otherwise. He said, "What is it this time?"

Wolkowski pointed a bony finger at the *Cape Cod Blue* hanging over the kitchen sink. "Tell me, Mr. Curtiss-Pelham." He took particular pleasure in sarcastically emphasizing

Jason's real name. "How long have you had that?"

"Not long."

"Where did you get it?"

"Friend gave it to me."

"What friend?"

"Can't remember, exactly. And unless you've got a warrant, I suggest you leave, okay."

"Can't remember. Well, I think you'd better try, Jason, because that painting could cause you a lot of grief."

Renata decided enough was enough. "Don't answer him, Jason. He's here without a warrant, and when I call the commissioner, he'll be gone. We'll let my lawyer find out what's happened."

Wolkowski turned on her fast, his skeletal face flushed with viciousness for anyone daring to challenge him. "What's going on, lady, is a possible felony rap. You may be a big deal in the art world and around town, but that isn't going to excuse you from maybe being an accessory. Not a good thing for someone in the U.S. on a green card, right? My advice to you, lady, is to button up. And fast."

It was naked bullying, and too much for Jason. Some long forgotten gallantry boiled up in him. "Hey, man. Get off her back, okay. She doesn't need a puke like you all over her. So get the hell out of here. And I mean now."

It scared Renate. "Jason, don't."

"Don't what? Let this asshole burst in here and bully us around?"

Wolkowski said to his subordinate, "Cuff him."

The subordinate grabbed Jason, Jason swung around and shoved him off and turned on Wolkowski. "You, you sonofabitch, you heard me. Fuck off out of here!" He stepped toward Wolkowski, shoved the Lieutenant backward toward the door. "Right now, asshole! Out."

He moved to push Wolkowski again and was blocked by Georgie. She stepped in his path and deftly karate chopped his outstretched arm. Jason clutched it with a surprised howl, dropping his towel. The subordinate put an arm lock on him and he was cuffed. Georgie looked at his nakedness and picked up the towel, wrapped it around his waist and tucked it into itself so it wouldn't fall off.

Wolkowski broke into a cadaverous grin and said to Klein. "Aaron, where did you get her from? I want her on my team."

"With all respect, sir, no way," Klein said.

Wolkowski sauntered over to look at the *Cape Cod Blue* closely. "Well, well. Shades of yesterday's Carlyle auction. For seventeen thousand bucks. Tell me, Jason. Is this a copy, or an original?"

When there was no answer, Wolkowski's eyes, which had been filled with the pleasure of baiting both Jason and Renata, suddenly hardened and became two stones set in a sneering skull. "I really would like to know, because if it's the original, I might have to book you for receiving stolen goods. We're after a painting that's a dead ringer for this and was whipped from Chicago." He paused a deliberately menacing moment to let it sink in, and then said, "And while we're at it, Jason, when did you cut and dye your hair? And why? You don't know? Shall I tell you something interesting? There was a clown who looked just like you who came into the Carlyle Auction house yesterday and went up to see Chase Morse with that pornography over there on the easel, and then came out at precisely noon. Quite a coincidence, yes?" To his subordinate, he said, "Okay, get Picasso here out of my sight. I'm booking him for resisting arrest, assaulting a police officer, receiving stolen goods and holding him for questioning as an accomplice in a major art theft." A now silent Jason was thrown a pair of pants Klein had brought with him from the bedroom, and rapidly frogmarched out of the studio.

Wolkowski turned on Renata. "And you. Watch yourself. Got that?" At the door he looked back. "You, two," to Klein and Georgie. "Bring the painting. And look around for drugs.

Nail whatever you find and follow me to borough headquarters, close convoy."

Renata called after him. "Hold on. I'd like to like to buy the painting."

It was too late. The heavy metal door slammed mutely behind him. Georgie was firmly polite: "I'm afraid it's a no go, ma'am. It's stolen property."

It was a final blow to the sculptress. Everything went out of her. The mess Jason was in, the danger to herself. And now the painting that had reminded her of so much so many years ago, now lost to her. Her voice broke. "Please. Can you ask Wolkowski when he calms down to call me? He can fix things if he wants. Or better still, I'll get hold of the commissioner. The picture means a lot to me."

She suddenly looked ten years older and exhausted. She sat down heavily on the platform at the foot of the unfinished statuary. Alarmed, Georgie went quickly to the fridge, thinking something cold would help, spotted the vodka bottle, poured some into a tumbler and brought it over. "Here, ma'am. You'll feel better."

Renata numbly had a swallow of the vodka. "Thank you. I needed that." She drank again and said, "I told Jason not to do it. What a fool."

Georgie sat down next to her. "Do what, ma'am?"

"Make a copy. I mean, that's what he does for a living. Jason didn't steal anything. Just the same, deal with Chase? Forget it."

"He copied the painting up there?" And when Renata nodded, "What was the copy for? Do you know?"

"No, I don't. Jason didn't either. And he had no idea the original was stolen."

"What did he do with it?"

"The copy? He took it up to the auction house."

Klein had gone to the sink to look at the painting more closely. "Are you sure this is the original?"

"Yes. Jason was supposed to get rid of it."

"Why?"

"Who knows? But I asked him not to. He was supposed to take it to an incinerator along with the suit Chase made him wear, but I hung it up and told him I'd take it down if Chase came here again." She paused, and her voice broke slightly. "There's no reason you'd understand, but it's like my childhood on the Black Sea."

Georgie hugged her shoulder and said, "Let's see what happens, okay?" She looked up at the statuary. "I love the work you do. Your two women is absolutely terrific."

Renata brightened visibly. "Thank you. They're going to San Francisco."

Georgie stared another admiring moment and then switched back to the painting and Jason. "The painting's awfully good. But the whole deal is crazy. He just walked in with the copy, like that? He wasn't stopped? I mean, the original was up for auction, understand? It wasn't supposed to leave the building."

"He had hidden it under that painting of me"—Renata pointed to the nude on the easel—"so no one would see it. On the same stretcher."

Georgie snapped a sharp look at Klein, who looked hard back at her. She said, "See? I told you."

"I'm with you." He had suddenly understood along with her how the Millet was got out of Carlyle House.

Georgie said, "I'll put that it in my official report."

Klein nodded. Wolkowski wasn't going to get credit for this one. Then he said, "What about the junk on the shelf in the other room?"

"What about it?"

He shrugged. "There are times when I hate being a cop."

Georgie said, "I know what you mean."

Aaron went to take the painting down.

Georgie rose and headed for the bedroom.

Klein got the painting. There was the sound of a horn

blaring from the alley below. He muttered, "Oh, Christ," and then, not seeing Georgie, "Georgie, what the hell are you doing? Let's go. That's Darth Vader himself."

There was the sound from the other room of the toilet flushing. Georgie came back and looked straight-faced at Klein, and wiped one palm against the other. Klein understood and said, "Oh." And turned away to hide a smile.

Renata had risen. The color had come back to her face, and she looked in charge again. She put the vodka bottle back in the fridge and said, "Could you give me directions to the borough headquarters? I want to be there."

Klein said. "We'll take you. You'd never get there on your own in the traffic."

An impatient horn blared up again.

Georgie laughed and took Renata's arm. Klein followed them to the door with the painting.

THIRTY-FOUR

At twenty-five thousand feet and Mach 0.8, the sound of the Dassault Falcon 50 EX Trimotor Jet as it passed over the Hamptons, then Montauk Point at the end of Long Island, was heard as the barest whisper to those still enjoying the late afternoon sun on the beaches far below. Seconds later, it was over the open Atlantic Ocean on its way to Nantucket with only two thin contrails, expanding white streaks in the cloudless summer sky, marking its passage overhead.

Within the pressurized cabin of the plane it was almost equally silent. With the jet on automatic pilot, Doyle had taken off his headset, and his attention had been diverted from the maze of instruments on the panel before him by a tiny white blotch on the ocean far below, the sail of some intrepid yachtsman abandoning the protection of Long Island sound and Block Island, a few miles ahead, and standing out to sea. Next to him, Randy Speers had just finished reporting their position to air traffic and was receiving instructions for their approach to the airfield on Nantucket.

Behind them, Helen Chen was still in her seat from takeoff, her small, neatly manicured hands resting on the thigh of one slender leg that was crossed over the other. Normally she would have unbuckled her seat belt and gone at once to Chase to smilingly ask him if there was anything he wanted, then hurried to carry out whatever the request might be. Instead, her body rigid with suppressed anger, she waited for Chase to call her.

It was a routine flight, one the crew had done scores of times and, whenever called on, had performed almost as though automatons with hardly a conscious thought as to what they were doing. It had not been a routine departure, however, and there was ample reason for the hostess's distress.

Doyle had been given uncomfortably short notice that Chase wanted the plane for the flight to Nantucket. Several days before, Chase had said he wouldn't be needing the plane until after the weekend. Since it was Saturday and Doyle hadn't heard from Chase, he assumed that he wasn't going. He was spending the afternoon with some old friends he hadn't seen for a long time with plans for an evening at the theater when Chase's call came saying he wanted to leave at once.

"Chase, it may take time to get Speers. Same goes for Helen. I wasn't expecting you to fly today. My fault. I'm sorry."

"You can't fly without them?"

"Not without Randy. FAA rule."

Chase had sworn audibly and said, "Well, get him at least." And then had hung up, leaving Doyle to wonder. There'd been an angry, bullying tone in Chase's voice the pilot had never heard before. When he'd answered the call, instead of the usual "one of the boys" friendliness, Chase had been almost uncharacteristically abrupt. Doyle had said, "Hello?" and Chase's very first words were simply, "I want the plane right away." It had taken Doyle a moment to realize it was Chase, and that Chase wasn't joking, and another moment to try to adjust his mind to Chase being so unlike the boss he'd always known.

He'd had to make four calls in order to track down Speers, all the time praying that the copilot wasn't having drinks someplace. When he finally located him, it was to hear Speers volubly express what he himself felt at such short notice. The copilot had been about to drive out to an afternoon in Connecticut and dinner at a country inn with an important new girlfriend.

Doyle almost took Chase at his unspoken word that he wouldn't need Helen Chen, but inner sense told him that would be a mistake. Once on board the Dassault, Chase might forget he'd virtually passed on her and want to know why she wasn't there. If he continued in the same mood as when he'd called, he'd more likely than not hold it against her. While he and Speers were relatively indispensable, Helen was not. She was supporting an aged widowed father and couldn't afford to have her job even remotely jeopardized. The major airlines were cutting back and the private jet market was flooded with hostess applicants.

Another frantic series of calls and he'd found her, and she had made it to the Marine Air Terminal at LaGuardia even before he and Speers, but in jeans and a tank top. There'd been no time to go to her father's apartment from a cousin's Chinese restaurant, and she hadn't been able to get her uniform out of the dry cleaners.

Racing into the private pilots' lounge, Doyle and Speers found her nearly in tears and confronted by Chase, who had arrived before any of them. Turning away from the hostess without a word of hello and with an expression that matched the bullying tone Doyle himself had been subjected to on the telephone, Chase greeted them with, "Miss Chen's not in uniform."

As the hostess vainly tried to explain about her uniform, which seemed Chase's only consideration, Doyle barely managed to hang on to his cool. He braced himself to come to her defense, but it wasn't necessary. Chase, clutching a Barney's suit box, stormed out onto the tarmac where the ground crew had already towed the Dassault, and boarded.

There wasn't time to discuss Chase's mood. Doyle expressed his astonishment with a low whistle and gave Helen's shoulders a supportive hug. Speers miraculously borrowed a clean white shirt her size from a young Latina clerk who always kept an extra at work. A flight plan was hurriedly filed, and the crew rushed to join Chase on the plane.

They found him already buckled into his seat and

uncommunicative. Doyle, planning to have it out with him when they arrived at Nantucket, went at once to the flight deck followed by Speers. He and the copilot took their seats and, as Helen Chen closed and locked the heavy exit door that sealed the air pressure in the cabin at ground level, hurriedly went through their check-off list and prepared for takeoff.

Less than ten minutes later they were airborne over Queens. As the La Guardia complex rapidly fell away to diminutive size behind and below them, none of the flight crew could have realized that Chase Morse was in the grip of something far worse than terrified anxiety to get to Nantucket and The Moorings; that for Chase, a time of reckoning had come. They could not know that his demons had finally succeeded in pushing a troubled mind, long hidden behind artificial arrogance and social confidence, to the brink of madness.

The end had begun that morning shortly after ten o'clock. Returning from forty minutes jogging on the pedestrian pathway between the East River Drive and the river itself, Chase was met with the announcement by the summer housekeeper at the door of the Gracie Square apartment, where he had retreated for the night, that he was wanted on the phone. Thinking it was someone from The Moorings, Felicity or Perkins or even Haydn, he snatched up the phone and identified himself.

The caller was Alice Marks, who apologized with false obsequiousness for disturbing him on Saturday afternoon, but said she was obliged to tell him that they'd received a call from one of the police investigating the theft of the Millet. The painting he'd bought at the auction two days previous had been identified as stolen ten years ago from a Chicago gallery. He was to surrender it to the police as soon as possible.

The news had shattered Chase. He muttered something to Alice Marks and was barely able put the phone back. For minutes he felt nauseous and barely able to breathe. There was that terrible tightness around his chest, a cold iron band, and that roaring in his ears as though all the surf in the world pounded in his head. Surf and babbling voices.

Little by little, he got control of himself. Objects in the room which had dimmed became clear again. He began to think. One thing was certain: He had to get the Millet into hiding as soon as possible. Either of his apartments in New York had already been ruled out by threat of a police search warrant. What better place than The Moorings, where there were a score of places it could be stored away and safe even from the prying eyes of the servants? Fly the Millet to The Moorings immediately before the police could act, find a way then to stall: an urgent business trip abroad, perhaps, while he took the chance on paying some foreign art restorer a huge sum to separate the Millet from the beach scene, or get hold of some solvent and take the equal risk of doing it himself. The voluntary gesture of then surrendering the wanted beach scene himself, he thought, especially if done through the Commissioner, would surely lift any suspicion that he was somehow connected with the theft.

The relief he felt at this plan brought euphoria with it. Unable to stop laughing, sometimes almost wildly, he showered, then grabbed up the phone in the bedroom to notify Doyle he'd be flying back to Nantucket as soon as he could get himself to the airport. To his immediate anger, he couldn't find Doyle at the apartment Carlyle kept for both pilots in New York, and the anger turned to fury as he was frustrated in one call after another in trying to track the pilot down on his cell phone which, maddeningly, Doyle had either not turned on or had placed out of earshot. By the time Doyle finally answered, the pilot had assumed to Chase the proportions of the devil incarnate.

Frustrated for nearly three hours, feeling now that time was of the essence in his need to clear New York with the painting, Chase's sense of urgency had reached a point where it was hard to think lucidly. Desperate, he sought to get a grip on himself and think one step at a time: get the Barney's box from his clothes closet where he'd stowed it the night before, get himself and it down to his convertible in the basement garage as fast as possible, head straight for the airport.

Steeling himself and without a word to the housekeeper, who remained ignorant of his flight until sometime later, he did just that and, only minutes before police descended on the apartment, drove out from the interior gloom of the building's garage into the nearly blinding brilliance of summer sunlight, the Barney's box with its precious contents secure on the seat next to him.

Then it happened. He'd stopped for a red light on York Avenue on his way to the East River Drive and the Triborough Bridge to Queens and the airport. In the car next to his, a woman passenger was holding up a late edition of *The New York Post*, and Chase, glancing casually over, was confronted by the huge black headline that glared at him from the open front page—"Art Thief Seized." It was just a glimpse. The light changed, the car surged away. But to Chase in his stress, the glimpse was enough to freeze him momentarily into inaction.

What art? What thief? Jason?

Horns honked. A driver pulling around him shouted an obscenity. A traffic warden leaving the curb to see why he wasn't moving, brought him, panicked, back to his senses. He accelerated away, almost running down the shouting man.

After that it was all a blur, his thoughts a repetitive jumble. Of course—Jason. It had to be. Somehow they'd got onto him for the Millet. What else for that kind of a headline? But how? And had he talked? He must have, or if he hadn't, he would. Either he or his big-deal sculptress.

Chase couldn't think past that. Fear stopped his mind. He could feel it in every part of him like an alien, physical presence. The police would soon be after him, too, if they weren't already. Maybe even in Nantucket, but maybe not today. At the thought of the island, its distance from the nightmare of New York, the seeming inviolability of The Moorings, he felt a sudden glimmer of hope. He'd make it to The Moorings, surely, check the news on television. If Jason had implicated him, there was the *South Wind*. He could put out to sea tonight, get beyond the twelve-mile limit by daybreak easy. Be free, then safe. The Azores or the Caribbean. He could take David with him. They wouldn't dare stop him if he had the child.

But parking his car at the airport, confronting his crew in the pilots' lounge, getting himself aboard the waiting plane where he threw himself into the security of a lounge chair while still clutching the Barney's box to him, he began to hear again the surf-like roar of water, the babbling voices, the garbled laughter, the drumbeat. The iron vise tightened once more around his chest, and he was aware of nothing else until he realized that the Dassault was hurtling down the runway and surging upward.

One moment the roar of water, the babbling voices, a crescendo. The next, sudden and miraculous near silence, the only sound the soundproofed whisper of the plane's three jet motors. There was the safe familiarity of the passenger area, the lounge chairs, the conference table, the galley, the plane's curtained windows, Helen Chen sitting immobile in her seat, looking familiar but unfamiliar in a white shirt.

He pressed the call button on the arm of his chair. Once, twice. She heard and came to life with a start. In a moment she was at his side.

"I'll have a vodka, Helen."

"Yes, sir." Unsmiling she went aft to the galley to get it. When she came back, he stirred the ice cubes around with the silver swizzle-stick always found on the tray along with mixed cocktail nuts, some crackers and cheese spread, and a napkin embossed with the Carlyle logo. He'd begun to realize that he was finally free from New York and the hated police there, that his chances of successfully getting away with the Millet were better every minute. Virtually nothing he could think of could stop him now.

Euphoria began to creep back, tingling.

Doyle left the flight deck and came past on his way to the lavatory at the rear of the plane.

"Everything all right, sir?"

"Fine, thank you, Pete. Just fine."

"About another twenty-five minutes, sir."

"Would you call Thomas, Peter? Tell him to meet me."

"Yes, sir." Surprised at the sudden change in Chase's mood, Doyle went on.

Laughter grew in Chase again. And a high of happiness. Once away to wherever, and if it became necessary, he could buy a new identity for himself. He could disappear as Chase Morse. Others had done it. Even without his inheritance from Darwin or the foundation money, he could last until he collected for the Millet. Then he'd have enough to buy anything.

The Barney's box lay enticingly on his lap. Enticing and irresistible. Perhaps he could risk taking the frame out of the box, the paintings out of the frame and, if he was very careful, peel back just a little corner of the plastic separating them. Just a corner. If that little corner of the Millet was damaged by it, so what? It wouldn't seriously devalue the painting.

He looked up. Peter Doyle had returned to the flight deck and was shutting the door on himself and Randy Speers. Helen Chen was back in the galley, tidying up. Chase smiled to himself; she was just a little Asiatic, and if she did come by, he didn't think she'd know one piece of art from another.

He opened the box and took out the frame he'd bought, holding it up before him and gazing on the *Cape Cod Blue*. There was a brief moment of anxiety when the light burlap that Jason had pasted over the back to disguise the aged canvas of the Millet came detached and fell away. Probably, he thought, it had been loosened by that fool of an escort girl when she took it out of the box. Anger stirred in him just at the thought of her. Bitch. He'd pulled her up short, all right.

He put the burlap back in the box. He'd glue it on properly himself at home.

He studied the *Cape Cod Blue* first, slanting the frame up toward him so he could see it better. A nice painting, he thought. Very nice. He could probably sell it easily some place. He'd take it with him with the Millet. And why not? God knows, he'd paid enough for it. He could at least get some of his money back.

Making sure nobody was looking, he held the whole frame up for a last look at the beach scene and noticed something odd. What had that fool Jason done to it? There seemed to be a light spot on it that blurred the paint. Had perhaps the plastic shield sticking it to the Millet come through? He looked more carefully. When he moved the painting, the light spot moved.

It was a moment before he realized what it was. He was seeing the light Helen Chen had turned on in the galley through the canvas. But that was impossible. You could see through one canvas, perhaps, if the paint had been applied to it relatively lightly, but surely not through two.

Chase turned the frame over and looked at the back. No old canvas struck his eye. He saw only canvas that was new.

A hint of panic seized him. New canvas—that was the copy of the beach scene. He turned the painting, held it up to the light, full panic starting to grip now. Looking at the back of it and through the canvas, he could see the figure of a woman and a child in reverse under a beach umbrella.

That was when he finally realized that there was no Millet there. The copy of the *Cape Cod Blue* was the only painting in the frame.

THIRTY-FIVE

When Detective Sergeant Aaron Klein and his partner, Detective Georgina White, were finally able to return to the offices of the upper Manhattan major crime unit, it was to find that once again the air-conditioning system had broken down. Cursing appropriately, they settled behind their respective desks with the iced coffee they had picked up on the way back. Neither felt much like talking. It had been an action-packed day, and they were weary from being at the whim of Wolkowski on top of all the pressure and stress of finishing up the case that had literally put their jobs front and center with the commissioner.

Writing up their report fell to Georgie and would take hours. She was reluctant to start, and once again slowly scanned the single foolscap sheet covered with small handwriting that she removed from her shoulder bag.

"Go figure," she said. There was wonderment in her voice.

Klein looked across his desk at her. "Yeah. Crazy, no?" He couldn't blame her for reading the paper for what he figured was the third time at least. Everything written on it was a classic example of the totally unexpected, a clear statement that you could never read the future, just the way he hadn't been able to see beyond his nose when they'd started to leave the warehouse studio with Renata and the painting. They'd entered the dimly lit hall planning to take the freight elevator down because Georgie wouldn't go down the stairs. "Rats," she'd said.

He'd already pushed the elevator call button and had been about to close the studio door behind them when she suddenly said, "Wait." And had put her foot in the door, blocking its closure. And then said, "Aaron, did you not notice anything funny about Olenski when he was marched out of here?"

"Something funny?"

"You didn't did you? Well, for just a second when he had his back to Wolkowski, he cracked this weird smile."

"Sure, okay. If you say so. He smiled. So what?"

"So when I went to school, someone getting busted doesn't smile."

He'd felt his patience slipping. "Georgie, what are you driving at?"

She stared at him, her expression giving nothing, then said, "Olenski making a monkey of Wolkowski." And promptly pushed the door open all the way and marched back into the studio.

"Georgie, for Christ's sake."

He'd left Renata waiting and followed her in, complaining "Skull head's got a short fuse, you know that, don't you?"

His answer was silence. Georgie glanced quickly around and then went straight to the easel and the nude of Renata.

"Georgie …"

"I need your knife." She silently held out her hand.

A horn was heard again from down on the street. "There he is. You know he's going to kill us."

No answer. Reluctantly, he'd fished out his pocket knife, snapped open the blade and put it in her hand.

Georgie said, "You see this canvas on the stretcher? Here, not the new stuff. This old stuff underneath. There's a little bit that's peeping out from under it on the edge here. I spotted it when we first came in. The stretcher's old, too. But the canvas on its back is brand new and not even attached to the stretcher. It's just been pasted on to hide something. Okay?" She laughed, "Friend Jason pulled a fast one on Mr. *Social Register* Morse. Want to bet?"

He'd hardly had time to wonder how it was that she suddenly knew so much about the way paintings were mounted when she used the pocket knife to quickly flip out four or five staples. When none were left, she gently removed the Renata nude from the stretcher.

And Klein found himself looking at the painting of a peasant washerwoman kneeling by a stream with a basket of laundry beside her and, etched in every line of her tired face, the world-weary look of the downtrodden everywhere over the centuries.

His memory of that astonishing moment was interrupted now by Crandall shambling into the office while as usual wiping sweat from the ebony skin of his big moon face with a bandanna-sized red handkerchief.

"Congratulations, Georgie," Crandall said. "I heard all about it. Of course you know Wolkowski is going to hate you forever."

"I'll consider that an honor."

Klein laughed. Still fresh in his mind, and he guessed it always would be, was Wolkowski's stunned loss of aplomb when they presented him with the famous painting. Not being the star in the situation had so taken the wind from the bullying Lieutenant's sails that he'd for once been unable to speak with his usual ill-concealed disdain for anyone of lower rank.

Crandall said, "You don't mind, Georgie, that your glory moment turned out to be shared?"

Georgie gave him the kind of patient look one bestows on someone of pathetic ignorance and which she usually reserved for Klein. "Boss," she said, straight-faced, "Along with everyone of any cultural merit whatsoever, I am thrilled that one of the great works of art for the last several hundred years has been recovered safe and sound. That's quite enough for me."

Not quite knowing if she was directing the remark specifically at him or just at the world in general, Crandall made a mock gesture of defensively ducking before he dropped a sheaf of papers on Klein's desk. "Copies of various warrants," he said. "One a copy of the Cape's warrant for Morse's arrest as soon as they lay hands on him. Jesus, that guy is something. Embezzlement, robbery, murder."

"Parricide," Georgie said.

"Nothing less," Crandall replied.

"See?" she said to Klein. And then, reflectively, "It's like something out of Shakespeare, isn't it? A family like that, and one of them killing his own father."

"I don't know about Shakespeare," Klein said, "but we sure get it all in this department." On the way into the office he'd been told that the district attorney wanted a shelved six-year-old murder-suicide case reopened. Klein's job on this next case would be to bring up all the old records and study them.

"Cheer up," Crandall said. "The Commissioner told me he's going to see you both get a promotion." He started out and stopped halfway through the door. "Oh, incidentally, Bouchard got some biggie on the Carlyle board to put the screws on the commissioner to spring Olenski. He's out this afternoon. No charge."

Klein sighed and shook his head at the irony of it.

"I'm glad," Georgie said and buried herself in the scripted page.

For the fourth time, she read as follows:

Dear Bouchard:

I have the Millet. I got it away from Chase Morse, who was stealing it. He paid me to make an exact copy of a beach scene called *Cape Cod Blue* that would fit into a frame he'd bought and had me bring the copy to his office covered with a nude of mine because the *Cape Cod* wasn't supposed to be out of the building. In his office, he had me remove my painting as well as the beach scene from their mutual stretcher, and he produced the Millet and said to take it out of its frame, cover it with the beach scene, and put both into a new frame he'd bought.

Then I got a lucky break. He had a phone call and I was

able to pull a fast switch. I took the Millet from its fancy frame and covered it with my nude instead of with the *Cape Cod* and shoved it into my portfolio bag. Then I inserted the *Cape Cod* into the frame he'd bought for it and the Millet and pasted some old burlap over the back to hide the newness of the canvas. I knew he knew nothing about paintings, and when he finished with the phone, I gave him a crazy story about protecting the Millet behind the beach scene with a protective plastic coating, which I said had stuck it to the beach scene and that only an expert could separate them. When I left, the guard saw only my painting, which was covering the Millet. I didn't dare go to the police because they'd think I had stolen the painting myself and was trying to collect the reward, so I brought it straight home.

Bouchard, I don't want any reward for rescuing Millet's great painting. Okay? Especially from a bastard like Chase Morse. Give it to some charity and you can have every penny he paid me for the copying, too. It's taken me since Wednesday to figure out the best way to let you know all this. Please come and get it just as soon as possible.

Jason Olenski.

Georgie put down the letter which Olenski had faxed to Bouchard from a bodega down the street only a short while before she and Klein and Wolkowski arrived on the scene. What Bouchard said when they'd met him at borough head-quarters, where he'd rushed the moment Wolkowski called to say he'd recovered the Millet, still resonated with her.

"Of all people," the auctioneer had said. "Olenski spent the last twenty years of his life sneering at every great masterpiece and painter. His defense against failure, I guess. But when push came to shove, something in him nobody knew about took over. Reverence instead of resentment, and God bless him for it."

Bouchard had talked to Haydn Morse and told the com-missioner and the DA that Carlyle was prepared to fund Olen-ski's defense if he was charged. "My guess is he'll be set free," he added.

It was like that with more people than you ever realized, Georgie thought. A lot of people who were judged as bad news often had decency hidden away inside them, and it sometimes came out when the chips were really down.

Klein saw the far-off look on her face and asked her where her head was now. She told him, and said with a straight face, "You see, Aaron, there's hope for you yet."

He hid a smile and shot a wadded up piece of paper at her. She laughed and they both settled down to work. Later, she thought, she'd remind him there was still the trafficking in illuminated manuscripts to nail down.

THIRTY-SIX

The Dassault Falcon had reached a point over open ocean nearly midway between Block Island and Nantucket when Speers, checking his NDB and VOR navigational instruments preparatory to starting a descent from twenty-five thousand feet to twenty thousand, received a call from Air Traffic rerouting them to Hyannis on the Cape. He had hardly alerted Doyle to this and the pilot was wondering why, although immediately beginning to change course, when a flashing light on their communications panel notified them to receive an emergency call from the Hyannis tower on their air security channel. Responding, they found themselves ordered to proceed on landing to the far end of the field, away from their usual parking area, where they would be met by the state police.

Slightly bewildered, Doyle demanded to know what was going on and found himself talking to the police lieutenant in charge of meeting their plane.

"You have a passenger, one Chase Morse, on board?"

"Roger."

"We have a warrant for his arrest."

"You what?" Doyle glanced over his shoulder through the partially open door of the flight deck back to where Chase, slouched deep in his lounge chair, was staring at a framed painting. The Barney's box he'd not let Helen Chen put away for him when she boarded had fallen to the floor beside him.

"An arrest warrant. What for?"

"Grand larceny and second-degree murder in New York, and a murder charge in Massachusetts. We advise you to be careful. He may be dangerous."

Doyle couldn't find words to reply. His first thought was there had to have been some sort of a mistake. Chase? Wanted for murder? Whose murder, when? And dangerous?

Speers had patched in on the call, and he and Doyle for a moment just stared at each other, unanswered questions and astonishment widening their eyes and stifling any speech. Then, leaving Speers to acknowledge and sign off, Doyle dumped his headset, slid from his seat and left the flight deck to alert Helen Chen back in the galley that they'd been rerouted but, with Chase within hearing distance, not telling her why. Once he'd spoken to Chase, he planned to slip her a note. Surprised at the unexpected change in flight plans, Helen started preparing the take-away coffee she was sure everyone would want once they landed.

Doyle went on to Chase, not quite sure of what he should say to him but deciding just as he reached him that he'd confine himself to their being diverted to Hyannis and to say it was because the field at Nantucket had been closed due to an accident.

"Sir?" There was no answer. Doyle bent closer. "Mr. Morse?"

He touched Chase on the shoulder. Chase raised his eyes briefly and then looked back down at the painting lying across his lap. Doyle tried again, bending over closer. "That's a gorgeous painting, sir."

When there was still no response he straightened and, with a last glance at Chase, went back to the flight deck; his expression and a brief shake of his head, warning Helen Chen in the galley that there was some sort of trouble where Chase was concerned and not to bother him.

Speers asked him on the pilot's intercom what Chase had said.

"I didn't get to tell him. It's like he's in a trance."

"Yeah?" Speers glanced back at Chase and remembered how unpleasant he'd been in the pilots lounge and the way he'd stormed off to the plane before it was ready for him. And then not talking to any of them when they came aboard. The police warning that he could be dangerous burned in Speers's head. Had Chase suddenly gone crazy? He remembered a CO he'd had in the Navy who acted like that and had been taken away in a strait jacket. "What do you think we should do?"

Doyle was cryptic. "Nothing right now. We have a plane to fly. Where did you stow the Taser?"

"In the map locker."

"Let's hope we won't need it."

Behind them, Chase, in his lounge chair, continued to stare at the copy of the *Cape Cod Blue*. But what he saw wasn't the painting. What he saw was an unfolding series of confused pictures, jumbled memories: his office with Jason getting the nude of Renata and the copy of the *Cape Cod Blue* off the stretcher he'd brought them in on, Jason easing the Millet from its large ornate frame, Courtney's icy voice echoing in his head.

And Jason laughing at him.

But suddenly it wasn't Jason laughing. It was Darwin. Darwin sitting right there in the lounge chair opposite him. And laughing. Laughing at his misery.

How had he got there? He'd thrown him off the float, hadn't he? Pushed him and his chair back under the water when it had erupted to the surface in an explosive bubble of air.

Once, twice, before the water finally stilled with Darwin gone forever. But now back again. And laughing.

The endless deafening splash of water returned, giant waves surging, tumbling, and pounding through his head, with it the thudding drumbeat and the iron vise tightening once more around his chest, the babbling voices. And Darwin's laughter. On the dock, in his wheelchair, just the other side of the gate, and laughing.

Go ahead and laugh, then, Darwin. Laugh a last time. You

can't escape me now. I only have to get the gate open and you'll be down the dock and off the float. Then laugh underwater if you will. This time you won't come up again.

Helen Chen happened just then to look over at Chase Morse. What she saw paralyzed her with terror. Chase was up out of his lounge seat and tugging at the heavy emergency handle that would unlock the cabin exit door. In his final dementia, he saw not the door but the sagging old gate to the dock resisting his struggle to lift the rusty lock and swing the gate open.

She rushed for him. "Mr. Morse!" Her voice stuck in her throat. Then she screamed. Chase's hand, struggling with the handle, flew over to an emergency button activating an explosive charge needed to force the heavy door open against the strength of the slip stream outside. With an explosive roar, the door burst outward, the aircraft bucked, Chase vanished. At twenty thousand feet there was instant decompression. The hostess, seized by a giant force, was sucked toward the void, grabbing at anything, being torn loose, grabbing again in a cloud of debris—glasses, dishes, magazines, pillows, the Barney's box.

Slammed against the lounge chair Chase had occupied, she hung onto it for dear life.

Speers had turned at her scream, turned and saw. Ejecting his seat belt and fighting himself to keep from being sucked out of the plane, he made it to her just as she lost all strength. As pressure equalized with the cabin invaded by frigid air, he managed to get hold of an oxygen mask, released automatically from the cabin ceiling and dangling within reach. Speers fitted it on, strapped Helen, unconscious, into the lounge chair with its seat belt, got an oxygen mask on her also, then took off his and made it back to the flight deck, where he donned another one.

Doyle dumped the yoke. The Dassault plummeted down steeply five thousand feet a minute and leveled off at ten thousand. He called a "Mayday" and was cleared to land at New London in Connecticut, the closest airport.

That Chase Morse had ever been on the plane was witnessed only by the copy of the *Cape Cod Blue:* In the violent decompression it had been jammed between two seats.

EPILOGUE

It took months for the media to cease running, as front page features and on prime-time television, the extraordinary story of the theft of a world-famous work of art by the president and CEO of a prestigious auction house along with corporate embezzlement and the murder of his father and an escort girl from Lithuania. No trace of this central figure, whose demise in the ensuing aerial tragedy was officially declared suicide, was ever found. A private memorial ceremony for him was attended only by immediate family and a handful of friends sympathetic to the ordeal to which the family had been subjected.

With the help of the Nantucket police chief, aided by the respect for privacy among virtually all the residents of Nantucket, the media were kept at distance from the family home there. Such protection was unable to be afforded to the crew of the Dassault Falcon executive jet, however. Having survived an incident of almost unmatched terror, they almost immediately found themselves the most recognizable faces in the nation. At the request of the deceased's family, they were compensated for their loss of jobs and media ordeal by receiving, in equal shares, the reward that had been refused by the copyist who had aborted the theft of the famous painting, and which, helped by the drama to which it had been subjected, brought eighty-five million when it was auctioned.

Eventually, when the circus subsided, the younger brother

of the deceased took charge of the auction house, aided by the former assistant to the legendary murdered patriarch as an executive vice president.

Recovered, the seascape by an anonymous artist, copied to disguise the theft, was bought from the art gallery owner in Chicago from whom it was stolen twelve years previous, and who, when he learned of its subsequent history, refunded the sale price. The painting was then gifted to the widow of the deceased. At the specific request of a young woman police officer attached to the major crime unit involved in the case, the copy, virtually impossible to tell from the original except for the copyist's deliberate omission of one stripe on the parasol, was given to the companion of the art forger and copyist who painted it. And at the request of this same officer, the copyist painted a second copy, which was given to the veteran policewoman whose original discovery of the painting in a loft studio in the Bronx was instrumental in helping solve the case.

The young French journalist who had come to America to do a story about an auction house wrote a best-selling book on the subject and, as a journalist, never looked back. Today, besides being married into the auction house family and the mother of three young children, she is host on her own morning television show, *Report from Nantucket,* featuring the daily lives of ordinary Americans and which is beamed throughout Europe. It features, as its logo, the lovely painting of a Victorian woman and child on a cloudless summer day, sitting beneath a gaily striped beach parasol and looking across an expanse of quiet blue water at a distant sandbar and at a little lobster boat whose faded blue sail hangs limp in the still air.

ABOUT THE AUTHOR

 Born to wealth and privilege in New York, David Osborn chose to spurn both as false icons after World War II combat as a Marine Corps dive bomber pilot. On his own and following brief careers in television and public relations, he expatriated to France when falsely accused of un-Americanism in the infamous Senator McCarthy era, paying his way with a co-authored first motion picture script, *Chase a Crooked Shadow*. When its star-studded success took him from laboring in a rock quarry in France into Britain's film industry, he was launched on a long world-class writing career that saw him dangerously engaged during several Cold War years with Czech anticommunist resistance behind the Iron Curtain. Living in France and England as well as isolated for twelve years in a tiny Alpine village in Switzerland, Osborn authored numerous stellar TV plays and a score of major motion pictures, including *The Trap*, which earned an Academy Award nomination. Turning novelist with the critical success of *The Glass Tower* followed by the world best-selling classics *Open Season*, *The French Decision*, *Love and Treason*, and a half dozen more outstanding thrillers, he has had many imitators, but none reaching the startling originality of his stories, the stunning impact of his flawless page-turning plots, and his literate prose in each that packs a powerful punch with nearly every line.

ALSO BY DAVID OSBORN

Novels and Screenwriting

Novels

The Glass Tower – Hodder & Stoughton

Open Season – The Dial Press

The French Decision – Doubleday

Love and Treason – New American Library

Heads – Bantam

Murder on Martha's Vineyard – Lynx

Murder on the Chesapeake – Simon & Schuster

Murder in the Napa Valley – Simon & Schuster

The Last Pope – Source Books

The Cape Cod Blue – Dagmar Miura

Alicia's Secret (young adult) – Dagmar Miura

A Cold Wind from the Andes – Dagmar Miura

The Head Hunters – Dagmar Miura

Looking Back: The Long Life of a Writer (a memoir)

Delta Red – Dagmar Miura

Eventide – Dagmar Miura

The Somersville Bodies – Dagmar Miura

Cold Case 369 – Dagmar Miura

The Lighthouse (a novella)– Dagmar Miura

The Saugatuck Conspiracy – Dagmar Miura

For Children

Jessica and the Crocodile Knight (a novel) – HarperCollins

Jessica and Her Adventures in Fairyland (collection of five novellas) – Dagmar Miura

Ophelia and Her Forest Friends (series of ten stories) – Dagmar Miura

Jessica and the Witch's Broom – Dagmar Miura

Jessica and the Flying Unicorns – Dagmar Miura

Jessica and the Golden Swan Feather – Dagmar Miura

Feature Films

The Trap (original story and screenplay; Academy Award nominee for Best Foreign Film) – Columbia

Open Season (screenplay, adapted from Osborn's own best-selling novel *Open Season*) – Columbia

Chase a Crooked Shadow (original story and screenplay co-written with Charles Sinclair; listed by the British Academy of Motion Picture Science as "One of the ten best suspense scripts ever written") – Warner Bros.

Moment of Danger, a.k.a. *Malaga* (screenplay adapted from the novel) – Warner Bros.

Malaga (screenplay) – Warner Bros.

Maroc 7 (original story and screenplay) – J. Arthur Rank

Deadlier Than the Male (original story and screenplay) – J. Arthur Rank

Some Girls Do (original story and screenplay) – J. Arthur Rank

The Road to Dusty Death (screenplay) – J. Arthur Rank

The Games (screenplay) – Associated British

Follow the Boys (original story and screenplay) – MGM

Beat Girl (original story and screenplay) – Renown Films/British Lion

Stop-over Forever (original story and screenplay) – British Lion

Winter Holiday (original story and screenplay) – MGM

Penny Gold (original story and screenplay) – J. Arthur Rank/
Columbia

Whoever Slew Auntie Roo? (original story and screenplay) –
Paramount & American International

Murder, She Said (screenplay, Agatha Christie adaptation)
– MGM

Murder at the Gallop (screenplay, Agatha Christie adaptation)
– MGM

Feature-Length Documentaries

Fangio, The History of Formula One Racing (original screenplay;
executive producer) – Volpi Productions

Why Ireland – Irish Tourist Bureau

Films Canceled While in Production

HMS Ulysses – Volpi Productions (screenplay adaptation of the
Alistair MacLean novel about protecting North Sea convoys
to Russia during World War II; production halted when a
key warship was unavailable)

The Mad Motorists – Volpi Productions (screenplay adaptation
from the Allen Andrews novel about the 1907 Peking to
Paris race)

Eagle at Sundown – Dragon Films (original screen story about
Napoleon's escape from Elba; starring Douglas Fairbanks; in
production when canceled)

Les Petits Rats – Disney (original story and screenplay about the
Paris Ballet school; production begun, then canceled)

Hunters' Horn – McCahon Productions (screenplay adaptation
from the Harriette Simpson Arnow novel; production
canceled; financing failure)

Blood on the Rose – British Lion (screenplay adaptation from the
Phyllis Hastings novel)

Television

Bouquet for Miss Olive (three-act play; British Television Producers Association nominee for Best Play of the Year) – Granada/ITV

Three on a Gas Ring (three-act play; British Television Producers Association nominee for Best Play of the Year) – Granada/ITV

Why George Brown Hanged (three-act play) – Granada/ITV

Arthur of the Britons (pilot and three scripts on the life of King Arthur; Writers Guild of Great Britain award winner for Best British Children's Series)

The Antiquers (original story, pilot, and six episodes in the sitcom series) – Irish National Television